Fall of Light

Nina Kiriki Hoffman

ACE BOOKS, NEW YORK

THE BERKLEY PUBLISHING GROUP
Published by the Penguin Group
Penguin Group (USA) Inc.
375 Hudson Street, New York, New York 10014, USA
Penguin Group (Canada), 90 Eglinton Avenue East, Suite 700, Toronto, Ontario M4P 2Y3, Canada
(a division of Pearson Penguin Canada Inc.)
Penguin Books Ltd., 80 Strand, London WC2R 0RL, England
Penguin Group Ireland, 25 St. Stephen's Green, Dublin 2, Ireland (a division of Penguin Books Ltd.)
Penguin Group (Australia), 250 Camberwell Road, Camberwell, Victoria 3124, Australia
(a division of Pearson Australia Group Pty. Ltd.)
Penguin Books India Pvt. Ltd., 11 Community Centre, Panchsheel Park, New Delhi—110 017, India
Penguin Group (NZ), 67 Apollo Drive, Rosedale, North Shore 0632, New Zealand
(a division of Pearson New Zealand Ltd.)
Penguin Books (South Africa) (Pty.) Ltd., 24 Sturdee Avenue, Rosebank, Johannesburg 2196,
South Africa

Penguin Books Ltd., Registered Offices: 80 Strand, London WC2R 0RL, England

This is a work of fiction. Names, characters, places, and incidents either are the product of the author's imagination or are used fictitiously, and any resemblance to actual persons, living or dead, business establishments, events, or locales is entirely coincidental. The publisher does not have any control over and does not assume any responsibility for author or third-party websites or their content.

FALL OF LIGHT

An Ace Book / published by arrangement with the author

PRINTING HISTORY
Ace hardcover edition / May 2009
Ace mass-market edition / May 2010

Copyright © 2009 by Nina Kiriki Hoffman.
Cover art by Aleta Rafton.
Cover design by Annette Fiore DeFex.
Interior text design by Laura Corless.

ISBN: 978-0-441-01873-4

ACE
Ace Books are published by The Berkley Publishing Group,
a division of Penguin Group (USA) Inc.,
375 Hudson Street, New York, New York 10014.
ACE and the "A" design are trademarks of Penguin Group (USA) Inc.

PRINTED IN THE UNITED STATES OF AMERICA

10 9 8 7 6 5 4 3 2 1

continued . . .

MAY - - 2010

"A very beguiling and magical coming-of-age tale. The author has a flair for the dramatic and unusual." —*Midwest Book Review*

"Bradbury without the literary ticks: the same fondness for haunting, winsome prose passages and quirky characters, but with a firmer grip on plot. This is a fun bit of lighthearted caprice that isn't afraid to slip into the shadows." —*SF Site*

"A feel-good call to learn to love all aspects of self and to gain an appreciation of family." —*VOYA*

"An absorbing read." —*Library Bookwatch*

"The book's real attractions arise from its portrait of the family dynamics and its sympathetic heroine." —*Booklist*

PRAISE FOR NINA KIRIKI HOFFMAN
Bram Stoker Award–winning author
Nebula Award and World Fantasy Award finalist

"[Nina Kiriki Hoffman's] stories and books are lyrical to the point of poetry, with exquisite writing, and are replete with urban magic that seems, somehow, as she tells it, quite natural." —*The Sunday Oregonian*

"A Nina Hoffman story is, by definition, a thing of high quality and mesmeric appeal." —Roger Zelazny

"Most writers show and tell. Nina Hoffman sings." —Algis Budrys

"A writer of quirky fantasies that brim with warmth and charm." —Charles de Lint

"Nina Kiriki Hoffman is a magician. Her words create worlds no one has seen before. Her characters are charming, her prose lyrical. She is one of the fantasy field's greatest talents." —Kristine Kathryn Rusch

To my sister. Thanks.

Acknowledgments

I am eternally grateful to E. Larry Day, special effects makeup artist of Chimera Studios (www.chimerastudios.com), who let me ghost him for a day on a movie set and was nice in every other way. My thanks to his crew as well, especially Molly, who answered many questions and showed me makeup tools and continuity Polaroids of actors being very silly.

I also owe a huge debt of gratitude to my sister, Valley Via Reseigne, production manager (among other things), and her husband, Richard Reseigne, construction coordinator (among other things), for help with the technical details of life on a movie set.

To Valley I am also grateful for introducing me to E. Larry and letting me tell movie people I am related to her. After that, people told me how great she is to work with and answered my questions.

What I got right, I got right because of these people. The wrong stuff is all mine.

1

When Opal LaZelle arrived at the Makeup trailer on the set of *Forest of the Night*, she found her personal employer, Corvus Weather, asleep at her station. The chair had been specially designed to hold his seven-foot two-inch length and generous, muscular frame. It had to be comfortable for hours at a time, the period it took her to transform him from a strangely stretchy-faced, gentle man into the monster of whatever movie they were working on.

She and Corvus had one end of the trailer to themselves. Four other makeup chairs stood in a line between the brightly lit mirrored walls and the many-drawered desk cupboards below them, where the makeup artists stored their supplies. Doors opened into the trailer at either end. Both doors were propped open; a cool breeze spiced with pine eased through the trailer, accompanied by the hum of generators.

Opal could have transformed Corvus in minutes using her special skills, but she and Corvus had only worked together on one film so far, and, though she was afraid she loved

Corvus, she didn't trust him yet. Applying the latex prosthetics to turn Corvus into the Dark God of *Forest of the Night* would take four hours; they were heading into a night shoot, so she had to start now. This was the first day of shooting for her and Corvus; most of the rest of the cast and crew had been on location in backwoods Oregon for a week.

Girl One and Girl Two were in other chairs in the trailer. Rodrigo Esposito, a dark, shaggy-haired man and the key makeup artist on the shoot, was working on Girl Two, the fair one, and supervising his first assistant, Magenta, as she worked on Girl One, the dark one. Opal knew Rodrigo from *Twisted* and *Deviant*, where he had been her boss, and she one of a small pool of makeup artists. He hadn't worked on *Dead Loss*, the film where Opal had met and been hired exclusively for Corvus. Corvus had been the ghost of two merged serial killers, an interesting challenge for Opal's skills as special effects makeup artist and Corvus's skills as actor. Unfortunately, though they both did worthy work, the writers' skills hadn't been up to creating a memorable movie. DVD afterlife was the only thing that saved the movie from being a dead loss itself.

"Opal," Rodrigo murmured as she set out her equipment. "Come meet the girls."

She glanced at Corvus. He sprawled in his chair, a dark blue fleece blanket over him, with black-jean-clad legs and giant black boots sticking out the bottom. He smiled in his sleep. His breathing was so quiet. It surprised her; most of the big men she'd known snored.

She slipped down the trailer to where Magenta, a short, stocky woman with short black hair that had broad pink streaks, stood by Girl Two. Opal knew Magenta from *Deviant* and *Twisted*.

"This is Lauren Marcos, our Serena," Rodrigo said. Lauren had large, dark eyes and a generous mouth, not yet colored; its natural color was dusky pink. She was a character actor with a string of successful comic sidekick roles behind her.

In *Forest of the Night*, she was tackling a different role, a serious, even depressing character, one of the two leads. Her dark, curly hair was pulled back from her face by a stretchy foam band so Magenta could lay the foundation.

"Hi, Lauren," Opal said.

"Hey, doll," said Lauren in a warm, low voice. "You got the big job, huh?" Her eyebrows twitched, and she glanced toward Corvus, her mouth edging into a small smile.

"Opal's a genius," Rodrigo said. "She has magic hands. She could turn you into a warty old witch your mother wouldn't recognize and the witch's mother would."

"That so?" The edges of Lauren's eyes crinkled. "Could we maybe do that sometime, Hon? Like, when my mother's actually visiting the set?"

Opal laughed.

"This is Blaise Penny, our Caitlyn." Rodrigo nodded toward Girl One in the other chair. "Blaise, Opal LaZelle."

"Hi, Opal," said Blaise. She was a gorgeous green-eyed woman with high cheekbones and a mass of crinkled silver blond hair. Blaise and Lauren played sisters in the film, but no effort had been made to cast for family resemblance. Lauren looked Hispanic; Blaise, Caucasian. They were different body types, too—Lauren solid without being fat, Blaise ethereal, the sort of person you expected to see tripping through the woods in a filmy gown and fairy wings. In *Forest*, Blaise was playing against type as the evil sister, which Opal thought promising.

Blaise had just come off two hit films. Opal wondered why she'd chosen a monster movie for her next project; she could have easily been cast in another big budget movie.

"Why aren't you in one of these chairs yourself?" Blaise asked.

Opal glanced at the nearest mirror, wondering if she'd made herself too pretty today. Sometimes she did that inadvertently, since she'd done it on purpose every morning for several years while she was a teenager. But no, she looked like her birth self, clean-faced, violet-eyed, her hair brown with gold highlights, cut even with her jaw so as not to get in her way. She had the same distinctive good looks that made her mother a successful newscaster, but mostly she didn't inhabit her face the way a star would.

Blaise was probably just being polite. "I could never do what you do," Opal said, and smiled.

Blaise tilted her head. Something edged the air between them, a recognition, or perhaps just an electric prickle. "I don't quite believe you," Blaise murmured. "I guess we all tell ourselves the lies we need to believe. Nice to meet you, Opal."

Disconcerted, Opal nodded. She glanced toward Corvus. "I better get to work. Excuse me."

"Later," said Lauren.

Opal returned to her workstation. She got out the full-sized head of Corvus she had made when she built his Dark God; it held all the pieces of his facial prosthetics. She had made stacks of each piece, enough for him to have a new mask every day he was shooting, and a few extra in case things went wrong. "Hey, big guy," she murmured, and Corvus opened his deep brown eyes.

He smiled. "You smell like apples."

"Shampoo. How long have you been awake?"

"Since the others got here," he murmured. His voice was deep and velvety, one of the things she loved about him. He had a career in audiobooks most of his coworkers didn't know about; he was especially popular as a reader of children's books, since he could do so many different voices. His voice had been wasted in *Dead Loss*, which had been about the menace of appearance, not about lines. Corvus's character had a lot to say in *Forest of the Night*. The Dark God had the ability to seduce, a welcome challenge for Corvus after years of playing unspeakable and unspeaking menaces. "Didn't feel like talking."

She smiled at him, folded back the blanket to expose his neck and bare shoulders, and got out her razor and shaving cream. She shaved him, even though he had shaved himself earlier. She talked to his hair follicles while she did it, asked them to lie dormant for a while. She cleaned his face and neck carefully, then applied a long-lasting moisturizer that would keep his skin safe under the adhesives she was about to use.

"Hang on," said a shadow against the afternoon sun in the doorway at their end of the trailer.

Opal's back stiffened. Erika Dennis.

The film's publicist swept in in a cloud of musky perfume and lifted one of her cameras from the interlaced straps of them around her neck. "First transformation," she said. "Gotta document it for the DVD."

"No," said Corvus. His voice held so much menace Opal would have run if it were directed at her.

Erika was oblivious, or maybe just strong-willed. "Yes." She aimed the video camera at Corvus's face and pressed the record button. "It's in your contract."

"No."

"Erika, get out," Opal said. She hadn't started making Corvus into the Dark God yet. They had done all the prep work during preproduction—studied the script, the storyboards, the costumer's concept of the character. They'd talked to the art director, exchanged sketches. She and Corvus had discussed what Corvus wanted to bring to the role, and what he hoped Opal would do to augment it. They had made Corvus's life-mask, the armature on which Opal built her monster. He had built the character inside himself. She felt it rising in him now as she prepared for his transformation.

She didn't think Corvus had magical abilities—he'd never exhibited anything overt—but something about the chemistry of interaction in the trailer charged the air. Opal felt a surge under her skin, her own power readying for a fight. It frightened her. She never had this kind of fight away from her gifted family. People said there were others with powers out in the world, but Opal hadn't yet met many.

Rodrigo took Erika by the shoulders and pushed her out of the trailer. "Not this time," he said. "Film it some other day and say it's the first time. This time they need to focus. Get out of our workspace, Ere. You're upsetting the talent." He closed the door in her face.

The scent and feel of threat faded.

Rodrigo said, "It probably *is* in your contract, Corvus. She'll have to film it sometime."

"It's not in my contract." Corvus had his eyes closed. "I specifically struck that clause. I always do. I'm going to play monsters all my life. I decided early in my career that I wanted to do it mysteriously. Nobody outside of cast and crew gets to see me transform."

"Yikes. That raises the stakes for *National Enquirer* opportunists."

Corvus sighed. "I know. Could you help me, Rodrigo? No cameras in the Makeup trailer."

"That's already the rule, except for my continuity cameras."

"Finished work is okay. It's the process I want to guard."

"You got it. I can't police the area all the time, though. If someone's determined to plant a camera in here and has the tech, I don't know that I can stop them. Cameras can be so small now. You can get spytech at Sharper Image, for God's sake, and this is not a secure shoot; lots of holes."

"Noted."

"I'll guard the workspace," Opal said. She could add a level of awareness every time she entered the trailer, check for hidden things. She was hypersensitive to anything that watched; it would be simple. She opened one of her extra senses and glanced around. "Who put that there?" She moved to the mirror and plucked a suction-cup-backed rubber eye from it. It had been staring down at Corvus.

The back of her neck prickled. No one else should touch her things or invade her space. She had proprietary processes. She realized she needed to set traps.

Rodrigo's eyes widened. "I vaguely remember somebody coming in and sticking that up. They said it was a joke."

Opal closed her hand into a fist. The eye looked like rubber, but things inside it crunched. She opened her hand again, revealed a crushed mess of machinery. "Man or woman?"

"Male," said Rodrigo. "Not somebody I know yet, but someone whose presence here didn't surprise me. One of the electricians, I think." He closed his eyes. "Seal brown hair, olive tan skin, shadowed eyes. Rangy frame. White T-shirt, jeans. Toolbelt with the requisite rolls of tape. I don't think I noticed him before or since, but I don't pay a lot of attention to them."

"May I see that?" Corvus asked. He held out a hand and Opal dropped the mashed electronics into it. His hand could have closed around both of hers and hidden them completely.

"God. I hate this. I guess we'll need to set watch here, or lock up when we're not in. I better check for others," said Rodrigo. He went down the trailer, looking everywhere. Opal expanded her awareness the length of the trailer. No sense of any more invading eyes.

Opal shrugged and went to work on Corvus. They sank into collaboration then, all her focus on his face as she applied the adhesive and then attached the different prosthetics that would alter him but leave him with the ability to govern his expressions. His deep, shadowed eyes watched her face most of the time. It was unnerving. Other actors she'd worked with fell asleep while she was applying their prosthetics and makeup, or listened to music with their eyes closed. It made them much easier to deal with.

She didn't notice when others entered or left the trailer, though she was half-conscious of surrounding murmurs, and then, finally, silence.

Corvus sighed.

Opal wanted his head to belong to her, to be the armature for her artwork. She wasn't ready to let him be a person yet. *You are mine,* she thought as she narrowed her eyes and stared into his. *You are calm and receptive. You wait without complaint.* He became very still then, but his gaze never left hers. She worked with adhesive and latex, and after she had applied all the pieces (some of her magic slipped out her fingertips, she couldn't stop herself; but only she would take off the mask, so she should be able to undo it), she painted on the colors. Last of all, she put in his monster contact lenses, glittery metallic green with no whites or pupils except for clear spots in the centers so he could see through them.

At last she stood straight and stretched, her shoulders creaking from her working stoop. She glanced at the clock. Their call time was for 6 P.M., and it was 5:30 now. Not much time to dress him! But he looked perfect, and the costume for his role was simple, an enveloping black robe. In the scene scheduled to film tomorrow, she'd need to put on the upper body and hand appliances, and that would take more time.

She flexed her fingers, stepped back, and studied the overall effect; she had been too lost in the details to notice the whole before.

She was looking at someone new.

Working off images of the Green Man and legends of the Bogeyman, she had crafted someone leafy and scary, overhanging brow, jutting chin, details of oak leaves and maple leaves starting at his nose and raying out across his cheeks, forehead, and chin; his skin was light brown, layered in leaf veins with green highlights and scatterings of powdered gold, intermittent gleams that would catch the firelight of the night filming. The strange eyes almost frightened her as they stared into hers. He looked like something from a dream.

The mouth moved. She jumped.

"Opal," Corvus murmured.

"Yes?"

"Did you paralyze me? I can't move."

"Oh. Oops. Sorry, Corr." She touched her palm to his newly leafy forehead and released him. She didn't remember spelling him still. She could tell she had done it, though; her signature was on the magic. Maybe a thread of something else.

He shook his shoulders, turned his head. "How did you do that?"

"Hypnosis." One of her stock answers. She usually didn't do things like involuntarily paralyze other people anymore, unless the circumstances were dire. Why had she done it to Corvus?

It had certainly made the work easier.

"I don't like hearing that," he murmured. "I'm not supposed to be an easy subject. You didn't do this to me on the last picture."

"No."

"I guess I must trust you." He blinked. His eyelids were brown, now, blended with the rest of his face. When had she colored his lids? All she remembered from their session was his unblinking stare.

And the magic that had seeped from her fingertips into his skin . . . She must have done it then, tinted his face the color she wanted.

With his eyes closed, Corvus looked almost like forest floor. Opal shot some Polaroids for continuity, asked him to open his eyes and shot a couple more.

Corvus turned and stared at his reflection in the wall of mirrors beside his seat. "Oh. My." A hand rose to his mouth, hovered but did not touch. He noticed the hand was normal, held it out, and frowned at it. The facial prosthetics worked well; she could read his expression without trouble.

"You're not going to need the hands in tonight's scene," she said.

His eyes closed, opened. "You're right. Do you have the mock-up gloves, though? I'd like to put something on. It'll help with the character."

She opened the drawer that held the hand work and got out the prototype gloves she had made. The real prosthetics were pieces again, finger sheaths, backs and palms of hands, a several-layer process to apply, but she had made the gloves to get the overall look, a template she could cut apart. She held the gloves open and he slid his large hands inside. She had worked from casts of his hands; the gloves fit absolutely.

She had used the leaf pattern and earth colors to craft the gloves, too. The fingernails were long, horny, and dark.

"Lovely," he murmured, his voice dark, rich, velvety. He gave her a Dark God smile. She swayed, wanting to fall forward into his lap.

"Are you all right?" He pushed up out of the chair, braced her shoulders in his gloved hands, and steadied her.

Opal blinked up into his face, pulled herself together. "I've got to get Wardrobe in here," she said. Had she laid an Attract Spell on him and not noticed? What was wrong with her? Usually she leashed her powers completely in situations like this.

She sniffed. No smell of an Attract Spell, but there was something at work here, something strange. It must be her, in love with her own creation and how Corvus embodied it. She'd had this problem before, especially at the start of a shoot, before she got tired of all the time it took to create her creatures over and over again. He was just so—perfectly monstrous.

Better ditch this attitude fast.

She picked up the "Ear," the communications headset that linked her to the rest of the crew, slipped it on, and hooked the battery/control box to her belt. She hated the headset. Its electric energy field messed up her thinking. She wore it as little as possible, but right now she needed it to drop back into the web of everything going on with the film.

She called the head of the teamsters and put in a request for Corvus's driver to be ready soon. Then she switched channels. No local traffic on the Makeup channel. She switched to Wardrobe, clicked the transmit button. "Betty?"

"Who is this?"

"Opal, makeup for Dark God."

"I'm still at the B&B set. You need something?" The key wardrobe artist sounded gruff and irritated.

"Costume for Dark God. Call time in half an hour."

"You're one of those last-minute emergency people, huh? Great," said Betty.

Turf wars, thought Opal. *Wonderful.*

"I'm still needed here," said Betty, still grumpy. "Pick up Kelsi, my assistant, at the trailer. She'll get you geared up."

"Is she on this channel?"

"She probably doesn't have her Ear in. She hates it."

"That makes two of us."

"Great. More idiots out of the loop. Go to the trailer and tell her I said she should help you. She can confirm if she wants."

Opal sighed and switched off. "Don't go anywhere," she told Corvus. "I brought you some water." She handed him a sports bottle with a straw, something he could sip from without upsetting the prosthetics. "I'll be right back with Wardrobe." She dashed out of the trailer, locked the door behind her.

In the Wardrobe trailer, Opal introduced herself to Kelsi Martini. Kelsi, her short bobbed hair lime green, her skin pale, her lips painted black, helped Opal track down Corvus's costume. "I'll suit him up," Kelsi said as she draped the long black robe twice over her arm.

"All right."

Opal's Ear crackled. Rodrigo's voice said, "What's your status? Ready to head out?"

She pressed the transmit button. "Not dressed yet."

"We're wrapping with Unit One, but there's been some traffic on another channel about the forest shoot. You should hurry."

"On it," she said.

"Can't wait to see what you've done to the big guy," Kelsi said as they left the trailer. "Sure looked spooky in the storyboards."

"Yeah, well . . ." Opal unlocked the Makeup trailer.

"What's with the extra security?" Kelsi asked as she entered the trailer.

"We found a hidden camera. Somebody's going tabloid on our asses."

Kelsi gasped, and Opal turned from locking the door to stare.

The Dark God loomed at the far end of the trailer. He was a large, ominous shadow against the light—all the other makeup stations had been shut down; only Opal's was still lit. His naked upper body looked bull-like, dense with muscles, and the silhouetted shape of his head was odd and wrong, different from her vision of him. Fear thrilled in feathering ripples up Opal's spine.

A sucking sound came from the Dark God's direction. "Got any more water?" Corvus said, his voice higher than usual.

"*Gaah,*" said Kelsi. "You scared me, dude!"

"Good." He had dropped the register into deep and rich again. Opal wondered if he'd spoken high to break the tension. She wouldn't put it past him. He was always sensitive to emotional atmospheres. "That's my job."

Kelsi headed toward him. Opal followed. As Corvus turned toward the light, she saw that he was just as she had left him, a demon—wood god mix, his mane of black hair raying out around the prosthetics that covered his face and neck. She had carried the dark brown/gleaming gold skin color of the Dark God a short way down his black-furred chest; below that, he was light tan, normal. She hadn't seen him out from under the blanket yet today; she didn't remember him being this buff during their last movie.

Kelsi walked all the way around Corvus. "Wow, Opal! Wow! That's amazing! I'd heard you were good, but I never—"

Corvus posed while Kelsi examined him.

"Fantastic," Kelsi whispered.

Opal crossed her arms. "Thanks. It helps to have good base material."

Corvus grinned, his Dark God expression more sinister than reassuring, but she could read beneath the layers she had applied to his face, and knew he was teasing her. She was glad they'd forged a good connection. Some of the actors she had worked with in the past had been horrors in several senses of the word.

Kelsi held up the black robe. "Well, so, want to slip into this, Mr. Weather?"

He put down the sports bottle, and Opal grabbed it. There were crates of water bottles on the Craft Services truck. She should stock some by her station.

Corvus stretched his arms behind him so Kelsi could slip on the sleeves. She slid the black robe up over his shoulders. "Any of this stuff bleed?" she asked Opal. "Do you have solvents to get it out of cloth?"

"It shouldn't stain; it's set until I use the removal goop."

"No stains, huh?" Kelsi fastened the robe at Corvus's neck with a silver brooch shaped like a five-pointed star, center point down. She straightened the hood. The back of her hand brushed the colored part of Corvus's neck. She studied her hand, flashed it at Opal: no makeup adhered. "Neat."

"Ticktock," Corvus said.

Startled, Kelsi glanced at Opal's Batman clock. It was almost six; they were due at the forest clearing location. "Sorry." She used hidden snaps to fasten the rest of the robe down the front, then reached way up to lift the hood and settle it, veiling most of his head. The hood left his face in shadow; only the extended chin, with its leaf beard, jutted out far enough to catch much light. "Okay. I'll ride over with you guys, if that's all right."

"Sure," said Opal. Then she glanced at Corvus: it was really his decision. He was the star, the one who could have tantrums and snits if he liked, so long as they stayed on schedule. He was so laid back she had forgotten he was talent and she was second- or third-class citizen. On some shoots, nobody ever let you forget your status; other shoots were more relaxed. Opal hadn't spent enough time on this shoot to get a sense of how it worked.

"Glad to have you," Corvus said to Kelsi.

"I'll get my kit. Meet you at the car."

Opal packed solvents and brushes and touch-up equipment in her makeup kit, along with duplicates of the pieces of latex she had applied to Corvus's face, in case of wardrobe malfunctions. "I have to stop at Craft Services and pick up more water—"

"Could you get me something to drink with calories in it? I don't want to eat with this on," Corvus said.

"Yeah. Patty stocked protein shakes for you. I'll walk you to the car and get you settled, then run for it."

"Good. I can see, but my vision is limited, and I don't want to bump my hands."

"Rest your hands on my shoulders." She stood in front of the door and waited until Corvus was right behind her, his large, warm, rubber-gloved hands heavy on her shoulders.

They had done this before, too: she had acted as guide dog on *Dead Loss*. The doubled head he had worn for that role was much more of a challenge for him visually.

Opal opened the door at her end of the trailer and flicked off the lights. "Three steps down," she said, "and the last one is—yikes!"

Erika's camera flashed, blinding her. She would have stumbled without Corvus's steadying grip on her shoulders.

"Stop it!" she yelled at Erika.

"No way. I've waited all afternoon for this." Erika shot a stream of pictures, alternating between two cameras on straps around her neck.

"If we're late because of your interference," Corvus said, his voice a low rumble, "we'll redirect the wrath to you."

"I'm done for now," Erika said. She smirked. "Thanks so much. Catch you later. Nice job, Opal." She strolled away, taking her musky scent cloud with her.

Opal shivered with suppressed rage. The wrappings on her powers unwound; she felt red rivers rise. Energy pooled in her palms. She hadn't been this angry since she was six-teen, newly powerful, and her younger brother and sister had teased her beyond bearing. She could hold up her hands and let the power jab out of her into Erika's back. Erika would melt into a puddle of steaming flesh, her cameras slag.

Opal clenched her fists to restrain the eager power.

Corvus's hands on her shoulders steadied her. He leaned down and whispered in her ear, "Not yet," in a Dark God voice, and that gave her the strength to chill her power and send it back to sleep. In the shocky aftermath, she swayed, and Corvus held her steady.

How could she even contemplate such a devastating thing? She was Opal, low-powered Opal who only used her gifts to change how things looked. Who inside her rose up in a kill-ing rage?

Corvus's rubber-taloned fingers massaged her shoulders

a little. His regular voice said, "You okay, Opal, hon? I guess we should have expected that. She's a pit bull."

She hugged herself, settled down. "Sure. Sorry, Corr. Let's go. Three steps down, and the last one is steeper."

"I'll find it by feel."

They descended the steps. Once they touched down on the parking lot between the bed-and-breakfast, where the first unit had been filming all day, and the abandoned grocery store the production company had taken over as a housing for sound stages, Corvus moved up to walk beside her, one hand still on her shoulder. They walked to the black Lincoln the production manager had rented for Corvus's use.

A short dark man leaned against the car, reading a magazine. He wore pointy boots, jeans, and a brown leather jacket. "Hitch," Corvus said. "This is Opal, my makeup artist. She comes with me every time. Opal, Hitch, my driver."

"Pleased," said Hitch, holding out a hand. Opal shook it and smiled.

Kelsi joined them. "I'm geared up! Let's rock and roll."

"Boss?" Hitch said.

"Kelsi. Wardrobe. She's with us, too."

Hitch shrugged and held the door for Corvus.

"I've got to get food and water," Opal muttered.

"There's another Craft Services van at the site," said Kelsi. "Dinner break's at nine. Somebody'll bring a load of sandwiches."

"Oh, good."

Kelsi jumped into the backseat. Opal joined her. Hitch piloted them away from the trailer village.

From the supermarket parking lot, people could walk anywhere in town; it was that small. Corvus, the director, and an actor Opal hadn't met yet were staying upstairs in the B&B. Most of the crew and any day players they needed stayed at a budget motel ten miles out of town, in the larger city of Redford off the highway. The production manager had rented a house across the square from the B&B in Lapis where she set up the office, reception, accounting, and a small room where the director, the director of photography, and anyone else who needed to could watch the dailies on DVD. The director of photography and the producer lived upstairs in the house. Other principal actors were living with various families around town.

Lapis had been small but busy before the Interstate was finished in 1966 and business and traffic moved a few miles west. One main road ran from north to south through town; two smaller roads ran east–west past the outskirts. Hitch took Sixth Street to Lost River Road. A mile east out of town, they came to a post with a paper plate stapled to it. One of the crew had written FOREST and an arrow pointing away from the road on the plate. There was a rutted track where the equipment trucks had churned up late spring mud on their way to the clearing where demonic rituals involving the Dark God were going to be filmed.

Mud spat up into the undercarriage of the Lincoln as they took the squishy road into the forest. The terrain was slippery. Opal wondered why the location manager had picked this place—until they broke out of the trees into a perfect clearing, firm ground, clear of trees, with a small brook running through one corner, and a stone altar and lichen-starred standing stones at the far end.

It was Magic Hour. Twilight still lightened the sky; the trees were visible but dark against the lingering light. Someone had brought in small bronze censers on tripods, suitably smoking, and an open fire danced in a ring of stones in front of the altar. A group of extras in long white robes were bunched up at the far end of the meadow. Light racks, camera tracks, and sound equipment stood ready near the altar. Chairs, the Craft Services truck, and equipment vans were arrayed at the near end of the meadow, hidden behind a photographed forest backdrop.

One of the young men directed Hitch off the road into a makeshift parking lot where someone had cleared a few trees. He pulled in and turned off the engine, which didn't silence the night. Portable generators roared near the equipment.

Hitch rounded the car and opened the door, helped Corvus out. Opal and Kelsi emerged. "The ground's pretty good here, but you better let me lead you anyway," Opal said, turning so Corvus could rest his hands on her shoulders again.

"Anytime, hon," said Corvus. He sounded distracted.

"Come on, come on," yelled Neil Aldridge, the director, "we're eating energy here." He wore black slacks and a black shirt. He was tall and muscular, with a shock of dark hair, heavy brow ridges, and a dissatisfied, thin-lipped mouth. He stood with his arms crossed, looking irritated. He appeared about forty-five. She hadn't seen any of his earlier movies. She and Corvus had wanted to consult with him about the Dark God in preproduction, but he had fobbed them off on the production designer, Dathan Riley, who was excited about the concept and worked with them to define and fine-tune it. Aldridge's voice was mellifluous, and carried well. He sounded kind. That was not his reputation.

The script supervisor, a sturdy woman with a clipboard, stood one step behind him. "The call was for six," Neil said.

"Sorry," said Opal. She checked her watch. They were a minute late. "Erika."

"Damn," muttered Neil. "Well, get out here and let me see what we've got."

Opal led Corvus past Neil into the full glare of the lights near the altar. Something itched her feet, some dazzle or discomfort she didn't recognize.

"Ladies, gentlemen, and others, our monster," said Neil. Like a ringmaster, he swept an arm toward Opal and Corvus.

All sound aside from the generators stopped.

Corvus gripped Opal's shoulders once, then gently pushed her aside. He stood with his arms crossed and looked over the assembled cast and crew. He moved his head and the hood fell away, revealing a stranger.

The horns weren't part of her prosthetics. They looked right, though, two short forward-thrusting spikes growing from Corvus's leafy temples, gleaming gold in their grooves. Opal opened her senses wide. Stranger magic tickled the bottoms of her feet, met her own force without meshing with it.

It climbed Corvus, enveloped him, resided most strongly in the places where she had changed him. Her alterations had left toeholds for it.

"Corvus," she whispered.

The face turned toward her. The eyes were dark now, not so green, and the soul looking out was not the man she knew.

He smiled. His teeth were pointed, serrated like a shark's.

Applause burst out around the circle.

Corvus lifted both arms, basking, circled with his hands, then took a very theatrical bow, one leaf-skinned hand lifting a segment of his robe behind him.

"He's going to steal the picture," Neil muttered. Then, louder, "All right, everybody, find your marks for a run-through. Can you see all right, Weather?"

"Perfectly," said Corvus.

"I want you looming on the far side of the fire, behind the altar, looking hungry while your minions dance for you. Menace and lust."

Corvus nodded. Opal raised her eyebrows, her gaze on his face. Did he want her to help him across the clearing to his mark? He nodded, gesturing from her toward the location. She stepped closer, and he settled his hands on her shoulders. They walked in tandem toward the fire and the altar. "Corr, are you all right?" she murmured.

He laughed. "Better than ever." He didn't sound like himself.

A tall man in a black robe backed away as they approached, Corvus's stand-in. He had the height, and his face was the same color greeny brown as Corvus's mask, but nothing else about him looked like Corvus. "Evening," he said.

"Hi, Fred," Opal said. Fred had been Corvus's stand-in on *Dead Loss*, too.

"Whoa, Nellie," said Fred when he saw Corvus. He hurried off to where the other stand-ins stood, behind the camouflage backdrop and out of sight of the cameras, smoking and whispering.

"Can you see your mark?" Opal asked. There was a piece of black electrician's tape on the ground beyond the altar.

"I know my place. Thanks, honey." He let her go, and she edged away from him, turned to look back. She stared at the pointy-toothed smile, the too-dark eyes, as a flicker of firelight ran over his face.

She hoped he was okay.

"Stand by for rehearsal. All nonactors off the set," Neil yelled.

Opal fled. She ran back to the car and pulled out her traveling kit, then joined Wardrobe, Makeup, and Hair at the cluster of canvas-backed chairs on the edge of the clearing, behind the backdrop.

"Cue music," called Neil. Someone punched a tape player. Eerie music full of whining wind instruments from unnamed countries and the thud of deep drums started up. "Action!" The frozen people in white, the looming figure in black all responded to the music. their motions small and restrained at first, growing wilder and looser.

"Okay, great," said Neil. "Let's do it from the top with the cameras."

"Last looks!" called the first assistant director, George Corvassian.

Opal grabbed her kit and joined a rush of Makeup, Hair, and Wardrobe people to the actors. Corvus started the scene with the hood up; midway through, when the minions had loosened up and didn't look like bad 1980s dance party victims, he would drop the hood.

He lowered the hood when she approached him and bent so that his face neared hers. She studied his face and could find nothing to correct.

"This is so strange," he murmured, in almost his own voice, and then, the Dark God spoke: "I like you. I like this. I wasn't sure at first, but now I'm glad you're all here."

She backed away again, her heart beating too fast. The hair on her arms stood; her skin prickled everywhere.

"Starting marks," yelled Neil. "Here we go, people. Start the music again."

A bell rang. George cried, "We're on bell. Roll sound, please."

"Rolling."

"Roll camera."

"Rolling."

"Action," Neil said.

Opal settled into Corvus's giant custom canvas-backed chair, opened her senses, and reached for what disturbed her here.

The ground was alive with more than scuffed grass. She had a sense of profound sleep, with an edge of waking, of old wounds, covered but not healed, and of something unhuman, a mind that didn't work like anything she had ever encountered.

She had had a brief career as a tree talker when she was sixteen—the family invited a tree to live in their house over the Christmas season every year, and the youngest with gifts was the one who issued the invitation. She had only done it once before her younger brother Jasper came into his power and took over the job. Communicating wasn't one of her stronger gifts; she had had to listen hard to find a tree that volunteered to travel. Even then she wasn't sure if she'd chosen the right one, not until her mother spoke to the tree and confirmed it. Since then—twelve years ago—she hadn't tried to talk to anyone but humans, and that using her mouth.

"What are you?" she whispered.

The ancient sleeper surged beneath her, alive with an energy she could sense but not see. It didn't answer.

It was this that was seeping up into Corvus's skin, shifting him in ways Opal hadn't. She wondered what it wanted, whether it would hurt him.

Magenta, in a chair next to hers, cradled a tiny portable TV that showed a black-and-white version of what the hot camera on the set was filming. At the moment, the camera was focused on Corvus's face. Magenta whispered, "What you did with him? That's amazing. How did you do it? Can I watch you next time? I want to learn."

"If it's all right with Corvus," Opal whispered.

"Cut! Let's run it again," Neil called.

Usually everyone had magazines to flip through while they waited, but tonight, Wardrobe, Makeup, Hair, and drivers all watched whatever monitors they had, even three takes in. Opal couldn't stop staring at Corvus. Whatever was in him worked on her, inviting her to fall in love with him even more than she already had.

During one of the touch-up moments between takes when everyone rushed to fix whatever had gone awry during the last take, Opal said, "Corr, are you okay in there?"

He just smiled. She lifted a gilt-dipped brush, lowered it. He needed no help from her.

"Starving," he whispered then, and she went to the mobile Craft Services van and got him a protein shake. He sipped while they reset the cameras, but he didn't speak to her again.

They closed down at midnight, just before the rain started. Hitch drove Corvus and Opal back through sweeping rain as other crew broke down sets and sheltered equipment under tarps. Someone rushed the exposed film off to be developed.

In the Makeup trailer, Corvus sprawled in his chair. Opal got out the Polaroid camera and shot more pictures of him, compared them to her earlier shots. She wrote time and date across the bottoms of the new Polaroids in Sharpie permanent ink.

The horns on his forehead were the most obvious change, and they still looked good. The rest of her forehead pieces didn't have them, though. She'd have to spend the rest of the night making new appliances.

Or maybe she could cheat. As long as she had the photos for continuity, she should be able to manage. She wasn't sure how to manage the wild magic out in the clearing, though.

"Ready for removal?" she asked Corvus when she had satisfactory shots from several angles.

"Please," he said. He held out his hands. She pulled the latex mitts off gently. They came off all in a piece. She handed Corvus a towel, and he wiped sweat and moisturizer off his hands. She set the gloves up on spikes to dry; she would powder, maybe blow-dry them tomorrow, as necessary.

She got out her special solvent and prepared to take the first section of his facial prosthesis off. It clung to his face. She eased a brush loaded with solvent along the edges. As the outside edge of her finger brushed over the prosthetic, she felt not latex but flesh, warm, with pores and tiny hairs.

She set the brush down across the solvent tin. Her hand shook. She stroked Corvus's leafy cheek, pointed chin, horns. The eyes, a solid dark green color, watched her, and the mouth quirked in a small smile.

"Let him go," Opal whispered. Warm power gathered in

her fingertips. She touched them lightly to his face, and the foreign power that had been riding him since they had arrived at the clearing seeped away. Her fingernail flicked up the edge of a cheek piece.

She reached for her brush and worked carefully, pulled the pieces off, and tossed them in the trash. The horns came off as though they were part of the forehead pieces. She set them on the counter near his life-mask so she could match tomorrow's mask to them. She worked with haste, hoping the new energy wouldn't return and force Corvus back into character.

She took care with his skin, finishing with another round of moisturizer.

"Feels good," he said as she massaged lotion into his face. He still wore the dark contacts and watched her face more than her hands.

"Good," she echoed, distracted. "How are you, otherwise? Did you notice anything different?" She finished and capped her bottles.

Corvus popped out the contacts, set them into the solution-filled container she held out. He studied the more recent Polaroids. "I don't know. It doesn't look like the prototype, or even what I looked like when we left the trailer. Looks much better, actually. When did you change it?"

"Um—last looks, right before the first shot."

"I don't remember. Guess I was distracted. Did you watch the monitors while we shot?" asked Corvus.

"Sure."

"How'd I come across?"

"Amazing."

He smiled, seemed entirely himself again. "Good. I wonder if the D.P. will let me see the dailies. Do you know when they're supposed to arrive?"

"Three sets tomorrow night, but I'm pretty sure Aldridge

doesn't want any of the actors looking at them. News at supper was he's an overcontrolling asshole." There had been a half-hour meal break in the midst of the night's filming; Corvus had been restricted to protein shakes, but Opal had wolfed a sandwich and listened to other crew members talking.

It wasn't the first time she and Corvus had heard these rumors about the director. They had done research on cast and crew while Corvus contemplated the project, mostly quizzing other people who had worked with the principals before. The part was too good to turn down, even though it wasn't a great script.

"Frustrating," Corvus said. He moved his shoulders, still clothed in the black robe. "A good night's work."

"Time for your beauty sleep," Opal said. She checked the call sheet the assistant director had handed out just before they stopped filming for the night. "Call's for four P.M. tomorrow—we'll have to start makeup around noon."

He sighed and pulled himself to his feet. "Thanks for taking care of me." He gave her a hug, then ambled out of the trailer.

She policed her area, straightening, cleaning, restocking supplies. She got out the new set of latex appliances she'd use on Corvus tomorrow, draped them over the life-mask, checked to make sure there was no one nearby, and then, studying the Polaroids and the previous pieces of altered mask, she let her power seep into the forehead pieces to form the horns. A tiny touch of alien power still lingered in the horns from that day's mask; when she touched their tips, the power jumped into her fingers. She touched the new horns and the power flowed into them.

Disturbing. Yet it helped, added some quality that made the horns match absolutely with the earlier set.

When she had finished, she curled up in the residual warmth Corvus's body had left in his oversized chair. She studied pictures of the face she had built, with its later additions. Who had shifted her work? She'd never encountered outside magic on a set before, even though she had done most of her work in weird supernatural movies.

The face, with its blank white eye sockets, stared back at her. A corner of its mouth quirked up into a smile.

2

The following day, Corvus had a scene on the soundstage with Lauren Marcos, who played the older sister, Serena, in the film. Opal was thrilled. He almost never got close-ups—she'd spent hours watching his old movies on DVD after she met him on *Dead Loss*, and he was mostly a shambling monster in the distance, obscured by fog and darkness and attended by scary musical cues. Even when his face appeared full screen in the scary psycho shots, he was always projecting rage or madness. This was going to be different.

Corvus and Lauren had run lines during a late breakfast just before Corvus's makeup call time, off in a corner, hunched (at least, Corvus hunched; Lauren, two feet shorter, had cricked her neck to keep his face in view) together. Opal, eating a breakfast burrito with Makeup and Wardrobe, had felt a familiar flare of jealousy, and had, with a practiced mental motion, tamped it down. Corvus wasn't her creation at breakfast; he was entirely his own self, and he could be interested in Lauren if he liked. Or just work with her.

Opal fell in love with everyone she worked on. She had to love them. Otherwise what she did to them wouldn't look convincing. She loved them, and she had to convince herself to leave them alone. She throttled her urge to claim Corvus and ate the rest of her burrito, then went to the Makeup trailer and rechecked her preparations.

Corvus was quiet when he came in, silent as he stretched out, shirtless, in his chair and lay back so she could work. Today, because of the close-ups, Opal was applying neck and chest prosthetics as well as face and hands. Lauren, in the next chair being tended by Rodrigo, was quiet, too. Opal cleansed, shaved, moisturized Corvus's face, letting the magic seep from her fingertips into his skin only a little. The pieces of the false face slid on smoothly. When she pulled up out of her creative trance and glanced at the clock, she saw she had finished an hour early.

Lauren was still sitting in the nearest makeup chair, flipping through a fashion magazine. Rodrigo was gone.

"That was intense," she said. "You always get so wrapped up in your work?"

"Yep." Opal shook her head to wake herself, checked Corvus. He looked great. She studied the Polaroids she'd taken the night before and compared them with Corvus now, was satisfied with the match. She took more shots and dated them.

"Opal," whispered Corvus. "You did it to me again."

"Oh, God," she said, and pressed her palm to his enhanced forehead, released him from paralysis. "Sorry. Are you all right?"

"Feeling strangely fine." He stretched and rose to his feet, all the visible skin on his front altered into Dark God, though Opal had done less work on his upper arms and lower abdomen. "It's not something I enjoyed, that sense of utter helplessness, but it didn't leave me stiff the way I expected. I almost trust you enough to relax, and it does make it easier for me to stay still. Nothing even itched. Posthypnotic suggestion?" He paused, arrested by his own image in the mirror. "Oh, I *am* someone else now," he murmured low.

Lauren set aside her magazine without looking and studied him. Her eyes widened.

Corvus smiled at her, his look strangely tender. The energy in the air feathered against Opal's skin, unspoken messages involving warmth and desire, persuasion and invitation. She fell under the spell herself, and wondered if Lauren had any defenses against it, or wanted any.

She couldn't let Corvus and Lauren make out now; it might mess up the makeup. "Wait until after your scene," Opal said, her voice cross.

"What?" Corvus's voice was deep and Dark Godly, but startled.

"Oy," said Lauren, and shook herself. "Yeah. Focus, Laur," she muttered.

"I need to put one last piece on the back of your neck," Opal said to Corvus.

"Right." He dropped to his knees on the floor and leaned forward, braced his arms on the seat of his chair. She applied the last piece of the prosthesis, almost certain not to be seen, but still necessary.

When she had finished, Opal thumbed a button on her walkie and switched to Wardrobe frequency. "Betty? This is Opal. The Dark God is ready for wardrobe."

Corvus stood, his back still tan and human-colored below the darker brown, green, and gold of his neck and the black of his hair.

"Okay, Opal, good. You're early. Kelsi's in the trailer. I'll tell her to come to you. They're still filming scene nine on the stage, but what the heck."

"How close are they to done?" Scene nine was supposed to

wrap by four, when Corvus and Lauren were due on the set. Opal checked her watch. They were still an hour early.

"Aldridge is throwing a hissy fit about rounded vowels," Betty whispered. "Millie has the wrong accent."

"Great."

"He might finish this scene on time, though. Better be here."

"We will." Opal signed off. "Kelsi's bringing the robe here."

Lauren stood. She was already dressed in her costume for this scene, flat black kung fu shoes, jeans with wear-whitened knees, and a chocolate brown blouse that buttoned all the way to her throat. Her street makeup was minimal, subdued, almost not there. In her first confrontation with the Dark God as an adult, she was restrained, self-protective, making no attempt to look good. Her childhood encounter with the Dark God had driven her character underground, hiding from herself and the world. She would shift over the course of the film, and so would her costume, hair, and makeup.

Kelsi knocked. Opal let her in. "Hey, big guy," Kelsi said. Corvus stooped, and Kelsi settled the robe around his shoulders, adjusted its folds, mated the hidden snaps to each other, and fastened the upside-down star at his throat. Covus lifted the hood. His horns tented the material.

Opal grabbed her set makeup kit and went to the door. "Wait," she said. She closed her eyes and tuned in to the air. She had already checked for spies in the trailer, and now she pushed her senses farther out. Was Erika lying in ambush again? It occurred to Opal that the pictures the publicist had taken the day before were now inaccurate, but maybe Erika didn't know that yet. It would be better if no one knew, but she wasn't sure how to manage that.

No one waited outside, so Opal opened the door and led Corvus down the steps. His hand on her shoulder was warm again, but he squeezed her and let go at the base of the stairs.

"I don't know what it is," he said, "but I can see better today. Thanks for your help."

The construction crew had built a mock-up of the forest altar on the soundstage inside the old supermarket, so they didn't have far to go.

This shoot had a bigger budget than most of the other movies Opal had worked on. She felt a brief pang for previous pictures, when, as chief makeup assistant, she had had more to do, helping out with makeup for everybody from the stars to the extras. Even though she loved Corvus, it was a pain being attached to one person; everybody else got variety in their work.

The crew had been out in the forest all day shooting a flashback to Serena's earlier life, when she had participated in the demonic rituals of her mother's coven in the forest, summoning the Dark God. Splices of Corvus's image from the previous day's filming would be cut in later. Gemma Goodwin, a fourteen-year-old child actor, was playing thirteen-year-old Serena.

People were already complaining about Aldridge in corners during meal breaks, though Opal thought he had been businesslike on the set yesterday. People said he was a stickler for getting done on time, whether it was quality work or not, and he had a reputation for reducing people to tears by yelling at them. It was part of his theory about getting the best performance out of an actor: break them down completely until he could build them back in the form he desired. Corvus wasn't his first choice for monster. Aldridge had a protégé he had wanted to use, but the studio executives had overruled him.

They crossed the parking lot toward the abandoned supermarket. Under a canopy tent that made the old parking lot look like a garden party, the stand-ins smoked or drowsed or played computer games at a picnic table. The red light over the door to the building was off; no filming was happening at the moment. They passed a security guard on their way into the chilly building, then headed over to the clutter that wasn't one of the sets, a hanging clothing rack, stacks of flats full of bottled water, masses of Medusa wires coiling across the floor and dangling from the ceiling, and all the canvas chairs with actors', producers', and directors' names on them. The director's, assistant director's, and producer's chairs huddled on a platform a short distance from the cast's chairs.

Opal and Corvus went to Corvus's specially constructed chair. She helped him settle into it and got him the novel he was reading, complete with its own book light; the waiting area was indifferently lighted. A few of the other actors were there, sipping water; Rod and Magenta perched in chairs with absent actors' names on them.

Opal went back outside to the Craft Services trailer to fetch a couple of the butterscotch protein shakes for Corvus, then returned and wandered over to the Props department monitor, a small black-and-white TV that showed the view through whichever camera was hot on the set. The camera was focused on a table topped with a doily, with a lamp sitting on it. The light was made from an old brass carriage lamp. Opal hugged herself. She had forgotten how cold they kept it on the soundstage to offset the melting heat of the lights.

"Fascinating, isn't it?" said a stocky older man, his hair solid, grease-tamed gray, his face set in a wide smile like a frog's.

"What's going on?"

"Wait for it, wait for it," he said. Someone put a small, carved wooden box beside the lamp, angled it sideways, held a Polaroid next to it and moved it again. "Excitement unlimited!"

"That's the magic box?" Opal asked. The script mentioned a magic box, left by the dead mother at the bed-and-breakfast, discovered by the two daughters when they returned after an absence of years. The box held the key to unlocking the daughters' magical natures. It was made of some varnished wood, and the figures carved into it were geometric rather than representational. Inlaid diamonds of mother-of-pearl gleamed under the light.

"That's the magic box. You like? Say, who are you, anyway?"

She held out her hand, and he shook it. "Opal LaZelle. Special effects makeup." She hitched a shoulder toward Corvus.

"Joe Lazarus, prop master."

"Pleased to meet you."

A bell rang. "Roll sound," called someone. "Rolling," called someone else. "Roll camera." "Rolling." A clapperboard showing production, scene, take, roll, date, sound, director, and cameraman came into view on their screen. Someone bumped it. It pulled out of frame. "Action!"

Opal stood beside Joe and watched as a slender hand moved into the shot, rested on the box a moment, then slipped it out of frame. Blaise Penny, as Caitlyn Lost, the younger sister, was stealing the box.

"Cut," cried a voice. Two bells rang.

"Sixth time he's done that one," Joe muttered. "Is it over yet?"

"And print! Break, everybody. Ready set two for scene nineteen!" one voice called, and a second voice echoed it. Activity surged around another part of the soundstage, and the sound of hammering and an electric saw.

"Better scoot," said Joe. He headed into the storm of activity around the forest altar set.

Opal went back to the gathering of canvas-backed chairs. Corvus's oversized chair had accompanied him from *Dead Loss*. While he was on the set, Opal curled up in his chair, but now she settled into the chair assigned to Blaise. Blaise wasn't going to be in the scene with Corvus and Lauren, so she would probably quit for the day. If not, Opal would move. This might be a good time to take a set temperature, see how Blaise treated the help. Lauren was friendly, which was good to know.

"Stand-ins," yelled someone. Corvus's stand-in, Fred, and Lauren's stand-in headed for the set, a tall man in a black robe and a compact woman in brown blouse and jeans.

"How you doing?" Opal asked Corvus, who sprawled in his chair, his hood low over his face, his altered hands sticking out the ends of his black sleeves, the leafy fingers curled under into loose fists. The novel she had brought him earlier lay closed on his lap.

"Strangely," Corvus murmured. "Did you give me post-hypnotic suggestions to help me find the character? I don't know that I signed on for that."

"No," said Opal. "Honestly, Corr. I didn't even know I was hypnotizing you. I didn't tell you to do anything."

"I'll vouch," said Lauren, lazily. "I was watching the whole time she did you. She didn't tell you anything."

"I'm not exactly myself, here," he said.

"Who are you?" asked Opal.

One of the great hands clamped over her wrist. "I think you know," said a low voice from under Corvus's hood. His mouth, the only visible part of his original face, smiled slowly. "You are my handmaiden, are you not? The facilitator who brought me this more-than-perfect vessel? You will be rewarded." The voice had dropped to a whisper.

Opal twisted her arm, tried to free it from the vise of his fingers. He gripped her more tightly.

"Hey, big guy. Save your energy for the shooting," Lauren said.

"Corvus," Opal whispered.

He released her, then ran his clawed fingertips gently

down her arm, ended with them resting on her knuckles. "I don't wish to frighten you," he said. "Yet."

"Could you *be* any more creepy?" Lauren asked. "Leave the handmaiden alone, will you?"

"What?" Corvus asked in his normal voice.

"You're getting eerie, Corvus. Stop it. At least until we're acting."

"I'm eerie?" He sounded surprised.

"Opal, come sit by me," Lauren said. "Could you check my eyelashes?"

Opal left the chair beside Corvus and moved to the one on the far side of Lauren. It was Dirk Baptiste's chair—he played the mysteriously ambiguous sheriff in the film, and Opal hadn't met him yet. His only scene with Corvus happened during the climax, which wasn't scheduled to be filmed for a week.

Opal leaned to look at Lauren's eyelashes.

Lauren winked.

"Thanks," Opal whispered.

"I've got some questions for you later," murmured Lauren. "For now, could you take a quick look at my makeup?"

"No, she cannot," said Rodrigo, beside them suddenly. "That is not her job. It is mine."

"Sorry," said Lauren. "*You* check my eyelashes, then."

Rod put a Set2Go kit labeled "Caitlyn" in his black duffel and took out one labeled "Serena." He leaned close and peered at Lauren's face. "Close your eyes," he murmured. She did, and he blew across her eyelids. A loose lash lifted, drifted. "As for the rest, let's wait until they call for last looks. Everything looks pretty good for the moment."

"Scene nineteen. Ten-minute warning," called one of the assistant directors over by the forest altar set.

Opal got to her feet and grabbed her own kit, a small wheeled suitcase. Special effects makeup called for a lot more equipment than street makeup. She returned to Corvus, wondering who would meet her there. She fished one of the protein shakes out of her bag. "You hungry?" she asked.

"Not really, but I'll drink. It might be a while before I get another chance." He sounded normal again, no more creepy whispering.

Opal popped the top of the can and slid a straw in, held it up where Corvus could easily sip. He steadied her hand with his own, but didn't close his hand on her again; he drank from the straw. She watched his mouth to see if the makeup survived its encounter with the straw. His mouth looked different, and real. The straw didn't disrupt it at all.

"Here we go, people," called the A.D. "Stand by for blocking rehearsal."

Corvus pushed Opal's hand away gently. He and Lauren rose and headed for the set. Opal set the half-finished drink on a nearby table, grabbed her kit, and followed, with Rod.

The stand-ins moved off the set. The boom operator adjusted a microphone to give Corvus more headroom.

SCENE 19

EXT. ALTAR STONE. TWILIGHT.

The DARK GOD stands at the head of the altar stone, which is stained with dark splatters. SERENA, clutching a big sack of a purse, stands beside the stone, not too near the Dark God.

DARK GOD
You've come here for a reason.

SERENA
That's right, to find out what happened to my mother in this forest. Something killed her . . .

Neither Cait nor I believe she committed suicide. Who are you? Some Halloween nutcase who goes around dressed like that all year? You get a kick out of scaring people?

                    DARK GOD

We have known each other before. Don't you remember?

He reaches out, tips her chin up. Eye contact. They transfix each other. Serena breaks contact, shakes her head.

                    SERENA
(agonized whisper)
No.

                    DARK GOD
(low, hypnotic)
You were dedicated to me at your birth. I tasted your blood when you were thirteen, and you pledged to serve me then. Don't you remember?

                    <u>SCENE 19b</u>

EXT. ALTAR STONE. NIGHT.

Flashback sequence. YOUNG SERENA at the altar stone where a small fire burns in a circle of black stones, with bowl, goblet, gold disk with mystic writing on it, three red roses. SERENA'S arm is held steady by a FIGURE in a hooded green robe, her mother, her arm stretched above the altar, a gleaming bronze knife flickering in firelight above the child's wrist. Other ROBED FIGURES dance in the background, eerie FLUTE AND DRUM MUSIC, flickering light indicating firelight, torches. CLOSE-UP on child's eyes, with wildly dilated pupils.

MOTHER
(portentous voice)
Do you give yourself to the God for the greater
good of us all?

YOUNG SERENA
I do!

The knife descends, slashes a shallow cut on the child's wrist, and
blood splashes into the fire. Horrid cries of ghoulish delight from all
the robed figures; music picks up a notch, and dancing grows more
frenzied. Dark figure looms behind them, head nodding to the music. It is the DARK GOD. For a moment his face is visible, smiling,
the eyes glowing green with satisfaction.

BACK to present.

SERENA
No, that never happened! It was just an awful
dream!

DARK GOD
You cannot deny it. You bear the mark of that
day.

He traces the scar on her wrist with his index talon.

DARK GOD
It is written here, and also on your heart. My
name. Speak it.

SERENA
(whisper)
Is . . . bry . . . Isbrytaren.

DARK GOD

Yessssss.

He raises her hand to his face, presses his lips to the scar on the
inside of her wrist, then to the back of her hand.

DARK GOD

Now you remember. You know. You can deny your
destiny no longer. You are mine.

SERENA

No! No!

DARK GOD frames her face with his hands as her mouth goes wide
to scream. He stares into her eyes and she stills like a hypnotized
rabbit facing a snake.

DARK GOD

Do not imagine serving me will be terrible. I treasure your fear, but I will also give you gifts. Gifts that
can help you in your quest. We will work together.

DARK GOD strokes SERENA'S cheek gently. Her face shifts through
a range of responses from horror to acceptance, then finally to anticipation. He tilts her chin again and leans down to kiss her. His
hood falls forward so that the kiss is implied rather than overexplicit.

"All right, everybody, stand by for rehearsal." "Rehearsal's
up!" "Here we go . . . and . . . rehearsing!" "Rehearsing!"
"And . . . action."

Opal had retreated with Rod and the other Hair, Makeup,
and Wardrobe people to the tangle of cast and crew chairs
behind the walls that simulated night forest. They could hear

but not see as Corvus and Lauren ran their lines. Rod got a small portable TV set from his duffel and tuned in to UHF channel sixteen, which, in the vicinity of the soundstage, carried the signal from the hot camera, visual without sound. All of them bent their heads to watch the rehearsal from the view of the master shot camera.

"Dark God looks so real," Magenta muttered.

"You're a genius, Opal," Rod said.

"Thanks," murmured Opal. She felt both proud and disquieted; she knew she was good at her job, no matter how she did it, but this time she couldn't take total credit. Something had worked through and with her to turn Corvus into who he was now.

"But the lines," Betty muttered. "This is so cheesy. I hope they can pull it off."

The rehearsal ended.

"All right, kids," said the director, "Last looks."

Opal got Corvus's Set2Go bag out of her suitcase. It held sponges, gilding powder, adhesive, and other things she could use to tweak Corvus's prostheses and bring them back to their original look. She and the other Hair, Makeup, and Wardrobe people took their kits and continuity Polaroids and went on the set to make any necessary last-minute touch-ups.

Opal made the transition from the shadows around the edges to the set, where everything was subject to observation. The lights were bright and hot. Two different worlds existed side by side, the visible world that created the film's fictional reality, and the invisible world where the illusionists lurked. Opal didn't like being on the set; she kept most of herself submerged while she was working, and even though she knew she was skilled enough to maintain her mask of normal, being onstage made her nervous. Nobody would be interested in her; she was part of the scenery that moved, and yet, a camera might turn her way, capriciously, and show a part of her she hadn't hidden well enough. She glanced at the cameras. None had a red light lit. Not a guaranteee.

Coming on set to make sure everything was right was an important part of her job, so she did it. Corvus dropped his hood and leaned forward so Opal could inspect the prostheses on his head. She couldn't find anything she needed to fix. He held out his hands, turned them up and down. Again, they looked perfect. "Any problems?" she asked.

"No." He stood to his full height and pulled the hood up.

"Ready? All nonactors, clear the set," said Aldridge.

Hair, Makeup, and Wardrobe retreated. Opening bell rang; sound and camera rolled, slate bumped, action called. Rod got out his TV again. Everybody watched the first three takes of the master shot, but then interest dwindled. People settled back in the canvas-backed chairs, pulled out books or magazines. Rod worked on a crossword puzzle. Craig Orlando, key hair, had a book of sudoku puzzles.

Opal opened her letter case, got out a pen and a piece of stationery with red maple leaves across the top.

"Dear Mom," Opal wrote. Maybe she was nuts to write an actual physical letter. Magenta thought so. E mail was easier and faster. Opal's mother liked something she could hold in her hand, and ever since Opal's younger sister's accident with one of the household computers, Mom had been suspicious of them. Maybe even before the computer went wild and caused plants to overgrow the guesthouse. Mom had never been fond of technology, though, as a TV news personality, she tangled with it every day. When she got really mad, studio equipment around her broke down.

"Lapis is tiny and dusty. The sets look good, though, and so does my Monster. You met Corvus Weather at the premiere of *Dead Loss* last fall, remember? This costume is much better. He doesn't have to kill anybody in this movie, either, just corrupt them, so less mess to mop up."

Maybe she better not mention the human sacrifices. Her mother hated film representations of witchy religions, especially the bloody ones that made witches look bad. Her dad laughed about all the things the movies got wrong, but sometimes Mom had no sense of humor.

Not that her family were technically witches, or used magic as a religion; magic was something they were born with, though it didn't manifest until they reached their teens. Their family had many traditions associated with magic use. They had met witches—a variety of them, some professing Wiccans or Pagans with power and without, and some, well, just witches. The word *witch* didn't explain the LaZelles, but Mom could get upset about almost anything.

The Dark God didn't commit any of the film's murders—that was all human stuff. Opal had read the script a number of times and she wasn't sure if the humans were supposed to be acting under the influence of the Dark God, or on their own, thinking they could tell what the God wanted without asking him. She was pretty sure the film had, as part of its agenda, a veiled indictment of organized religion. Which was pretty silly for a horror film no one important would ever see. Then again, the director had pretensions to art. Always a problem, in Opal's experience. People who thought they were doing art were much harder to work for.

Second bell rang twice, signalling the end of the take. "All right," called the A.D., "we're switching to Dark God's POV of Serena. Last looks."

Opal set her letter aside and grabbed her bag. Corvus wouldn't be in this shot, but she might as well check on him anyway.

He smiled at her, and his green eyes glittered. Unnerved, she ducked away from him and left the set. The rest of the day was like that: nothing ever went wrong with the makeup, and each time she faced Corvus, she felt a chill—this was a stranger, and she wasn't sure if he was friendly.

3

∾

Shooting finished at eleven, and afterward, it took Opal an hour to photograph and then remove Corvus's face and hands. The pieces came off easily. The good thing was Corvus slept through most of it. By the end, he looked like his normal self. She astringed the last of the glue from his face, moisturized his skin, and prodded his shoulder gently. He woke with a start.

Except for them, the Makeup trailer was empty. A production assistant had been by earlier to leave off call sheets and script pages for tomorrow's scene. Lauren had an early call the following morning, and had left as soon as she was clean. Rod and Magenta had cleared all the counters and locked all the drawers and cupboards, then left. Hitch had left the Lincoln's keys with Opal before he clocked out; he was done for the day and Corvus wasn't working any longer, so Corvus had control of the car.

"Are you hungry?" Corvus asked as he levered himself out of his chair. He went to the clothes valet and pulled on a shirt.

"I suppose," said Opal. "Are you? I have a couple more of those liquid diet things." She checked the tiny fridge that was part of her counter. A few diet drinks, some protein shakes, and some makeup items that needed refrigeration.

Lapis had a coffee shop and a family restaurant, but neither stayed open late at night. There was no place nearby to get food. "I'm hungry, but not for another shake," Corvus said. "Want to go out for dinner?"

Opal checked the call sheet for the following day. Corvus had a scene where he incited the sisters to fight with each other. They wouldn't need to get to makeup until ten A.M. "Sure," she said, feeling a little strange. She had spent hours and hours with him, but mostly in the context of playing with his face, or waiting to play with his face. They had lunch together, catered meals—along with all kinds of other people at the same table. Most dinnertimes, each of them took their per diem and went separate ways, but that was when they were on a more normal schedule.

The nearest open restaurant Opal knew about was on the highway, ten miles from Lapis, near the characterless hotel where most of the crew and the lesser cast had rooms. Opal drove the Lincoln there with Corvus relaxing in the passenger seat. The restaurant was an IHOP truck stop, and none of the strangers sipping coffee inside had ever seen someone Corvus's height before, from the reaction they got when they walked in. Everybody gawked. Corvus was used to it.

"You movie people?" the waitress asked. She was young and blond and looked wilted but game.

"Yep," said Corvus. "How could you tell?"

She grinned and avoided the obvious answer. "Don't get many black Lincolns in the parking lot, not till you folks started dropping by. You want to sit with the others?"

"Where?" asked Corvus.

She gestured with a pink-feather-poof-topped pen toward the corner booth. Travis Roy and Bethany Telfair, the *Forest of the Night* scriptwriters, were holed up there with pots of coffee, laptops, and color-coded pages of script. Opal had met with Bethany in preproduction to discuss her concept for the Dark God. In those meetings, the young scriptwriter had been energetic and confusing, full of contradictory details. Opal had gotten a clearer picture from the production designer, who would dictate the look of the whole picture anyway.

Now Bethany looked frazzled. Her hair, ginger, thick, and shoulder length, stood up in tufts, as though she had been tugging at it.

Travis, Bethany's husband and mentor, blinked blearily at his screen. He was older than Bethany. His hair was a thick shock of gray, and he had deep character brackets around his mouth. He wasn't smiling now.

"They look busy," Corvus told the waitress. Then Bethany glanced up, brightened, and beckoned them over.

Opal wondered what Corvus really wanted to do. He was good-natured enough to head for the table.

"Want something to eat?" asked the waitress, following them.

"Yes, please," said Opal.

"You one of the stars, hon?" asked the waitress.

Opal smiled and shook her head. "I do makeup. Mr. Weather is the star."

Corvus slid into the booth beside Bethany, then shook his head. "The makeup is the real star, Jenny," he said.

Opal checked the waitress's nametag, saw that Corvus had her name correct. She sat next to Travis, who scooted over to make room. He stacked some of the pages and pulled them closer to his laptop.

"You been in anything I might have seen?" the waitress asked Corvus.

"Depends on whether you like horror films," Corvus said. "I play a lot of monsters."

She shook her head, handed them menus. "Naw. I got

enough scares in my daily life. Rather see romances. Your voice sounds familiar, though."

"I don't usually have speaking parts. Could I get some coffee, please?"

She started. "Oh, sure. You want some, too, hon?"

"Please," Opal answered.

The waitress went to a neighboring table and grabbed mugs and silverware wrapped in white paper napkins, set them on the table in front of Opal and Corvus, and headed for the kitchen and the coffeepot.

"What are you guys doing?" Opal asked the writers.

"Rewriting scenes twenty-five, twenty-six, and twenty-seven," said Bethany.

"Adding in scene twenty-five A. Aldridge wants more monster, Corr," said Travis. "After he saw yesterday's dailies, he decided to beef up your part. You got an extra week?"

"If they have the budget for me, sure. What am I supposed to be doing now?"

"He wants you to do an extra scene with child Caitlyn, really mess her up."

"It makes dramatic sense," said Bethany. "I always wondered about her motivations, anyway, Trav. She has everything going for her, looks, talent, youth, and she's just so *bad.*"

"Caitlyn and Serena both have father issues," said Travis. "Their mom killed their father, remember? Years before she killed herself."

"What? That's not in the script," Corvus said.

"It was part of the brainstorming we did early on. Serena was out there at one of the rituals. She was five or six. Mom was high on something. Dad was, too. In the grip of the drug, Mom sacrificed Dad. Lots of blood. Dark God shows up. Serena saw what happened, but she suppresses it. Caitlyn never found out. To Caitlyn, Dad went away one night and never came back. She's been searching for him or a reasonable facsimile ever since."

"*Eww.* Serena thinks Dad's blood was spilled to summon Dark God? So maybe she thinks of Dark God as her replacement father?" Bethany tugged at her hair, then attacked her laptop's keyboard.

"Which is pretty disgusting, since *he* thinks she's his *bride,*" said Travis.

Bethany shrugged. "Hey, they're creepy witches. What more do you need?"

"Where do you guys get your ideas about witches?" Opal asked, with a touch of acid. She regretted the question the moment after it came out. It wasn't her job to critique scripts or supply magical reality.

Travis and Bethany grinned. "Watching other peoples' movies," said Travis.

Bethany lost her smile. "Yeah, but Trav, this particular project—"

"Oh, right. We actually did some original work on this project. Bethany got the idea while she was staying at the Lapis B&B," Travis said.

"You visited Lapis before you wrote the script?" asked Corvus. "Why on earth?"

Bethany said, "My folks live in Lapis. I grew up around here. A couple years ago, we were having a big family party, and not everybody could stay at my folks' house, so I spent my first night ever in the scary B&B. When I was a kid"— Bethany's gaze softened—"I thought the B&B was run by ghosts. Mr. and Mrs. Gates—well, they're still there. I thought they were old when I was a kid, but now they're positively ancient. You can see the cobwebs on 'em. They manage to keep the place clean, though.

"Anyway, I had such a dream in that house. More like a nightmare. Most of the plot for the movie, in fact. The next morning I got my cousin to drive me out to that clearing, which was a place we never went when we were kids. It was supposed to be haunted, too. I mean, when I'd sleep over at my girlfriends', all the kids knew some story about something horrible that happened there. And it was creepy out there. That altar, those stains. The story kind of—well, I talked it over with Trav, and we figured we could make something out of it. It's one of those gift things. Kind of drops into your lap."

The waitress finally brought them coffee and took their sandwich orders.

"You thought that clearing was haunted when you were a kid?" Opal repeated after the waitress left.

"Yeah. My brother wanted to sneak over there one Halloween, but I was petrified and wouldn't do it. Everybody said kids had died there in some horrible way—bled out on the altar rock, or something worse. There were lots of rumors of Bad People in the woods. Nobody said the *W* word, though. They were more like bogeymen and bogeywomen."

She went on, "Now that I think about it, there are lots of places around here that felt off when I was a kid. We had a few places it was safe to go, like the lake and the library, and the rest of the world was filled with scary places."

"You have any trouble getting permits for the locations?" Opal asked. She knew some sites where people practiced magic; the sites had their own powers, and made it hard for nonmagical people to find them or stay on them. Was Lapis trying to protect itself from her or from others?

"I don't know. Not my department. The locations were perfect, though, which I guess they would be, since this is the place I was describing in the script."

"I wonder if they scouted anywhere else," Opal muttered.

"Is there something wrong with here? I thought everything was going great," said Travis.

"This place feels weird to me," Opal said. "Which doesn't

make a bit of difference to anybody who matters. I just—I think there's something going on under the surface."

"You *trying* to creep me out?" Bethany asked.

"No. No, sorry. Corr—"

"Maybe I know what you're talking about," he said. "The non-posthypnotic suggestions?"

"Right. Really, I'm *not* trying to force you anywhere near your role."

"You guys are speaking code now," said Travis.

Opal bit her lip, tried to figure out whether to share her concern with anyone. What the heck. Travis and Bethany were writers. They were close to being wallpaper, too . . . depending on whether the director and his team included them. "Corvus falls further into character than he needs to, even when he's not on the set," she said. "And that Dark God guy—not really a fun person."

"I thought he was fun," said Travis. "I love writing for him. Stuff almost writes itself. Deliciously creepy."

Opal frowned and checked Corvus's reaction to this. He looked puzzled.

The waitress brought their sandwiches, and they ate.

"So," said Bethany when Opal had finished half her sandwich, "what's not to like about Dark God? Personally, I think he's not creepy enough. Trav made him all seductive instead of terrifying."

"It's a trend," Travis said. "Horrifying heroes. Vampires and werewolves are really hot in romance right now. Why not gods?"

"We're writing a romance?" asked Bethany.

"Of course. Twisted, but that resonates with people at the moment."

"Oh. I wish I'd known. Well, anyway, Opal—"

"He called me a handmaiden and thanked me for selecting such a perfect vessel for him."

"I what?" said Corvus. "Are you saying I said that?"

"You did. Ask Lauren. Also, his face is alive," Opal said. The minute it was out of her mouth, she thought, *This is a mistake. I shouldn't be talking to outside people about this stuff. Never break the wall of silence that surrounds our magic.*

But this is not our magic. I don't have to keep it secret.

"My face is alive?" Corvus asked, more confused than ever.

"The face I put on you is alive."

"Can I use this stuff in the script?" Travis asked.

"How are you going to use something about a mask being alive?" said Bethany. "It's been done, and it's not our movie."

"Not the mask," Travis said. "The handmaiden and vessel stuff."

Opal sighed, and decided that on the whole, it was probably a good thing they weren't taking her seriously.

"I called you a handmaiden?" Corvus said, and pressed the knuckle of his index finger against his lips, then dropped his hand. "I wonder what I meant."

"I *am* a handmaiden," said Opal. "I wait on you and serve you."

He studied her, his brows lowered. Finally a smile flared, as though he knew she was kidding. His gaze was warm, and she felt again the queer tight twist in her chest, the love she couldn't stop. She wanted to help and protect him, give him all the tools he needed to be great.

She had felt like this about Gayle Graceland, the first star she had been personally attached to on a project, in *Weather Witch*, even when Gayle was a raving bitch, throwing things that broke and couldn't easily be replaced, and occasionally hitting crew with them. Adoration had engulfed Opal. She had put up with all kinds of lunatic behavior from Gayle; the love pressed her into servitude, pulled her best skills out of her, forced her to make sure Gayle was perfect in every take, even when others whispered commiseration to Opal behind the scenes.

After Gayle's part wrapped, Gayle had invited Opal on a spa vacation. The grip on Opal's heart had vanished. She envisioned the trip: Gayle behaving badly, abusing Opal, Opal picking up after her and trying to calm everyone hurt by her. Opal had refused the invitation. Later, she read all about Gayle's supposed spa antics in the tabloids—slapping a masseuse, starting a mud fight—and she felt nothing but relief that she hadn't gone. The picture came out; Gayle's performance got great notices, while her personal life was chewed up and spit out by the media.

Opal got a better job, and fell in love again. Her next film hadn't been a monster film and she'd been one of a core of makeup artists under the supervision of a key artist. She'd fallen for Gerry that time, even though she didn't always make him up. He looked good enough not to need much help. They'd gone out after the film wrapped. The relationship had died a natural if public death.

Corvus was the only person she'd worked with so far who kept a grip on her heart, all unknowing, even after they finished a picture. She had gone on thinking about him, wishing she were with him, even after *Dead Loss* was made and out.

He had never given her a reason to think he reciprocated her feelings.

Now they were working on a second job together. She hadn't had to let go of the love.

In the break between pictures, Opal had gone home and talked to her mother, a newscaster and social commentator, who knew about being famous and loved for how she looked and behaved on camera.

"Crushes are strange," her mother said. "I have fans who send me all kinds of things. Photographs. Poetry. Pastry. Underwear, some of it used. Impassioned letters begging me for fingernails or locks of hair or a lipstick kiss on the return envelope. I use my talents to turn on the charm, but I always try not to turn it too high. People watch me. They feel they know me. They want to own me. Sometimes it's disturbing, and other times it's my dream come true, the height of my desire. If it gets sick and twisted, I can deal with it: I have the skills to shut the fans down before they hurt me or themselves.

"So, my dearest daughter, have you asked yourself what you get from this love, why you let yourself fall into it?"

"No," Opal said, after consideration. "I wondered whether I should try to cure myself of it."

"You could shut it off with a thought," said her mother. "It's a choice you've made. It must pay off somehow."

Opal thought about Gayle. Everyone else on the *Weather Witch* shoot had hated the star, but she looked so good on film they had to work with her. Not hating her had helped Opal get her job done, no matter what Gayle did. If Opal had stood her ground against unreasonable behavior or demands, or even asked for the respect she deserved, everything would have taken twice as long. Her love for Gayle had been useful; it kept the film close to budget and gave Opal the power to do her job even after it would have become unbearable for anyone in her right mind. She had cruised through work in an altered state of fatuous adoration and done fine.

Later she had bumped into the key makeup artist from *Weather Witch* at a party, and been confused by the contempt the man showed her. It took her a while to remember what she had been like under the influence of Gayle.

Corvus was a different story. Gentle, likable, helpful, talented, and willing to work with her. Somebody she wasn't embarrassed to be in love with.

"You do an amazing job no one else could do," Corvus said to her now. "Somehow I don't think 'handmaiden' covers it."

"Thanks," she said. She stared down at her plate, then raised her eyes to meet his gaze. The smile he gave her was her favorite, the one that promised laughter. "I'm not so worried about the handmaiden part. It's the part where he said he was using you for a vessel that really bothers me. It was like you were possessed."

His laugher came, deep and infectious. "I was pulling your leg," he said.

4

Opal slid up her sleeve below the table, checked the bruises on her wrist where the Dark God had gripped her. Pretty strong pressure for a joke. Didn't jibe with anything she knew about Corvus: he had never hurt anybody that she'd heard of, and she'd spent months in his orbit.

More was going on here than an actor acting like someone he wasn't. She knew the feeling of power settling on someone, knew it had come from outside of him.

She tilted her head to look at him again, and found him leaning forward, the smile gone, his heavy brows pinched together in worry. "I didn't mean to upset you."

She sucked on her lower lip. "Big guy, I'm the one who knows who you are under the mask. You shouldn't even *think* about messing with me."

"Define *messing*."

"Yeah, Opal, define *messing*," said Travis.

Opal flushed. Stupid writers, always looking for hidden

meanings. "Pulling my leg. Corvus, you wouldn't play a mean joke on me for no reason. Why pretend you would?"

"I'm not comfortable with the direction the conversation's going."

"Oh." She thought about that, smiled. "Let's change the subject, then." She needed to collect more information before she decided what to do about it.

"All right."

"Let's finish eating and I'll take you back to your room," Opal told Corvus.

"I'm done." Corvus rose, loomed over the table.

Opal unfolded her paper napkin and wrapped the second half of her sandwich in it. She stood, too, and tucked it into her coat pocket to eat after she had dropped Corvus off in Lapis. "Good night," she said to Bethany and Travis. "Hope you can finish and get some sleep."

"We never sleep," said Travis. "Thanks for the ideas."

Corvus got the check from the waitress and paid before they headed out into the night. Opal drove with him sprawled in the passenger seat beside her. By the time they reached the bed-and-breakfast, he was asleep. She debated the merits of waking him versus using a persuasion on his sleeping self, and, after a scan of the area to make sure no one else was around, decided on the second option. She went around the car, opened his door, and spoke to his body, bypassing his mind. "Gently, gently, and all in concert," she whispered, "rise from where you are, walk in beauty, stealth, and grace; carry yourself to where you can rest."

Corvus got out of the car, his eyes closed. Opal took his hand. "Come," she whispered. He didn't take much persuading; somehow he was tuned to her already, receptive to suggestion, and that worried her. Maybe it explained the paralysis she had put on him without meaning to earlier.

Early in her dating career, Opal had learned to be wary of where her unconscious talents took her: she had tranced boys

without even trying, had not realized that their perfect behavior toward her was the product of her own desires rather
than their characters. Her younger brother Jasper was the
one who alerted her to what she was doing. He'd asked her if
she really needed to spell a guy to get a date. "Jeez, Opal, you
can look like their dream girl; how come you need to put
them under to get them to go out with you?"

The front door to the bed-and-breakfast was locked. Opal
and Corvus stood under the orange porch light while she
pondered this.

The house distracted her. The door felt almost as though
it were warded. The house, too, put out some nonvisual darkness. With Corvus swaying slightly beside her, Opal studied
the face of the house. The front windows were lace-curtained.
Dim orange lights glowed behind the two windows to either
side of the front door. Opal felt as though the house were
watching her.

The script described this house as possessed by a spirit of
evil. Maybe Bethany was sensitive. Opal wasn't sure the house
was evil, but she thought it was possessed. One of her cousins
had a gift of sensing the histories of places. Some houses made
him sick; he could tell that people had been murdered in
them, or hurt in other ways. Opal had never thought she had
that kind of sense.

She flattened her palm on the front door and felt an uneasy shift under her hand. Huh.

Still, she needed to get Corvus to his room.

Corvus had the key on him somewhere, but asking him to
find and use it might wake him up. He looked so peaceful. She
murmured to the lock. It opened for her. Again she sensed a
shift in the house, not like the lurch of an earthquake, more
like something stirring under the surface of a street. When she
touched the door handle, she felt a slight squirm, as though
the metal were the skin of some smooth reptile. Then a low-
level rumble, like purring.

Uneasy, she crossed the threshold with Corvus in tow.

In the front hall they had to maneuver between movie equipment; parts of the B&B's downstairs were being used as a set. Corvus moved just as she had told him to, gracefully and stealthily. "Go to your room," she said. He led her up the stairs, his hand still in hers, and down the hall to one of six doors. She talked to the lock on his room and opened the door, and then the door to the next room down the hall opened. Neil Aldridge leaned out.

"What the hell is going on out here?" he said.

"We just got back from supper. I'm putting him to bed," Opal answered.

Aldridge glared at her. "No games," he said. "I need him fresh tomorrow." He glanced at his watch, shook his head, and retreated into the master bedroom. As he shut the door, Opal heard him say, "The monster is bedding the makeup girl," and a murmur from someone else, a woman.

Opal sighed and drew Corvus into his room. It looked nice, spacious, brown-walled and ruffly, everything gingham or patterned with tiny flowers and edged with fussy lace. The bed was huge, a good thing; Corvus could fit on it if he lay diagonally from one corner to the other. The weird household spirit, ominous yet welcoming, was present under the surface here, as well. It didn't really feel as though something was ready to pounce or menace. Just as though something was watching. Maybe licking its lips. Opal shuddered and closed the door behind her.

"All right," she said to Corvus. "Do everything you need to, to put yourself to bed comfortably."

He went into the bathroom and only partially closed the door. Water ran, and toothbrushing sounds drifted out to her. The sound of a long and abundant piss. The toilet flushed, the water ran again. Good. Even in his sleep, he washed his hands after using the john.

Now was a good time for her to leave. She glanced around

the room, wondering if she should do anything else for him
before she headed back to her own hotel. Tell him he could
wake up when he'd rested or when the alarm went off, she
supposed. She went to the bedside table to check the alarm
clock. They had to be in Makeup at ten. She had no idea how
long it took Corvus to wake up, shower, eat. Should she set
the alarm for eight thirty? Nine? Maybe it was time to wake
him up and let him run his own life. Then again, that might
just confuse him. She set the alarm for eight thirty.

He emerged from the bathroom, naked, eyes closed. He
gathered her up and pulled her onto the bed with him. There
was a folded quilt at the bottom of the bed, and he tugged it
up over them, then settled on his side, his arm tightly around
her, snugging her back against his front. He was so large she
felt as though she had a warm, breathing mountain behind
her. His arm was muscular and heavy. She had seen his upper
body before, but now she thought about what else she had
just seen when he came out of the bathroom: respectable, but
not intimidating. Oddly attractive, like the rest of him. Not
at all erect, however.

He sighed into her hair and dropped more deeply into
sleep.

She lay in his embrace, her heart bumping, and wondered
what to do next. Wake him? Escape by persuading his arm
to let go? Stay where she was? The director already thought
they were sleeping together, and hadn't told them they
couldn't.

This was a bad idea, though. Corvus didn't know what he
was doing. Besides, she was still fully clothed, including her
shoes, and she was lying on half a squashy sandwich in the
pocket of her coat. She hadn't brushed her teeth or gone to
the bathroom.

"Let me go," she murmured to his arm. At first it tightened. "Please let me go," she whispered, with persuaders, and
he sighed again and lifted his arm. She scooted out. "Rest

well," she told him, "and wake when you need to." She slipped out of the room, got it to relock itself, and then left the house, locking it behind her.

———————

At the hotel ten miles away where the lesser cast and crew were staying, Lauren was waiting in the utilitarian, sterile lobby with her feet up on a coffee table, reading a novel. She put it down as soon as Opal entered. "Did it really take that long to take off his makeup?" she asked.

"What are you doing here?" said Opal. As a lead actor, Lauren had her own private room in someone's house in Lapis. All the principal cast and crew had been quartered close to the locations and soundstage.

"Waiting for you," Lauren answered.

"Did you get supper? We went to the restaurant and ate."

"My host family left me a meal. I stopped at the restaurant to look for you, though, on my way here, and you weren't there. Where've you been?"

Opal checked her watch. Two A.M. She needed to get up in about six hours. "Is there something I can do for you?"

"Can I come up to your room? I'd rather not discuss this in public."

There was no one behind the front desk, and no one else in the lobby. Opal supposed someone might come in at any moment. She looked across the parking lot to the restaurant where she and Corvus had had dinner, which was open twenty-four hours and had lots of glass. Travis and Bethany were still ensconced in the corner booth, arguing about something.

"All right," Opal said at last, and headed for the elevator. Lauren followed.

Opal switched on the light in her room and glanced around. She spent so little time here she had made no effort to soften it away from its budget motel one-size-almost-fits-people-with-no-expectations. The maid had made the bed.

There was a small round table with a couple of chairs, and a television bolted to a wall shelf. She had to pay extra if she wanted the cable turned on. Her per diem would cover it, but she didn't need TV after a day working on the film.

Opal gestured toward the chair. "Please have a seat. I'm sorry. I don't have anything to offer you. There's a pop machine down the hall. . . ."

"I don't need anything," Lauren said. She took the chair, though.

Opal dropped onto the bed and fished the squashed half sandwich out of her pocket. "What's on your mind?"

"I was wondering if I could hire you for a side job."

"I think I'd get in trouble with the union if I did that."

Lauren considered. The corners of her generous mouth stretched into a small frown. "Cash under the table? It's not complicated. Just a simple disguise. Here's what's happening. I got involved with one of my costars on my last film. His name's Norman Davis. What I didn't know going in was he's a nutcase, kind of an obsessive stalker type, and right now he's unemployed. Somebody said they saw him at the supermarket down the road. I'm kind of afraid of him. I wondered if there was something simple I could do to hide myself from his regard. What if he's been savaging things for fun ever since I broke up with him? I don't want to be one of them."

"Oh," said Opal.

"Security's tight enough on the shoot to keep him out. I'll talk to the chief about this. But I'd also like to be able to go out and wander around, shop, whatever, without being paranoid all the time. Can you help me?"

"I'm sure Rod—"

Lauren leaned toward Opal, her large dark eyes intent. "I watched you work," she said.

Opal waited.

"My grandmother's a witch," said Lauren, "and my sister has a little talent. Not like you."

Opal straightened. Calm flowed into her. It was a first for her, being discovered by someone she didn't want to know about her talent. Since she had started in the business, she had revealed herself to a few people, but never by mistake. She could take care of an unintended revelation. The family had techniques to deal with outsiders. Opal had mastered persuaders. She hadn't used them much until tonight, with Corvus and the locks, but she knew her own strengths.

"I'll never, ever tell," said Lauren.

"Even if I don't help you?"

Lauren shook her head. "Your choice. I'll ask Rod for disguise advice if I have to, and Craig. I know a blond wig would change me, and I can walk and act differently. I just thought—"

"How much would you pay me?"

"How much would you want?"

Opal sucked on her bottom lip, rose, and wandered to the dresser. She opened the top drawer and looked at her underwear, shook her head. She opened another drawer. More clothes. What was she expecting? "Money's not much of a motivating factor for me," she said. She got good pay doing special effects makeup, and she didn't spend much. Her bank balance was almost big enough to buy real estate in California.

"Is there something you'd prefer? I don't have a lot of pull with the Makeup people. It's not like I could get you a promotion."

"I don't want a promotion. I have the job I want." Opal wandered into the bathroom and looked at her toiletries. She picked up her hairbrush, then her comb. She set them down again. She had no cosmetics of her own, just soap and shampoo and moisturizer. "Oh," she said, "I know." Out in the room again, she went to the closet and opened her suitcase, pulled out a bag of new makeup brushes, her spares. She selected a broad brush, the kind one used to whisk powder onto a face.

"What can I do in return?" Lauren asked.

"You were there when the other person talked to me," said Opal. She sat on the bed with the brush cupped in her hands. She strengthened its psychic shape so it would be able to hold power, and then she sent power into it.

"The one who talked through Corvus?" Lauren said.

"You understand that there was someone else?"

"I don't know what to think, except that was a lot different from the way he usually talks. But he's such a good actor, he could do a voice and persona like that without any trouble. Was it a joke?"

"He said it was, but I don't believe it. Something worked through him and through me, something I don't know. I'm afraid of it. What you can do for me . . ." She finished imbuing the brush with power and set it on her thigh. "Listen to my fears. I don't have anyone else I can talk to about this right now."

"I can listen. Of course I can listen," said Lauren. "Does this mean you trust me?"

"I don't know yet. I'd like to trust you. But how can I?"

"I don't know," Lauren said. "My *abuela* said she could tell when a person was being straight with her, but my sister, not such a good lie detector. Lots of boys fooled her into thinking they meant everything they said when they were trying to get into her pants. You do any truth detecting?"

"My talents lie in the opposite direction," Opal said. "Come in the bathroom and let me show you how to use this."

"What?"

"C'mon." Opal rose, and Lauren followed her into the bathroom, where the mirror was just wide enough for both of them to see themselves at once. "Sometimes I use tools in my work," Opal said. "I've just made this one different. I hold it, and think about the effect I want to achieve, and then I apply it." She thought about pale, crystal green eyes. When she had the image clear, she closed her right eye and brushed the brush over the lid. She opened her eye and stared at herself:

one violet eye, one pale green one. The effect was spookier than she expected. The green eye looked wicked, somehow, as though it saw too much. Her color sense was a little off, too. She closed her violet eye and looked at the world with the green one; suddenly the utilitarian, beige-colored bathroom had secret sparkling diamonds hidden in its corners, and strange patterns in its wallpaper. "Whoa."

"My god!" said Lauren. "That's amazing. Amazing!"

"It's peculiar," Opal said. She held out the brush. "This thing is charged right now. What you should do is think of something simple. The more complicated and extreme you make it, the faster the charge gets used up, and if you run out of charge, you can get stuck that way."

"This'll work for *me*?" Lauren took the brush gingerly.

Opal nodded. "Once I put the power in the tool and tell the tool how to work, anybody can use it, if they know what they're doing. Think about the change you want, then brush it into being."

Lauren held the brush up as though it were a magic wand or a conductor's baton. She closed her eyes, took a deep breath, and opened them. She brushed her cheeks. The shape of her face changed, became thinner. Her jawline softened. She brushed her lips. They also thinned.

She was unrecognizable.

"Oh, God," she whispered. "Unreal." She set the brush down and placed her hands on her cheeks, pressed her fingertips to her mouth. "Oh, God," she repeated. "It feels like it looks. Oh, God!"

Her eyes were still large and dark, wide in their astonishment. "How—"

Opal stood back, her arms crossed over her chest.

Lauren swallowed. "How long does it last?"

Opal touched Lauren's cheek and thought about it. "I guess about two hours. It's hard to tell. You can change back with the brush, too. You don't want to try this too often. I can't put too much into the brush—I need to save power for my own work."

"Is this what made Corvus strange?"

"I don't think so. I only change the outer layer, what the light falls on. It shouldn't go any deeper. Do you feel like someone else?"

Lauren stared at her new self. "I think I'm myself inside, but if I went on looking like this for a while, I'd feel different. Wearing this face, I'm not so sure of myself or what signals I'm sending. This is *so* strange."

Opal checked her watch again. Nearly three. "I've got to get some sleep or I might mess up tomorrow."

"Oh. Oh, yes, sorry. Thanks, Opal. This is unbelievable."

"You might want to practice undoing it before you leave, so I can help if anything goes wrong."

Lauren nodded. She picked up the brush, held it, thought, then stroked the brush gently over her cheeks and mouth. Her face filled out, generous, sensuous, arresting, and Opal felt a twist in her chest again. Though she hadn't made any choices about Lauren's changes, her power had worked them, and now she was engaged, like it or not. A warm affection welled up in her, a longing to protect Lauren and help her, spend time with her in any capacity Lauren allowed.

She felt stupid. Why hadn't she foreseen this outcome?

Maybe it was for the best.

"I look like myself again, right?" Lauren asked. She patted her cheek. "I did all right?"

"You did great."

"Do you need this for your eye?" Lauren held out the brush to her.

"No," said Opal. "I wonder." She closed both her eyes and thought her other eye green. She studied herself with the new eyes. "It's weird, isn't it, how such a small thing can make someone look completely different?"

"You look lethal, somehow."

"Hmm." What would the Dark God make of that? "Hey, wrap the brush in a handkerchief, if you have one. Because it's a touch power, it might affect random things it comes in contact with, like stuff in your purse."

"You're giving me this?"

"Sure. You can pay me back for the cost of the brush if you like. That's one of the expensive ones. Be careful with it."

"I will." Lauren went back to the bedroom and rummaged in her purse, found a small silk Japanese pouch with coins in it, dumped the coins out and put the brush gently in. "Thank you," she said, and hugged Opal awkwardly. "See you in the morning." She let herself out.

"Good night," Opal said. She just remembered to set her own alarm before she fell exhausted into bed with all her clothes on.

"You sleep all right?" Opal asked Corvus when he arrived at the Makeup trailer at ten. She had gotten there about twenty minutes earlier and had almost finished prepping for him.

"Great. Suspiciously great, when I don't even remember how I got to bed last night. What happened?"

"You fell asleep in the car. You took direction, though, even asleep. Did you know you sleepwalk excellently?"

"No one has ever told me that before. Opal?" He reached for her hand, tugged her away from setting out her brushes. "Things seem much stranger on this shoot. What's going on?" He stared into her face, started. "Good lord, what happened to your eyes?"

She had forgotten the change. She glanced at the mirror and saw pale, crystal green eyes staring back. They looked like someone else's eyes, mysterious and unsettling. "I'm trying out a new effect. You like?"

He frowned. "It's interesting, anyway."

"What's he talking about?" Rodrigo asked from the second chair. He and Magenta were taking a break before Blaise and Lauren arrived. Their call for makeup was much later. Opal had more to do for Corvus.

Opal opened her eyes wide and stared at Rod. "Whoa!" he cried. "Where'd you get the contacts? They're great! You look so different!"

"It's not a commercial company. I'm a beta tester. Guess I better take them out before I spook anyone else."

"Thumbs up for looks," said Rod, and Magenta nodded.

Opal gave them a big smile. She knelt over her counter and pretended to pop contacts out and put them into an illusory case, letting her eyes go back to their natural violet. She locked the intangible case into one of her drawers and turned to look at Corvus. "You ready?" Opal asked.

He leaned back and stared at the ceiling. Finally he clasped his hands over his stomach and nodded to her. "Apprehensive, but ready, I guess."

"I'm sorry I've broken your trust," she said gently to him as she shook a can of shaving cream. "I never meant to."

"Things are happening I don't understand."

"Me, too."

"I never sleep well on a shoot. Too much to obsess about."

"Do you consider that time well spent?" she asked.

"In fact, I do; it's those after-midnight skull-sweat sessions that lead me to character breakthroughs—when I get a chance to act a character. They don't stop me from doing a good job, not when you can't see my real face."

She sighed. "I chose not to wake you when it turned out you could walk while asleep, and get ready for bed, too. It's my fault. Seemed like you were tired enough to need whatever rest you could get. I apologize."

"You're going to take responsibility for my sleeping so deeply?"

She hesitated, then said, "I made a suggestion to you while you were under."

He caught her hand before she could apply the shaving cream. "What was it?" he asked, his voice grating.

" 'Rest well,' " she said. "Just 'rest well.' "

His face went more still than she had ever seen it. He stared at her, motionless, her hand caught in his. She felt the hot track of a tear streak down her cheek and blinked to stop any others from falling. He might hate her now, but that wouldn't change how she felt about him, which meant she was in for misery.

He opened his hand and released her, then lay back in his chair and closed his eyes. She shaved him and prepped his skin and laid the prosthetics on gently and silently. This time, she noticed when Blaise and Lauren came in, was remotely aware of their being prepped by Rodrigo and Magenta. She did nothing to Corvus but attach necessary things to his face, arms, hands, and upper body; she made sure she didn't paralyze him this time, but he didn't move; he barely breathed. She ornamented him the way she would have painted a statue.

Lauren, ready for her scene, sat in the next chair and watched, silent.

"Time for the contacts," Opal said at last, her voice choked.

"Can I put them in myself?" he asked.

"Not with the hands you've got now."

"Oh." He stared down at his hands. This time she had done his whole chest and arms, and the hand prostheses. Today there would be close-ups. He blinked twice. "Go."

She couldn't help saying a small spell to herself, that she would slip the contacts in perfectly, not harm him, that he would be comfortable with them as long as it took. She lifted his leaf brown eyelids and slid the contacts in, which gave him the stare of a stranger.

"Good job," he said. He pulled the lever that straightened his chair so he could stand up easily. He shook his shoulders, and said, as if to himself, "Good."

"I'll call Kelsi."

Corvus studied himself in the mirror while Opal called Kelsi on her walkie to come over with the Dark God's robe.

"I need jewels," said Corvus, his voice low and thrilling. "Why would I not adorn myself? It is too simple. Have you people no sense of pageantry? Handmaiden." He turned to Opal.

Opal glanced at Lauren, who had straightened, her eyes wide.

"I want something that sparkles. A diamond star for my forehead."

"I can't do that, sir. It would ruin the continuity."

"You *can* do it," he whispered. "You *will* do it." He gripped her wrist again, bent forward, and brought her hand up to touch his forehead. "Give me a small fraction of your power. A tiny taste, a promise of what we will share later."

"I don't want to share with you. I don't even know you."

"You know my vessel," he whispered. "You love it."

"You're not that person."

"I can give you that person."

"I only want him if he gives himself."

"Foolish denier of dreams."

"Yep, that's me," Opal said. "Give up this dream of jewels, will you? You're here to play a part, that's all."

He grinned, suddenly, just as Kelsi's knock sounded on the door. Lauren jumped up and opened it.

"How little you know," the Dark God said to Opal. "It's delicious."

Lauren closed and locked the door after Kelsi came in, the Dark God's robe over her arm.

"I am surrounded by beauty," said Corvus, smiling at all three of them. "It's a fine time to be awake."

"Mr. Weather, could you hold out your arms behind you so I can slide this on, please?" Kelsi asked.

Corvus posed. She slid the robe onto him. After she had

snapped it shut and fastened it with the silver star, he took her hand and pressed his lips to the back of it.

"Won't you screw up your—" she began, but then her eyes met his, and she blinked and swayed, leaned into him. His arms folded around her; her face pressed against his sculptured abdomen. He closed his eyes and drew in a long breath, his smile widening.

Kelsi sagged in his arms. He lifted her and set her gently on his abandoned chair, where she curled up, snoring softly.

"What did you do to her?" Opal demanded.

"You wouldn't give me what I needed, so I had to go elsewhere." He stretched as best he could in the cramped quarters of the Makeup trailer. "I feel stronger now."

"She going to wake up okay?" Lauren asked.

"Of course. She will just—*rest well.*" He turned his luminous eyes to Opal, who had flinched at his words. "You could both rest well, if you liked."

"Get out of here. We have a job to do. Do you have your lines memorized?" Lauren said.

"My lines?" He cocked his head. "My lines. Oh, yes, they're in here."

"Well, I hope you can act," said Lauren. She unlocked the door, flung it open, and stomped down the stairs.

Opal packed her makeup suitcase for the walk across the parking lot to the soundstage. She was conscious of Corvus's body hovering above her, of the absence of his spirit and the presence of someone else's. She wasn't sure how to handle that. She wanted to rescue Corvus, bring him back to himself, but—what if she confronted the new guy and lost? She had never been the most powerful person in her family. She had no idea how to kick a spirit out of a body where it didn't belong. No way could she act like an exorcist. No religious training. She used her power to alter appearances, not to change the cores of things.

Her options were to try something desperate that might

not work or wait him out. See if the new guy could act. Maybe the new guy was the character, and wouldn't need to act.

The new guy had been present before, and Corvus had returned to the body without any damage but lost time. Maybe the new guy had a time limit on how long he could stick around. Although the fact that he had sucked something out of Kelsi and left her asleep didn't bode well. Powering up, stealing energy, it looked like. If he could do that to Kelsi, he could probably do that to other people. Opal wondered how hungry he was, and how far he'd go.

Kelsi was still breathing. That was good.

Opal had done her best to leave the magic out of changing Corvus into the Dark God this time, but she had let a little trickle in at the last moment, and the new guy had brought his own. Looking at the Green Man face on him, she didn't think it was latex any longer.

Corvus didn't trust her. This wasn't going to help.

She needed to figure out how to deal with the new guy. Though she had known some roughhousing techniques when she was younger—she had needed them to deal with aggressive siblings and unkind cousins—she was out of practice.

She had a cell phone in her pocket. As soon as she got a minute—and there were lots of hurry-up-and-wait minutes on the set—she'd call home, see if her relatives had any ideas on how to deal with this.

She turned toward the door, and the thing in Corvus's body said, "Just one taste," pulled her to him, pressed his lips to hers.

His mouth had a flavor like a ripe, juicy peach, something she had never tasted in a kiss before. She struggled with several impulses: slap him and maybe mess up four hours' work, cost the picture who knew how much time and money to repair the face. Relax into it: she'd dreamed Corvus would fall for her, in the way of hopeless fantasies. Her sensible streak said it would never happen naturally (it could be made to happen without much effort, she knew), and she wouldn't force it. This wasn't Corvus, though; it wasn't even someone she liked. This was the opposite of her fantasy, an unpleasant reality she didn't want. While she debated, she felt him drawing power from her. Not good. She needed to cut him off. She could change herself into something without a mouth and break the connection. Shock him away from her. Slide sideways—

Light flashed, a camera's shutter clicked, and then more flashes and clicks. "Work it, work it," said Erika from the door.

Opal gripped the Dark God's shoulders and pushed him away. She wiped her mouth with the back of her hand. "Stop."

"This is terrific stuff," Erika said, staring at the screen on her digital camera. "Couldn't have asked for anything better—bye, now!" She raced away as Opal advanced on her, and just then, Opal's Ear crackled. "Where are you?" asked one of the A.D.s.

Opal glared at the new guy. "You're coming," she said, grabbed her suitcase, and headed down the stairs.

Laughing, he followed her.

5

∞

The new guy in Corvus's body went to the altar set for blocking rehearsal with Blaise and Lauren, and Opal slumped into a chair next to Magenta, who watched a monitor as the cast ran the scene.

"You probably don't need to hear this again," said Magenta, "but he looks absolutely awesome."

"Thanks."

"You getting ideas about him?"

"What?"

"I am. I thought he was weird-looking at first, but man, he's hot, in or out of makeup. I usually skip the stars—can't deal with those messed-up egos, and most of them don't respect us—but him, there's something about him—"

"I know."

"There's a rumor you were in his room last night."

"I was."

"Business or pleasure?"

"Business. I put him to bed. But just now, Erika shot us kissing." Her hands closed hard on the chair arms. "It's not just us in an awkward moment," she muttered, "it's the makeup. Nobody's supposed to see that until the trailers. If she leaks any of those—"

"Uh-oh," said Magenta. "What were you doing, messing around when you were due on the set? How could you do that when he's already in makeup?"

"It wasn't my idea. He just grabbed me."

"Whoa. He doesn't seem like the type."

"He's kind of schizo. I like the other one, not this one."

"He musta grown up weird, had to deal with all kinds of body image shit from other people. No wonder he split himself in two."

"Hmm," said Opal. She pulled out her cell phone, but just then, someone called out, "Last looks!" She grabbed her suitcase, and she and Magenta went to the set.

"Can he act?" Opal muttered to Lauren as she passed her.

"Enough," Lauren answered, then tilted her head to catch light so Magenta could look her over and see if she needed powdering or lipstick repair. Rod hovered near Blaise, who looked amazing, an angel, though her expression was marred by some form of distaste. Rod said something to her and her face cleared. She closed her eyes as he whisked powder across her nose and cheeks.

Opal faced the new guy. "Come on down, big guy," she said. "Let me check your looks."

Obligingly, he bent over. She studied her Polaroids from the night before against his face. He looked better today, though nothing substantial had changed—continuity should be all right. She touched one of his horns, and it felt solid and rooted into his forehead. The point of his chin, the built-up brow ridges had the heat and solidity of living skin. There was no rubbery give to them.

He pressed his hand over hers as she felt his face. His palm was warm, the gesture gentle. Had her problem solved itself? Unlikely, with her latex acting alive.

"Corvus?" she said, hoping anyway.

He smiled, but didn't answer.

"Clear the set. Let's go, people. Starting marks. Starting marks." Opal and the others fled back to the chairs in the outer darkness.

"Blaise is a bitch," Magenta whispered to Opal as they settled. "I'm lucky she wants Rod to do her. 'Nothing but the best,'" she mimicked.

"Do you like Lauren?" Opal whispered back.

"She's not fussy. She looks good, too—not much to correct for."

"Quiet," yelled one of the assistant directors. "We're on bell. Roll sound, roll camera, please." The starting bell for filming rang. Casual conversation died. The voices of the actors spoke their lines from behind the walls of the altar set.

Opal wished she could go outside and phone her family, but now was when she had to be present and silent, in case anything went wrong. She slid a notebook out of her suitcase, opened it to a blank page, and wrote down everything she knew about the person who was not Corvus but wore his body.

It wasn't much of a list.

What if Magenta was right, and this was a case of multiple personality, some other facet of Corvus taking charge? She didn't have to like him, she just had to work with him. It would explain Corvus Prime's lost time, but not the new guy's use of magic. He could be a natural, she guessed. But Corvus had never behaved anything like this on *Dead Loss*.

Option two: local phenomenon. Bethany's story about how

she wrote the screenplay added weight to this option. They were messing with sites that might hold old history, old tragedy, old power. Opal had heard stories about places of power. She knew how to send power into objects. Maybe someone had sent power into the ground at the altar location, and Corvus had accessed it somehow. She hadn't seen that happen before, but it seemed plausible.

Option three: some inimical and possibly noncorporeal person was stalking someone on the movie, and picked this weird way to get at them. She, Opal, seemed like the most likely candidate for a haunting, since Corvus had spent the bulk of his haunting time with her. She couldn't remember anything she had done recently that would have upset anyone magical. Since magical people tended to hide their talents, she could have offended someone with power and never noticed. She never set out to offend people, though.

Maybe the power was haunting Corvus. Maybe Corvus had a curse on him, and this was how it manifested. Maybe he'd angered someone who could do this sort of thing. Hard to imagine. His reputation was solid: a professional in every way, easy to work with, someone who would put up with a lot and give you a good performance even in adverse conditions. She'd never heard a negative story about him.

"Cut!" yelled Aldridge. "Dark God, could you play this a bit more sinister?"

"Of course," said the new guy.

Opal closed her notebook and went to the Prop Department monitor. They were shooting a master shot, an overview of the scene, with everyone in frame; the viewpoint was from the foot of the altar stone. Dark God stood at the head of the altar stone, with Serena (Lauren) to his left and Caitlyn (Blaise) to his right. Magenta joined Opal and Joe.

The slate moved into frame: Roll 32 Scene 23A Take 2, FOREST OF THE NIGHT Dir. Neil Aldridge Cameraman: T. Yamanaka.

CAITLYN

She doesn't deserve you. She abandoned you years ago. I'm the one who's been faithful! I'm the one who's honored you since I was a child! Give me the power!

DARK GOD

She is my promised bride. We have a blood connection. It is her destiny.

CAITLYN

But she doesn't even want it! Pick me instead.

SERENA

I do want it.

CAITLYN

That's not what you said yesterday!

SERENA holds her wrist above the altar stone, turns it so the underside is up. She pulls a knife from a sheath at her waist. It gleams. She touches the tip to her skin.

SERENA

Isbrytaren, I am ready to pledge myself to you again.

DARK GOD

I accept your pledge.

He takes her hand.

The Dark God took the knife from Serena. "Wait a sec," Magenta whispered. "That's not in the script." She glanced at

Opal and Joe, but they shook their heads. Opal had read the script, but not recently. She supposed she ought to read the scenes listed on the call sheets, but her job didn't change; the Dark God had pretty much one look all the way through the film; she just had to make sure it was consistent. The only question from day to day was whether he'd be in close-up or distance shots, which governed how much of the other prostheses and body makeup she applied and how long the call sheet budgeted for application.

"Are you ready?" the Dark God asked, with peculiar intensity.

"That's in the script," Magenta whispered.

On the set, Caitlyn said, "Wait. This isn't right. She's supposed to cut herself."

"Not in the script," muttered Magenta.

The Dark God said, "Do you presume to tell me my business?"

"Not script."

Caitlyn: "But the book says—"

"Not script."

"Serena," said the Dark God.

"I'm ready," Serena replied.

"Script," whispered Magenta.

The Dark God drew the tip of the blade from Serena's palm a little way up her arm, and blood welled in its wake. He leaned forward and licked the blood, his eyes half-closed in ecstasy. Serena swayed, held upright only by his grip on her arm. Her eyes closed. Her face showed something that could be pain or absolute joy.

"Ick," whispered Magenta. "*So* not script."

Opal jumped to her feet, galvanized by a fear come to life. How could they trust someone else inside Corvus's body? There was no indication he cared about the same things everyone else cared about. Why should he?

If he wasn't following the script (and she didn't

remember—but Magenta did), he must have his own agenda. He was a power person, and she didn't trust him. Her great-uncle Tobias, her family's magic teacher, said blood carried power and could be used in both good and bad ways to transfer energy and other influences. She strode toward the set, marshaling her resources.

George Corvassian, the first assistant director, grabbed her arm and pulled her away. He dragged her all the way to the second set, then put his mouth right next to her ear. "We know it's not in the script," he whispered to her, "but Neil wants to let it play out and see what happens. It's looking great."

"It's a real wound," she whispered, furious.

"Special effects knife," George whispered. "Ask Props."

"I don't think so. What if he really hurt her?" She decided to speak in a language he could understand. "She could sue the company!"

"Anyway, it happened, and we might as well see if we can use it."

"But he—"

"It was superficial," George said.

"You don't understand," said Opal. She pulled loose, but he grabbed her again.

"Wait," he whispered in her ear. "If there's something seriously wrong, Neil will stop and take care of it."

Opal didn't trust Neil to do any such thing. "The Dark God'll get Lauren. He'll own her."

"It's only a movie," muttered George. "There are worse tragedies at sea."

Opal opened her mouth to scream and interrupt the filming, but just then two bells rang, signaling the end of the take, and George let her go. Opal raced to the other set. The set doctor was treating Lauren's arm. The actress stared at it blankly.

Opal touched Lauren's shoulder, sent as much spirit protection as she could. She remembered doing this for her sisters and brothers when they were little; sometimes she had had to protect them against each other, and sometimes she gave them a layer of safety against their mother. It had been a long time since she had done it.

Lauren blinked and woke, gasped and jerked her arm. The doctor held it firm: he was applying antiseptic. "What?" Lauren said. "How'd that happen?"

"Dark God did it. During a take."

"Damn it!" Lauren jerked free of the doctor's grip, marched over to the Dark God, and shook her arm at him. "You did this to me?"

"You said yes," he said, speaking in Corvus's voice, gentle. He smiled, almost benevolently, despite the monster face he wore.

"Looked great on film," said Neil. "Print that." The script supervisor made a mark on her script. "We'll do the other shots with fake blood, naturally," he said. "Did you get down the new dialogue?" he asked the script supervisor, and she nodded.

"All right, actors take ten or fifteen while we set up for the next shot and get some typing done," an assistant director called. "Stand-ins to the set. Lighting crew. D.P. and camera crew. Next shot POV Caitlyn on Serena and the D.G."

Magenta approached Lauren. "We have to cover the scratch with something for the next take."

"In a minute." Lauren turned to the Dark God. "How'd you make me stand still for this?"

"You have many desires, all competing. This was one of them; I only teased it closer to the surface."

"Don't do it again."

"I make no promises."

She glared up at him, then turned and took a few steps, lost. Her hand rose to touch the new wound, now dabbed with ointment. Lauren glanced around until her gaze encountered Opal, and then she went to her, pulled her away from the others. "Help," Lauren whispered.

Opal touched her shoulder, tried to sense what had happened the way she used to. When she was younger and most of the childcare in the family devolved onto her, she had come up with shortcuts for finding out who hit whom, and later, when some of them got their powers and one of them didn't, she'd learned to trace power use even more.

"It's bad," she said. "There's a reason why the devil gets you to sign a contract in blood. It carries a blueprint of your identity with it. Now he has that, and he got you to give it to him."

"I feel like I was drugged."

"Yeah, I think you were. Maybe not drugs, but some kind of altered state. Hypnosis."

"He doesn't play fair."

"I know."

"What's he going to do with me now that he's got me?"

"I don't know. I think him kissing me was the same kind of deal. Saliva has all that genetic information, too. Not as popular in mystic circles, but still potent, and he stole some of mine."

"He kissed you?"

"Right after you left. While he was doing it, Erika caught us. Photo op city."

"Great," said Lauren sarcastically.

Opal shook her head. "I don't know what she's going to do with those pictures, but maybe I better tell somebody about them. Someone with actual veto power might be able to block her using them."

"Talk to the production manager. Fran. You know? She's in charge of all the stuff that happens on location, and she might be able to control Erika. I don't know. Erika's a really good photographer, Opal. She gave me some great head shots."

"Thanks for the tip. I'll see what I can do. I might be able to take care of the pictures another way. They involve the fall of light." She thought about that. She could affect film, and probably digital media, too. She'd have to get specific, though; just fog the ones of her and the new guy, and see if Erika had backed up her photos anywhere.

"What can we do about D.G.?" Lauren asked.

"I'm going to ask my mom for advice."

"I'll call my *abuela*."

"Tell me if you find out anything."

"Will do. You tell me, too, okay? Not that I'll be able to do anything about it. You think he plans any more conquests?"

They both looked at Blaise, pouting by the fake altar stone.

"Has he shown any interest in her?" Opal wondered.

"Nothing obvious. I think that pisses her off. Before he turned into D.G., she was trying to get his attention, but he's, you know, all reserved and quiet. You can't tell where he's looking, or if." They watched Blaise, who seemed to feel their regard. She glared back at them. "She really gets into that character," Lauren muttered, "and sometimes she doesn't come out. It's disturbing. Her character hates and despises me. Or maybe my character. It's not always clear."

"We have to find out what he wants," Opal muttered.

The Dark God put arms around both their shoulders, and came to stand between them, startling them. Opal had thought he was still by the altar stone with Blaise, but that was Corvus's stand-in, Fred, with his hood up, a respectable distance from Blaise.

Should have known it was Fred from the way she's not paying attention to him, Opal thought.

"What who wants?" the new guy asked. "Do my hand-maidens conspire?"

"Stop it, for God's sake. That's creepy," Lauren said. "My

mom didn't spend years cleaning other people's houses to turn me into some handmaiden."

"What *do* you want with us?" said Opal.

"Do you know the child who wrote this play?" he asked.

"Sure, Bethany. We talked to her last night in the restaurant." Opal shook her head. She and Corvus had talked to Bethany, anyway. The new guy hadn't been around for that discussion. She thought.

"You know she grew up here?"

"You're not going to make us live the script, are you?" Lauren asked. "If that's your plan, I'm quitting right now. I don't care what it costs."

He laughed. Then he patted her head. "You can't leave," he said, still smiling.

"Just watch me, buster. No way am I going to turn into some sexy vamp girl and go around killing people to serve your need for blood."

"I won't ask you to," he said. "It's not really blood I need." He stroked her hair. She stood rigid, but then she relaxed into it, shoulders lowering, her head tilting toward him so that his hand had easier access. She blinked, and closed her eyes, a contented smile on her face.

Trance technique, thought Opal. *Hair involved.* The new guy's arm still rested on her shoulders, but he wasn't stroking *her* hair. She glanced up at his face, the lace of leaves across his skin, the horns, the jutting brow and chin, the lakes of shadow, the internal glow of the eyes, the quiet smile. He did not look malevolent or dangerous, despite the monster outer layer. She and Corvus and the art director had wanted him to be strange rather than terrifying. How informed had they been about his real nature? He was local; he had almost said so, talking about Bethany and the script. Opal had built the pieces of his face in Los Angeles, nine hundred miles away. Maybe his true face was completely different, and now he was just a squatter behind her creation. The horns, though—those weren't hers.

Magenta stalked over to them. "Stop that," she said to the new guy. "You want to mess everything up for the next take? Serena's on camera for it. I still need to fix her arm, and now I have to call Craig and get him to redo her hair. What is *wrong* with you?"

The Dark God stared at Magenta, his face expressionless. Her breath caught, and then she held a hand to a reddening cheek. "What are you doing to me?" she cried. "Why does it burn?"

"You mustn't speak to me that way." He continued to stroke Lauren's hair.

"This is crazy," Magenta said. She looked at Opal. "Am I crazy?"

Opal shifted, uncomfortable with the new guy's arm over her shoulder. Strange overlays webbed them: the power structure of the film, where the stars ruled, sometimes on a level with the director, sometimes above or below, but all the service people, she and Magenta, were lower-class citizens, not supposed to speak sternly to those above. Plus, whoever the presence behind Corvus's mask was, he seemed at home as an aristocrat. He took without asking, and considered everyone else his playthings. Handmaidens. Like one of the worst stars, although he hadn't been mean or really petty yet, just bossy and demanding.

Lauren, waiting for Opal at her hotel the night before, well, that had been odd. The structure had tilted. Lauren knew Opal was a magic user, and that changed their status in the eyes of each other. Right now, since Lauren had spoken to her on a topic other than makeup or special effects, in full view of the other cast and crew, people would be making up stories about that, if they had the attention to spare.

Opal had hooked up with stars before, in a variety of ways. She'd almost thought she was marrying one. A mistake. Location shoots often threw people together in odd combinations. The intensity and isolation drove them into each other's arms and beds, and sometimes exhaustion made them mistake physical release for something more important. As soon as their reasons for living in each other's shadows evaporated, so did the connections.

Her connection to Corvus hadn't behaved like that. After this, though, who could tell? The new guy was messing everything up, in more than one way.

"I don't think you're crazy," Opal told Magenta. "I think he's hypnotic. D.G., please don't hurt Magenta. She's just doing her job."

"I don't care for her tone."

"She gets that. She won't talk to you like that again." Opal nodded to Magenta. Magenta didn't respond.

One of the assistant directors called, "Ten minute warning, everyone."

"We have to fix Lauren's hair and that great gaping slash you made on her arm right now," Magenta said, "your majesty."

The new guy stopped stroking Lauren's hair, gripped her shoulder, gave her a gentle push. "Go and be repaired," he said. She only half awoke. She glanced back at him, her dark eyes sleepy, before she wandered off in Magenta's wake to one of the canvas-backed chairs behind the scenes, where Craig, the key hairstylist, waited with a Polaroid and a set of combs.

"Are you going to do the work, or screw up the production?" Opal asked.

"I am going to do many things," he said in a low voice. "Right now, it amuses me to put my face and my voice inside these machines. This is a new way to work. It may aid me greatly. It's a wonderful time to be awake."

"Are you ever going to let Corvus come home?"

He smiled, stroked her hair, offered no answer.

6

As soon as the stars were safely trapped acting in front of the cameras, Magenta grabbed Opal's hand and dragged her as far from the altar set as they could get inside the building. They huddled inside the bathroom, soundproofed enough that they could talk in low voices, with walls thin enough they'd be able to hear the two bells that signaled the end of the current take. "What the hell is going on?" Magenta asked. One of her cheeks still blazed.

"Have you ever worked on a picture that was cursed?"

"Cursed? I've been on one where everything went wrong. We were filming in Mexico, and bandits stole the equipment trucks while they were driving to the location, and one of the stars died, killed by a freak accident with a dollycam, and the weather kept screwing us up. Nobody got any sleep, and everybody got mean. Cost overruns, sniping tempers, infighting—we all hated what we were doing by the end. Then, you know, they couldn't save it in post. The thing was a huge flop. Worst shoot of my life. Is that what you mean?"

"Sort of." Opal frowned. "In a more supernatural way, though."

"What, that old you're-doing-something-commercial-on-top-of-an-Indian-graveyard riff?" asked Magenta. "Who believes *that* shit?"

Opal touched Magenta's reddened cheek.

"Ow!"

"He burned you by looking at you," said Opal.

"I've seen that happen in hypnotist acts. Okay, not the burned part, but I've read about that. Freaky powers of the human mind, turned against itself. You said it was hypnosis."

"It might have been, I guess, but I'm exploring other options. You asked what the hell's going on. I think Corvus is possessed."

"Oh, please!"

"That's my explanation. I can't make you believe it, but there it is. Bethany wrote the script here, where she grew up, surrounded by things she was scared of. Whatever's creepy here got inside her head and helped her write it."

"What about Travis? He cowrote."

"Bethany did the first draft while she was staying at the B&B. Travis doctored it. They find a producer and put together a package, and hey! Creepy evil guy gets people right where he wants them so he can use them to further his creepy agenda. I build the mask. Corvus steps into the role. Creepy guy crawls into Corvus, and here we are."

"That is so lame."

"I would love," Opal said, "to be wrong about this."

Magenta mini-paced. Two steps one way, two steps the other. The sink and the toilet precluded her having room to really pace. "Okay," she said, "your explanation covers his bad behavior, my cheek. What the *hell* is happening with Lauren?"

"The not-script part. He drank her blood, and now he can control her."

"Melodrama!"

Opal snorted. "All right. Melodrama. And yet. Can you picture Lauren standing there like an idiot while someone strokes her hair and ruins her look, in the time it takes to set up a different camera angle? She strikes me as much more professional than that."

"She's his love slave."

"Since when? She wasn't dopey like that yesterday."

"Nope."

"Would she have looked at him twice yesterday?"

"Yes, of course she would, and did. Now, maybe you didn't notice this, because you get so wrapped up in your work, but the whole time you're slapping bits of rubber on Gigantor, Lauren's perched in the next chair, watching, even after the rest of us have left the trailer. You don't call that a crush? Admittedly, you can work magic—"

Magenta halted, turned, stared at Opal with narrowed eyes. "Damn! All that time Rod spied on you, then tried to repeat what you were doing later? He could *never* get it to work, even though he got hold of every ingredient you ever used. He snooped your trash! You mean nobody can replicate your processes because you're *cheating*?"

"What cheating? The whole point is to do something nobody else can do."

Magenta growled, then paced away and back.

Finally, she said, "Well, the crucial question is, are we going over budget?"

"Creepy evil guy says no. He likes being in the movies."

"Well, okay," said Magenta, and two bells rang. "The show must go on." They left the bathroom and rushed to their equipment.

Blaise, Dark God, and Lauren came off the set and settled into their chairs. Rod was ready with bottles of water for everybody. Opal fished one of the protein shakes out of her suitcase. She presented it on her open palm to the Dark God.

"What is it?" he asked.

"Nourishment." She shook it vigorously, then popped the top. "I think you could probably use this about now."

He took it, studied it, sipped from it, and frowned. "Tastes vile." He sipped again. "But I take your meaning. It satisfies a certain hunger." He drank the rest and handed her the empty can. As soon as she set it down, he took her wrist and tugged her toward him. "I have another hunger," he said, staring at her lips.

"Please," she said, conscious of Rod and Blaise and Lauren and Magenta, conscious that she had no interest in another kiss from him. "No."

He lifted her hand to his lips and pressed them to the back of it. Her shadow self, the one who held her magic, startled and tried to retreat, but he had forged a connection with her earlier, and she didn't know how to break it. He drew a long draft of her magical energy, leaving her wilted and confused. She swayed and sat down beside him.

"Thank you," he said, his eyes glowing even brighter.

She pressed her hand to the cell phone, a lump in her pocket. She had to call home.

This time, when the actors were called back to the set, Magenta came to her. "What happened? What did he just do?"

"Kind of a vampire thing." Opal pressed her palm to her forehead. "I don't know if I'll ever get Corvus back." She dug through her bag for another protein shake, opened and drank it. She checked her watch. They should break for lunch in twenty minutes. She felt better after the shake, but she could tell she was still depleted.

They did a quick last looks after the rehearsal. Opal didn't even touch the Dark God. The A.D. called for silence, and the bell rang.

Rodrigo and Magenta joined Joe at the Props monitor again to watch the filming. Opal stayed where she was. She needed time to think.

He got the drop on me. I've let him have his way too much. I have to fight. I have to fight! For Corvus, for Lauren, for herself, against whatever plans the Invader had, she had to pull herself together and remember who she was and where she came from.

When she was younger and first came into her power, tired of being the good child, the oldest, the caretaker, the one who put up with shit from her mother and all the younger kids, she had flirted with turning really, really bad. She had explored dark powers her great-uncle had frowned at and warned her against. Maybe that made her more susceptible to the Invader's powers. Maybe it gave her tools. Her magical self had been living so far underground since she left her family's house that she'd practically trained herself to be normal. Time to loosen up and find her secret self again.

First, she needed distance, a shield, so the Invader couldn't just walk up to her and suck her dry.

He's taken my identity inside him, but he gave me his, too. Their morning kiss had been hours ago, and she'd eaten and drunk since then, but at some point she had swapped spit with the Invader—or Corvus's body and that should give her some kind of hold over him. She tasted the interior of her mouth, a little sour with the aftertaste of energy drink, and could find no trace of him. She needed to seek with a different sense. She closed her eyes.

Who has entered into my house of self without an invitation? She saw a room, comfortable, with a desk she could work at, a swivel chair more like a throne than office furniture, shelves along the wall holding all sorts of materials she could use to shape masks, craft colors, make salves, ointments, creams that could dull skin or shine it, draw attention to or divert it from any feature of the human face, pencils and putty, spirit gum and mustache hair, terror and beauty.

Life-masks of previous clients stood on pedestals on a second desk, with bright but diffuse light shining on them, a place where she could create. Books of reference photos stood in staggering stacks along another wall. In a corner was a second chair, broad and adjustable and comfortable, with a red velvet pillow on it for her to hug while she sat and thought. Nearby was a fireplace, clean now, with a ball of green witchfire burning coolly in it.

Above the desk, a wide window that looked out into a sunlit garden.

Her interior office, her safe place where she met her muse for tea.

In the back corner across from her thinking chair stood a tall featureless shadow, a stain on the air. It had a scent of metal and machine oil that didn't belong in her place. She rose from her office chair and turned toward the shadow, but it flickered, only visible from the corners of her eyes; she couldn't look directly at it. It faded from direct gazes.

She needed to know more about him if she were going to defeat him. So a shadow of him had invaded her private place? At least she knew one place to find him.

"Opal." Rod joggled her shoulder. "You okay?"

"Not really. I'm worried and tired."

"Oh."

"Not what you were asking." She straightened. "What's up?"

"Lunchtime. Betty went on ahead, and reported back on the walkie that it's that rosemary chicken thing again, with the greasy potatoes."

"Oh, boy!"

"She's not sure if it's leftovers from yesterday, or the only thing they know how to cook. You ready?"

She rose, locked her case. "Cast already went?"

"Yeah."

"I didn't take my continuity Polaroids."

"Magenta did it for you. You missed some last looks, too,

but he looked fantastic. Didn't need any touch-ups. Magenta checked. Not that she wanted to. She's scared of Corvus now."

Opal wondered if Magenta had shared Opal's theory of Corvus's possession with Rodrigo. She decided to wait before she broached the subject with him. After they finished shooting for the day, maybe they could meet for dinner and talk about what was going on, and whether there was anything they could do about it. She said, "Well, I owe her, and I know it. I've got to make a call, and then I'll be right there. Thanks for waking me."

"You're welcome. Say . . ."

She waited for it.

"I thought you got the easy job, but now I see it isn't so. Is your guy on the rag or something?"

"I don't know."

"Sympathies, anyway. Still looks good, even when he acts nuts."

She smiled and headed outside. Around back of the building, she got out her cell phone and dialed the number of a house she hadn't lived in for seven years.

"Hey," said Flint, one of her younger brothers.

"Hey yourself. Mama home?"

"Um, no. She left for the TV station about ten minutes ago."

Opal checked her watch. "Damn! Uncle Tobias there?"

"Hang on. I'll find out." There was a clunk as he set the handset down—probably on the kitchen table, Opal thought—and then his footsteps receded. She waited, checked her watch, waited. She should eat. They only had half an hour for lunch. Then again, she'd had that protein shake . . . Presently footsteps approached, and she heard heavy breathing. "Hey," Flint said, "astonishing as it is, Uncle Tobias is not in his tower. I don't know where he went."

"Damn! I really need to talk to someone!"

"I'm someone," said Flint plaintively.

"About dealing with magical possession."

"Oh. Okay. Not one of my things. Are you possessed?"

"No, my friend is, and the possessor guy is a—well, I need help."

"Do you want me?"

She smiled and stared into the forest behind the old supermarket. Her younger brother was a screwup. He had trouble getting his powers under control. They were good powers, but nobody understood them—they were different from anyone else's. She loved him dearly, but even she, in her role as second mother, hadn't been able to help him figure out how to make his powers work reliably. "I might. Not just yet, but thanks for the offer."

"You want someone else? Jasper? Gyp? Beryl?"

"Are they home?"

"No."

"If I get desperate, I'll call you back," she said. "Thanks, little brother."

"Must be serious. You never asked for help before," he said.

"Never?"

"Not in living memory. Hang on."

"Flint, I have to go to lunch."

"Hang on," he said again. "I'm going to try something."

"Flint—no, don't—"

He grunted.

Something punched Opal in the stomach so hard she fell down. She dropped the cell phone, and it skittered away. She lay on the damp, packed earth and tried to catch her breath. She could barely hear Flint's voice: "Hey? Did that work? Something happened. Are you okay? Opal? Opal?"

She wondered if she was okay. Why would her little brother send her a body blow? Her stomach felt—hurt, and warm. Warmth spread through her like a liquor afterglow. She closed her eyes and went to her inner office. In the middle of the room, an exercise-ball-sized fireball hovered, glowing orange and red in streaks, sending out arcs of random heat. She held a hand out to it, and a prominence flared up, scorched her fingertips. She tried to pull her hand back, but the light locked onto her. The burn spread up her arm into her shoulder and then— cooled, effervesced, moved through her like water flowing up the stem of a dehydrated plant. More than half the ball burned its way into her and cooled down, refreshing and reinvigorating her in an unfamiliar way. Even after she felt restored, the fireball floated in her office, diminished but lively.

Presently she sat up and reached for the phone, which hadn't stopped squawking.

"Don't do that again," she said in her big sister voice.

"Oh, God, are you okay?"

"I think so. It hurt me, but then it helped. Thanks for the thought, anyway, little brother. The delivery method needs work. We operate from different places. Your energy needs to be converted before it can turn into my energy."

"You'll be okay?"

"Yes. After the initial shock, I recognized what it was, and you know, I *do* need energy right now, so this is a help. You need to ask before you do things like that, though, bud. Okay?"

"Okay." He sounded so forlorn she wished she could hug him.

"Tell Mama I'll try calling later tonight. I'm not sure how late. We don't get many breaks here. You might tell Tobias, too. Okay?"

"Sure." He still sounded subdued.

"Got to run," she said. "Love you."

"Love you."

By the time she reached the out-of-business café the caterers had taken over while they were in town, the buffet was almost empty of food and she had five minutes to grab something, eat, and head back to the Makeup trailer. She wolfed a banana and grabbed a chicken leg to eat while she walked.

The Dark God wasn't there when she arrived, nor was Kelsi still curled up asleep in his chair. Opal opened the door and glanced across at the trailer next door, a three-banger Star Waggon with private rooms for Lauren, Blaise, and Corvus to use when they weren't required on the set. Corvus had the room at the end nearest his special station in the Makeup trailer. All three rooms were veiled with curtains, and no lights were on in any of them.

Magenta and Rod came in and set out their tools. Magenta dropped off a set of Polaroids with date and time written across the bottom in Sharpie.

"Thanks," Opal said to Magenta. "Thanks for picking up all my slack. God. Sorry I was so out of it."

"Vampires," said Magenta, with a shrug. "What can you do? You feeling better yet?"

"Yeah. Who knows how long that'll last. You didn't touch him, did you?"

Magenta shook her head. "For one thing, his makeup was fine. If it hadn't been, I would have woken you. Union rules. I'm not allowed to touch him."

"I know."

"And, after seeing what he did to you and Lauren, my hots for him went right out the window."

Opal nodded.

"Good luck. If you know how I can help you if he sucks on you again, tell me now."

"Keep your distance. No sense both of us going down."

Magenta bumped fists with her and went back to her station to finish laying out her brushes.

Opal set up her station. She didn't expect to have much to do, unless Invader had lost hold of Corvus since she last saw him. He had just stolen energy from her; he could probably hold out for a while.

She had to prevent him from stealing more energy from her. Flint's fireball—how could that boy transfer energy along a phone line? Maybe she shouldn't ask. He often couldn't repeat his feats. Trying just made him mess up in more spectacular ways.

Flint's fireball still warmed her insides, still felt like a transplanted organ from someone whose blood type she didn't share. Maybe she could use its foreignness to protect herself from predation. She dropped into Corvus's chair, went inside herself, and sat cross-legged in her mental study. A fireball half the size of the original one still burned there. She looked around for the shadow the Invader had left in her study earlier, but didn't see even a flicker in the corner of her eye.

She focused on the fireball. *Please give me an outer skin of unfriendly fire,* she thought, and the fireball brightened, almost smiled at her, and sent out a sheet of fire that formed a thin glowing layer around her.

Thanks, she thought. *You are beautiful. You are good. You are my friend.*

The fire laughed at her in Flint's voice.

He will come with a kiss and a siphon, Opal thought. *Do not enter him. Keep him back. Burn him.*

I hear, the fire sang, cheerful flames dancing.

She felt someone looming over her and looked up into the green glow of the Invader's eyes. She rose from the chair and gestured toward it. "Have a seat?"

Lauren and Blaise were in the other chairs. Rod and Magenta went to work repairing the damage lunch had caused without conversation. Magenta watched Opal and the Invader covertly.

The Invader settled into the chair and looked up at her, a faint smile on his leafy face. She got the Polaroids Magenta had taken before lunch and studied them, holding them near his face. Perfect match—nothing had come loose. She wondered if he had eaten greasy potatoes and rosemary chicken

with the rest of the cast and crew. Corvus couldn't eat solid
food with appliances on his face, but if it was the Invader's
real face, he could eat anything he liked, she supposed.

Would the prostheses ever come loose again? She opened
a drawer and took out the Polaroids she'd shot the first day
and studied them against his face. He had still been Corvus—
though already troubled by the intrusion of the Invader. He
had changed since—the color of his skin was a trace greener
now, the horns more pointed, the eyes larger and the brows
more peaked. Subtle changes. She wasn't sure she should tell
anyone. Possibly it could pass as normal character change.
They were shooting the scenes out of sequence, but a lot of
them were dim light, so it probably wouldn't make much
difference.

The finished film was shipped to L.A., where the editor cut
it together into rough scenes, transferred them to DVDs, and
overnighted them back. Only three copies were made; they
went to the director, the director of photography, and the producer, to share with subordinates as necessary.

Opal remembered earlier days in moviemaking, when everybody who was interested gathered to watch the processed
dailies from the day before. The system had changed; too
many actors, seeing their earlier work, wanted to do it over.
Big names like Schwarzenegger and Cruise could do that, but
none of the actors on this picture had that kind of clout.

She decided to wait until someone mentioned the difference
in the Dark God's looks from shot to shot, if anybody did.
They couldn't be as alert to his face as she was.

"Well?" he asked.

"You look perfect," she said.

"Of course."

"Have you always looked like this?"

He turned and studied himself in the wall of mirrors
above her built-in makeup cabinet. "Never have I looked like

this until now. I admire the design. This is a good face for me, I think; it startles those who see it for the first time, but does not send them away screaming. I want them to sit still for my approach. You are an excellent mask maker."

"Thanks," she said.

"So you don't need to touch me now?"

"Not unless there's something wrong with the facade."

"You'd touch me if I lost something vital?" He reached up with his transformed hand and wiggled one of his horns. It was too solid to come loose. He glanced toward Magenta, who suddenly focused intently on painting Lauren's lips. "Your friend also doesn't wish to touch me."

"We're not running away screaming, but we've learned to fear you."

"I am not doing my work correctly, then. I don't wish you to fear me, my handmaiden."

"I'm afraid of people who steal vital energy without asking, or put people into trances with a touch, or cut people without permission, or burn someone with a look because she said something disrespectful. How am I not supposed to be afraid of that?"

"I should give you something in exchange for your energy. I would, if you would let me." His voice was caressing, low and warm. "I would give you pleasure," he murmured. "I would give you almost anything in my power, my glorious wellspring of delight."

"Right now, your cooperation is really sexy," Opal said. "Do a good job on the picture, and I'll try to relax about the fact that you've displaced someone I love."

"Do you love me, Opal?" he asked in Corvus's voice.

"Corr! Are you in there?" She gripped his shoulders and leaned to look in his eyes. The green glow had dimmed, but he was still hidden behind the mask she had put on him that morning.

"Do you mean it?" he asked.

"Yes, I love you." Now was not the time to explain what kind of love it was, or that it wasn't exclusive. "Are you okay?"

"I don't know," he said. "I don't seem to be tracking very well."

"But you're not suffering?"

"Suffering? I've been asleep, I think. Did I mess up my scenes? I don't remember doing them. Was I sleepwalking?"

"I don't think so. Do you realize you're not alone in your body?"

"What? I don't understand."

"You're possessed by some god-thing. Maybe it's the Dark God of the script. He's been acting the part, anyway, maybe as well as you can, with more motivation."

"I don't understand," he said again, and then his eyes changed, and it was the Other staring out at her. "He doesn't have to understand, if you are good to me," whispered the Invader. "If you resist, I can help him understand in many unpleasant ways. Shall I let him sleep, or wake him up and make him suffer? The choice is yours."

Why had she brought up suffering to Corvus? Had she given the Invader ideas? Damn it. "What do you want?"

"Touch me."

She touched the horn he had wiggled, found that it was still seated well on his forehead and wouldn't move without—without, perhaps, a bone saw. He reached up and took her hand, brought the palm to his mouth and pressed his lips to it—

Then cried and thrust her hand away, tapped his lips gently with his fingertips. "What did you *do*?"

"I got some help," she said.

"Well, dispense with it, unless you want me to do something to your beloved."

She clenched her fists. She wanted to pound him. How

would that serve Corvus? It probably wouldn't help him. If she had her sister Gypsum's power to curse things—

"Where the hell are you guys?" yelled one of the assistant directors from the door. "You were due on the set fifteen minutes ago!"

"Give me something," whispered the Invader as Blaise and Lauren—both fully made up and ready—stood.

Fire, leave me a finger free, Opal thought, and her fire skin retreated from her right index finger. She touched the Invader's lips with it, and he took it into his mouth, sucked on the first knuckle, and released her. She felt only a little faint this time. He surged to his feet and swept out of the trailer, followed by Opal, Blaise, Lauren, Magenta, and Rodrigo.

Lauren gripped her arm. "Did Corvus really come back?"

"You heard that?"

"We were all listening as hard as we could."

"I don't know if it was Corvus or a trick. I don't trust the new guy at all."

"None of us do," said Lauren. Blaise, beside her, shook her head. Rod and Magenta had gone on ahead.

"Blaise?" Opal said.

The fair-haired woman stared after Corvus's tall, black-clad form. "He has a good professional reputation. That's not the behavior I'm observing. I don't want him to sabotage the picture. If you can come up with a way to handle this, deal me in."

"Thanks," said Opal. She felt a weight settle on her shoulders. They were all worried, and they thought she was the one to deal with the problem. Well, maybe she *had* given the Invader an opening to Corvus by using the techniques she had used to create his face, so she *should* fix the problem. She had more magical resources to fight the Invader with than anybody else on set, as far as she knew.

At least everybody was on the same side, or said they were.

Filming resumed with different angles on the same scene. The Invader behaved very well, saying his lines over and over again; he didn't forget the dialog he had improvised. They had a stunt knife for the part where he sliced open Serena's arm, and some stage blood for him to lick when they did the new takes, and he seemed okay with that, too. Opal went on the set to do last looks any time they paused long enough to need it, and she never had to work on the Invader's face. After a while, her tension evaporated.

It was only after filming had finished for the day, around eleven P.M., and the Invader was sitting in his chair in the makeup trailer, that she went back on high alert.

He had taken off the robe and given it to someone from Wardrobe, and he sat there in his black jeans and leafy skin and horny hands, smiling. "What are you going to do with me?" he asked.

"You tell me. Are you going to stay in there all night?"

"Would you like me to?"

"No," she said, unsure whether a statement of her desire would help or hinder. She wanted Corvus back so much she was going to ask her mother for help, something she couldn't remember doing since she had reached the age of eight. She didn't have the tools to force the Invader out by herself. She needed her mother or Tobias. Would either of them be up this late?

"If I come out, you must promise me you will restore me tomorrow," he said.

If you come out, how can you make me let you back in? she wondered. They had two more weeks of work on location, though, maybe longer, depending on the rewrites Travis and Bethany were doing. Every time she put the face on Corvus, it was another invitation to the Invader.

"Make me a promise or I won't leave," he said.

She clenched her fists and looked away, down the trailer

toward the chairs where Blaise and Lauren sat, Magenta and Rod standing beside them, no one else moving.

She could lie. Make a promise and not keep it.

That went against everything she believed about herself. It had always been vital to her to keep her word when she gave it. She tried not to ever give it if she didn't mean it, even though she saw people around her break promises all the time.

Still, she could do it. Maybe.

"All right," she whispered. "I promise."

7

∾

The Invader heaved a deep sigh and relaxed in the chair, his shoulders slumping and his eyes falling shut. She hadn't known he was so tense. It was a clue. Possessing another was exhausting. She might be able to use that, or at least take note of it to report to her mother.

She got out her solvents and makeup removers and went to work on Corvus.

He slept through the removal. A production assistant brought in the call sheet and new script pages for the following day early in the process. Opal paused long enough to glance at their start time for the next day. The weather forecast was for rain, so they were filming on the soundstage again. Corvus was supposed to be in the Makeup trailer by ten A.M.

She stuffed the call sheet and the script in her messenger bag and moisturized Corvus's hands, arms, upper body, and his face, which was empty of the Invader but also of consciousness.

Lauren and Magenta hovered as Opal finished.

"Corr?" Opal whispered, gripping his shoulder.

It took him a long time and some serious shaking to wake up. "What?" he said at last, opening eyes still hidden behind the Dark God's contact lenses. "What happened? How'd I get back in the trailer?" He glanced toward the clock on the mirror. "Is that A.M. or P.M.?"

"It's midnight," said Lauren. "What do you remember about today? Anything?"

He groaned, and said, "This morning. Opal and I were—you said you told me to rest well, and I was a little upset. I don't like to sleep soundly. It makes me nervous. Have I slept through the whole day?" He gripped Opal's arm. "Did you hypnotize me into it?"

"No, I didn't!"

"I'm sorry." He let her go.

"Corvus, you spent most of the day being someone else," said Lauren. "Someone incredibly creepy, a lot like the role you play, a manipulator who gets off on other people's pain."

"What?"

"The good thing is, he can act," she continued. "He's doing you proud. But we'd much rather have *you* around."

He looked at his watch, pressed a button to get the date. "It's November, not April First," he said. "I don't like this joke, Lauren."

"Are you hungry?" Opal asked.

Distracted, he glanced toward his stomach and frowned. "Ravenous. Opal—"

"Come on, big guy. Let's go get some supper."

He let her pull him to his feet. He accepted the shirt she handed him. Magenta and Lauren were watching him so intently he turned his back to them and whispered, "What do they want?"

"They want to make sure you're okay."

"It's not just my shoulders or my ass, eh?" He flexed his biceps and glanced back.

"Those, too," Opal whispered, and smiled.

He put on the shirt and buttoned it to the top button. He set the back of his hand on his forehead. "I'm so tired," he said.

"Let's get you to the car. You can nap on the way to the restaurant." Hitch had left Opal the keys again once Corvus was off the clock. "You've got to eat, though, Corvus. I don't know if you had anything all day aside from a protein shake I forced on you."

"You were really talking and interacting with me all day?"

"Not you. Someone else in your body." She snagged the last set of Polaroids she'd taken before she removed his makeup, rubber-banded them together, and stuck them in her messenger bag. The Invader had posed for the Polaroids, showing his teeth, his horns, and the unlikely gleam in his eyes. She would show them to Corvus at the restaurant; maybe that would help bring this home to him.

"This feels like a bad extended jape," he said. He shook his head. "It's hard for me to take seriously."

"It's outside your experience. Of course it'll take you a while to get used to it," Opal said. She remembered the steps she and her family had to take every time they introduced outsiders to who they really were. "You don't have to believe us, Corr. You *do* have to decide what to do next."

He followed her down the trailer stairs, Magenta and Lauren in their wake. Opal pressed the keychain button to unlock the Lincoln, and Magenta and Lauren climbed into the backseat. Corvus stared at them. "You're coming?"

"We've been waiting all day to talk to you," said Lauren, "and we're not letting you out of our sight."

He shrugged massively. "I'm not up to much conversation, I'm afraid," he said.

"That's okay. Whatever you've got."

"All right, then."

Opal held the door so Corvus could climb into the passenger seat, then went around the car and got behind the wheel. She started the car and drove.

"Did you dream?" Lauren asked from the backseat.

"What?" Corvus said.

"While you slept through the day, did you have any dreams? Say, one where you woke up for a second and talked to Opal?"

"Was that not a dream?" he asked. Opal, watching the view out the front window of light blades on a dark road, with tree shadows crowding close, was conscious of Corvus's regard. His gaze prickled against the skin of her right cheek like sunlight.

"What do you remember?" she asked, without looking toward him.

"Did you tell me you loved me?"

She closed her eyes, then opened them so she could watch the road. "That was really you I was talking to? I wasn't sure."

"It wasn't a dream?"

"No, I really said that."

"Did you mean it?" He shifted in his seat, turned to peer toward the backseat. "Or should we have this conversation later?"

"They heard everything I said before," she said. "I meant it, sure. How could I not love you? I don't like the one who's been using you, though, and he has me over a barrel now."

"What do you mean?"

"He only let you out tonight after I promised to help him back inside you tomorrow."

"*You're* the one who put him in me?"

"Not exactly. I put the Dark God's face on over yours, and he used that, somehow. I don't know what to do. Do you want to quit the film?"

"No," he said. "I still have dreams that this'll be a break-
out role for me. I want to act this part."

"But when I put the face on you, you're gone—I think."

"Lauren?" Corvus said.

"You and I and Blaise did scene twenty-three all day today, Corvus. Do you remember any of it?"

"No," he said.

"Well, you were great, whoever you were, creepy as hell,"
said Lauren. "I have to tell you, if you quit now, the whole
production will fall apart, and it won't be doing your career
any favors, either. But if it's a matter of survival, well, you
should do whatever you have to."

"I'm not doing my own acting," he muttered, "but I'm doing all right. That troubles me. I want to do the work . . . I
feel okay now. As soon as you put the face on me, I return to
being this other guy?"

"That's the impression I get," Opal said. "Magenta and
Lauren and I have been speculating about how it works. We
have ideas, but no certainties."

Corvus shook his head. "This is crazy."

"Yeah," said Opal. "Just deal with as much of it as you
can. Ignore the rest."

"How's that going to help us get rid of the Dark God?"
Magenta asked.

"We can't force Corvus to believe something he's not ready
for," Opal said, "no matter how urgent it is."

"How urgent is it?" Corvus asked.

"It's hard to say. Is he hurting you? You don't seem to have
suffered today, but he says he might hurt you tomorrow unless I do what he says."

"What he makes her do is let him suck on her like a vampire," Lauren told Corvus. "Except it's not blood he takes, but
her life force. He did that to me, too, or something like it.
I'm not sure what he did to me, but it was horrible."

"Shit, Lauren, he drank your blood," said Magenta.

"Didn't drink it, more like licked it, and then he put a spell on me that turned me into a drooling idiot, worshipping him just like Serena. All the rest of today's filming! I didn't come out of it till you stripped off my makeup, Madge. I remember it all, though. I was awake and watching. I just couldn't come to the surface."

"You all believe this happened today," said Corvus.

"We were there, and you weren't," said Magenta.

"But I—" He pressed his face into his palms. "I can't think about this now."

"Don't worry, Corr," said Opal. "We're almost at the restaurant. Guys, give it a rest. Let him eat."

"We need a plan," said Magenta.

Opal said, "The call sheet said we're filming scene twelve C tomorrow, and I got a stack of new script pages for Corvus. Are you in that scene, Lauren?"

"No. That's afternoon, Corvus with Gemma and Bettina. It's a new one about how messed up the sisters get as kids. In the morning, Blaise and I are filming in the B&B. One of our fabulous bitch-fight scenes."

"What's your call time tomorrow?" Opal asked.

"I need to be in Makeup by seven thirty," said Lauren. "We're supposed to be on the set by eight. What's yours?"

"Corvus goes into Makeup at ten so we can film at two. They give me four hours to put together Dark God. With the Invader's help, it takes less time. If there's any time after you finish and before we start filming, maybe we can talk, if Corvus is too out of it tonight." She pulled into the restaurant parking lot and turned off the engine.

Magenta and Lauren got out of the car. Opal reached for her door handle, but Corvus grasped her wrist. "Wait," he murmured.

Opal opened her window. "You guys get a table, will you? We'll be in soon."

Magenta saluted and headed into the restaurant with Lauren.

"I'm fuzzy on a lot of details," Corvus said in the relative darkness of the car, "but I remember you said you loved me."

"So what?"

"What does it—where do we—I'm not sure—"

"It's not a trap or an obligation, Corvus. It's just part of the way I work. To change someone so completely, I must love them in both their personas, before makeup and after. It usually wears off when the picture's over."

"This happens to you a lot."

"Only when I'm at the top of my game."

"Do you ever follow up on the feeling?"

"Oh, come on. Who needs the tsuris?"

He stared out the windshield, his large hand still loosely circling her wrist. "Did you feel like this during *Dead Loss*?"

"Immediately," she said. "You're not hard to love."

He sat silent, his fingers warm around her wrist, his palm a warm, dry pressure against the back of her hand. "Did it wear off afterward?"

"No."

"Why didn't you—"

She blew out a breath. "You try to maintain a low profile, but those people at *Entertainment Tonight* and *Access Hollywood* just love pictures of you with starlets, you know?"

"I think that's why those girls call me. Guaranteed exposure. The Beauty and the Beast captions write themselves. It means nothing."

She laughed. "Oh, *they* call *you*, eh?"

"Most of the time, I'd rather stay home and read a book," he said. She heard an undertone of laughter. "Opal," he said, the laughter gone.

She waited. She had gotten involved with one of her other special projects, a popular leading actor who could have picked anyone. He professed to be tired of high-maintenance relationships—not the most promising opening, but she had loved him deeply, or the character he was playing, anyway, a tortured soul with interesting facial scars she applied as necessary. He had been sweet, tender even; on idle days, they had spent time in the wilderness, where he could be someone he wasn't: unrecognized. But she always knew who he was.

He took her to a couple of premieres, too; he wasn't ashamed to be seen with someone who gave him no extra clout. He never treated her as a lesser being, the way some stars treated all the people whose names came at the end of the movie rather than the beginning, but she never cut her self-imposed tethers while she was with him and showed him she could fly.

Later, the news stories weren't kind to her: another in the chain of broken hearts he'd left behind, but this time, they said, given her profession, at least she knew how to conceal the tracks of her tears. Dreadful stuff.

Corvus tugged gently on her wrist. She unbuckled her seat belt and waited. He looped an arm around her, and lifted her (with some help from her) over the center console to settle in his lap. She relaxed against his chest; she had dreamed of being there, curled in his arms, his heart beating in her ear, and now she could hear it. She nestled against the huge warm mountain of him. His arms circled her, and his breath stirred her hair. He smelled like the sandalwood-scented moisturizer she'd rubbed on him, and underneath it, his own scent, that of a large, powerful, clean male animal.

A voice whispered: *Don't be stupid; we've been down this road before. Nothing good can last. You don't know him. You don't know anything about him. How can you trust him?*

Who needs trust? some other part of her asked. *I just want to fool around.*

He tipped her chin up and lowered his face, touched his lips to hers. His kiss was gentle and tasted sour. She gripped his face and explored his mouth, then pushed away. "I can taste how hungry you are," she whispered. "You should eat. We can do this later."

He groaned and hugged her almost too tight, then unlatched the door and helped her out of the car.

The same waitress was working again.

"Hey," she said. "I read your name off your credit card and rented one of your movies when I got off shift this morning. I watched it over lunch."

Corvus smiled. "I wouldn't eat while watching any of them. Did you like it?"

"You were really scary!" she said.

"Thank you."

"But I'm not scared of you now. I think that's strange. Oh, don't mean to hold you up. You guys want a table to yourself tonight, or are you joining someone?"

Corvus pointed toward the corner booth, where Magenta and Lauren sat, eating French fries and drinking soda.

"Her I've heard of," said the waitress, nodding toward Lauren. "She was great as Bitsy in *Fooled Me Twice*. Is she really as nice as she was in the movie?"

"She is," said Opal.

"Oh, good. We had a couple other stars in here around dinnertime, and they were—well, you don't need to hear. Please, seat yourselves. Here's some menus. I'll be right over to take your orders."

"Thanks, Jenny," said Corvus. He and Opal headed for Magenta and Lauren's booth. "Opal, you said something about new pages?"

"Yes. Sorry." She fished a sheaf of marigold-colored paper out of her messenger bag and handed it to him. Opal slid in beside Magenta, and Corvus beside Lauren.

He took reading glasses out of his shirt pocket and skimmed through the pages. There were six. "I've never seen this before."

"They were writing it last night, remember? In this same booth."

"Any good?" Lauren asked.

He flipped back to the start and frowned. "I—"

Jenny came up, pencil poised over her order pad. "Steak?" Corvus asked, peering at her over his glasses.

"Sure. T-bone or top sirloin?"

"T-bone."

"How you want that?"

"Medium rare. And a big salad if you have one."

"Sorta," she said. "Anything to drink?"

"A pitcher of coffee." He flipped through the marigold pages. "Gotta stay awake awhile longer. Got some memorizing to do."

"How about you, hon?" Jenny asked, turning to Opal.

For the first time Opal remembered her own hunger. It had been a long time since lunch, which she had barely had. She ordered a turkey sandwich, salad, and a glass of milk.

"Be right back," said Jenny, and bustled off.

"So what did you figure out in the car after we left?" Lauren asked.

"Not much," said Opal.

"Took you pretty long," said Magenta.

Lauren kicked Magenta under the table. "Meanwhile, we're still trying to figure out what to do about the D.G.," she said. "I don't want him to get to me again the way he did today. Tomorrow I'm safe, because we're not working together, but I think day after tomorrow, we're scheduled to do another forest shoot, if the weather cooperates. What I want to know is, are you *completely* unconscious the whole time he's here?"

"I don't remember anything about today, aside from sitting down to get made up, our fight, the dream about Opal," he said, "and then waking up after the day was over."

"I wonder if there's some part of you that remembers," said Lauren.

"What's your point?" asked Opal.

"If they're two separate people, we have to figure out how to manipulate the D.G. without Corvus's help—if he's stuck down in the basement and can't affect the D.G. while he's in charge, that's no good. If there's some kind of connection, we might be able to get Corvus to work on the guy from inside. Assuming Corvus is on our side, and doesn't want the D.G. torturing us all day while he's gone. But if there's a connection, that might mean the D.G. could figure out everything we plan, so I don't know whether to talk about this anymore in front of him."

"This film has been an eye-opener, and I've been here less than a week," Corvus said.

"What do you mean, big guy?" asked Magenta. She sipped soda from the bottom of the glass through her straw.

Jenny came and put food down in front of Corvus and Opal.

Corvus salted his steak, sat with his fork poised, frowned at his food. "Why did I say that?" he asked himself. "I'll tell you why. My flight lands in Portland, and I'm in charge of my life, about to start work on a new project. Good step on my career path, a role with meat to it. I know I can do a good job. I've memorized the most current version of the script. I've got a good room right in town, with a bed that's big enough for me for once, and my trailer's decent. First weird thing I learn on this shoot: Opal can hypnotize me."

"Oh?" Lauren glanced at Opal, eyebrows up.

Opal shrugged. "Not on purpose. Just so he could lie still comfortably while I was changing him into Dark God."

"I'm helpless in her hands," Corvus said. He straightened to his full height, which was impressive, sitting or standing. He shook his head slowly. "Long time since I've been helpless for anybody. I hate that."

"How come you can hypnotize him?" Magenta asked. "Is that part of your general witchiness?"

"I guess," Opal said.

"Wait," said Corvus. "You're a witch?"

"Close enough."

Corvus glanced at Lauren and Magenta. "Not news to them," he said to himself. "Okay. Maybe I knew it, too. So anyway, that's the first step to my discovery that I don't rule my own life. Now this other person is running around wearing my—wearing me, and alienating my coworkers and friends."

"You could leave," Opal said. "While you're still you. I'll drive you to Portland if you want."

"Breach my contract? Mess up this multimillion-dollar production and screw over everybody working on it?"

"Yep," said Opal.

"I don't think so. Talk about a career-killing move."

Opal had the impulse to stick it out, too. The shoot had to end sometime. They might be able to figure out how to deal with the Invader, keep him tame enough to work with. He was her best creation to date, though she couldn't take full credit for him.

"Is this movie going to be any good?" she asked the others.

"It'll be okay if they don't completely screw it up in post," said Magenta. "Nothing everybody hasn't seen before, but that's good, if it's something everybody wants to see again."

"Like everything I've done so far," Corvus said. "Anyway, in terms of career, I'm working my way toward where I want to be. Maybe next picture, I get to wear my own face, who knows? I know that's not likely; not many roles written for seven-foot leading men, but it could happen, right?"

"If anybody can do it, it's you," Lauren said. "You've got a great face. I wonder if Travis and Beth would write you a picture."

"To get to that point," he said, "I should probably get through this picture first. Agreed?"

The women looked at each other and nodded.

"All right, then. I vote we wait and see what happens tomorrow. Though I'm not looking forward to it." He sighed and settled into eating.

Opal had finished her sandwich. She checked her watch—after midnight—then opened her messenger bag to search for her cell phone, even though she was sure her mother had already gone to bed.

Lauren leaned across Magenta and touched Opal's arm. "Sorry to change the subject," she said. "But there he is."

"Who?" Opal asked.

"The ex." She nodded toward the front of the restaurant. "I wonder how long he's been here."

They all looked. A dark-haired man was sitting at the counter with a mug of coffee in front of him. He held something in his hand, stared down at it. It winked.

"Is that a mirror?" Magenta asked.

"Subtle, isn't he?" said Lauren.

"Who is he?"

"The guy who's stalking me, Norman Davis."

"You have a stalker?" Magenta said.

"Yep. Not just trendy, but nerve-racking."

"Do you know what he wants? An autograph?" asked Corvus.

"Not hardly," said Lauren, while Magenta said, "He's a movie star, big guy, not an autograph hound."

"Oh?" Corvus looked at the back of Norman's head again. He frowned.

"He was the male lead's sidekick in *Fooled Me Twice*," said Magenta. "Mr. Comic Relief. The B-story romance with Lauren's character."

"Oh. That was a charming subplot," Corvus said.

"You've actually seen the movie?" Lauren said.

"Of course. I like to know who I'm going to be working with. You were great. He was good," Corvus said.

"Thanks. Yeah. Snowed me enough I said yes when he wanted to take the relationship outside the script."

Jenny leaned forward at the counter, smiled at Norman while she refilled his coffee mug, laughed at something he said. She gestured past his shoulder toward their table and asked a question. Norman shook his head without turning around.

Still staring at Norman, Lauren said, "Will you guys leave with me?"

"Sure. Anyway, we have to, don't we? I've got the car," said Opal.

"Oh. Yeah," said Lauren. She smiled.

"Corvus will pretend he's your boyfriend," Opal said.

"I will?" said Corvus. "Of course I will, if that's what you want."

"Not sure that's a good idea," Lauren said. "I know Norm is whacked. I don't know exactly how. He might get weird and destructive toward you, as well as me, if he thinks we're together. Anyway, tabloids will be announcing you two as a couple any day now, right?" She smiled at Corvus and Opal.

"Are there actual press leaks on this shoot?" asked Magenta. "Erika is irritating, but she doesn't seem to have sent out a story yet. We had some security scares in the Makeup trailer, but I haven't seen anything in the tabloids about this shoot yet, and yeah, I'm checking out the *World Weekly News* and the *Enquirer* every time I'm at a cash register in the supermarket."

"I could start some stories," said Lauren.

"Please don't," Opal said. "Been down that road. Hated it."

"Really?" Lauren asked.

"That was with Gerry?" Corvus said.

"Gerry who?" asked Magenta.

"Gerard Shelley." Opal hunched her shoulders. Her relationship with Gerry hadn't ended badly. They were still friends, but he had moved on. Really, so had she; she'd been working with Corvus by the time she and Gerry wished each other well. The tabloids had invented their own sour ending. "Why do you know about that, Corr?"

"I told you, I research the people I work with."

"You hooked up with Gerry?" Lauren said. "I worked with him once. One tiny scene. I was a funny library lady and he had a question. He's awesome. Or—does it turn out he's not?"

"No. He's a good guy," Opal said.

Jenny came by with a coffeepot and a pitcher of cola, offered refills. She glanced over her shoulder toward the counter, then looked at Lauren.

"Sweetie, we're not together any longer, and I'm totally uninterested in him," Lauren told her. "So please don't tell him what I'm doing or who with, okay?"

Jenny flushed. "He said he wanted to surprise you."

"Yes, but not in a good way."

"Oh," said the waitress. "I'm sorry."

"No way you could know that. He's an actor. It's his job to convince people he's nice. Underneath—well, my advice would be don't go there, but it's up to you."

Jenny's eyes widened. "No." She gave her head one shake. "I wasn't even thinking that. I thought you were a couple."

"Nope. So don't tell him any more about me than you have to, okay?"

"All right. Boy, having you guys around sure makes life interesting."

"We live for that," said Lauren with a grin. Jenny topped off everybody's drinks and went away again.

"Well, I've got pages," Corvus said. "Or does the other guy need to memorize them?" He shuddered.

"He knows what you know," Lauren said. "We found that out today. If you get your lines in your head, he can get to them. Hmm. That may answer my earlier question. You guys are connected somehow. Any plans we make with you, he can figure out, maybe. That's not good."

Opal dropped her hands to her thighs and fisted them under the table. She needed to talk to her mother. The previous Christmas, her sister had done a strange spell that revealed how people connected to each other in her family, and Opal had seen strings leading from her mother to everyone else. If she could connect to Corvus that way, maybe she could talk to him, even while he was submerged under the Invader. She dug out her cell phone. "Excuse me," she said. "Gotta make a call."

"Don't go too far," Lauren said. "Please."

"Right out front," said Opal. "I'll keep an eye on you through the glass."

They all watched her leave, and she realized everyone was depending on her. It felt like she was back at home, herding her younger siblings around, being their mother because Mama wasn't really good at that, listening to every complaint, fixing things that went wrong. Familiar, and in a way almost sweet, and also annoying.

She stood just to the side of the door. She could see the back booth from there, and she also saw Norman's profile. He was handsome, and looked grumpy.

She called home.

"Opal, is that you? I've been waiting to hear from you," said her mother after one ring.

"Oh, good. I'm sorry to call so late. Glad you're up."

"I'm not, really. Your father and I are reading in bed. What's the problem? Flint wasn't very coherent."

"Mama, I put a face on my friend to turn him into a monster, and a monster came with it. What do I do?"

"Can you give me some real information, honey? It's hard to diagnose from this distance."

Opal explained as much as she understood about the Invader, how the location had influenced the writing of the script, the script had dictated the nature of the monster, and the monster she had assembled had taken on a life of its own. She also talked about the Invader's blackmail scheme. "How did you make those strings that hooked us all together, Mama?" she asked.

"What are you talking about?"

"Remember Gyp's Reveal Spell, how it showed strings between us? She broke the string you had to her, and—"

"What are you talking about, Opal?" Mama asked again. "I don't remember any Reveal Spell."

"It was at that special meeting we had before last Christmas, just before Gyp got her curses under control. Actually, it was the meeting where she figured out how to control them, and she—" Opal thought about the meeting, remembered her own astonishment when her sister and her sister's new lover had showed the family many things, most of them unpleasant.

So many things had happened during the meeting that Opal didn't remember it very clearly, but she remembered the image of her whole family draped in webs of many colors, and how her mother had spun most of the webs to snare the rest of them. Looking at the webs had told Opal so much: why her younger brothers and sisters never moved out, and how scared her mother must have been, to hang on to them so tightly.

Opal had carried the web image to the extended family party in Los Angeles after Christmas, had wished she could see the webwork among her cousins and grandparents, aunts and uncles. Mama had four sisters and two brothers, and she didn't get along with any of them. Opal had lost her special vision by then, though, and she had to guess rather than know. She had studied her grandparents afresh, noticed how Grandmère pitted her children against each other. "Well, Anise," Grandmère had said to Opal's mother, "I hear your oldest boy is learning to use his talents in music. Sage, what's wrong with your daughter? She was studying flute last year. Why did she give it up?"

Aunt Sage had been upset. "How did you know?"

"I know everything," Grandmère had said. And then, to another aunt: "Well, Lily, I understand your youngest daughter transitioned at last. At fifteen! I hear she has cooking talents. So sad, Anise, about your girl Gyp, having to do it all without talent—"

But that was where the party got interesting. "As to that," Mama said, "Gyp brought her usual array of cookies and brownies to the party. We had more to share this year than usual, but I notice there are almost none left. I wouldn't say she's not talented."

"Not talented with a capital *T*," said Grandmère, with a tiny shark smile.

"I suppose," Mama said brightly, "it depends on how you define talent. Gyp finally transitioned, although her talent is like Aunt Meta's."

"What?" Grandmère spoke so loudly everyone turned to look and listen.

"Gyp has the power of curses," said Mama, almost proudly.

Opal was surprised the whole family didn't already know. She remembered how distracted Mama had been before Christmas, and realized part of her distraction must have been due to planning how to introduce the family to this new development. Play it up? Play it down? Mama had picked the first alternative.

Opal checked for Gyp. It should have been her information to share. Gyp was talking to two of the cousins, admiring a brag book one held, maybe photographs or artwork. Like everyone else nearby, the cousins heard Mama's declaration. They stepped away from Gyp.

Opal had headed toward her. So had Flint and Jasper and Beryl. Opal slowed when she saw other cousins gathering around Gyp, asking questions, touching her arms and shoulders, one or two embracing her. Gyp was smiling.

Mama continued, "She even uses her power in cooking, though she has to have help, or what she makes comes out cursed. Don't worry. We made sure our contribution to the potluck was curse-free."

"Curses? Curses?" Grandmère muttered.

Mama took top news honors with that information, no matter what this cousin or that cousin had managed to do with their powers last year. In fact, Grandmère was so surprised she lost control of the party for at least half an hour.

"Strings," Mama said on the phone, bringing Opal back to the present. "I don't remember any strings."

"Oh. Well, do you have any other good ideas?"

"I just have bad ideas, like flying up there to help you, and bringing the kids with me. Do you want any or all of us with you?"

"How would that work with your job?"

"It wouldn't be convenient, but I can escape if I have to. Do you want me to send Tobias?"

Opal's great-uncle Tobias was the family teacher. He knew more magework than any of the rest of them, and had been practicing longer than the rest of them had been alive. He was a stick in the mud, though; didn't even leave the house to accompany the family on vacations. Hell, he claimed he liked having the time alone, and he probably meant it.

"I don't know," Opal said. "If he could come, that would be great. I don't know if we're in enough danger to warrant emergency measures, though."

"I'll check with him in the morning," said her mother. "Call if you need help sooner than that. Here's your father."

"Opal? What can I do to help?" asked her father, and suddenly she felt like crying. Dad was great. But he had no more than normal human powers.

"Same deal as always, Dad. Be yourself. Listen and think. If you come up with any ideas, let me know."

"All right," he said. "Love you, Opal."

"Love you," she whispered, closed the phone, and wiped her eyes.

8

Opal peered into the restaurant—she had forgotten to watch what was happening between Norman and her friends—but everything looked the same. She opened the door and went back to the corner booth.

"Thanks for the offer, Lauren," Corvus was saying when Opal settled next to Magenta again. "I'll ask Opal to run lines with me." He turned to Opal. "You'll spend the night, won't you?"

"What?"

"You'll stay with me tonight."

Immediately she felt like saying no. Did he think a declaration of love made her stupid or weak? Did he think it gave him permission to order her around?

"Please," he said.

"Sure," she said, shaking her head.

"And on that note, maybe we better get back to town," he said, "so I can practice and get some sleep."

"I'll want my toothbrush and a change of clothes," said Opal.

"Of course."

Corvus paid for everybody, and linked arms with Lauren on the way out. They swept past a frowning Norman. Lauren never even looked at him.

Across the parking lot at the budget motel, Magenta bid them goodnight and went to her room. Lauren and Corvus followed Opal into her room. Having Corvus there made Opal conscious of how low the ceilings were, how small the room really was. She liked his room better, despite the brown gingham and chintz, and the sense of the house watching.

"How much should I pack?" she asked. If Corvus had an agenda, she wanted to know what it was.

"Doesn't that kind of depend on who he is after shooting tomorrow?" asked Lauren. "You don't want to move in with D.G., do you?"

"Good point." Opal packed essential toiletries, the oversized T-shirt she wore as a nightgown, and one change of clothes. It all fit into her messenger bag.

She drove them both back to Lapis. A car followed them— Lauren pointed it out.

"Don't worry," Opal said. "I can take care of this."

As soon as they reached town, Opal parked and conjured an image of their car, while hiding the real car in unreal shadows. The imaged car drove on past them.

"What was that?" Lauren asked as she watched the image of a car drive away from them, with Norman's car following. She leaned forward in the backseat, gripping Opal's seat.

"An illusion," said Opal.

"But how—Oh. You can do that?"

"It's light. I can work with light. That's my gift."

"If you can do that—you could make your own movies. Without the benefit of actors or sets."

"Not interested," said Opal. "At least, not at the moment. Where are you staying, again?"

Lauren was quiet as Opal drove her to her host family's home, speaking only to give directions. She gripped and released Opal's shoulder before she climbed out of the car. "Later." Opal watched as Lauren went up the front walk and into the house. One light burned beyond the front door; the rest of the house was dark.

No other cars drove down this street. Opal pulled out and drove slowly back to the bed-and-breakfast, watching for Norman's car, but her illusion car had apparently led him far from downtown Lapis. All to the good.

At the B&B, Corvus took her bag out of the backseat and carried it up. The house didn't feel menacing tonight, more curious. Again, when they reached the upstairs hall, the director glanced out of his room as their footsteps sounded. He frowned and shook his head, disappeared back into his room without a word.

"Who's he shacking up with?" Opal asked as a woman murmured beyond the wall Corvus's room shared with Aldridge's.

"They're very discreet," said Corvus. "I've never seen her, only heard that voice. Can you tell from listening?"

Opal leaned her ear against the wall, but couldn't make out the words, only the tone. She glanced at Corvus.

"I think it's Blaise," he said. "Trav and Beth just rewrote a key scene and gave her five more lines. They cut Lauren's part by three lines. Lauren was looking over her new pages while you were on the phone. She's mad."

"She should be. Serena's the main character," Opal said.

"That could change."

It was true. Lots of things could change during production, and even more drastic changes sometimes took place in postproduction.

"That sucks," said Opal.

"We'll see what happens," Corvus said. "From everything going on, nobody knows how this will play out. Too many wild cards. Will you read lines with me?"

"Yeah, I guess," she said. "I have to brush my teeth."

"Go on. I'll change."

She changed into the T-shirt nightgown she usually didn't wear—when she was alone, she slept naked—and wrapped herself in a man's triple-X corduroy work shirt, the closest thing she had to a bathrobe. She washed up.

When she came out of the bathroom, Corvus was lounging on an overstuffed brown and white gingham couch; it was big enough to support him without parts of him hanging over the edge. He wore blue pajamas and his reading glasses, and he was studying the script. Love swept through her, startling and inconvenient. He glanced up at her over the tops of his glasses, and her throat tightened. He could immobilize her with a look; better not let him know. She forced herself to walk forward and sat on the bed across from him.

"It's only six lines," he said. "I think I've got it. Would you help me?"

"Sure." She took the script from him and read the parts of Young Serena and Young Caitlyn. The Dark God was already sharpening up the rivalry between them, pretending he favored one, then the other.

Opal was intrigued by the young girls' parts. They had seen this monster accept the sacrifice of both their parents. Well, according to Beth and Travis, Serena had seen her mother sacrifice her father to him, and both of them had witnessed their mother's suicide on the Dark God's altar. Why were they even talking to him? Neither of them seemed scared of him. Young Serena even clung to his hand. By the end of the scene, he had stooped and gathered her to him. Young Caitlyn stood outside of the embrace, her face cold.

Did this make psychological sense? Opal wasn't sure it

did, but then, maybe it didn't need to. Most horror movies she'd worked on weren't that long on sense. People always wandered off alone in time to get killed, when any sensible person would cling to the others and head for someplace with lots of light.

"Both of you may be my handmaidens and help me," said Corvus, "but I will always love one above the other." He was almost whispering by the time he finished.

"Love me," said Young Caitlyn. "I'm strong and beautiful."

"Love me," said Young Serena. "I'll do whatever you want."

Corvus laughed a villain's laugh. It went on too long. Opal dropped the pages and stared at him. His eyes glowed green.

"Go away," she said. "You said you wouldn't come back until tomorrow!"

"What?" Corvus blinked, and the extra light in his eyes faded.

"Let's go to bed," Opal said. "Which side do you prefer?"

"The left side," he said. "Now *I've* got to brush my teeth. Did you want to—? Because I'm not sure I have the energy."

"I'd rather just get some sleep," she said. While he was in the bathroom, she curled up under the covers on the right side of the bed.

Water ran. She needed to collect more power. She might need enough to offer some to the Invader and keep some for herself, or she might need enough to fight him. Either way, she needed to engage in power collection.

She thought about the person she had been in her teens, her brief period of rage and revenge, when she had attacked her irritating brother, Jasper, in ways creative, devious, and mean. It had been so foreign to her character she hadn't maintained it for long. Also, Jasper had gone through transition soon after she had, and once he had his own powers, he was too formidable for her to fight. She had read some of the

Forbidden Texts during her brief flirtation with the dark side, though, and learned a few handy things.

She reached into her shadow and summoned the Sifter Chant, the one that threw out a net to snare any stray power in the environment and store it in her power reservoir. There was nothing inherently evil about this chant. It could work in the background once she set it going; she would only need to check on it now and then to make sure what she was collecting wouldn't make her sick. The world was full of different-flavored powers in various stages of existence, and some of them weren't good for anyone.

She scribed three symbols on her palm with her index finger and spoke the Sifter Chant three times, felt the opening out of her nets and the first tiny tugs as she collected. The power flowed into her reservoir and stored itself, quiescent. *Good,* she thought, drowsy now, warmed by the very act of summoning.

The next time she opened her eyes, it was because she smelled coffee. Corvus stood beside the bed holding a mug near her face. "I don't even know if you drink coffee in the morning," he said as she sat up. "I do. Copious amounts, usually, unless I'm about to put on a costume it takes an hour to get out of. Thank God this picture isn't like that."

She took the mug from him and drank from it. It had lots of cream and sugar in it; usually she didn't use either, but she liked it this time. The coffee tasted like hot ice cream.

"Thanks," she said.

He was already dressed, black jeans and a blue shirt, and his hair was wet from a shower. Opal lifted her wrist to check the time. Six thirty. She groaned and glanced at the pillow, imagined flopping down to sleep another couple hours.

"We gather for breakfast between six and nine. The hostess is kind of strict about that," Corvus said.

"You go ahead," said Opal. "I'll go back to sleep and drive out to the IHOP later."

"Come on. You can eat here. Bess always makes too much of everything."

She downed the rest of the coffee. "Okay, if you want to be public about this, us being a couple, if that's what we are. I'll be down after I shower. You sure?"

"How secretive have we been so far? If you think Magenta and Lauren aren't going to tell anyone, think again."

"And anyway, it's only half a couple. You never said anything," she muttered. "I feel like your all-access stalker."

He sat on the bed beside her and pulled her into his arms, kissed her with his eyes shut; she knew, because she kept hers open, and saw the trouble in his face, the lowered brows, tightened cheeks. She flattened her hand against his chest and pushed him back until he lifted his face away from hers. "Please. Don't torture yourself. I said a stupid thing, all right? I meant it before, about this not demanding any specific response from you."

"Am I that bad a kisser?"

"Go on down to breakfast. I'll shower and sneak out. I can get something to eat at Craft Services."

"No. We need to straighten this out before I turn into that other guy you don't like." He shook his head. "Still not sure I believe that, but I'm afraid of it anyway. What's wrong?"

She blew out a breath, got up, and paced. "It's much easier to love you when you don't know about it. I don't want everything to shift around because this information is in the way. I can love you from a distance, from the other hotel. I can love you whatever you do, including if you get involved with someone else. I can have this as my own background feeling and do my job just fine. This foreground stuff isn't working for me. I don't want to think about whether you care about me. If you do care, I don't want you worrying about how to treat me, or whether I'll explode if you make the wrong move, or whatever's going through your head that makes you feel like you have to prove something to me.

If you want to prove something to me, this isn't the way.
Okay?"

"What do you think I'm trying to prove?" he asked.

"God, I don't know. You don't have to act like you want
me, Corr. That's not what I need."

"But I—I *do*—" He dropped his forehead to his palm.
"What do you need?"

"Go back to normal. Think about the role, worry about
your lines, be here because you're doing a job. You do yours;
I'll do mine. We'll be fine."

"Except for the other guy who walks around inside me."

"Well, there is that."

"Give me a kiss before you leave," he said. "We might not
have another chance."

She huffed, exasperated, then went to him. He embraced
her and kissed her, and this one went better; with him sitting and her standing, they were well matched in height.
This time she tasted desire and desperation, two things she
felt, too. Eventually, he eased away from her and smiled. She
smiled, too.

"Okay. I'll see you in the trailer at ten." She grabbed her
bag and went into the bathroom to shower.

On her way down the back stairs ten minutes later, she ran
into Blaise. They slipped out of the house in silence. Blaise
walked away down the street in the early morning light, then
glanced over her shoulder. "Come on," she said.

Opal followed her to a small but ornately gingerbreaded
house in the next block. Blaise gestured her up the front porch
steps. "Neil initially set me up with a room at the B&B, but I
didn't want it," she said. "Didn't want to be housed with the
movie people. Said it'd be too noisy. More fool I."

"So this is your lodging?"

"Right, a nice lady in her seventies with cats. A fan. Sick-
ening, really, in a way, but handy, too. She always gets up and
makes me breakfast if I'm here, no matter what time the

call's for. She made me a four A.M. breakfast one morning.
She stocks my favorite foods. I bet she'd be thrilled if I
brought another movie person to breakfast."

Opal raised her eyebrows.

"Yes, you're enough of a movie person to impress her.
Come on in." Blaise tapped on the door and opened it.
"Myrna?" Blaise called softly as she and Opal entered the
foyer. The walls were dark maroon with sparkles in the paint,
and a strange, complicated coatrack stood against the right
wall, with dangling garments hanging on it that looked a
little like the cult robes in the film. A large, fluffy, tabby-
striped cat stropped Opal's legs, purring. "You up?" Blaise
called.

"In the kitchen, dear," called a pleasant alto voice from the
back of the house.

"I've brought a friend. Is that all right?"

"Oh, who? Who?" A door flapped open in front of them.
A stout woman with short curls of bright, copper-washed
hair stood there in a gray silk dressing gown covered with
blue butterflies.

"This is Opal LaZelle, who does the creature makeup for
Forest," Blaise said. "Opal, Myrna Partridge, my excellent landlady. Myrna, is it too late for breakfast?"

"Too late? Of course not. I was hoping you'd make it
home in time." Myrna held the door open and they walked
past her into the kitchen, all white counters and yellow, flower-
sprigged wallpaper and sunny floor tile. A black cat clock
with wagging tail and shifting eyes ticked loudly on the wall
by the fridge. Everything looked unnaturally clean, considering there were six cat dishes on the floor near the back door,
each with a little kibble remaining, and three large water
dishes on the floor near the sink. "What's your pleasure this
morning, Blaise? My goodness, Ignatious certainly has taken
a liking to your friend."

The big tabby had followed them into the kitchen, where

he settled on Opal's feet. The cat's purrs were audible from the floor. He stared up at Opal with wide green eyes.

"Is there any more of that strawberry Special K?" Blaise asked.

"I bought a new box just yesterday," said Myrna, "and more skim milk for you."

"Thank you, Myrna. You're much too good to me," Blaise said.

Opal knelt and stared into the cat's eyes. Their green glow looked familiar. The cat licked her nose.

"Oh, please," she said.

He did it again, the rasp of a wet tongue against her nose. She sighed and stood up.

"What would you like for breakfast, dear?" Myrna asked.

"Cereal sounds good," said Opal. "Thanks so much, ma'am."

"You're so welcome." The landlady got down two large pottery bowls and poured cereal in one, eyebrows quirked as if to ask *how much?* Blaise held up her hand after only a little cereal had gone into her bowl. She took the bowl to the fridge and poured milk into it, then grabbed a couple of spoons from a drawer and returned to the kitchen table.

Opal waited until the bowl was half-full before cutting off the flow of cereal. "Okay if I get my own milk?" she asked.

"Surely. Help yourself." Myrna sat down at the table with a large mug of coffee. "If you want coffee, there's a full pot in the coffeemaker, and mugs in the cupboard above it. So you're making the Lapis monster?"

"Well, the monster for the movie, anyway."

"That creature is a local celebrity."

"Oh? Did the writers base him on an actual local legend? They didn't tell me. Are there any descriptions of him?"

"Tall and dark, they say, and he stalks the young girls. I remember when I was fifteen, all the girls talked about him, and none of us were allowed out alone at night. We had some shivery sleepovers, I can tell you."

"Did he have a name?" Opal asked. She poured milk onto the cereal and set the bowl on the table next to Blaise's place. Blaise handed her a spoon.

"There was something romantic we called him. Let me think." She sipped coffee, narrowed her eyes, and stared into the past. "So sad, it was. The Last of the Lost."

"Last of the Lost," Opal repeated.

"There was a girl I knew then—what was her name? Linda, I think—who felt sorry for the Last."

Opal got some coffee and sat beside Blaise. "What happened?"

"She had some idea that he was a sad and lonely creature someone had abandoned. This was the early fifties, and there were lots of things we didn't talk about. Linda never had us over to her house after school, and she came to school with bruises she never explained. She had a terrible time at home; I think that's why her heart went out to him. Anyway, at one of our sleepovers—now that I think about it, I remember she didn't make it to many of those; her mother didn't let her out of the house—she wanted us to sneak out the basement window and go to the forest with food for the Last. None of us would do it. We were all terrified. She snuck out after the rest of us went to sleep, and we never saw her again."

"Whoa," said Blaise.

"Was there a search?" Opal asked.

"Oh, yes. Everybody and their dogs were out in the forest looking for her. Somebody found her hair ribbon on a bush. Someone found a few bloodstains on those strange rocks out there in the clearing where you all are filming, but they looked old. I think some of the boys went out there and played weird games. Nobody who had a cat let it out of the house at night, I recall." Myrna drank more coffee, sleep-walked to the coffeemaker for a refill. "They said it wasn't the first time something like that happened. People went missing—that was why our parents were always telling us not to go out at night."

She settled in her chair. "Sometimes I envied Linda. I thought she went off somewhere and found another life, and it had to be better than here. Maybe she found someone to care about. Maybe someone did her in. I did think about that, too. Might have been better for her, either way.

"Even these days, I don't much sit on my porch after sunset. I'm still afraid of the night. I remember my husband and I went to Mexico on a trip one time, and there were all kinds of people out after dark, and music and drinking and dancing. It was like visiting another planet."

Opal ate cereal and drank coffee and thought about the Invader. "Why did you stay here?" she asked. "Why not move away?"

"Oh, well. I inherited this beautiful house, and it was all I ever knew, really. My husband and I both grew up here. He went away to college, but something scared him and he dropped out his junior year and came home. He worked in the gravel pit here ever since. Died last year." She shrugged. "I asked him what happened out there in the world, but he never did tell me. Boys do all right here, but we had no children, and not for lack of trying. If we'd had girls to look after, we might have made different choices."

"Can I ask you more about the Last of the Lost?" Opal said. "Did anybody ever know where he came from or why he was here?"

Myrna closed her eyes and thought. "Collected girls," she muttered. "Nobody ever said what he did with them, but it was probably about sex, which we never talked about, or murder, which we did talk about, but only from what we saw in the movies. Nobody ever found bodies or bits of them. We said the missing girls were runaways in the police reports. Why was he here? Well, because he'd always been here, forever and ever. Before there was a town, he was here. He was here because of the people who were here before." She opened her eyes, stared into Opal's eyes. "Isn't that odd? I don't think there *were* any people here before. Maybe Kalapuya Indians, but I don't think so."

"Opal, I've got to get to my seven thirty makeup call. I'm going to head over now," said Blaise.

Opal checked her watch. "Shoot. I better go, too. Mrs. Partridge, thanks so much for everything. Is there anybody else around who might be able to tell me more about this Last guy?"

"Old Bessie Gates at the Early Bird Bed-and-Breakfast, where you folks are filming. She's even older than I am, and she's lived here all her life. Haven't spoken to her in a long time, myself. Don't get along with her. But if anybody knows local history, she's the one."

"Thanks. Should I wash this?" Opal held up her bowl.

"No, no, don't worry about it. You kids just go. A pleasure, Opal."

"Likewise," said Opal. She grabbed her messenger bag and followed Blaise out.

"So that was quite the fishing expedition," Blaise said.

"You know there's something going on with Corvus," said Opal. "This is all background."

"You think the thing she was talking about is the thing that's taken him over and molded him into a better actor?"

"He could always act!" Opal said. "You are such a snot!"

Blaise laughed. "You're easy to tweak," she said.

"Why would you want to?" asked Opal.

"I need to find out who you are," said Blaise. "If we're arming for some kind of war, I like to know who I'm fighting with."

"Okay, maybe you're right. Who are *you*?" Opal asked.

"It's not that easy," said Blaise. "It's not my habit to get along with anyone, and I have my reasons for that."

"You're sleeping with the director, and suddenly you have more lines."

Blaise laughed again. "Sure. I want to shine in this picture. It has potential. People aren't expecting much, but some of the writing is sharp, and I must say, your work with Corvus, however it's happening, is quite astonishing. I wouldn't be surprised if you were nominated for an Oscar— or, I guess Dathan would get nominated for art direction, and take all the credit. Of course I'm angling to get more and better lines. Lauren's not good at guarding her territory. Right now, the picture has two leads, and I don't like that. I'd like to emerge the winner, the one people remember. The writing isn't quite aimed that way yet. But I can work it around."

"So you really are a bitch."

"Yep." She smiled. "We all would be, if we weren't so busy being nice. Let that be a lesson to you. You could use a little bitching up, too."

9

∾

They arrived at the Makeup trailer. "Be right back," said Blaise. "Gotta make a pit stop." She headed toward the B&B.

Opal unlocked the trailer door. She figured she could nap in Corvus's chair until he arrived—that would be easier than sneaking back into the B&B or driving her little economy car back to the motel in Redford.

Lauren, Rod, Corvus, and Magenta were already in the trailer. Corvus sprawled in his chair, his reading glasses perched on his nose, a novel in his hands and one of her lights angled so it shone on the pages. He straightened.

Opal wondered why he hadn't gone either to his room or to his private dressing room in the trailer next door. Maybe he was feeling social. She said good morning to everyone and hopped up on the makeup counter to think about Blaise. She had seen principal actors behave in ways that led to increased roles for them, decreased roles for others, but she'd never had an actor be so up front about it. You were supposed to maintain an attractive surface.

Well, in public. Lots of stories made the rounds about stars whacking their personal assistants with phones or other handy objects. Opal had observed some bad behavior, experienced some herself, and heard many stories about much worse.

Corvus watched her. "Where'd you go?" he asked.

"I had breakfast with Blaise," she said.

He quirked both eyebrows.

Lauren was already in her clothes for the shoot. The fight Serena was having with Caitlyn today was apparently early in the picture, when Serena was still dressed in dowdy, repressed clothes—a khaki skirt, a bulky oatmeal-colored shirt with long sleeves—before her relationship with the Dark God opened her up to her dark side, and she went wild and vampy. She was in her chair, waiting for makeup. Magenta was still setting out her tools.

"How'd that happen?" asked Lauren.

"We were leaving the B&B at the same time," said Opal.

Magenta and Lauren looked at each other, then at Opal with varying degrees of dismay.

"Well, okay, I heard something like that was going on," said Lauren, "but I didn't want to believe it."

"Believe it," said Opal. "Corr said you mentioned rewriting last night, losing some of your lines, Blaise getting extra."

"Yeah. It makes sense now."

"She's angling for even more, Lauren. I hope you figure out how to handle this."

"I'll come up with something."

"Meanwhile, at breakfast, Blaise's landlady told us about a local monster that stalked women here in the fifties."

"What?"

"We need to ask the woman at the B&B about this. Blaise's landlady said she would know about the monster if anybody did."

"You could ask me," said Corvus, "sometime in the near

future." His voice was deeper than usual. He stared at the new face of the Dark God, on its life-mask head on Opal's counter where she had set it out the night before. She had already altered the rest of the stack of latex to add the horns and the other slight changes the Dark God had made, matching the rest of her mask supplies to the Polaroids, using magic without qualm because there was no other way around the continuity problems.

"I'll do that," said Opal. "You ready for this, Corr?"

He closed his eyes, sighed, and nodded. "Let's go. Wait. A kiss for luck first?"

She held his head between her hands and touched lips to his. He ringed her with his arm and drew her closer. She thought about what she had learned about him overnight, and some of it was funny and sad. She still loved him. Plus, he tasted wonderful, even flavored with coffee. At last he loosened his hold around her, and she pushed up and away.

She pressed the back of her hand against her mouth, as though to print his kiss on memory, and said, "Try to hang on while I'm doing this, okay?"

"I will."

She shaved him and moisturized him, and he watched her, smiling. "How can I not love somebody who treats me this way?" he asked as she mixed the adhesive.

"How many of your barbers have you fallen in love with?" she asked.

"All of them."

She lifted the brow piece and applied fresh adhesive to the back of it, then laid it carefully across his temple. She checked the Polaroid she had taken the night before and nudged it a little sideways, then lifted the second piece of leafy latex skin. By the time she turned around, his eyes had changed, and it was the Invader looking at her with most of Corvus's face. The effect was eerie. She hadn't seen him using Corvus's real features before. He looked almost natural there.

"Thanks," he said. "I respect your honor."

"Well," she said, and laid the next piece of his face on over Corvus's. "Are you an ancient entity?"

"I don't care to discuss that."

"Did you steal girls fifty years ago from this town?"

"Let's get to know each other better before I tell you my personal history," he said. "Where's my kiss?"

She wondered if she still had Flint's energy to shield her from him. It hadn't stopped her from kissing Corvus, or even sleeping with him. She held out her hand, trying to ignore the shudder in her flesh. He took it in hands she had just been embraced by and brought it close to his mouth. The burn of Flint's blessing heated her hand as the Invader drew her hand toward his mouth. "Clear a little space," she said to herself, reassured and again charmed by Flint's gift. She gave him the back of her hand to kiss, but then brought back the shield before she lost much energy to him.

"Strict," he said.

"We have work to do," she said. "If you're hungry, I'll get you food. Right now, let me finish putting on the mask, okay?"

He stared up at her, and leaves pushed up out of his skin, tracing themselves in the same paths as those on the mask she had made, changing his face from within.

"Don't!"

"It's more comfortable this way," he murmured.

She saw Lauren watching her and Corvus. Magenta watched in the mirror. She looked pale.

"Turn him back and let me do it my way," she said. "You have to be honorable, too, or I'll leave right now."

"You won't," he whispered. "You can't."

She set down her tools and walked toward the door.

The whisper followed her. "You'd leave him to me?"

She gripped the doorknob, turned it, and opened the door. He asked a good question, but she had to stay strong, or she might lose Corvus altogether. She stepped out of the trailer onto the landing. The door almost closed behind her before she heard the voice of the Invader.

"All right," he said. "Come back."

She stood on the landing under the overcast sky, savoring a brief moment of the other choice. Walk away from all of this. Never do this job again. Her mother still kept her room for her at home. It would drive Opal insane to live at home for any length of time, but she could rest there and figure out a different way to use her gifts, begin a whole new career. It wasn't too late.

Or, less dramatically, just get a job on a movie filming on another location.

Lose Corvus, with whom she was still hopelessly in love. There was a chance he would be back. Maybe she could increase the likelihood of that if she stuck around.

She turned and went back into the trailer.

Corvus looked like himself again except for the two pieces of prosthesis she had attached. His eyes had extra light in them, so she knew the one she loved wasn't present.

"I *will* walk," she said.

"I understand," said the Invader.

"All right, then." She went back to work, and he left the face in its natural state, letting her do the crafting to make it unnatural. She did not let even a little magic help her.

By the time she had almost finished fitting the Invader into his face and looked up again, Lauren was gone; Blaise had come and gone without her noticing; and the two girls who were playing Serena and Caitlyn as adolescents were in the chairs. Magenta was working on them; Rod was undoubtedly on the set with Blaise and Lauren.

"Have you met the girls yet?" Magenta asked Opal, her tone flattened.

"Not yet," said Opal. She dipped a brush in gilt, another in adhesive. She painted a thin outline around one of the leaves on Corvus's cheek and scattered gold over it. The Invader watched her, smiling. She checked his face against last night's Polaroid and decided he would do.

Opal called Kelsi, who said she'd bring Corvus's robe right over. There was something to be said for the convenience of a simple costume without changes. She wandered over to where Magenta was working.

"Hey, guys," Magenta said. "This is Opal. She's the creature wrangler. Opal, this is Gemma Goodwin and Bettina Lysander."

"Nice to meet you," Opal said.

"Hey," said the darker girl, slightly plump, who looked pretty much like a younger version of Lauren. She looked about twelve. Her voice was deep. "I'm Serena the younger, a.k.a. Gemma."

The other girl, who looked even younger, was a match for Blaise in cherubic beauty and silver-gilt crinkled hair. Maybe she also matched Blaise in temperament; she scowled at Opal, turned back to Magenta. "Yeah, so? Finish up, will you?"

"You're done," said Magenta.

Bettina slitted her eyes and glared at Magenta. "You spent ten more minutes on Gemma than on me. I'm telling."

"Please do."

Projecting anger with every motion, Bettina pushed herself up from the chair and stalked out of the trailer.

"Well, that was dramatic," said Gemma.

"It *is* nice to meet you," Opal said.

Gemma laughed. "Thanks."

Kelsi came in and stood beside Corvus's chair, not too close. Corvus rose and put on the robe. Kelsi hesitated, then fastened the star at his throat. He didn't reach to touch her, which relieved Opal's mind. Kelsi had reason to be skittish. He lowered his chin and smiled at Gemma.

"Whoa!" said Gemma, staring.

Opal said, "This is—what *is* your name?" Kelsi slipped out of the trailer.

"Isn't it Corvus Weather?" Gemma said in a slightly choked voice. "I've seen some of your work. I was going to say it was awesome, but I get the feeling this project's going to be different, and even more intense."

"I want a name to call him when he's in this state, because he doesn't act like Corvus," Opal said. "Is your name Last of the Lost?"

He smiled at her, his eyes glowing green and hot. She had not put the contacts on. That much costuming, she figured, she could leave to him. It gave her a quick way to know who was behind his eyes.

"That's a trifle cumbersome. I'll give you a name which isn't mine, but to which I'll answer. Phrixos."

"Phrixos," Opal repeated.

"Prick," said Magenta.

He glared at her. Her cheeks reddened. She gasped and turned away, her hand rising to hover near one cheek.

Opal gripped his arm. "Stop it."

"God!" said Gemma. "What was that?"

"Overreacting," said Opal. "Stop it, Phrixos. Magenta—"

"Damn, I keep forgetting," Magenta muttered. "All right. Phrixos. What the hell kind of name is that?"

"One I like," said the Invader. "Child, I am pleased to meet you." He held out a hand to Gemma.

"I'm scared to meet you," she said, and slowly placed her hand in his. He lowered his head, lifted her hand, kissed the back, a linger of lips, and she suddenly relaxed and smiled at him.

Before she could worry about Phrixos brainwashing a child, Opal's Ear crackled from its resting place around her neck. Magenta tapped her Ear. Opal put the Ear on. "Where are you people?" asked the assistant director.

Magenta checked her watch. "Shit."

Opal pressed the transmit button. "On our way," she said, and then, to the others, "Let's go." She grabbed her messenger bag and makeup suitcase and followed Gemma, Magenta, and Phrixos out of the trailer, and locked it behind them.

Magenta fell back to walk with her. "Figures the little princess would actually get to the set on time," she muttered. "Brownie points for her and demerits for the rest of us. Are my cheeks red?"

"Wait a sec." Opal had a spell she had used often on her younger siblings, a healing for scrapes, cuts, and bruises. She held her hands palms out near Magenta's face and murmured. The red faded.

"Wow. Lots better. Thanks, Opal."

"You're welcome. I think your nickname for him is right, but we can't use it when he can hear us," she muttered.

"Yeah. I get that. I'm a slow learner, but I learn."

The red light over the door to the soundstage was out. A security guard held the door open for them. They went to the backstage grouping of chairs near the clearing set. Bettina was already in her own chair, hunched tight and frowning, so that she looked more like an unpleasant old lady than a young girl. An older, baggier version of her sat in a nearby chair reading a fashion magazine.

"Gemma?" said a slender, dark-haired woman in another chair. "What was the delay?"

"Sorry, Mom," said Gemma, settling beside the woman. "This is Magenta, my makeup lady, and Opal, who does the Dark God makeup, and that's, uh—Phrixos? Everybody, this is my mom, Doreen Goodwin."

Phrixos came forward and held out his hand. "Corvus Weather," he said. "Pleased to meet the mother of such a talented child."

Gemma's mother did not look as pleased as Phrixos

sounded, but she was polite. "Nice to meet you. Please call me Doreen." She extended a hand to Phrixos, gave a slight shudder when he accepted it. He didn't try to kiss the back of her hand, which Opal thought was interesting.

"My pleasure." He glanced toward the woman who was apparently Bettina's mother. She didn't look up from her magazine. Phrixos smiled and sat in Corvus's chair.

"Hey," said Neil. "Lighting's up. Cast to the set for blocking rehearsal."

Gemma, Bettina, and Phrixos headed for the set. Opal slumped in Corvus's chair, hugging her messenger bag, and Magenta took the chair next to her.

Craig Orlando sat in one of the other chairs. He smiled at Opal and Magenta.

Doreen sat in Gemma's chair and stared at Magenta.

"What is it, Mrs. Goodwin?" Magenta asked.

"Why do you choose to look so strange when your job is to make people beautiful?" she asked.

"Because I don't have to be in front of the camera. I can look any way I want," said Magenta, smoothing back her heavy black and pink hair. "I did a fine job with your daughter, didn't I?"

"Yes," said Doreen. "I was just wondering. If your job is—"

"Yes, but I already got the job, ma'am. I don't have to keep interviewing for it. This is the me I feel like being now." She ran her fingers through her hair and smiled.

"Ah." Doreen subsided.

Magenta got a pad of paper out of her duffel and wrote, *Was that weird, or is it just me?* She slid the pad into Opal's lap.

It was weird, Opal wrote back. She rose and set her messenger bag in Corvus's chair. "I'm going to check the camera," she said.

"Me, too," said Magenta. They went over to the Props area

and joined Joe at his monitor. The camera was set for the master shot, showing everything. Bettina and Gemma sat on the altar stone, side by side, Bettina looking fierce, Gemma hesitant. Phrixos stood at the head of the stone, face-to-face with them. They spoke, but the monitor had no sound. Opal mouthed the lines, having memorized them from practice with Corvus the night before.

"Louder," said Magenta, and Opal whispered them a little louder, lip-synching as well as she could.

"This scene's new, huh?" Joe said after the first run-through.

"Yep."

"Creepy as hell. The more they write on this, the worse it gets. Only good thing about this scene, no props to manage, and I still get paid."

"Hey," said Opal. It was true. All she saw in the camera's view were the actors and the standing stones. The stones were set decoration. The actors didn't pick up or move anything in this scene. Although they did interact with the stones—touch them, sit on them. No knives or cups or censers or braziers. Daylight in the forest—a whole different animal from the night rituals.

Opal left the Props area and edged around the backdrop of photographed forest to watch Phrixos as he ran through the scene with the girls. No doubt about it, he looked the part, and he gave her the creeps. In the script, he didn't actually seduce the underage girls, but he was asking them for a commitment to belong to him in later life. "Handmaiden," whatever the hell that was supposed to be. Damn it, Travis had used it after all. Phrixos was infecting her brain, and she was infecting the writers.

He had been infecting the writers all along.

"A little more hunger, Caitlyn. A little more revulsion, Serena," said Neil.

"But I don't—" Gemma said.

Phrixos placed his palm on her forehead. She blinked in confusion. "What?"

"You're supposed to be more afraid of me," he said, his voice low and thrilling.

"But I—"

"You fear me," he murmured, "you resist me, you are fascinated by me."

Her face changed as he spoke. Fear dawned, and she couldn't look away from him. She did not blink.

"Thanks for the direction, Corvus," the director said dryly. Phrixos smiled at Neil as though taking his remark at face value. "All right, we're almost ready to shoot. Last looks!" he said.

Opal got her bag, and she, Craig, and Magenta went to the set.

Phrixos knelt and stared into her eyes. As always, his makeup looked perfect, if that was what it was. "I'm hungry," he whispered.

"You pick now to tell me?" she whispered back. She dug an energy drink out of her bag. "It's not very cold."

"You know that's not what I want," he said.

She studied her hand. She could almost see the flaming shield Flint had given her, still strong after a day—self-sustaining, or was she feeding it? Either way, she was grateful for this warm invisible cocoon. She stroked her smallest finger until it emerged from its shelter. It felt strangely bare. She curled the other fingers toward her palm.

He leaned forward and took her finger in his mouth. The touch of his tongue, his lips, was strangely erotic. She felt the draw on her magical energy, and that was erotic, too, the mother's power to feed another from her body.

"What are you doing?" whispered Bettina. She sounded appalled.

Opal felt a little faint. She touched Phrixos's face as though redrawing one of his cheek leaves and slid her finger from his mouth. His eyes glowed brighter than they had, and he smiled.

"Thank you, my handmaiden."

"Hey. She's not your handmaiden. I am," said Bettina.

"Save it for the take," said Neil. "Come on, people, let's get to work! Clear the set. Starting marks. Okay. We're on bell . . ."

Opal joined Magenta and Joe at the Props monitor and watched the scene come alive. Now that the actors were projecting, they could hear the lines. Gemma went through a series of emotions. Opal found her so fascinating she couldn't look at Bettina or Phrixos.

"Wow," muttered Magenta. "She's really good."

"She's in a trance."

"Prick can hypnotize other people into acting, too?"

"Apparently."

"Cut. Good work," said Neil after the second bell had rung. "Got it in one, people. Print that. Take a break while we light for close-ups."

The actors came off the set. Someone went outside and summoned the stand-ins.

Phrixos claimed Corvus's chair. Gemma's mother tugged Gemma toward a chair beside hers. The woman who might be Bettina's mother took her a little way off and lectured her. She didn't go far enough that everyone couldn't hear every word she said. "I saw the whole thing on the Casio," she said, "and that girl stole the scene. What's the matter with you?"

"She has better lines," Bettina said.

"You're making excuses."

"What do you expect me to do? She has the interesting part."

"There are no small parts, only small—"

"Minds," said Phrixos.

The woman glared at him. "This is a private conversation," she said.

"Perhaps you should take it farther away," he said. Then his voice silkened. "Perhaps you should leave the child alone. She gave an adequate performance."

"Adequate is not good enough," said the woman.

"Cast back to the set," called one of the A.D.s. "Last looks."

They all went to the altar, except for the mother and the maybe mother. As she touched up the powder on Gemma's nose, Magenta muttered, "Who is that woman, and why is she tormenting Bettina?"

"That's her on-set guardian," Gemma said. "I forget her name. She's always mean, and she torments our tutor, too."

"Shut up," said Bettina, beside Gemma. "You don't know anything."

"What, you *like* the way she treats you?"

"She wants what's best for me."

"Clear the set," called Neil. "Let's go, camera two."

Back in the chairs, Magenta got out an *InStyle* magazine and flipped quietly through it. Opal thought about watching the Props monitor again, but ended up curled up in Corvus's chair instead. Doreen came and sat beside her. The woman took a small pad of paper out of her purse and wrote a note on it, then shoved it in Opal's face.

What is that man doing to my daughter?

Opal took the pad and pen. She wasn't sure what to write. Finally she settled on *Coaching her.*

I don't like the way it looks. Is he a Svengali?

Opal tapped the pen on the pad. She couldn't remember how the movie had turned out. *I don't know. Maybe. ???* she wrote.

Don't you leave him alone with my daughter.

Opal stared at the note, then snatched the pen and wrote, *I can't control him.*

I see how he treats you. He's more interested in you than anyone else. Keep him on a leash.

Opal shook her head. *He's the one pulling strings.*

Doreen clutched the pen and pad in her hands, stared at the backdrop separating them from the set. Her hands tightened until the pad bowed. Finally, she wrote, slowly, *Do what you can? Please. Help my daughter.*

If I can, I will.

"Cut," yelled the director. Two bells rang. "Print. Good work, people! Caitlyn, you're a little stiff; let's do another one. Relax. Don't be the actor playing the girl. Be the girl."

"Yes sir."

Phrixos's voice murmured something, and Bettina murmured something in response. A moment's silence.

"Last looks," called someone, and Magenta, Craig, and Opal headed for the set.

Phrixos was kissing the back of Bettina's hand this time. She stared into his eyes.

The director grabbed Opal's arm as Opal passed him. "Is the monster schizo?" he whispered.

"Not exactly. More like multiple personality," Opal whispered.

"Damn it. This upsets me. But it's working on film. Damn it! Nobody told me!"

"It's a recent development."

Neil blew air out through his nostrils, a subvocal snort. "Rein him in."

"How? Why does everybody think *I* can control him?" Opal's whisper came on a gush of breath.

"You're sleeping with him."

"In a master-servant way," Opal muttered.

"Oh? Damn. That's no help. Anyway, do what you can, will you?"

"I already am, and it's not a whole lot."

Neil released Opal and pushed her toward the set.

Opal went to Phrixos. He leaned forward. "Trouble?" he muttered, and for a second she felt comforted by his concern, as though she had a co-conspirator.

Then she remembered what everybody was complaining about. "You're creeping everybody out, and they want you to stop it."

He smiled, and his eyes glowed brighter. "Don't worry," he said, but not in a way that convinced her. "Things will fall into place."

"And then what?"

"You'll see."

10

He dropped a brief kiss on her cheek—no draw, only a touch—then turned her by her shoulders and aimed her off the set with a push on her rear. She stumbled two steps, then whirled and walked backward as she studied him. She hadn't touched him up again. If it were Corvus, that kiss on the cheek would have mandated some kind of makeup repair, and so might the swat on the butt, but Phrixos was fine.

In the next take, Bettina and Gemma gave fantastic performances, and Phrixos was superb.

"Cut and print," Neil said. "Now we need some hand shots. Off the set, everybody! We need to reset the cameras."

They wrapped early, around eight in the evening. They had shot every shot listed on that day's schedule, and, partly because of Phrixos's influence on the young actresses, they had shot fewer takes. Everything seemed aligned to give the best results. Neil had consulted with the production manager about whether they should try something that wasn't scheduled, but each scene took hours to set up. A production assistant came by with call sheets and script revisions for tomorrow as the actors headed toward the Makeup trailer or the Wardrobe trailer to escape the people they had been playing all day.

Opal hadn't found a minute to call her family. She only thought of doing it when a scene was shooting or when she was summoned to the set. She had spaced it during lunch, worn out by wondering what could go wrong next. Plus, Phrixos had drained her with another kiss, despite the new power collecting she had been doing. She needed to collect even more energy, but she hadn't found time and space to do the necessary meditations. Tonight, she promised herself.

Phrixos followed Opal into the Makeup trailer. She wondered if he would leave Corvus's body tonight, or if she had another fight on her hands. She didn't want to spend any more time with him than she had to.

He had taken the call sheet before she could look at it, and was studying it as she nudged him toward the chair. She had been fighting him all day and was tired of the constant energy it required. She'd look at the call sheet later.

Lauren waited in one of Rod's chairs, looking rumpled, unmade up, and worried. Bettina and Gemma came in and sat down, Bettina glaring at the older actress, but there were enough chairs for everybody. Rod and Magenta went to work taking off the girls' makeup.

Lauren didn't seem to notice Bettina's irritation. She didn't even pay attention to Phrixos; her look was all for Opal.

Opal settled Phrixos in his chair. "Go on," he said. "Check with her." He leaned back and closed his eyes, call sheet and script pages—pale blue this time—in a loose pile on his lap.

"Thanks." She felt again the momentary and confusing sense of collaborating with the enemy. Why did she trust him even to this extent? She needed to, she guessed. She went to Lauren and took her hands. "What's wrong?" she murmured.

"Norman's here, and I can't get the brush to work. I forgot what you told me about it."

"How'd he get on set?"

"He's not, really, but he's found a place to stay in town, and he's lurking outside every time I walk across to the B&B."

"Has he approached you yet?"

"I've been shadowing Blaise, and she's shadowing Aldridge, so we're always surrounded by people. Traveling in a pack is more tiring than you'd think. Plus some of the pack keep breaking away and I can't figure out who to follow. So the answer is no, but now we're done for the day and I need to go home and rest, which makes me feel vulnerable. Also I'm starving. Did you try that pasta at lunch? Could anything taste more like glue and Styrofoam?"

"It was bad," Opal said. "Okay, you relax here and I'll see what I can do with the big guy."

"Thanks." Lauren sighed and dug through a hobo-style purse, produced a battered paperback romance.

Opal returned to Phrixos. She tugged the papers out of his grasp and set them on the counter.

"Lauren is in danger?" he asked.

"Do you remember about that?" asked Opal. "You learn what Corvus knows, right? He heard about her stalker last night at dinner."

The green glow in his eyes dimmed a fraction as he looked inward. Then he returned and stared up at her. "I remember now." He gripped the arm of his chair as though to rise.

"What?" said Opal.

"The man is a gnat. I can dispose of him."

"No disposing, all right? Not that I know exactly what you mean by that. If you could send him off to mind his own business, that would be good. No murdering, all right?"

"You prefer he leaves here alive?" said Phrixos.

"I insist on it," she said. A chill shivered in her shoulders. She had been frightened of Phrixos before, but hadn't let herself think about whether he was truly dangerous.

He smiled at her, the leaves shifting on the planes of his face until he looked truly demonic.

"Stop that," she said.

He raised his eyebrows, but he still looked scary. She grabbed the Polaroid and took some continuity pictures, dated and time-stamped them with a Sharpie. In the process, Phrixos's face relaxed back into the role of supernatural monster, losing its disturbingly human cunning.

Good. Phrixos responded to routine.

Opal got out the solvents that would loosen the adhesive on his face.

"I could approach him as I am now," he said before she started removing the top layer of appliances.

"You think he's going to be scared of a costume? He's a professional. Relax. Nothing's going to happen right away, except I'm going to take off your mask, okay? Then we're going to dinner."

"Whom do you want to escort you?" he asked.

Was this an opening? Could she just ask for Corvus and get him back? How useful would Corvus be in dealing with Norman? Corvus had physical presence; he worked out. Opal had never heard of him getting into fights with anyone.

On the other hand, maybe Phrixos really could solve their problem in a nonlethal way. He had certainly hypnotized people into doing his bidding on the set today and yesterday. Possibly he could give Norman a mental twist that would keep him away from Lauren forever.

"You," Opal said. She tried not to be disturbed by the smile he kept all through his unmasking and subsequent cleansing and moisturizing.

By the time she restored him to Corvus-normal, everyone

had left the trailer except for her, Phrixos, and Lauren. As Phrixos buttoned himself into Corvus's shirt, Opal packed her messenger bag, stuffing call sheet and script pages in, in addition to everything else she imagined she might need. Their call for tomorrow was five A.M. The weather was supposed to clear so that they could film in the forest. This was an early scene, the coven in the forest summoning the Dark God, and involved Gemma and some actors Opal hadn't met yet, including Ariadne Orullian, the woman who played Caitlyn and Serena's mother; this was her bloody death scene.

Five A.M. They had left the set on time and a half, since the shoot plus makeup application and removal had taken eleven hours. First three hours of tomorrow would be time and a half until they reached turnaround. Well, a person had to take advantage of the weather when the opportunity arose. They'd been waiting to shoot on the forest set for too long already. It was possible they would shoot a piece of the scene with Dark God and Lauren on the altar rock if the light held out, her "come to the dark side" scene.

Lauren was curled up in the chair, the book in her lap, her eyes shut and her mouth slightly open, soft snores coming out. Opal shook her shoulder gently and she gasped and sat up. "Huh?"

"Let's go to supper," said Opal.

Lauren looked up at Phrixos, narrowed her eyes. "Who are you?"

"Phrixos."

"Have you been that before?"

"That's his Scary Dark God name. It's not his real name," Opal said, "but it comes in handy."

"Oh. Okay. So anyway, not Corvus. How come you're not Corvus?"

"Opal asked me to stay," he said, and smiled his demon grin. "I understand you have a problem with someone. I can help you deal with it in ways he can't."

"Why would you?"

"I protect my own."

"I'm not yours," she said.

"Do you wish to test that assertion?"

"Stop arguing," said Opal, "and let's go take care of this guy."

"Wait a sec," said Lauren. "How do we plan to do that? Norman creeps me out, but I'm not ready for full-scale violence."

"It would solve your problem," said Phrixos.

"Not going to work for me," Lauren said.

"Opal says the same thing. It's a timid generation you are. Very well. I will settle for a less permanent solution, and merely persuade him away."

"Okay. Thanks."

"First I want a kiss."

"What?" She shrank back. "No."

"Payment in advance. What's wrong with that?"

"You gonna knock me out the way you did Kelsi?"

"I won't," he said.

"I'll be able to walk and talk and think afterward?"

Phrixos sighed. "Very well."

"I don't like you," she said. He smiled gently, cupped the back of her head in his hand, and leaned forward to press his lips to hers, gently, gently, working slowly up to more pressure. Lauren stood passive at first, her eyes closed. Her hands crept up to grip his shirt. Their mouths engaged more fully, and Lauren's posture softened.

Opal struck Phrixos on the back of the head with the flat of her hand. "Stop that!"

He pulled away from Lauren, licked his lips, grinned sideways at Opal. "Jealous?"

"Oh, please," said Opal.

Lauren moaned, opened her eyes. She looked dazed. She

blinked, shook her head. "You are so—" she said, her voice rising with each word.

"Tasty? Helpful? Pleasurable?"

"Infuriating."

Phrixos laughed. "You, on the other hand, are another source of pure pleasure. Let's go." He threaded her arm through his and went to the door, helped Lauren down the steps. They left the trailer-laden parking lot with its saggy insta-fence and a guard sheltering under an overhang on one of the Star Waggons from the constant misty drizzle. As they crossed the street toward where Hitch had parked the car, a form detached itself from one of the droopy-branched evergreens in the town square and came toward them.

"Norman," said Lauren. She gripped Phrixos's arm more firmly. Opal came up on his other side, and he crooked an elbow so she could hang on him, too. What the hell. This was why she endured his presence without protest. She hooked her arm through his.

The man walked into the light of the nearby streetlamp, staring at Lauren's face. He had an engaging best-friend type of face, not leading man; slightly disheveled and good humored, friendly blue eyes and a wide smile. His bangs flopped half over his eyes. "Evening," he said.

"Norman," said Lauren.

"Lauren."

"What are you doing here?"

"Well, waiting for you, I guess."

"I told you to stop that," she said. "It's over, Norman. Find someone new."

"It's not that easy." He came closer. "There's no one else." He bent to peer at her. "No one else is you."

"Well, okay, I'll live with that hypothesis. I'm the only me. And I'm telling you to leave me alone, Norman. Seriously. Get over it and move on."

He smiled as though that would change things. Opal, an educated observer, had to admit that he had an excellent and inviting smile.

"I'm not ready," he said. "I can't stop thinking about you, Lauren. You won't leave my mind. I need you."

"I don't need you, and I don't want you," said Lauren. "Do you hear me?"

He shook his head. "I hear you, but I don't believe you."

"Phrixos," Lauren said.

"Come here, little man," Phrixos said, his voice gentle and rich.

Norman backed up a step. "I'm not getting in range of those fists of yours. I'm besotted, not insane."

"I won't hit you. I just want to shake the hand of the man who recognizes treasure when he sees it."

"I'm not touching you," said Norman.

"Very well. I'll touch you, then." Phrixos eased out from between the women. In one stride, he stepped into Norman's breathing space, crowding him. He cupped his hands around Norman's head, tilted it back until Norman was staring up at his face. Norman shoved at Phrixos's chest, but the taller man didn't budge, even when Norman pounded on him. "Quiet," Phrixos said, his voice gentle and thrilling. Norman slowed and stopped, hung limply in Phrixos's grasp.

"Good," said Phrixos. "Listen to me. Hear me. Your memory and desire for this woman fade. They seep away. She is not in your blood. She is not in your brain. You do not need or want her. She is just another woman you worked with once. A pleasant acquaintance, nothing more. You have somewhere else to go, something else to do. She leaves your mind and you find another star to fix on. Say it."

"She is not in my blood. She is not in my brain," Norman whispered.

"You release her from your thoughts and let her go her own way."

"I release her," he muttered, almost too low to hear.

"You are content."

"I am content."

Phrixos lowered his hands from Norman's head to his shoulders, stabilized him. "Are you all right?" he asked.

Norman shuddered, shook his head as though he could cast off thoughts like water, and said, "Okay."

"Can you stand?"

"Okay."

Phrixos lowered his hands. Norman swayed a moment, then found his feet. "What am I doing here?" he asked.

"We don't know. You were following us," said Phrixos.

"I was? Where are we?" He glanced around at the nearby forest, the mist, the night. He looked closer to home. "Hi, Lauren. Who are you?" he asked Phrixos, ignoring Opal. "You were in a horror movie, right?"

"Several. We're in Oregon, shooting a movie, but you're not in it. You just showed up here. Where's your home?"

"Los Angeles." Norman frowned and got out his wallet, checked the currency compartment, pulled out some receipts. "Looks like I ate at an IHOP this morning, but I don't remember it at all. Here's a keycard for a hotel, the Bugle Arms. Wonder which room I have. What time is it?" He looked at his watch. "That late?" He glanced around. "I don't know what's the matter with me. Maybe I'm having a psychotic break. What's the date?"

Lauren said, "November seventh."

Norman looked confused, unfocused. "I've lost a week. Last thing I remember was calling the airline to book a flight. Guess I was coming here, but I don't know why."

"Maybe there are clues in your hotel room," Lauren said. "What are you driving?"

Opal tried to remember what kind of car had followed her last night when they left the restaurant, but it had been dark.

Norman reached into his pocket, came up with a key attached to a plastic tag with writing on a slip of paper inside: Enterprise Rent-A-Car, and SILVER CAPRICE LIC. # KKO 951.

"Huh," said Norman.

Lauren glanced around at nearby cars. She pointed. The Caprice was parked down the block from the B&B. They strolled over and checked the license plate. The numbers matched. Norman unlocked the passenger-side door and looked in. A litter of fast-food wrappers and white paper bags with a doughnut shop logo emblazoned on their sides lurked in wadded disarray in the footwell, and on the seat were a pair of binoculars, three bottled waters, a half-eaten sandwich falling out of its paper wrapper, a notebook with crabbed blue ballpoint handwriting in it, and a handheld digital recorder.

"Jeez," said Norman. "What the hell have I been doing?"

Opal reached in and snatched the notebook and recorder.

"Hey!" Norman said.

"I'm pretty sure you don't need these anymore," she said.

"How would you know? Have we even met? If that stuff belongs to me, I want it back."

"No, you don't," Phrixos said, a hand on Norman's shoulder.

"I sure do. Are you people robbing me?"

Phrixos rested a hand on Norman's head again, only this time Norman sidestepped. "Quit touching me! What are you, a pervert?"

"That and much more," said Phrixos, gripping Norman's shoulder in one hand and his head in another. He aimed Norman's eyes toward his own again, and stared down with that peculiar intensity. "Let go of any records you have of Lauren. She's just someone you know, not someone you obsess about. You don't need anything you wrote down or spoke about her. Let it go. Repeat that."

"Let it go," Norman whispered.

"You feel all right, and you don't suspect us of any ill intentions toward you. You feel we are your friends."

"You're my friends."

Opal slipped the notebook and recorder into her messenger bag.

"You remember what number your room is in the hotel, and where it is. You remember a creative reason why you came up here that has nothing to do with Lauren. Maybe you're researching something for your career. Understand?"

"Yeah," said Norman.

"Good," said Phrixos. He stroked Norman's hair, then released him again.

Norman shuddered and said, "Where were we?"

"Hard to tell," said Phrixos. "You ready to go back to your hotel now?"

"Yeah. I feel tired. Can't remember what I've been doing, but I'm worn out."

"We'll see you later," Phrixos said, and gave Norman's shoulder a little shove.

"All right. Good night." Norman slammed the passenger door shut and rounded the car to climb in behind the steering wheel.

Opal stood beside Phrixos in the cold evening air and watched Norman drive away. When the car turned a corner and the taillights were no longer visible, Lauren let out a sigh.

"I don't know that that is permanent," said Phrixos, one arm dropping to lie across Lauren's shoulders, the other resting on Opal's. "I didn't want him to forget forever, because there might be something in his memory we need later. Also, I'm low on energy right now. I could do a better job if you would feed me more."

"Quit whining," said Opal. "You drew from him, didn't you?"

He laughed and squeezed her shoulder. "A little. He can't

supply the quality of energy I get from either of you. So, Lauren, a kiss as thanks?"

"Must I? I'm tired, too."

"I see I have not sufficiently impressed you with my awesome majesty," Phrixos said, but it was hard to tell whether he was joking. "In any case, my internal self grows restless, so I'll say good night. Opal." He bent and pressed his lips to hers, and she let him, because no matter how tired she was, she was glad he had solved Lauren's problem, even if only temporarily. When his lips touched hers, though, he jerked back, and she realized Flint's shield of fire was still working, bless the boy for giving her weird energy that didn't get used up. She thought her lips free of the shield and reached for Phrixos, pulled him down and kissed him, sending him some of the extra power she had collected during the day.

He moaned with delight and drew more, but just when she was going to struggle and stop him, the draw halted; his taste changed, and so did his posture. She was kissing Corvus, who held her closer, then finally raised his head and looked around. "What a nice way to wake up," he said. The green glow in his eyes had dimmed but not extinguished. "What are we doing now?"

"Solving Lauren's stalker problem, at least for the moment."

"Oh?"

"Let's get food," she said, and they headed back to the lot by the supermarket/soundstage where Hitch had left the Lincoln. On the drive to the IHOP, Opal brought Corvus up to speed on the Dark God's new name, Phrixos's behavior on the set with the girls, and his confrontation with Norman.

"He wanted to kill him?" Corvus asked as Opal parked on the edge of the IHOP lot.

"He didn't exactly say that," said Opal.

"But he implied it," Lauren said.

"Do you think he could?" Corvus asked. He held the restaurant door for them as they went in.

Tonight a different waitress seated them, a small, young brunette with black-framed glasses, a narrow smile, and a mouthful of chewing gum. "Hi, Erin. Jenny off tonight?" Corvus asked.

"Yeah." The girl glanced down at her nametag, as though confirming her name was Erin. "You guys in the movie?"

"Sure," said Corvus.

"Cool. This table all right?" She showed them to a table for four, not the corner booth they'd been in the last two nights.

"Sure."

Opal hesitated to look around, wondering whether she would see someone she knew and get drawn into someone else's drama. She had plenty of her own. She hadn't seen any of the cast or crew's rental cars in the lot, but that didn't necessarily mean no one was here. It was a short walk from the crew hotel to the IHOP.

She saw only strangers. She sat facing the door, and Corvus seated himself beside her, Lauren on his other side. After the waitress asked them about beverages and went to get them, Corvus leaned forward, inspiring the women to lean forward, too. "Do you think he could kill someone?" he repeated.

"We don't know enough about him," said Lauren.

"This morning one of the town old-timers told me a story about a monster who used to haunt Lapis during the fifties," Opal said, then remembered she had mentioned this to both of them that morning. "He was called the Last of the Lost, and he stole young girls. Nobody ever found any bodies though. Plus, it's one of those stories you tell tourists to make your town more interesting. But what if there's some truth to it?"

"Did you ask him?"

"Yeah. He only answers questions when he feels like it."

"We need you to be more active," Lauren said. "Be our spy. Pay attention to what he's thinking. Were you awake at all today?"

"I was asleep again the whole day," he said. "I kissed Opal in the morning, and then I woke up kissing her in the evening. Nice, but odd."

"Your eyes are still glowing," Opal said, "so I think Phrixos is still awake. Can you tell?"

"What?" He sat back, stared beyond her, then looked up at the ceiling. He put his hands on his cheeks, touched his lips. He held his palm in front of his eyes and stared, as though looking for a reflection of the glow. Frowning, he lowered his hand.

Opal dug a mirror compact out of her bag and presented it to him. "Take a look."

He stared into the little mirror, blinked at his own green-enhanced eyes. "You left the contacts in."

"Didn't use them today."

"That's eerie," said Lauren. "I never noticed."

"I think you're blending now, Corr, and you should stop pretending you're not. Phrixos, are you present?"

Corvus frowned. He looked so like himself and so unlike Phrixos she felt like backing down, but she changed her mind. They needed to know who they were talking with.

"I don't feel like he's here," said Corvus at last. "Still, there's the evidence of my eyes. Maybe we should talk about something else. Lauren, how did your day go?"

The waitress came and took their order, and then Lauren talked about the fight scene she had shot with Blaise that day. "Neil yelled at both of us equally. The writers were there, and he made them rewrite a piece of the scene so Blaise lost a couple of lines. They both seemed kind of irritable."

"I wonder what's going on," said Opal. "Tonight, I'll try a

glass against the wall to see if I can hear them better. Trouble in paradise?"

"They have my corruption scene scheduled for tomorrow afternoon if you guys can finish up with the kids on time," Lauren said, "which, considering how things are going so far, seems likely. Did you look at the pages?"

"I did," said Corvus.

"It's mostly the same as it was before, but we have one set of rewritten lines," Lauren said. "I asked Travis to do it, because there was a jawbreaker line in there. I think your line's the same, though."

"Yes. 'What do you *really* want?'" he quoted, in Phrixos's voice, thrilling, deep, and compelling.

"I want to be discovered by you movie people, get a role in the film, and then run away with you to Hollywood," said Erin the waitress as she set salads down in front of them. "Oh, God. Did I say that out loud?" She flushed and darted away.

"Interesting," said Corvus, looking after her. "I have the power to cloud women's minds. *Moo hoo hahahah!*"

Opal thumped his arm with her fist. "Don't laugh about it, big guy. What if it's true?"

He smiled the big goofy smile she considered pure Corvus, light dancing in his eyes, then sobered when she didn't smile back. "I pledge to use my powers for good."

"That's nice," said Lauren, "but I don't think it stops the other guy from using them for whatever he wants. What do you think *he* really wants?"

Corvus stared at his salad, his brow furrowed. He stroked a spiral pattern on his forehead with the first two fingers of his right hand. Finally he shook his head. When he looked up, his eyes had no extra light in them. "There's something there, but I can't get hold of it. It's red, though."

11

Before she drove them back to Lapis for the night, Opal stepped outside with her phone and called the family again. Her mother answered, peevish at the late hour. "There wasn't a single other time you could try us?" she demanded.

"I'm sorry, Mom."

"Yes, well, all right. Tobias considered your case and threw some auguries and said it's serious, but he can't leave until tomorrow. He'll fly to Portland and find some way to get where you are. He got Gypsum to MapQuest it for him. Expect him tomorrow night. You'll have to leave word with security."

"Did he get a cell phone yet?"

"He refuses to carry something on his person that concentrates signals from the ether," said her mother. "You'll just have to let him find you."

"If you see him before he leaves, please tell him thank you for me."

"I will." Her voice softened. "Opal, call anytime if the need is great. Call if you need reinforcements. We'll find some way to work it out."

"Thanks, Mom." She had to hang up before she started crying. For years she'd been handling her own problems. She felt silly going to the family for help when she wasn't even sure it was real trouble. It surely felt good to know someone else was concerned, though.

In the restaurant, Corvus was paying the bill again, smiling at Erin, who blushed while waiting for credit card approval.

"We ran through our scenes for tomorrow while you were outside," said Lauren. "Any satisfaction from your phone?"

"My uncle's coming tomorrow night."

"*Brujo?*"

"*Sí.*"

"*Bueno.*"

"Your *abuela?*" Opal asked.

Lauren shook her head. "She's sending me some charms to protect me, but she doesn't feel well enough to travel."

Opal drove them back to Lapis and let Lauren off at the house where she was staying, then parked the Lincoln in the guarded lot by the soundstage and walked Corvus back to the B&B. She lingered on the sidewalk in front of the building, and he stood beside her. Together they stared up at the front of the Victorian building with its tooled gingerbread eaves and strange bits sticking out where modern houses were smooth. The house was pale in the streetlight, with darker trim. No lights shone inside; lace curtains draped the lower floor's windows like an arrested fall of flour, hiding the interior.

"You coming up?" Corvus asked in a low rumble. He stood near her but didn't touch her.

Tonight the house didn't purr, but she still had the sense that something coiled inside it, and that the front door was a mouth that would swallow her and Corvus. She gripped his hand, and his fingers closed gently around hers. When she looked up, she saw green glow in his eyes. "Once we go in, we can get out again, right?" she said.

"You're safe with me," he said, using his Dark God voice.

"I don't believe that at all." Yet somehow she felt reassured.

He laughed and released her hand. "Stay the night or don't, my dear; it's your choice."

She had left her toiletries bag in his room after her shower that morning, unsure of anything, though it wasn't exactly a lifelong commitment. The hotel where most of her things were gave her fresh shampoo, soap, and conditioner every day in tiny plastic bottles, and she could always get a toothbrush and toothpaste from a nearby 7-Eleven, or even the front desk.

She glanced up at his face, saw the rueful smile that always captivated her, the faint tilt to the eyebrows indicating a person waiting for an answer. The glow was gone again.

"I'd like to," she said.

His hand rested on her shoulder, then, the heat of it welcoming and welcome, and they walked up the flagstone path together. He let her into the house. This time they got all the way to his room without rousing the director or anyone else.

"Wait here," he whispered at the threshold, then crossed the dark room and turned on the bedside light. He nodded and she came in and eased the door shut, locked it. The atmosphere was different in the room tonight; the light lower, and no sense of tiredness or settling for comfort.

Corvus picked up the alarm clock and set it, placed it on the bedside table again, then only looked at her, most of him in silhouette with the lamp almost behind him. She stepped away from the door without speaking. Her breath quickened as she kicked off her shoes, dropped her messenger bag on the couch, and went to him. His huge hands were gentle and deft, the knuckles brushing her breasts as he unbuttoned her shirt. She worked his belt free of its buckle. Only their breaths sounded in the room, ragged and harsh, along with the small thuds of discarded garments dropping to the floor.

Everything that followed had its own logic and rhythm. She ended up drowsing across him afterward, riding the rise and fall of his chest, one of his hands resting on the small of her back. He pulled the covers up over them and was gone into sleep like a candle snuffed out.

The alarm woke them far too early, while the sky was still dark. Corvus groaned, a sound and a vibration against her cheek. She lay soaking in his warmth, comfort, and scent, until he finally rumbled, "Opal? I think we better get going," and she remembered where and who she was.

They shared the shower and brushed teeth beside each other, dressed out in the open space of his room. She was on her third day with this set of clothes; they stank. She glanced at Corvus to make sure his back was turned, then ran her clothes through a Refreshing Spell, and stroked pale green into the shirt.

"We don't have time to go anywhere but here for breakfast," Corvus said, and she checked her watch. Almost four fifteen A.M., and they had to be in the Makeup trailer at the location by five. "Bessie sets out coffee and toast and cereal and juice. Sometimes more, if she's feeling perky. Neil or George will have told her we're getting up early today."

"Okay."

Neil and Blaise were in the dining room when they arrived. None of them spoke. Neil had a plateful of scrambled eggs and sausages, things Corvus hadn't mentioned in his menu report, and Blaise had a big mug of coffee and a piece of dry toast.

Opal got coffee and a buttered English muffin from an array of food on the sideboard. She sat at the table to slather the muffin with blackberry jam. Corvus got a huge bowl of oatmeal into which he dumped raisins, milk, and syrup. "Sleep well?" he asked Neil.

"Well enough," said Neil. "You?"

"Yeah. Blaise, you're on hold today, right?"

Blaise shrugged. "Yes, but I'm going to the location with you anyway. I want to watch you seduce my sister."

Opal glanced at Neil to see if he had any objections, but he was absorbed in his breakfast.

An old woman with silver hair, a softly wrinkled face, and a cushiony, comfortable-looking shape clothed in a red plaid dress and a white apron came through the swinging door from the back of the house, bearing a plate of crisp bacon, which she set down in the center of the table. "My, my," she said, looking from Blaise to Opal with a smile. "More company. You ladies care for anything you don't see here?"

"No," said Blaise.

"The bacon looks great," Opal said. This must be Bessie Gates, the woman Mrs. Partridge said she didn't get along with. Opal wondered if now was a good time to ask about ancient history, but before she could frame her question, the woman turned to Corvus.

"Master?" Bessie said.

He paused, a spoon loaded with oatmeal on its way to his mouth, and cocked his head at Bessie. "Ma'am?"

"What may I feed you?" There was silk in her voice, Opal thought, spider silk or something else, something worshipful and seductive and a little sticky.

The house was watching and listening to them.

"I'm happy with oatmeal and bacon," said Corvus, his voice at its most gentle.

The woman smiled, bobbed her head, tucked her hands into her apron pockets, and headed toward the door back to the kitchen.

Neil looked grumpy. No one had called him *master* or asked what he wanted.

"Ma'am?" Opal said.

Bessie paused with her shoulder against the swinging door. She turned reluctantly. "Miss?"

"I was wondering if you could tell us about the Last of the Lost?"

Bessie laughed. "Where'd you hear that old wives' tale? From an old wife, I'll wager! Who was it? That tattletale busybody, Myrna Partridge?"

"She did say some girls disappeared in the fifties and were never seen again."

"It makes a good story, doesn't it?"

"Do you know what happened to them?"

"Well, now." Bessie came back into the room and stood beside the table, looming over Opal, her hands still hidden in her pockets. She seemed taller than she had before. Her eyes were hungry. "Sometimes a woman has to get away from a place," she said. "There was just no help for her there. I think it's likely those girls hiked over to the highway and hitched a ride up to Portland. I know it seems like we're at the back of beyond here, but even back then, the big city wasn't so far away. Who knew what happened to any of them once they left?"

"You don't think they went to the forest to join the Last of the Lost?"

Bessie laughed again. "There is no Last of the Lost." She strode toward the door. "He's not lost, and he's not last anymore," she muttered, with a glance at Corvus before she disappeared.

Opal looked at Corvus, too. He was shoveling oatmeal into his mouth; it took him a couple of seconds to notice her regard. When he did, he raised an eyebrow.

"Maybe she'd answer if you asked the questions," Opal said.

"What *are* the questions?" asked Corvus.

"There are no more bloody questions," said Neil, "only

timing, and you need to shove off if you're going to make your call."

Hitch drove Blaise, Opal, and Corvus to the location. Blaise didn't say anything snide on the way.

The Makeup trailer, Cast trailer, Craft Services trailer, generator, camera truck, all the equipment had been moved to the location during the night. The morning was misty but not drizzling, a relief to everyone. Gemma and Bettina weren't in Makeup yet; their call was for eight A.M. Transportation had started the Makeup trailer's generator and turned on the heat already, but Rod and Magenta hadn't come to open up the trailer, since they didn't have to arrive until Gemma and Bettina did. Opal turned on the lights as Corvus and Blaise settled into chairs. She unlocked the cupboard where she stored the prosthetics and set up for work. Blaise lounged in one of the chairs, opened a copy of *Harper's* and effectively vanished, but Opal, conscious of her presence, didn't talk with Corvus. There was nothing she wanted to say to him where anybody else could hear.

She wondered if she wanted to do a postmortem on their first actual night together anyway. Maybe she should just let it lie.

She was ready for Corvus's transition into Phrixos, she thought, but this time it happened while she was shaving him, before she had applied any of his face. The glow grew in his eyes, and his smile widened. She hesitated, then finished the stroke she had started. Blaise glanced up, but she was behind Corvus's head and couldn't see his eyes.

Phrixos closed his eyes and relaxed under her hands. Only once did he break her concentration, when she had leafed over his nose and let one hand rest on his leafy cheek while she thought about her next step. He pulled her hand toward his mouth. She sighed and drew the shield away from her smallest finger, let him feed from her. The Sifter Chant had been running in the background; her reservoir felt pleasantly full. She narrowed the channel, though, so he could not draw too quickly or too much. She shut down the feed before he released her, testing the limits of their boundaries.

"Unfair," he muttered.

"Live with it." She wiped her hand on her jeans and finished matching his face with yesterday's Polaroids. "Arms, please."

Gemma, Bettina, their guardians, Magenta, and Rod all arrived at the trailer at the same time, as Opal was finishing Phrixos's chest leaves. Another actress Opal hadn't met yet arrived as well, a dark-haired woman who displaced Blaise. Blaise hopped up on a counter near Corvus's chair, still clutching her magazine. Magenta went to work on Gemma, while Rod started with the strange woman.

When Opal finished turning Phrixos into the Dark God, Rod called her over. "This is Ariadne, the mom who gets to die in today's scene. Day player—she's only got the two scenes, this one and one with the kids we're shooting on a different set tomorrow. Today we have a call in for all the other coveners, but they'll be wearing hooded robes, so not much makeup on them. Ariadne, Opal LaZelle, special effects makeup."

"Hi," said Ariadne. "You doing my blood?"

"If I am, nobody told me," said Opal.

"She's special to the Dark God. Fake blood is not her department," Rod said.

"Oh. Well, hi," said Ariadne.

"Hi." Opal smiled and went back to Phrixos, who was drowsing.

The mist had lightened by the time they came out of Makeup and headed for the stones. The clearing was silent, the air cold. Opal felt again the undertone of hum, an anticipatory sensation. Something waited.

She walked with Phrixos over to the altar stones as the stand-ins came off the set. Then, suddenly, he lifted her and set her on the altar. She felt a vibration all through her. "What are you doing?" she asked.

"Lie down," he whispered. He gripped her shoulders and pushed down on them. "Just for a second."

"What? No!" She tried to wrench free, but he didn't let go.

Lightning flashed. Or, no, it was a camera flash. Erika stood just outside the circle of stones, taking pictures one after another.

"Hey," said George, the first assistant director and Neil's shadow. "What's going on here? No horseplay, Corvus! You're going to knock something out of alignment if you're not careful."

"Lie still," Phrixos said, his voice soft and fierce.

She couldn't break his grip. Furious, she lay on the stone and glared up at him.

He spoke a phrase in a language she didn't recognize. Something burned and buzzed against her back. She felt the flare of Flint's shield along her skin as something tried to enter her and failed.

"Corvus!" said Neil.

"Let go!" she said. Finally he released her and she sat up, shoved off the altar stone, and ran from the set to the cast corral behind the backdrop. Shuddering, she curled up in Corvus's chair.

Erika ambled over, camera still in hand. Opal hid her face in her hands and Erika strode past.

"What was *that*?" Magenta asked.

"Things getting worse," Opal whispered. "He stopped playing nice."

"Oh, God." Magenta touched her shoulder, glanced toward the set. They were behind the backdrop and couldn't actually see what was happening at the altar directly. "Did he hurt you?"

"He tried to get something to—possess me. I mean, I'm not sure about that, but he—" Opal shuddered again, pulled arms and legs tight to her center, hugged her knees to her.

She remembered one of her high school boyfriends. Once she had come into her powers, she had experimented with boys, changing her appearance in little ways to see which features attracted which boys, then trying some of the nastier spells in her repertoire, the ones Great-Uncle Tobias had scolded her for studying, to see how much she could bend people to her will. She had had no idea back then what kind of boyfriend she really wanted.

Somebody sweet like her father, the only one in the house who could actually make her mother slow down and think before she acted? Opal could force boys to be sweet, but she couldn't make them sweet and strong enough to stop her from doing anything she wanted to them. She didn't know what Dad's secret was.

Somebody who could resist her? No, she got enough of that with her younger brother Jasper and the rest of the kids. Even when she was just trying to help them, they fought back. It wasn't fair. She wasn't really their mom, just the one who took care of them. Mom was gone most of the time, and even when she was home, she was absorbed in her own affairs. The kids had minded Opal when they were little, and she loved them so much it hurt. Now they were teenagers and didn't mind much anymore.

And then she met Keith. At first he behaved like the other boys she'd experimented on, falling under her spell, responding to her smaller manipulations. Her friends thought he was so agreeable. Her most recent ex-boyfriend, still obsessing about her, wilted and faded away: Keith was stronger, better-looking, smarter. Plus, Opal suspected, but never confirmed, that Keith had beat up the previous boyfriend at one point. That sort of thing could drum even enchanting girlfriends out of people's brains, and a good thing, too, because Opal hadn't yet learned other, cleaner ways of dumping boys.

Keith behaved like all her previous boyfriends . . . up to a point. They'd been on the beach at night when she realized he wasn't like the others. They were alone on a blanket, the repeating hush of waves not far from them, faint fog rising to mask the stars. He had given her the kind of sexual experience that was all she knew, a gentle, prolonged session she had orchestrated with subtle precision, culminating in a small orgasm for her and a release and collapse for him. They lay silent. She stared sleepily up at stars. He sat up and said, "This is your idea of a good time? Let me show you something, babe."

None of her spells affected him. Nothing she did even slowed him down. He took her hard. He hurt her. The things he whispered to her hurt, too, almost worse than the physical experience.

Afterward, when she curled up and cried, he sat beside her and said, "You have no right to complain, babe. That's what you've been doing to all those boys. They were okay before they met you. Think about it."

She couldn't get herself to go back to school for a week, though she knew she was setting a bad example for the other kids in the family. When she did go back, she practiced a new way of altering her appearance: she made herself invisible. She watched the boys she had messed with and saw that some of them hadn't recovered particularly well. Keith would meet her gaze if he caught her looking at him, but he never smiled at her. Every time she felt herself drawn to someone new, though, she'd glance around and realize Keith was watching her.

She finally went to Uncle Tobias and forced herself to tell him everything. He set her new studies, strict lessons about how to unspell people and free them. She worked hard.

Her final assignment was to find as many of her old boyfriends as she could and take whatever spell threads she had left on them off. Tobias helped supervise. Afterward, most of them were mad at her, if they had memories at all. Tobias gave her permission to protect herself with illusion when necessary.

But it was uncomfortable living in a place where so many people had the wrong kind of history with her. She reengineered herself: moved to Los Angeles, ninety miles from home, got a real job—in the movies, like many in her family, but not with any of her cousins or aunts or uncles. Not with anybody she'd ever met before. She started at the bottom, assisting a makeup artist on a low-budget horror movie, and kept her talents under wraps while she learned how normal people worked. Anonymity and distance gave her the strength to examine everything she'd done so far, think about it, make different decisions.

Now *she* was like one of those ineffectual boyfriends she'd mistreated in her teens, at the mercy of a power greater than her own. She hadn't even tried to resist yet. She needed to resurrect Evil Opal.

"He tried to get something to possess you?" Magenta whispered, her grip on Opal's shoulder tightening.

"Keep away from him if you can," Opal said. She took a deep breath. Evil Opal. Her shadow self. Somewhere in her memory house, probably behind a closed door in the basement or the attic, Opal had locked her away. Time to dig her out.

"You bloody fool, you don't go messing with anyone in public," Neil said to Phrixos, behind her. "Especially you don't manhandle any talent necessary to the successful completion of the picture, not unless it's something she wants, and then you do it in private. I won't have this kind of upset on my set."

"Just a joke," Phrixos said.

"Nobody's laughing. Now straighten up and find your character. Time for blocking rehearsal. Ariadne? Where's my mini Caitlyn and Serena?"

Magenta loosened her grip on Opal's shoulder as the other

stars went onto the set. Doreen, Gemma's mother, stared at Opal. Perhaps she hadn't seen or heard what had just happened. Maybe she had. Nothing to do about it now.

The actors walked through blocking rehearsal. Neil yelled at them a lot.

"The big boss is grumpier than usual," Magenta muttered. "Wonder how things went with him last night."

Neil didn't have a light touch with the actors; instead of getting them to work with him, he made them resentful and defensive. The rehearsal repeated several times.

Blaise drifted over from the trailer that held her dressing room, along with Lauren's and Corvus's. "Trouble in paradise?" she asked.

"Did you kick the boss out of bed last night?" Magenta asked. "What chemistry there is is all bad."

Blaise raised her eyebrows, but didn't answer.

"Might as well shoot the fucking scene and hope for a miracle," Neil yelled. "Last looks! Somebody make these people look better than they can act!"

Opal collected her kit, but she waited until Magenta, carrying a different Set2Go bag for each of the teen actors, joined her before she headed for the set.

Opal mentally stroked Flint's shield, made sure it surrounded her completely. She checked her reservoir for power: plenty. She flexed her fingers, remembered ribbons of invisible smoke she had sent out to do her bidding when she was controlling people. A tiny puff of smoke from her index finger reassured her.

As usual, Phrixos didn't need touch-ups. He stood silent, looming above her, his expression unreadable, observing, as she focused on the separate details that made up his character's whole. He touched her face without making any attempt to draw from her. His eyelids flickered. She wondered if Corvus was trying to surface. At least he didn't grab her and lay her on the altar again.

One of the special effects crew was on the set to orchestrate the blood spatter from the mother's horrifying death. He had practiced with a Styrofoam mock-up of the set inside the soundstage building, and thought he knew where all the spray and spatter would go, but when they actually started filming, things kept going wrong with the direction of the blood. Some of the blood spattered across the camera lenses, which entailed an extended cleanup. The altar stone got liberally spattered and needed scrubbing every time, though they couldn't get all the stain off—some of it was original, and old. They decided to leave it, but the continuity shots looked different every time.

The onsite showers in the trailers didn't have strong enough water pressure. The stars were miserable after every take—and wardrobe was running out of copies of the clothes, even though they were pretty generic, white robes for the coveners, including Ariadne, the girls' mother, the black robe for the Dark God, and special ritual dresses for the two girls in honor of their induction into the Dark God coven. The girls weren't supposed to be in range of the blood spatter, though Neil had reserved the right to drench them if he thought it made dramatic sense. Bettina and Gemma had changed out of gory dresses twice already, and there had been big gaps in the filming while their hair was restored. Special Effects was using peppermint-flavored stage blood, so at least everybody would have clean-tasting mouths if they ate any by mistake.

"Break for fucking lunch," the director finally said. "I don't know if we can salvage anything out of this fucking mess. Come back ready to work." He wandered off, muttering curses, while people mopped up behind him. Everybody went to the folding tables set up behind the drapes that hid the trucks, trailers, and cast corral from the cameras. Catering had dropped off a big box of mixed sandwiches wrapped in plastic an hour earlier, and a tub full of varied canned beverages buried in ice.

The hum under Opal's feet had grown more insistent during all the mishaps of the afternoon. As everyone else left the ritual rocks, she wandered toward them, hands stretched before her, palms aimed downward. Something under the ground was awake. She'd never felt anything quite like it before. Her family home was full of spirit-haunted things, some of them active, because people with power had been using them for years; but none of them purred like this. The energy didn't get through her shield, yet still she sensed it, a warmth, a summons, almost a song.

The altar stone, still damp from being cleaned of special effects blood, vibrated with enticing energy. A sweet taste thrummed on Opal's tongue. She reached, for what she didn't know; she only knew something invited her, promising things.

"Open to me," it whispered. "I will be your strength. I will be your spine. I will be your friend and protector. I will be your wings."

She flattened her hands against the altar stone, felt the surge of a warm sea of power under her palms. Only Flint's shield kept it separate from the sea inside her. She could make the shield retreat, bare her skin, wrap herself in that warmth, finally find something that would take care of her instead of her taking care of everyone else—

"What are you doing?" asked someone behind her.

She blinked, glanced back. Phrixos stood silent a foot behind her, his hood up, his face shadowed in the black robe of his character. She was startled. She hadn't known he was there.

He was not the one who had spoken. Beyond him stood Erika, frowning, no cameras raised, curiosity marking her face.

"What?"

"Something special about the rock?" Erika asked.

"I'm sorry?" Opal said.

Erika came forward, stared at the altar stone. She sucked in her lower lip, then touched the stone. "Ow!" Her hand jerked, a drop of blood spilling free of her finger to splash on the rock. "What? How'd that happen?"

The music streaming from the rock rose from a single voice to an orchestra, full of ominous chords, woodwinds, and triumph, strings singing, deep notes of percussion.

Erika froze. Then her hand lowered, drops of blood welling from her fingertip and dripping on the stone, where they wet the surface and vanished. She set both hands against the stone, leaned on them, her shoulders hunching.

Manipulating her arms as though she were a rag doll, Phrixos gently stripped the cameras and her shoulder bag from her, then lifted her and laid her on her back on the stone. She stared up at him, only her eyes moving. "What," she said, her voice a thread now as the music of power lapped at her, loudest where her blood fed the rock. "Don't," she said. Her hand jerked, though, pressed the bleeding finger to the rock, pressed the palm, and then the wrist. "Stop it," she whispered.

12

∞

Opal stood, battered by wild waves of energy coming from the rock, from the ground below. Even the grass was dancing. Phrixos stood beside her, an absence of light and sound. Before her on the altar stone, Erika closed her eyes, her face drawn into a grimace. As her blood dripped into the stone, something flowed from the stone into her finger, a trickle of blue green energy Opal could not quite see but could sense. It sparked up Erika's arm, seeped through her torso, climbed her spine, and burst into her brain. Erika jerked again, and Opal woke out of the trance the music had put her in.

She stepped forward, lifted Erika's wounded hand from the stone, and broke the connection. Erika's body stiffened, all muscles tight, then relaxed. The music faded, still present but not so overpowering.

"Hey!" yelled someone from behind them. "What are you doing?"

"Are you okay?" Opal asked Erika.

"No," Erika said. Her voice was strained, as though her

throat had closed around the word and didn't want to let it escape. Her hand encircled Opal's forearm, the grip hard enough to hurt. "Yes. No! Help me!"

Opal helped Erika sit up, supported her as she slid off the altar stone. Phrixos stood silent, while Neil stumped across the clearing toward them. "You people know better than to mess with the set between shots! Have you gone mad?"

Opal lifted Erika's arm over her shoulder and snaked an arm around her waist to help her walk. Phrixos still held Erika's camera bags and shoulder bag. He followed.

"What the fuck is this?" Neil cried. "Someone better answer me, or there'll be hell to pay."

Phrixos halted beside him and stared into his face from under that dark hood.

"Don't you play a part with me, you great lurching golem. I admire what the camera does with your image, but I was against hiring you from the start, and I haven't changed my mind yet—what's that look? What? Stop that! Stop . . ."

Opal left them both behind. Erika's muscles had been stiff when she came off the altar, but they loosened as she walked, and her breathing eased, opened. "What happened?" she asked.

"You tell me," said Opal.

"I don't know. I feel like I walked into an electric fence. Everything in my head is still going *kabong*." She lifted the hand she had bled from, stared at her finger. "Can a rock be a vampire? What's wrong with this shoot, Opal?"

"You're the professional observer," Opal said. She was relieved Erika was talking like a person with sense after whatever had happened to her on the rock. It didn't make her feel like sharing anything with a woman who had been nothing but an irritation in her life so far.

"Yes, but you're the one with all the secrets."

"Let me know when you decide to respect my privacy," Opal said. "Until then, I'm not telling you a thing."

"But I—but—" Erika gripped her forehead with her free hand. "My head hurts."

The crew had finished devouring all the sandwiches, and most were on their feet again, leaving behind wads of plastic wrap, dented aluminum cans, crumpled paper napkins, and crumbs on the folding tables the caterers had set up for lunch.

Magenta rose from the table. "I saved you a cheese sandwich. Something happen?"

Opal glanced behind her. Phrixos had his palm on Neil's forehead now, and the director wasn't fighting him anymore; his eyes were closed.

"I think it's bad," she muttered.

Magenta looked where Opal was looking. "Uh-oh. What's D.G. doing to our director? What's with Flashbulb here?"

"She bled on the altar stone. Then Dark God put her on it."

"That does sound bad," Magenta said.

"Whyever would you say that?" Erika asked. "Because that shambling monster as good as assaulted me? Or because the rock bit me, then Tasered me, and Miss Too-Big-for-Her-Britches let it happen?"

"What?" Magenta asked Opal. "This was going on and you just stood there?"

"I was sort of—in a trance myself."

"The rock Tasered Erika?"

"I touched it and it paralyzed me! It drank my blood! Then that giant goon laid me out on it like a sacrifice, and"—she put her hand to her forehead, gripped it as though she could squeeze a memory out—"and I'm not sure what happened next, except it hurt, and I feel really weird. Kind of—not alone."

"Opal," said Magenta.

The first assistant director called, "All right, people. We're burning daylight. Let's get back to it. Stand-ins, we need to check the lighting again. Cast, go to Makeup for repairs. Crew, assume the position!"

The pull of work tugged them back to their stations. Erika, her cameras once again draped around her, trailed Magenta and Opal back to the trailer, but Rod turned her back at the door. Her screeches of rage in response were only halfhearted, trailing off with one last nonspecific, "I'll get you, bitch!" before Rod shut the door in her face.

Phrixos sat in his chair with his hood down, his eyes burning, looking like some wild thing captured against its will and ready to attack. Bettina and Gemma waited in their chairs, both pale and unhappy. Doreen hovered near Gemma, though technically she wasn't supposed to be in the trailer during makeup unless there was trouble. Rod had already gone to work on Ariadne. No one spoke, the sign of a truly troubled shoot.

Opal stood at her workstation facing the mirrored wall, her back to the trailer. She could see the others reflected as they went to work. She placed her palms flat on the counter. The tools of her trade were around her, and she pulled together the identity she had built for herself since she left home: skilled, respected, solid and reliable, invisible, accomplished, creative, resourceful, inspired.

Not enough, she thought, and remembered the new people she had become on this particular project: witch friend to Lauren and Magenta, Corvus's girlfriend, Phrixos's walking nourishment supply, information collector.

Not enough, she thought again. She closed her eyes and found her inner study. Some of Flint's energy still floated there, a bumbling fireball. *Come,* she whispered to it. *Help me open to my shadow self.*

Obedient, the fire seeped through her, sent bright warmth into all her dark corners, found the door she had shut on the self who knew how to manipulate and hurt other people, the part of her that most resembled Phrixos. Fire formed the key to pick the lock for her, but she had to turn the doorknob herself. She reached out and did it, pulled the door open and stepped through.

A skin of darkness settled over her, snugged against her in every expanse, crease, recess, every fine hair and blemish. It seeped under her surface. She twitched, settling it, then scratched an elbow. The new self itched! *Hey, hey,* it said, *what have I missed? Whoa, lots of life! Wow, what's going on here? How neat is that?*

She lifted her eyelids and stared at herself in the mirror, saw darkness staring back. She closed her eyes and asked herself what the hell she had just done. *What I needed to,* she decided, and shuddered. She studied herself again, smiled, and saw the extra intensity darkness gave her, the beckoning that said, *Come closer. I have such interesting things to tell you.*

Hey, said her second self, *show me the guy.*

She turned. Phrixos stared at her, his face unreadable beneath its overcoat of leaves and glitter. He sat up straighter. "What have you done?" he asked.

She felt wings at her back, flames at her fingertips, a blaze behind her eyes. All defenses, because her second self could tell how dangerous Phrixos was. She smiled at him, too, because second self felt the pull of attraction between them. It wasn't Corvus her second self wanted.

"Ready?" asked one of the production assistants from the trailer door.

"She never even touched him," Bettina said, pointing to Opal and Phrixos.

"He doesn't need any help," said Opal. "He's perfect."

"You didn't even look at the photos," said Bettina. "You're a total slacker."

Opal raised her brows and looked at Bettina with the glare of an older sister who can do things to you while you're asleep if you piss her off. Bettina lost color. She leapt to her feet and fled the trailer.

"How'd you do that?" Gemma asked, rising from her chair as Magenta tried to pat her cheek with a powder puff.

"I'll demonstrate, if you bother me," Opal said. Her voice had deepened just a little.

Everyone in the trailer turned to look at her. In the resulting silence, the P.A. said, "We needed you ten minutes ago, people! Come on!"

Phrixos rose, tipped Opal's chin up, and kissed her. Instead of letting him draw from her, she drew from him, sucked off a draught of his energy. He tasted sweet and sour, smoky and sharp, scary. He tried to move into her as his essence crossed her tongue, but Evil Opal knew how to drag all of him out of Corvus's body. Something in her spun darkness to wrap him tighter and deeper in a cocoon of night, though she couldn't paralyze him; she felt him struggling, and countered with more until at last he lay silent.

Corvus staggered when he let her go. She stared up at him and saw that Phrixos's green glow had faded from his eyes. "What?" he said in Corvus's voice.

She smiled. "Well, that's a handy trick. You're wanted on the set, Corr."

"I am?"

She turned him and aimed him toward the door. "I'm right behind you." She felt drunk and a little staggery herself. The taste of the banished god was still on her tongue, intoxicating to her second self. She grabbed her bag and followed Corvus down the steps in the wake of Ariadne, the two girls, their Makeup and Wardrobe people, the mother, and the guardian.

"Which scene are we doing?" Corvus asked Opal as they rounded the backdrop and headed for the altar.

"Mom's death scene. You studied it last night with Lauren at the restaurant, remember?"

"Vaguely," he said.

"So far it hasn't been working out very well. Everybody's

in a mood, especially Neil. We spent six hours getting it wrong, and then we broke for lunch."

"How did I get to be me in the middle of the day? I'd pretty much given up on that."

"I forced it," said Opal.

"You did?" He studied her as they walked. "How?"

"I used a trick that probably won't work twice," she said. "Now you're going to have to act happy while you're sprayed with special effects blood. Oh, and just before lunch, Phrixos actually woke the rock by spilling Erika's blood on it." The grass was still vibrant with energy, and the rocks glowed with it. The music was there, too, half a melody that played, cut off, started again. Beneath it all was a slow pulse, the heartbeat of something huge, old, and resting. Resting, but awake now.

The hairs on Opal's arms and legs bristled. The muscles in the back of her neck twitched. Whatever lay under the ground recognized her presence, and wanted her.

"Over here," bellowed Neil. "Quit lagging!"

They reached the altar, where the coveners in their recently dried robes, Ariadne in period clothes as the mother doomed to die, and Gemma and Bettina in their white lace dresses as witnesses and innocents waited. Corvus took his mark at the head of the altar, straightened, and turned into a close approximation of Phrixos; it was hard to distinguish them by sight when they were in full makeup, but Opal could sense the spiritual difference.

Phrixos was inside her, and not lying quiet, either, though she had tried to lock his essence away. Her second self was intrigued by him; she let small bits of him out to play, enjoying his dark impulses, though not giving them any weight or power. Opal felt things going on in the back of her mind while she was focused on what was in front of her: Neil harangued his cast about their previous inadequacies and demanded better of them.

"Does that kind of screeching ever work?" Magenta muttered, from beside Opal.

"Sure," Opal said. "Fear works. You should know that by now."

Magenta stared into her eyes, then stepped back.

Opal considered this. She had opened to her dark half, and anybody smart *should* be scared of her, if that change was visible. Maybe she should mask it better. She closed her eyes and thought *disguise*, one of her best and most practiced skills. She felt the spin of energies as her looks reformed into something nonthreatening, knew each change; she had done this a lot when she was a teenager, to convince her parents she was innocent. Her great-uncle Tobias hadn't been fooled; he could see under surfaces. She looked toward Magenta again.

"What did you just do? I hate it that you can do makeup without tools."

"Is it working? Are you reassured?"

"Yeah, and I don't like that either. Jerk me around! Who were you a minute ago? Almost as scary as the prick."

"Takes one to deal with one," said Opal.

Magenta half smiled and glanced toward Opal's crotch. Opal laughed, and said, "Not quite that way, but yeah, I decided to be my own mean self. Somebody I haven't been in a long time."

"Well, that's weird. Makes me wonder who you normally are. Did it make a difference?"

"Yeah. I did a job on him, locked him up. Right now, he's Corvus, not Phrixos. Not sure that was smart, and I don't know that it'll last, but I managed it."

"Cool," said Magenta. "You gonna get nasty, too?"

"I hope not. Can't rule it out, though."

"Can you give me some protection?"

Protection. Why hadn't she thought of that before? She could make talismans for everybody—except Lauren, who had already been tapped by Phrixos, and Erika, who had been attacked by the altar. Maybe she could come up with something that would help even those who had been compromised.

She didn't have much experience with it, though. Her brother Jasper had worked on it more. Maybe when Uncle Tobias came, which should be any time now, he could help her.

"I—" Opal began, but then Neil yelled, "Is my goddamned blood ready to go?"

"Ready," said the pale-faced special effects man.

"And it'll go the right direction this time? It'll land where I say it's supposed to land?"

"Yes," squeaked the man.

"All right, then. One final blocking rehearsal without the blood, and then you lot have no excuses left!"

Opal kept her attention on Corvus, listened to make sure he remembered his lines and knew where he was supposed to go. The girls were flat in their delivery, having said everything twenty times already, but Corvus brought a new spirit to his gloating over the death of one of his character's most devoted followers.

"Good," Neil said at last. "Last looks, and let's make this the actual last, shall we?"

Opal checked Corvus over carefully, referencing Polaroids from the morning shoot. He looked a little less realistic now, but nothing needed work.

"All right, clear the set," said Neil. His call was repeated, louder, by the first assistant director. Opal fled with all the others to the cast corral. Rod got out his little TV, and they watched as the take went perfectly for the first time that day.

Everyone involved relaxed as soon as Neil called cut. He and the A.D. and the D.P. gathered around a monitor and watched a playback, with the script supervisor right behind them to take notes. Everyone else waited for the verdict.

"All right," George, the first assistant director, called out, "looks like we got the master shot, finally! Two angles on it. Thank God. Clear the set. We'll go to close-ups on the principals next. Coveners, you're done for the day. The rest of you, take five while we set up."

The actors went to the Wardrobe trailer, where they changed out of fake-blood-soaked robes into lounging wear. They came to the cast corral and settled into chairs, most leaning back as though exhausted. The makeup artists cleaned fake blood off everyone who had been spattered for the umpteenth time, and restored their pre-suicide makeup. Doreen, Gemma's mother, went to the Craft Services truck and came back with several bottles of water. She offered them to Gemma, Bettina, Ariadne, and Corvus, who all accepted.

"Do you want something to eat?" Opal asked Corvus.

He caught her hand and lifted it to his lips. She wondered if Phrixos had found his way back inside—she hadn't had time to tend to what she had pulled from Corvus earlier. The little dark flurries and explorations some part of her had entertained while the rest of her was being Opal LaZelle, special effects makeup queen, had slowed.

Something moved inside her, something that was not either of her selves. She closed her eyes and tried to wrap it in darkness again, but she felt the taint of it, itchy and exciting, glowing along her mental entrails and trails.

There was no sense from Corvus of threat or invasion, even as his lips pressed against the back of her hand, only a warmth that wakened memories of last night.

The ground was alive with excited anticipation, and it kept trying to send exploratory feelers up through her feet. Something inside her reached down toward the invading energy, but explorations from both directions stubbed against Flint's shield. She needed time and space to figure out what had happened.

"Actually," Corvus said, in his own voice, letting her hand

slip from his, "I'm starving. I don't know what he had for lunch, but I don't think it was enough. Could you get me one of those energy drinks? I don't have his power over the makeup, to eat with it on and not mess it up."

"Sure." Opal went to the Craft Services wagon and got some cold protein drinks and a couple of straws. She brought them back and then stood behind Corvus as he drank, contemplating her inner universe.

Magenta tapped her shoulder, startling her, and she looked up without thinking about who she was. Magenta sucked in breath and took a step back, and Shadow Opal smiled wide, the smile of seduction that said, *You're the most interesting person I've ever seen. Come closer.* Magenta wavered, not fleeing, not approaching.

Opal straightened, tried to find her usual face. "Sorry. Identity crisis."

"Are you a good witch or a bad witch?" Magenta asked after a pause.

"Hard to tell at this point."

"If you have a choice, could you veer toward the good witch end of the spectrum? We really don't need more bad blood on the set."

"That's my usual inclination, when I act like a witch at all," said Opal.

Magenta glared at her, then said, "Well, anyway, about protection."

"Protection?" said Corvus.

"Not that kind," Magenta said. "If this is the good witch I'm talking to, can you say a spell that will protect me from you and the prick?"

"Let me think." One thing that had worked for her was Flint's shield, but she didn't want to give any of that away; she needed it herself. She held up her hand, studied it, turned it over and back, and tried to see how Flint's shield surrounded her like a clear second skin. What were the components of this energy? It came from Flint, which made it something other people usually couldn't make or use. She wanted to make more of it. She stroked fingers across it, trying to taste its ingredients. Her younger sister Gypsum was a cook who could analyze components of baked goods by savoring a bite. Opal wondered if she could sample spells the same way, though her darker power might taint them somehow. Opal had never paid much attention to food, and she hadn't done much magical investigating since she was a teenager, hungry for skills and knowledge that would help her outfight her younger and more powerful siblings.

She lifted her hand to her mouth and pressed her lips to the back of it, touched the tip of her tongue to it. She could barely tell the fireskin was there; it wasn't trying to protect her from herself. She sucked on it, and then a taste flared in her mouth, a jalapeño scorch across her lips and tongue. *Analyze,* she thought to herself and to Evil Opal. *Replicate.*

Offer it energy, and ask it to change the new energy into itself, responded one of her.

Is it a living thing with its own mind?

Don't know. Can't break it down, but maybe we can get it to work with us.

She lowered her hand and closed her eyes, shutting out the sight of Corvus staring up at her from the chair, Magenta focused intensely on her, Rod down the trailer tending to Bettina, Gemma in one of the closer chairs with Doreen hovering over her.

In her mental study, Opal talked to the small ball of Flint-fire that remained after it had built her shield. "Can you make more of yourself to share with my friends?" she asked it.

Let's try, it thought.

She opened her power reservoir and trickled power toward the fireball. It ate the power and grew. When it was the size of a small weather balloon and she had almost exhausted her reserves, she opened her eyes. Magenta waited.

"I think I can give you a shield," she said. "My little brother gave me a kind of bodyshield that protects me from Phrixos's power, unless I take it off. I was rolling it back from just one finger, or my lips, when he made me feed him. I don't know about using this power on someone who isn't—isn't a witch herself—so this might not work. It might fail spectacularly. Do you want to try anyway?"

"How wrong could it go?" Magenta asked.

"I don't know. I've never done anything like this before."

"What if it cripples me, or makes it so I can't work?"

"Yeah," said Opal, "what if?"

Magenta frowned ferociously at her, then lifted a leg and propped her running-shoe-clad foot on the back of Corvus's makeup chair. "Maybe you could put it around my foot and see if it works."

"Take off your shoe and sock," Opal said.

Magenta glared at her, then did it. Opal cleared a section of counter. "Sit here." Magenta hopped up, and Opal took her foot—toenails neatly trimmed and coated in sparkling black polish, the long slender muscles and bones an elegance of form—between her hands. Opal went into overawareness, her body's eyes focused on her hands and Magenta's foot, her mind's self engaged with Flint's fireball in her study, consulting and interacting with it. "We want to protect someone who is not like we are," she told it, and it sent out a thin, questing thread that eased along the lace of her veins, arteries, muscles, and nerves to her fingers and palms, to lie like a simmering sea of fire just under her skin.

"Okay," she said, her voice tight, her attention split, "I'm going to start now. Tell me if it hurts and I'll try to reverse it. Ready?"

"I guess," said Magenta. She scrunched up her face.

Opal stroked two fingers along the arch of Magenta's foot, spreading the smallest flush of fire along the skin. She glanced toward Magenta's face, looking for signs of pain.

"Oh," Magenta said. "That's warm."

"Does it burn?"

"No. Feels nice."

"Okay, I'm going to be a little bolder." She tapped into the stream of Flintfire lying under her skin and spread it over Magenta's foot in a sweep of her whole hand.

"Yikes!" said Magenta.

Opal looked at her, but she looked more surprised than pained. Opal waited for a more telling reaction.

"It's okay," said Magenta.

Opal gloved her whole foot in shield, then let go. Magenta stared down at her foot, kicked it, flexed her toes. "It's a little warm, but other than that, I can't even tell anything's there. So now my foot's safe?"

"Safe as I can make it," Opal said, "with what I know right now."

"Do the rest of me?"

Opal sucked on her lower lip, then held out her hands. "Give me your foot again."

Magenta held out her foot, and Opal grasped it, spoke to the fireball. "Send energy from me to her, slide along all her skin, and protect her from outside sorcery."

"Including yours?" asked the fireball. As she spoke to it, it had acquired personality. She had a sense that she was talking to a separate self. One of hers? More like Flint's, though she didn't think he was inside her. The fireball was itself and could make decisions. So she had her usual self, her evil self, a semicorralled Phrixos, and the self-aware fireball colonizing her. It was almost like being back home.

"Probably best if you do," she told the fireball.

"This won't be me anymore once we sever the connection,"

said the fireball, "so there's no guarantee you'll be able to talk to the shield."

"Okay, maybe we'd better leave it vulnerable to me a little, in case something goes wrong." She wished she trusted herself more. Dark Opal might decide to make mischief; she already felt the urge percolating. "Ready?"

A sound outside her internal conversation penetrated her concentration; she woke to herself in the outside world, Magenta's warm foot in her hands, Corvus, his chair turned so he could see what she was doing. "We need Dark God on the set," repeated her Ear.

"Oh, God," she said. "I forgot." She looked Corvus over; he still looked flawless. "We've got to get out there."

Magenta gripped her shoulder. "Do me first."

"But—all right." Opal closed her eyes and focused on the fireball, big with all she had given it. "A shield for all of her," she whispered, and the fire flowed through her. It streamed up from Opal's hands along Magenta's skin under her clothes. There wasn't time for finesse; they would be in big trouble with the director if they were late to the set. She waited until she got a sense from the shield that it had enveloped Magenta completely, then cut it off and felt it flex and tighten around the other woman, settle against skin.

Opal grabbed her on-set kit and Corvus's leafy hand and pulled him toward the door. Magenta, dazed, sat behind them, breathing loudly. Opal chanced a glance behind her, unsure if Magenta was all right, but then they were out of the trailer and crossing the lively ground toward the altar again, and something dark and fiery battered inside her, trying to free itself. The attack was so sudden and surprising she couldn't counter it. In that way, Phrixos pulled back the shield protecting her hand, and flowed from Opal into Corvus. They both stumbled and caught themselves as their insides reorganized. Then Phrixos stared down at her with Corvus's eyes and his own unsettling half smile, and Opal had time to wonder what he had learned while she had held him inside herself.

"That's better," he said, and laughed. "You are so full of lovely things. I'm glad you're the first handmaid I found."

"Bite me," said Opal.

13

❧

She flexed her fireskin, made sure it was complete.

He lifted her hand toward his mouth, but then they stepped into a hailstorm of the director's disapproval. Phrixos pulled away from Opal and took his mark; Opal returned to the others who spent most of their time waiting; the cameras rolled, the scene unfolded again, smaller now, the cameras focusing on faces, hands, angles that menaced.

The Dark God maintained character this time, and gave the two girls looks that straightened them out—or reduced them to authentic fear and longing, appropriate to the scene. They did lines until the director was satisfied, and held the blood until the very end. Opal watched Phrixos lick blood from his leafy lips, saw the glow blossom in his eyes on camera, though this was stage blood—how could he get joy from that? Acting? Or maybe symbols spoke as loudly as the real thing to him, in which case, they were in even more trouble than she thought.

Magenta tugged on Opal's arm as Opal watched a scene unfold on Rod's Casio, and she looked up. "What?"

"I feel—strange," Magenta whispered.

"Good strange or bad strange?"

"I don't know. I'm warm—"

"But not burning up?"

"No, it's more, sort of, comfortable." Magenta shifted shoulders up and down, first one, then the other. She scratched the back of her neck. "But a little itchy. Could you—"

"What?"

"Could you cast a spell on me so I can see if it works?"

Opal glanced around. Rod was standing within hearing distance. He didn't look surprised. Maybe Magenta had told him about their experiment while Opal was busy working over Phrixos. She wasn't sure she liked Rod being in the loop.

Don't worry about it, said one of her. *The more people who know, the more we can do to them without having to break through disbelief. Less worry about repercussions. If everyone's expecting me to be a witch, what's the downside to witchy behavior?*

Being burned at the stake?

That's not going to happen to us, one of her thought. *One of us is of the fire. If they try to burn us, we can swallow the fire.* Flint's fireball stroked flame across her face. All she felt was warmth and comfort. *Good.*

Opal straightened and looked at Magenta, considered. A hair-color-changing spell would do, simple, not very energetic, nonthreatening. Turn Magenta's black, pink-streaked bob purple and green. Opal closed her fist, opened it, sent a small moth of spell toward Magenta. It stuttered out against the shield, a tiny purple spark.

Magenta gasped. Rod jerked as though pushed by an invisible hand against his shoulder.

"Did you see it?" Opal asked. She was never sure whether others could perceive magic working. Sometimes it hid itself, sometimes not.

"Fireworks in my face," said Magenta.

"The shield works well enough to block a spell like that, anyway," said Opal.

"What did you try to do?"

"Change your hair color."

"You can do that? Of course you can. I—"

All their Ears crackled, summoning them to the set for another round of fixing marred makeup. By the time they returned to the chairs, they had lost the thread of the conversation.

Opal curled up in Corvus's chair and closed her eyes. "Okay," she whispered. She had shielded Magenta. Should she extend that shield to others? She checked her power reservoir. Still low from supplying Magenta's shield, so she stepped her Sifter Chants up to more actively seek local power. She felt them hum as they teased strands of power from the lively ground. She sent some of the new power toward Flint's fireball to replenish it. It was the best thing she had going for her.

She wasn't sure the shield worked the way it was supposed to. Magenta had agreed to be a guinea pig; let her. Maybe after a day's trial to make sure there were no negative side effects, Opal would protect Kelsi, Lauren, Blaise, Rod, the girls.

Maybe.

Maybe she would only help people who were nice to her.

Maybe she should harm people whom she didn't like. She contemplated the universe of people she knew on the set. Bettina was the person she was most irritated with currently. Bettina's on-set guardian was worse than the kid. Erika was an irritant, too, though maybe she was already messed up enough by her contact with the rock, the mixing of her blood with whatever lay below the ground here.

Phrixos. Talk about troubling. She had locked him up inside herself, but he had freed himself. What had he done to her before she noticed his escape?

She went back to her study. Flint's fireball had settled on

the hearth and was now acting like an overactive but almost respectable fire. "Did you see where I put the Dark God while he was here?" she asked it.

"Some other room," it said, and sent a finger of flame to point toward the main door into her study. She went out, found herself lost in the castle of self. A tatter of black on the floor: she moved toward it, recognized a shred from the cocoon her dark half had used to bind Phrixos. She picked it up and ventured down the stone-floored hallway. Veins and striations of some other material striped the dark rock walls. Jewels glinted here and there, and other things gleamed in the matrix, shapes that whispered and promised.

Doors opened here and there in the living rock, different shapes, sizes, and compositions, most of them ajar. She had never been into any of these rooms. She peeked into one and saw a baby, apparently about two years old, asleep. It could have been any of her siblings; it was her favorite state for them, quiet, comfortable, completely trusting, beautiful in their innocence. So easy to care for; a hug could nourish them. She stepped into the room and contemplated the baby. Finally she realized it wasn't breathing.

She darted forward, arms out, ready to give it mouth-to-mouth. One of her selves stopped her. "It's not dead," said some other Opal. "Just frozen. They're easier to take care of that way."

"What?" she asked.

"If you could have, wouldn't you have frozen them once in a while? When they had colic, when they were screaming, when they turned into brats? If only you had had your powers while you were small. Our mother made you take care of them all by the time you were ten. Couldn't you have used a nice freeze ray on them then?"

"No. That would make me just like Mom!" she cried.

"Mom has her good points," said the other.

"Neglect and misuse of power aren't good points."

"Kinda depends."

Opal turned and found a Goth version of herself, dark brows, pale skin, golden eyes, and her naturally light hair darkened to black with one white streak above her left eye. She wore a gray body stocking. Had she ever been this self? Opal couldn't remember a time. Maybe for Halloween? *No.*

"Am I the shadow self or are you?" said Goth Opal. She smiled. Pointy teeth.

"Cliché and obvious," Opal said.

Other Opal shrugged. "I can be whatever I like. Right now, this is working for me. I'll change if you want me to; I don't care about the form."

"No, it's all right. I like that you're different from me."

"Just a surface. The fall of light."

Opal looked back into the crib at the frozen baby. "Why do you know about this?"

"You gave me this baby a long time ago. Sometimes I wake her up and play with her."

"Who is it?"

Dark Opal stepped past her and lifted the baby in her arms, cradled it. The baby breathed. Her brow wrinkled, her eyes opened. Violet eyes. She looked preternaturally aware.

Opal half reached for the child, and Other Opal handed it to her.

A strange frightening tenderness swamped Opal as she held her baby self in her arms. She wanted to wrap the baby in love and safety. The baby's own feelings of fear and abandonment swept through her. When Opal was this little, there hadn't been anyone to do for her what she managed to do for the others: guard them, hug them, whisper them past their nightmares, warm them when they were cold, feed them when they were hungry. Opal was the oldest. Daddy had gone to work every day, leaving Opal home alone with Mom, who liked being pregnant but didn't like taking care of babies once they were external to herself.

At some point an aunt and uncle had moved into the guest-house, and Mom often dumped baby Opal on them while she was out building her career as a television personality. The relatives were better about tending to Opal when she needed things than Mom had ever been. For a little while, Opal had felt cared for and beloved. But then the aunt and uncle had twins of their own, and their attention was split.

Opal learned not to need things. She grew up a little ahead of the twins. She learned how to take care of babies from watching her aunt and uncle.

The baby was quiet and still in her arms, eyes wide and watching.

Opal hugged her, filled with wordless longing for many things that had never happened.

The baby opened her mouth and screamed and cried, wracking sobs alternating with shrieks.

Opal rocked the baby and murmured to her, but nothing halted the shuddering, piercing cries. She held her out so she could see her. "What's wrong?"

"She's the first version of me," screamed the Other Opal above the noise. "Sometimes she wants to do all the things we never did, and that's one of them. You can't shut her up once she gets started, no matter what you do. That's why I always end up freezing her."

Opal held her smaller self as she sobbed. Each sob and cry grated against her heart. How long could this go on?

"Hours," said her other self, even though she hadn't spoken aloud. "I've timed it. I've never ridden it out. We stored up a lot of trouble, sister. You're more patient than I am."

Opal kissed the baby's cheek and set her in the crib, tucked the blanket around her small thrashing form. The baby paused in midscream and stared up at her with glistening violet eyes. Her cheeks were wet with tears, ruddy with crying.

"Love you," Opal whispered.

Baby opened her mouth, and Other Opal touched her forehead gently. She froze, stiller than death. Other Opal touched her eyes closed, tapped the chin to close the mouth.

"She'll be all right," she said. "She always is."

Opal backed away from the baby, fighting all the compulsions that said the baby was her responsibility and she had no right to leave it. What the baby needed was love and affection. She could give that. How could she walk away?

Roaring fire swept through her, a rage so big she couldn't keep it inside. Flames rose from her skin, formed a hot, flaring cocoon around her. The stone under her feet scorched, but she didn't feel the heat. She stared at the baby. Why should she be the one who took care of the baby? Where was the baby's mother? How could she leave such a tiny creature alone, surrounded by cold, uncaring stone?

"This is the safest place she could be," said Other Opal, and then, "no place is safe."

Opal stood on the threshold to the hallway, flames flickering the air around her, glanced once more at the baby, then crossed into the hall. Her rage died down. The door closed most of the way behind her. Other Opal stood beside her.

"What were we doing before we went in there?" Opal asked Other Opal.

"Seeing what Phrixos did while he was here."

"Where was he?" She liked Other Opal having a form she could question.

Other Opal pointed down the hallway toward a three-way branching. A fragment of black cocoon lay on the floor, and beyond it, down the left-hand branch, another. They moved that way. Down the hallway, soft gold light spilled from an open door, and another black tatter lay in the fallen gold. A shadow flickered past the edge of Opal's eye, and she almost turned, but Other Opal took her hand, tugged her onward. They hastened toward the open door—

Someone shook Opal's shoulder. She gasped and pulled free of the inner world. "God, Opal, where were you?" Magenta demanded. "I've been shaking you forever!"

"Sorry. What's up?"

"Last looks again!"

Opal jumped up, staggered; her legs were shaky from sitting. She grabbed her kit and followed Magenta at a run to the set.

The energy state of everything has changed, Opal thought— the ground more alive and awake than it had been, people in sharper outline and color to her eyes. Night was coming, and the lighting crew had put up banks of lights to replicate the amount of daylight they'd started shooting in. She felt as though she was moving through a liquid, something denser than atmosphere. Every move anyone made, every word they spoke, even their thoughts and feelings, reached out through the rippling air, responding to every other thing going on, all of them trapped together, working on each other at a distance. She turned to Magenta, wondering if she felt it, too, but Magenta only frowned fiercely at her and ran ahead.

Opal sped to the set. Phrixos caught her before she crashed into him. "Whoa," he said. "Something wrong?"

She looked up at him, checking for smug. Had he left traps in her head? She still didn't know. "I'm late," she said. "Sorry."

"Need a little blood cleaning," he said. "Splatter misfired again."

He had blood spots across the leaves of his face, and a big splotch on his chest. She muttered under her breath and opened her kit to do repairs. If things were normal, she would have had to take him back to the Makeup trailer, undo half of what she had done that morning, and redo it—hours of work. But because Phrixos was alive inside of Corvus and had chosen to manifest as something that looked just like the monster she had created, all it took was a little water sponged across his face and chest.

He pressed his hand over hers as she wiped a droplet of false blood from his cheek. The leaves of his face crinkled under her hand, not dry as fallen leaves, more like living leather. He pushed his face against her palm.

Scarves of red, yellow, and orange energy shimmered up around her, hovered around both of them.

"What the hell are you doing?" Neil demanded, his naturally loud voice even louder than usual.

The ground was alive with the exhalations of something that breathed out color and light. The air vibrated with anxious anticipation. Phrixos snaked his arm around Opal's waist and pulled her close. Light danced around them.

"Stop that! You're screwing up everything! What's with all this light? I didn't authorize that shit! Stop—oh, damn it, roll cameras."

Phrixos turned his face and kissed her palm. His tongue left a hot wet firekiss in the center. Slowly, he drew her hand from his face, pulled her up against him, lifted her from her feet. Her fireskin tightened all around her as colors sheeted up in plumes and sprays, fountains of light, the ground alive under her feet and pulsing hypnotically. Sparkles and streamers of light curled around them, sent questing fingers to stroke her, only to stub against her shield. Then the fireskin flexed and melted, fled into the air to dance with all the other colors of fire.

Other Opal opened golden eyes inside her and smiled, grew from an idea into an inhabiter, stretched out to fill Opal's skin, tingling in the fingertips and toes, a stitchery of silvery mesh under the surface. She pushed into Phrixos's embrace, sought his mouth against hers, and the energy from underground, the fire in Phrixos that had burned others, rose up to wrap them in heat, cinnamon and ginger, saffron and bittersweet, peach and henna, heedless of everything around them. He tasted of milk flavored with Indian spices, cardamom, nutmeg.

"This is what he left in us," Other Opal whispered to Opal. "A door." She wrapped their arms around Phrixos, embracing everything he was and wasn't. For the first time, she opened herself wide to him, and he came in, unrestrained now, flooding through her like shadowed water, drawing her to mingle with him. He laughed aloud, startled by who she had become since he escaped her. Other Opal shoved at him, and he encompassed the push, still laughing.

"I like this you better," he said.

She shoved him again, but ended up laughing, too, then pulled him back into a kiss, let herself disappear into the heat.

14

When Opal opened her eyes to the outside world again, she was lying on the altar. Night sky was above, beyond the reach of the banks of lights that shone full on her and on Phrixos, who lay across her, his arms around her, his leathery, leafy face against her cheek. Glow still surrounded them, hazy, golden and green.

The eyes of the cameras watched them.

She took a breath.

The one under the ground had sent Phrixos out as scout and envoy, point man and first negotiator in this latest of its ventures into the world above. All these people had moved willingly into its orbit, with only the most tenuous of invitations. They had danced on its head and let it taste them. They had come bringing treasures. Nourishment, playthings, converts.

Opal blinked, glanced around. Everyone she could see looked stunned and strange. She heard the muffled machinery of filming. People were scattered amongst the lights, cameras, tracks, boom mikes, all the hidden structures associated with capturing a momentary fall of light. Those who manned the machines seemed to still be on the job, though they looked blank, not present. None of them looked like themselves.

She pushed Phrixos back so she could sit up. He was limp, spent, still smiling, asleep or comatose, dead weight across her legs, a huge lump of flesh. She was naked. She touched his chest, made sure he was still breathing. She leaned forward, smelled the cinnamon on his breath, felt warmth under her palm when she laid it against his cheek.

She wasn't sure she wanted him to wake, so she eased out from under him and slipped off the rock. She leaned against the altar stone and tried to get her bearings.

She had been out of her mind, drowned in fire and water, lost to thought. Had they fucked? In front of the cameras? Apparently they had. Her coverall lay draped across the top of the altar, and her underwear had disappeared. She straightened, retrieved her coverall and stepped into it, carefully zipped up so she wouldn't snag her skin or anything else. She felt awash and sticky with the secretions of someone else, invaded, unalone, colonized. There was a salt taste in her mouth, a wet heat still between her legs, an uncomfortable itch and burn. She had a sense of incomplete separation; he was still inside her, though not physically; or he had left his flag planted, or some other sign of occupation: threads of him woven into her fabric, things he could call to that would open a door in her and invite him back.

"Rod? Magenta?" she said. She glanced at the nearest cameraman. "Ben?" He didn't even blink. "Neil?" She looked for the director. People stood all around the altar, with vacant faces and staring eyes, many in states of undress. Those who still wore clothes didn't seem at home in them; shirts were untucked, zippers not zipped, buttons in various states of joining with buttonholes, or not. Many went barefoot. Some were frozen in the act of coupling. Everywhere she looked, people were paused, trapped, as though she had arrived between one moment and the next.

Neil was nowhere nearby.

Magenta edged out from behind the backdrop, held onto the edge of the fake-forest-photographed cloth as though ready to flee. "Is it over?"

"What happened?" Opal asked.

"I don't know. It was hard to see through all that crazy special effects stuff. Light and magic. I thought they put that in afterwards now, but man! It was intense!"

"The light?" Opal asked.

"Yeah, it was everywhere, like fog. It kind of—people sucked it in their mouths, you know? Even little Gemma, she tried to run from it, but it followed her and got in her face until she had to breathe it. It came at me, too, but—I don't know. Maybe that shield you gave me? I didn't breathe any of it in."

"Oh. Oh. Good," said Opal. "So everybody else got caught in the light? Then what?"

"It was like they had a script. They were acting it out, like the coveners in the film, except the people running the lights, camera, and sound—they stayed on the job. The rest of them, all of them got into some kind of chanting and dancing, and you guys up there, too, kind of, dancing, and getting naked, and—did you know he was allover leaves? I sure didn't see you do that to him in the Makeup trailer."

"I got naked?" Of course she had. No use trying to deny it. Where had her mind gone?

"Uh-huh. I, uh, well. Didn't think I should watch that part, but I couldn't look away. Anyway, you two weren't the only ones. There was a lot of that going around, only nobody was home in their heads." She looked toward the forest. "I tried to stop Rod. I called his name, I pulled on his shirt. He acted like I was invisible! Off he went in the crowd."

"The girls?" Opal whispered.

Magenta licked her lips. "They, uh." She pointed toward the forest. "The girls ran off, but they had those blank eyes, too. There was so much going on I couldn't keep track of everybody. That Evil Guardian Witch of Bettina's, she was in the thick of the crew cluster, but Gemma's mom kind of panicked. She hid in one of the trailers. And then just now all those lights faded and everybody stopped. Then you're awake, but nobody else is. Huh?"

"What happened?" Opal muttered to herself. She reached out with hands and mind to feel where the energy lay. What had possessed her? Who was she now? She sketched a mirror in the air and stared into her own eyes, reassured by their violet color, then flicked it away and took in a breath, tasting for information.

"What did you just do?" Magenta asked. Focused elsewhere, Opal glanced toward her, and Magenta said, "Never mind."

The ground was quiet, the people absent inside themselves, maybe, except Magenta, whom Opal could now see was outlined in Flint's familiar flame.

"I need to think," Opal told Magenta.

"What am I supposed to do? If I try to wake people up, will it hurt them? I don't want to be here all alone."

"You're safe here," Opal said. "You have a magic shield, and it works."

"But—" Magenta looked around at a world on pause. "Nobody's themselves. What if they—You don't know. It was so crazy before. Where did it all go? They ought to be tired after what they did. Why aren't they sleeping?"

"I can't answer you until I figure out what just happened. I need to think."

"But—Oh, dammit, go ahead, then," said Magenta. She sagged in one of the chairs.

Opal sat in Corvus's chair, hugged herself, closed her eyes, went inside to see what she could learn.

Golden-eyed Shadow Opal sat on a couch in the mental study with a big cup of hot chocolate. She smiled and stretched out a hand toward the fire, which reached from the fireplace and wound through her fingers. "Have fun, honey?" she asked.

"I don't know. Did I?"

"Oh, yes, you did, in ways you never have before."

"Why did we do that? What happened?"

"Part of it was just letting go of all those wrappings you keep around your talents and your heart. Do you *ever* remember having fun, Opal?"

"Lots of times."

"Like?"

"Taking the kids to the county fair."

"Hands to hold, noses to wipe, vomit to clean up, children to keep track of, everybody asking for money, none of them happy for very long."

"Taking the kids to the beach."

"Sunburn, sand in their swimsuits, salt water in their eyes, always watching to make sure they're not drowning themselves or each other. Who carried the cooler? Who made all the sandwiches? Who shook the sand out of the towels at the end of the day? Who took the blame when we got home late because Flint ran off and got lost?"

"Bathing the kids. Tucking them in at night. Some of that was really—"

Shadow Opal waited for her to finish, and Opal inexplicably found herself in tears.

"You had tender moments," said Shadow Opal after Opal had rubbed her eyes without managing to stop the tears. "That's not the same as fun."

"When I was working on *Dead Loss*—when Corvus and I first met—"

"You focused on the job. Did you ever notice he asked you out for drinks after work? You always said no."

"He asked me out?"

"Six times. You filter out anything that might be fun. I'm tired of that."

"So you—so *we*—find ourselves on *Girls Gone Wild*? Scratch that—put ourselves there on purpose?"

Golden-eyed Opal looked past her. "Wilder than that," she muttered, "and oh, it was delicious. Delightful. Astonishing. He has powers he hasn't shown you yet, and he's part of a larger community here, with its own agenda. You weren't there, though. You still didn't have fun. You abdicated while I made you these memories."

"You made memories?"

"They're here." Shadow Opal glanced toward the study door. "Want to see?"

Opal shuddered, then shook herself like a dog shaking off water and headed for the door. Shadow Opal opened it for her and led the way into the hall beyond. They traveled down a hall that got darker and narrower as they went. At its very end was a thick steel door barricaded with bolts, bars, and locks.

"You're good at this sort of thing," said Shadow Opal.

Opal put her hand on a padlock the size of a pumpkin, with a cartoonishly large keyhole. "I did this?"

"You've got a lot of doors like this scattered around. Lots of things you don't want out roaming, I guess. I don't know how I got out."

"How do I open it?"

"Give me a key."

"A key?" Opal looked down at what she was wearing. The same olive green denim coverall she had just shrugged into back in the real world, with lots of pockets, and black boots. She pushed her hands into the pockets, pulled things out. Tape, scissors, lip gloss, a tin of Altoid peppermints, a Swiss Army knife, six quarters and two shiny pennies, a packet of airline pretzels, a wad of Kleenex. A pad of paper, a telescoping pen, two paper clips.

"Close enough," said Other Opal. She took a paper clip, held it in her closed hand, produced a skeleton key. "Are you ready?"

"No," said Opal, "but go ahead."

Other Opal touched the key to the locks—she didn't even have to turn it. They snapped open one by one. Finally the door was no longer locked. Other Opal stood back. She gestured toward the doorknob. "Your turn."

Opal gripped the doorknob, turned it, opened the door, and looked in at the altar in the forest.

Everything about the scene was different from the way it had been when she'd awakened. Here, the forest was a wilderness of strange, exotic trees, with leaves the shapes of violins, harps, hearts, arrowheads. The greens shone in many vibrant shades, and the tree bark was rich colors as well, red brown, cream yellow, slivers of peeling, textured silver. The altar glowed with gray light. A version of Opal stood on it, embraced by a version of Corvus in his Dark God shell. Phrixos's energy wasn't there. Opal stood rigid on the stone, though wrapped in his embrace. No one else was present.

"Relax," said the Dark God, in Corvus's beloved voice, the voice she had listened to many nights as she fell asleep, audiobooks that murmured to her in different hotel rooms, the voices of different characters, all, somehow, contained inside Corvus and let out to play. "Let go, Opal. Let go."

She watched her other self melt. The starch leached out of Opal on the altar, and she leaned against Corvus's chest. His arms supported her. His head dipped so he could speak near her ear. His voice softened; still, she heard every word.

"You don't have to be in charge. You don't have to take care of everyone but yourself. Let me take care of you," he whispered, and she melted more. Her eyes closed. Her mouth smiled.

He eased her down onto the rock, cupping the back of her head so that it didn't bump. He held himself above her, stared down at her face. "Let me hold you. Let me be in you. Let me be part of you."

Opal on the altar let him do all those things, moaning with delight. Her fingers unclenched, her shoulders eased, her body lay boneless, as though she no longer had to hold up the world. Her face relaxed into bliss. It lost the rigid look of someone who knows who she is.

Opal turned away, headed toward the door back into the hallway, but Shadow Opal gripped her shoulders and turned her to face the altar again. "Stop running away," she said. "Stop standing aside. Be there." Shadow Opal pressed on her shoulders, and Opal found herself compressing, deflating, narrowing into something not herself until she was something her other self could hold between her hands. Shadow Opal pressed her palms together, and Opal felt a disorienting upending of the world, a shriek of colors, a breeze brushing tastes against her, a swirl of scents, and then she blinked eyes open and looked up into Corvus's face, the monster she had made and grown to fear and love. His eyes glowed with green light around pupils slit up and down like a cat's. He closed them and pressed close, and then his lips touched hers and she gave herself up to that sense, his heat and pressure and tenderness, gentle in everything he did; he had buried himself in her, but he held himself up enough to not crush her; he had to tilt to reach her mouth, but he managed, despite his length. Something of the god worked in him to make it possible, and everything about him embraced her, made her feel safe in a way she could never remember feeling before.

She wanted to laugh, and she wanted to cry. How strange it felt, being here, at the mercy of someone else, having let loose of all the things she usually kept track of, her lists of things she needed, things she planned to do, things she would check to make sure everyone else around her had what they needed and knew what they were going to do next.

Most of her work was preparing. She spent hours setting

up the makeup and tools she used for her job, even though she could have worked faster and better without them. She planned ahead, usually, so she would be where she needed to be in plenty of time. Cars she drove never ran out of gas, and if she had to change a tire she always had a well-inflated spare. When she cooked, which she only did if she were expecting company, she had all the ingredients and instructions ahead of time and never missed a step.

She had spun webs of control around everything she touched.

A vision from Christmas vacation came to her.

Mother might not remember the strings she had threaded through everything and everyone around her, but the image of it was clear in Opal's memory, a horrifying truth revealed by her sister's magic during a family meeting: their mother had bound her children, husband, relatives up in magic threads that trapped them in the family home; only Opal had escaped. She had moved out into the world and spun threads of her own.

Opal opened her hands and let go of all those controls.

She opened her heart, let it lie revealed, unprotected. Corvus's whispers as he embraced her nudged her heart, as he drove into her, nested inside her. The edge of pain and yearning that rode him bumped into her heart, touched her own longing for something she had never yet found, wove into it. She found herself up against his heart as well, a large mass of all the colors of amber spiderwebbed in silver and gold, pulsing, with many chambers, slivers of secrets and wonders, memories and wounds, slender syllables of bliss and tiny grains of pain.

She slipped her hand inside his heart, let things flow across her palms and along her fingers. She tasted loneliness, longing, tenderness, fear. Solitude: long stretches of solitude.

"What are you doing?" he whispered. He had stilled above her and within her. His forehead rested on her cheek.

"I don't know," she said. Why had she thought it was his heart she touched? It wasn't shaped like any heart she had ever seen in an anatomy chart, or even in horror movies where people ripped the hearts out of each other's chests. She turned her inward vision toward what she had been thinking of as her own heart, and saw a landscape of walls. She went toward the first wall, looking for a door, but she couldn't find one, so she climbed up the wall—it had things sticking out of it, sharp things, but she found a way up them without cutting her feet.

Why did she have feet, she wondered, when she was shifting across impossible landscapes? There was no reason she should be one form or another. She paused, standing on a wall in her own heart, and thought, usually I work with surfaces; but I have practiced greater shifts. I have turned my siblings into objects of convenience on occasion, though not often, and not after they got their own powers. I have changed myself in all kinds of ways, sometimes so much that I had trouble remembering what my previous form was. Now I want to be something that can fly above walls and see beyond them.

She stared down at hands that looked like the hands she wore in waking life, then glanced down at her breasts, her front, her legs beyond the slope of her stomach. She was naked now, three steps away from the coverall-dressed self she had been and still another step from the physical body she wore in the waking world. How many layers down was she? She had left Corvus in midquestion, but it was Corvus in memory, not in real life; she could pause a memory without upsetting anybody, surely.

Shift, she thought, and she turned into winged mist, a thin and less connected-to-itself creature. *Eyes,* she thought after a moment's blind confusion, and she grew several eyes. She looked up, down, forward, backward, inward at the same time. It took a while to integrate all the visions into a coherent picture. The color of the sky had changed from standard blue to scarves of varied colors, blue, green, shades and nuances. Seeing many directions at once, vision was a three-dimensional experience. She was enveloped in sight the way she would be embraced by warm water in a hot spring.

She hovered above the courtyard protected by the first wall and saw a pale statue of a child in the center. The child had blind white eyes and short curls. It gazed toward the ground, its mouth in a faint frown, brows drawn together above its nose. The cloud that Opal was drifted closer to the child, saw her own features on the statue. Another younger, frozen self. She rose again and headed inward across the landscape toward another walled fortress. This one had a roof over it, but when she flew closer, she found that there were chinks in its armor; she flowed in through one of them and found herself in a chamber. Light shone in through the stained-glass walls, a mosaic of many different colors of red and dark orange, ruby, crimson, rust, coral, salmon, sunset colors. In the center of the chamber, on mounded velvet cloth, nestled a red jewel—or if it were a paler color, she couldn't tell, because the colored light coming through the walls and striking gleams off its faceted surface stained everything it touched.

She drifted down to the jewel. How vulnerable it was to anything in mist form. She had built all these walls, but did they really protect her? In this landscape, people could be so many other ways than merely human-shaped. She had protected herself so far, though—or had she? She and her shadow had still not found out where Phrixos had gone or what he had done while she held him inside, and now she was layers deep into herself and didn't know how to navigate.

She touched the red jewel. Passion flared through her, washed her up out of the walled landscape, back into Corvus's arms.

"Stop slipping away," he whispered. He braced her and

pumped into her, and it sent her spasming over the edge into complete loss of control.

He smiled when she came back to herself. "How was that?"

"Terrifying."

He kissed her, his lips soft. "Was anything about it good?"

"Are you fishing for compliments?" she asked, strangely detached from what had happened, but not outside of it anymore.

"No. I'm trying to learn you. Maybe next time I'll do better."

"Corr. This isn't even real. I don't think you're real. I don't know where we are, but look at these trees . . ." She lifted her head and looked, then gasped. She was back out in the real world, on the altar, with people and cameras all around them, and some of the people were waking up.

"I don't claim to be an authority on reality," he murmured, "but—"

15

"What the *hell* has happened to my production?" screamed the director, rising from a tangle of bodies in various states of clothed and unclothed just beyond the trees that ringed the clearing on the far side of the altar. "You! Put your pants on! Oh my gawd. Where are *my* pants? Oh my gawd. Where's the damned publicist? Someone lock her up before any of this gets out! What—"

"Say, boss," said George. "Is this a classic case of dope in the water or what?"

No one spoke. Neil found his clothes and hurried into them, as did anybody else who could locate what they or someone else had been wearing before the big meltdown. "All right," Neil said at last. "Dope in the water supply. That could work. Might even be true. Sabotage! Damage control . . . Loaders, I'm confiscating all the film we shot since—Juanita, when did you stop taking notes?" he asked the script supervisor, who was struggling to tie her hair back into a knot at the nape of her neck. It turned out she had a wealth of sleek dark hair, long enough to reach her hips. Opal had never seen her disarrayed before; she was in charge of keeping track of everything about the script—what was written before they filmed, what lines and angles changed in the course of filming, what time everything happened, and which take it happened on. She always wore her hair wadded at the back of her neck, with a baseball cap on top of her head.

Juanita buttoned her pants, tracked down her clipboard and a couple of pens from a scatter of things in the grass, then checked her watch. "Um," she said. "We had just finished take nine, scene twelve C, reaction shots to Mom's death. Another splatter misfire. One forty-five point thirty seconds. Three hours ago, boss. God."

"Everyone? Everyone, listen to me absolutely. You are gagged about this. Talk about it and risk being blacklisted. We have to figure out what happened. We have to . . . we have to examine the film for clues. No one who wasn't here is to know what happened. Understand?"

"But boss—"

"What *did* happen?"

"Who's going to pay for it?"

"Some of us are working overtime now," said one of the teamsters with satisfaction.

"If you call what just happened work!" Neil cried.

"Are you gonna?" asked someone else.

Neil growled, and then said, "That's enough for tonight! To your scattered domiciles go, you wretches! Where's my call sheet? Where's my A.D.s? We're going to have to redo the schedule for tomorrow, and you've got to let everyone know once we finalize it. The rest of you, clean up and clear out. Get off the damned clock!"

Continuity came by the set and shot pictures of everything there. Opal closed her eyes; Corvus lay quietly over her, shielding her from sight while keeping himself up on his elbows enough not to crush her. Her hand had settled just above his hip, and she left it there. The skin of leaves over him covered him everywhere. As Magenta had said, that wasn't something Opal had ever put on him. Phrixos must have arranged it. Where was *he*?

People moved, shutting down equipment, turning off lights, wrapping set pieces in waterproof protection for the night. Still, Opal and Corvus lay entwined, the center of the scene as lights shut off, generators powered down, and people moved around them, eyes lowered. People still surreptitiously searched for lost articles of clothing and equipment.

"Hey," said someone nearby. Opal opened her eyes and found Kelsi standing beside the altar. "Brought you some wardrobe." She held up a big black robe, one of Dark God's standard outfits, and a white covener's robe.

"Thanks, hon," said Corvus. "Could you drape the black thing over me? Maybe I can get up and wrap it around both of us. Not the first time I've been glad I have such loose robes for this role."

Opal tried to remember what she had been wearing before the forest took over. Before she let it take over.

One of her green denim coveralls with lots of pockets, and those black boots. She could not remember getting out of her clothes again, but she'd been walking between several worlds. She wondered who she had left in charge of the body. She rolled her head and looked around as much as she could. No sign of her clothes.

Corvus rose, draped in black, pulled her up with him, edged awkwardly around until they were both sitting on the altar with scarves of black lapped around them from behind. Opal glanced down at her body and saw stone scrapes, bruising, bite marks she didn't remember from the sex she had just had, awake, with Corvus, where everything had been a kind of gentle she wasn't used to in sexual encounters. The marks must have happened during the earlier sex, when Other

Opal was running things, and maybe Phrixos was around. If they got all that on tape—

She rubbed her face, reached inside for the healing she used to apply to scrapes and bruises on her siblings until they came into their own powers, and later, something she had practiced on the sly on various movie shoots. Usually on other people, not so much on herself. She didn't take these kinds of risks.

Kelsi stretched up and handed her the white robe, and she shrugged out of Corvus's embrace and slid it on, even as her skin repaired itself and bruised flesh healed. Power came easily. What had just happened hadn't drained her. She wanted to go back to her study and check how much Flintfire she had left, how much power her Sifter Chants had stored for her, but then she decided maybe she better come into the world for now and see what needed doing.

She wanted to figure out what had happened in the clearing, not just to her, but to everyone. What had the thing under the ground accomplished, and why? Had they fulfilled its desire, or was this just the beginning? It must have wanted all that energy for some reason, all that procreative power. She didn't know much about major ritual workings—that was not magic as her family practiced magic—but she had heard stories.

"Thanks, Kelsi," Opal said as she belted the white robe. "What happened to you?"

Kelsi's gaze dropped. Her head drooped. "I, uh," she said, and red flushed across her forehead and cheeks.

"Sorry," said Opal. "Shouldn't have asked. I guess everybody knows what happened to me and Corr, huh?"

"Not all of us were paying attention."

"Oh. Right." Opal looked up at Corvus's face, but he was staring past her toward the trucks. People were striking everything strikable. The security guards had arrived for the night so that they didn't have to move all the equipment back to the parking lot by the old supermarket. The guards looked confused.

"Better get to the Makeup trailer and take this off," Corvus said, stroking a cheek leaf.

"Right," said Opal. She led the way across the battered grass to the trailer, part of her mind wondering if the girls, Gemma and Bettina, had made it back from wherever they had gone when the wave of orgy energy hit. Maybe they had done things that would scar them for life under the influence of it. Opal hadn't done much memory mending, but she knew there were charms for it.

Uncle Tobias was supposed to arrive tonight. He could help. In fact—she checked her watch, then remembered she didn't know what time to expect him.

In the Makeup trailer, Rod and Magenta had closed up their stations and were gone. The trailer was dark except for a nightlight by Opal's station. Corvus settled into the big chair and Opal turned on more lights, snapped Polaroids of his head and shoulders and dropped them haphazard on the counter. "Does it even come off anymore?" she muttered to herself as she approached Corvus with her solvents. She wondered again what had become of Phrixos.

Corvus pulled his arms out of the robe and studied his chest and arms, leaved all over. These leaves weren't the ones she had applied to him at the start of the workday. They hadn't come off during the day, despite strenuous contact with other surfaces, including the altar stone and her. A memory of the leaves against her skin, rough, strange, smelling of autumn, abrading her like the scales of a dragon, chased through her mind and vanished.

She loaded a makeup sponge with solvent and lifted it, ready to press it against Corvus's chest. "Shed, skin," she whispered. She tugged gently at the edge of a leaf, and the leaf skin split and slid beneath her fingers, baring Corvus's chest, its halves sliding off him like silk to pool around the chair in heaps. Detached, the leaves looked like net fabric painted with color, dull and dark on the inside. It was like nothing she had ever worked with.

"Wow," she said. She touched his face. "Shed, skin," she whispered again, and the mask split down along the middle of his forehead, the spine of his nose, the philtrum beneath, the middle of his mouth, the cleft in his chin. It fell apart in two soft halves and pooled above his shoulders against the back of the chair. She gathered the halves and placed them on her plaster cast of his head, where they welded together and formed the face he had just worn.

She looked back at Corvus, restored to his nonmonster face, his smile steady, his hair rumpled, a few leaves still caught in it. He looked like her Corvus, except for the resident green glow in his eyes.

"Phrixos," she whispered.

He smiled at her with Corvus's tenderness, then rose and stretched, settled his robe on his shoulders again. "It's been an interesting day," he said, in Corvus's voice. "A pleasurable day, a profitable day in so many ways."

"What did you do to us?"

"What did I do? People did what they wanted. I just gave them an atmosphere of permission, maybe a few nudges in the right direction."

She shook her head. "No, I can't believe everybody wanted to do that."

"Why not?"

She flipped through memories, not all of them clear, of people in positions she'd never seen people in in real life, faces taut with pain or pleasure, the chant some of them chanted— nonsense words, or maybe not; words she didn't understand. Maybe they had all done what they wanted. But if that was the truth, why had they fled, shamefaced, afterward?

"Why did you do it?" she asked.

He looked at her then, and she saw that he was completely Phrixos, though he had all of Corvus in his gaze and look, the parts of Corvus he hadn't been able to successfully mimic before, tenderness and wry humor, sweetness, a self-effacing air despite his size.

A shadow self hovered above him, huge, glittering, and beautiful. It radiated power and satisfaction.

The ground? She had thought the ground was quiet, but now she realized it was warm, almost hot, with a long, slow pulse.

"We were starving, sleeping, hibernating with no spring promised," Phrixos said. "We lay here like husks a long long time, dreaming of waking. The girl came, the one who makes stories, with her promises of bringing others. She let us into her dreams. She listened to our story and took it out into the world. She told others and enlisted them into the service of the story." He glanced around the trailer, nodded toward the location beyond the walls. He spread his hands, as though to indicate everything about the production. "Many people work to make the story take form. Now we are awake again."

Opal pulled the covener's robe tighter around herself and stared at the man in front of her. "You gave Bethany the first draft of the script?" she said.

"She used her own skills to shape it, but we gave her dreams to draw from."

"The script is full of blood and terror and death."

Phrixos shrugged. "She seemed to think it needed it."

"So—no one has to die on the altar to satsify you in real life?"

"You and I have already done the necessary ritual there. Several times."

"But you used Lauren's blood, and Erika's—"

"Blood has its own power. I do seek and treasure it. There are some doors it is a key to unlock."

"What did you do to the inside of my head?" Other Opal had told her one thing about that—that he had left his own door into her there. Was that all? Maybe it was plenty.

He smiled and pulled the black robe up to cover his shoulders. "There are other hungers," he said, pressing a hand to his stomach. "Let's get something to eat."

"What did you do to Corvus?" she asked.

"Did anyone ever tell you you worry too much?"

"Worrying is an integral part of my character," she said, "so yeah, people tell me that all the time, but it doesn't change what I do. What did you do to Corvus?"

"I ate him."

"What?" she cried.

"Get your things and let's go." He nudged her shoulder.

She glanced around, frantic, wondering which spells to invoke to make Phrixos tell her the truth. If he had actually eaten Corvus, was there any way she could save him? Make Phrixos regurgitate him, the way Chronos had been tricked into coughing up his Greek god children after he had swallowed them? Was Corvus even still alive? Phrixos was full of power from what had happened in the clearing. Opal wasn't sure she could force him into anything.

"Kidding," said Phrixos. "Come on, let's get out of here."

Opal swallowed her terror and chose to believe him so she could focus on practical matters. She locked up her supplies, including the strange new leaf skin Phrixos had shed, grabbed her messenger bag, and followed him out of the trailer, turning off lights as she went.

She locked the door and glanced around. Most of the crew had driven away; a few were still packing up equipment. "The girls," she said. Worry flared, the same kind of worry she used to spend on all her younger siblings. "Magenta? Doreen?" Magenta had said Doreen, Gemma's mother, was hiding in one of the trailers.

Magenta had said that to Opal the first time Opal woke

up. She had had her clothes then. Gone inside herself, and awakened again in the real world, back on the altar. A time jog had happened, or something else. "How many times did we—were you always out here?" she asked Phrixos.

"No," he said. "Sometimes I was in two places at once. You took me with you."

"There's a clear piece of time in the middle of it all when Magenta and I were awake and everyone else was still under the influence."

"Yes," he said.

"When I woke up again—"

"It was fun, wasn't it?"

"You're gloating. I hate gloaters."

He smiled, stroked his hand down her hair. She jerked out from under his caress and strode toward the crew corral. It was deserted. The canvas-backed chairs with the names on them had been packed. Opal found Doreen's yarn bag in the half-crushed grass, with its crochet projects inside. Knitting needles might have made noise during takes, so Doreen had been teaching herself this new skill.

"I used to have clothes," Opal muttered, abandoning the bag. "What happened to my damned clothes?"

More important than clothes, what had happened to the young actresses? Into her mind rushed a spell she had often used as a teenage mother surrogate, a Locate-Lost-Objects Cantrip, because the kids were always losing things, and they got in deep trouble if the things were important and stayed lost. She visualized Gemma and whispered the spell. A thin thread of silver faded into view in the air before her, leading toward the forest. She raced off along the line, stumbling as she left the lighted clearing and headed into the trees.

No sound followed her, but she felt his presence behind her, Phrixos, a large displacement of space, a traveling nexus of energies. The thread led her past bushes and under branches, over roots and rocks. Some small animal startled out of her path, the sudden rustle of it scaring her so she stumbled, but he reached from behind and steadied her. She stilled, her elbow cupped in his hand, and paused to listen to the night, the diminishing racket of the animal crashing away, an owl calling from farther, and the sound of the stream. The night was damp and smelled of fallen leaves. In the still, she suddenly realized her feet were bare and battered, that she'd stubbed her toe against a rock. Pain signals flared, all the feelings she had blocked in her sudden panicked desire to find the children. Her calves were scratched and bleeding.

She muttered, set healing in motion, stood with the warmth of his fingers braceleting her elbow.

The crickets started up again, a song she had interrupted by running.

"They're all right," he said.

She was angry all over again that he could use Corvus's voice so well she couldn't tell the difference. "Whose definition of all right are you using?"

"Good point."

She pulled her arm out of his grasp and started forward again, slower this time. She flicked a small greenish globe of witchlight from her fingers so she could see where to put her feet down.

The silver seek-thread shimmered in the darkness ahead of her. It led her, eventually, to a nest of dried ferns and damp earth, where the two girls, still in their special ritual dresses, all tatters now, were curled up in each other's arms, their faces and arms smudged, their hair full of twigs, their breathing slow and steady.

Phrixos stood beside her as she stared down at the sleeping girls.

"They weren't part of it?" she asked.

"Not really."

"What does that mean?"

"The energy affected them, but I sent them away from it."
Now he spoke in a distant voice, the voice of someone else,
not Corvus nor Phrixos, someone she hadn't met. The glittering shadow she had seen hovering above him when she first
woke up.

"Why?"

"I knew you wouldn't like it," said the stranger.

"You care what I think?"

"You're a key element," it said. "I wish to keep you happy."

Good news and bad. She didn't necessarily want to be a
key, but if it wanted to keep her happy, maybe she had lever-
age. "Who are you?"

"I was asleep and now I'm wide awake, thanks to everything you've done for me." He stroked a hand along her
shoulder, down her back, trailing warmth and pleasure.

Creepy. She knelt and touched Gemma's shoulder. Gemma's
face contracted into a frown. She rubbed her cheek against
Bettina's shoulder, frowned again, and opened her eyes.
"What?" she asked, as though puzzled by everything. She
rubbed her eyes with dirty fists, then stared at Bettina's an-
gelic sleeping face so close to her own. She glanced around,
found and fixed on Opal's face. "What's going on?" This time,
her voice had sharpened into confusion and dismay.

"Lots," said Opal. "Strange things happened to everyone.
You and Bettina went off in the woods. Can you get up?"
Opal touched Bettina's shoulder. "Bettina?"

Bettina burrowed deeper into the hollow where she lay,
hunched her shoulders and hid her face.

"Bettina," Opal repeated. "It's dark and cold. I should get
you back to your hotel, or wherever you're staying. Wouldn't
you like a hot bath?"

Bettina slowly turned toward them. Her face showed traces
of muddy tears. She opened her eyes. A new tear ran down into
her hair. "I would like that above all things," she whispered.

Gemma sat up. She worked her legs free of Bettina's skirts, rested her hand on Bettina's shoulder. "Let's get out of here."

Bettina nodded, mashing her crinkled hair against the damp earth. She let Gemma pull her upright. She and Gemma worked together to scramble out of the hole they were in. Phrixos reached down and helped haul them to their feet. "You will never," Bettina said in a low voice to Gemma, "tell a soul what we did. Ever."

"What did we do?" Gemma asked. "I fell asleep and had really weird dreams. God, where are we?" She turned her head, glancing at the darkening forest around them.

"We're a ways into the forest." Opal touched the witchfire ball with a finger, fed it more energy so that it brightened enough to light the ground for a few feet in all directions. She lifted it so it hung in the air just above their heads, though not so high as Phrixos's head. "Let's go back."

"What's that thing?" Gemma asked in a flattened voice.

"Special effects," said Opal.

Phrixos strode in front of them, the light at his back, coating his robe with soft greenish yellow color. The two girls held hands as they walked just ahead of Opal. She didn't think they even knew.

As they forged toward the clearing, she said her cantrip again, this time focusing on Doreen. A slender thread of rose pink led toward Doreen; Opal broke away from Phrixos and the girls and followed her thread. It led to one of the crew Porta-Johns. The door was locked. Opal knocked several times and got no answer, so at last she unlocked the door with a tiny push, another skill she'd honed while caring for her siblings, though she'd only seriously used it a few times. Usually, she figured that if they were hiding, they needed to hide, not be found. Once in a while, necessity had pushed her.

"Doreen," she murmured. She opened the door half a foot. "Doreen?"

The door pulled out of her hand, opening wider. Doreen sat on the floor, a miserable ball, her eyes puffy, her face stained with salt tear tracks, her hair greasy as though sweaty hands had stroked through it too many times. She groaned and climbed to her feet.

"Whore," she said.

Opal flinched, straightened. She thought about what had happened that afternoon and wondered who and what she really was. Had she had any control over events? Had she given control away? She had definitely had sex in public, which was pretty skanky, but . . . "It had nothing to do with money," she said at last.

"Not you," said Doreen. "Well, you, but . . ." She ran her fingers through her hair again, pulled herself together. "God, I need a bath. A shower. Another bath."

"Mom?" Gemma said, tentative.

"Gemma! Oh my god! Are you all right?" Doreen came out of the Porta-John and reached for her daughter, who flinched and backed away, pulling Bettina with her. The girls still held hands; it was as if they didn't know how to disconnect.

"I'm fine," Gemma said, and held up her free hand in a "stop" gesture.

"Did you—where were you when—are you going to need therapy?" Doreen asked.

"Oh, who doesn't," said Bettina, her voice acid.

"Whatever it was, I kind of slept through it," Gemma said. She looked around. The clearing and the waiting area were trashed in some strange ways, but empty of people. Most of the equipment had been put away for the night. "What happened?"

"Thank God for small mercies," said Doreen.

"You really don't remember any of it?" asked Bettina.

"Why? What do you remember?"

Bettina's gaze went to their linked hands. She bit her lower lip. Her brow furrowed, and she said, "Well, I shan't tell you now. I wonder what it means in the long run. Perhaps nothing, if it wasn't as real for you as it was for me."

"But, on a more immediate note . . ." Opal glanced around. "It looks like everybody left. Or maybe they're hiding. I have a car. Doreen, did you drive yourself, or do the three of you want a ride somewhere? Phrixos and I were going to supper."

"After everything that's happened, you're going to eat?" Doreen asked, outraged. Her stomach rumbled and she glanced toward it. Her eyebrows rose. "Oh."

"Has anyone seen Rica?" asked Bettina. "I can't remember the last time I saw her."

Opal said, "Do you want me to find her now? I'll need something of hers. I don't know her well enough to track her."

"What are you, psychic or something?" Bettina said.

"Something," said Opal, as Gemma said, "She found Mom, didn't she?"

"Good grief, that's right." Bettina bit her bottom lip, swung Gemma's hand. "Well, I suppose I don't really want to find Rica. I suppose I hope she's all right. If what happened to her is the same as what happened to everyone else, I wish I'd had a camera. Pictures would be worth a lot in our future relationship."

"Eww," said Gemma.

"If you can drive us to our B&B, that would be good," Doreen told Opal. "I did drive myself and Gemma to the location this morning, but now it looks like my car is gone."

Bettina said, "May I stay with you two? I don't want to go back to my room alone."

"Okay," said Gemma, then glanced at her mother.

Doreen nodded, her face pale. "I don't want you to be alone, either."

Opal led the way to the Lincoln. Everyone piled in. She

didn't think she should let the girls and Doreen go without making sure they were all right, but she didn't know what to do for them. She was still appalled and confused about what to do for herself.

Doreen, her voice tired, directed Opal to another early-twentieth-century house in town, where the girls and the woman got out and slammed the car doors without saying good-bye.

"What do you think?" she asked Phrixos after they had sat in silence, parked outside the B&B. "Where do we go next?"

He smiled down at her. "Back to the nexus?"

"Is that the altar?"

"Yes. We could go back and add to the work we've started. We are close to completing all the necessary steps."

She didn't want to know about steps, or where they led. "I don't want to go back. I'm dirty and tired and hungry. The choices are your place or mine." She thought about running into Neil at the bed-and-breakfast. He'd been pretty mad when the confusion wore off. It was possible he would blame her for everything. He wasn't pleasant at the best of times. "Scratch that. We're going to my hotel."

"Do you have clothes for me there?"

"Nope, but I've got clothes for me. I can make clothes for you. I have an industrial-strength shower, too."

"You've made up your mind."

"I have." She started the car and they drove back to the hotel in silence.

The front desk clerk in the lobby opened his mouth to speak when he saw them, but they pushed past to the elevators without giving him time to say anything. Opal pressed the up button, then leaned on the wall, tiredness weighing her down. She knew how to deal with that, didn't she? She could draw energy from her reservoir and pull herself together. Just now, she felt too tired to do it.

Before the elevator arrived, she heard a voice greeting the desk clerk in jovial tones. "I'm looking for my niece," said Great-Uncle Tobias. "Opal LaZelle."

The clerk said, "I think she's registered here—"

Opal opened her eyes and straightened. "Uncle."

16

❦

Tobias crossed the lobby. He looked thin and tired and older than usual, though his thick white hair crowned his head like an energetic bush. He carried a small duffel bag and a jacket. "Oh, no," he said, studying Opal and Phrixos, his face stretched with dismay.

The elevator dinged and the doors opened. "Come up," she said, and she, Phrixos, and Tobias got into the car.

Opal's room had a deserted air, a little stuffy, the bed made up and everything hidden away. The air tasted sterile. Opal opened the curtains and then the window, which stopped after a two-inch gap. Damp, fresh, chilly air came in.

"There's a lot to tell you," Opal said to Tobias, "but I need a shower first."

"I'll wait." Tobias settled in one of the chairs by the little round table, with his bag beside his feet.

Phrixos followed Opal into the bathroom, out of his robe, and on into the shower as soon as she got it going. His head brushed the ceiling even when he hunched over, and he took up so much space she could barely turn around, but she decided she didn't care; she was closer to the showerhead and the delicious stream of hot water than he was, and that was all she focused on, until he helped her soap up and scrub. At which point she leaned back against him, both of them steamy, soapy, slippery, comforting, with warm water pounding on them. She said, "Let me think."

He closed his arms around her and stilled.

At last she had time to count her blessings. Hot water. The girls were safe. Tobias was here. She had enough power—

She closed her eyes and went inside herself, to the study. The fire—Flint's fire, augmented by some of her sifted power—burned in the fireplace. Her second self wasn't there.

She grabbed a poker and stooped before the fire. "Hey, you traitor," she whispered to it, stirring it with the poker. "You deserted me and left me open to him."

Open to a kind of mad transcendence she had never experienced before, a memory she wanted to consider and strengthen, even though it frightened her. "Let go," Corvus or Phrixos or both of them had said, and for once in her life she had. He had not let her fall.

The fire sent apologetic flames to stroke her hand, then flooded through the air to wrap around her, but she said, "Wait," and sent it back into the fireplace. It burned bright and comforting, the promise of protection.

Something outside her shifted, and she left her study. Phrixos's arm reached past her to turn off the water. She gasped and shivered as the warmth stopped, though they were both wrapped in steam, and he was warm against her back still, and her lower legs were also warm.

"Was that long enough?" he murmured. Water had gathered around their feet and calves, rising to the level of her knees, almost spilling over the edge of the tub; she had dropped a washcloth on the drain where he couldn't reach it, and it had acted like a plug.

She bent and pulled it loose. The water rushed away. "Is my hair clean?" She worked her fingers through it. She couldn't remember using shampoo.

"Clean enough," he said. He pushed aside the curtain and grabbed towels from a shelf of metal bars above the toilet, shook one open and draped it over her, then scrubbed at his head with another.

She stepped out onto the linoleum and dried off. She hadn't brought any clothes into the bathroom except the white robe. It was tattered and stained from her passage through the forest. She wrapped a towel around her and went through the steam to the bedroom.

Tobias had the overhead light on and was studying various drafts of the script, which she had left lying on the table. Opal sighed and pulled a brown coverall out of the closet, grabbed some underwear, and went back into the bathroom to change.

Phrixos stood there, flushed from the heat, a towel wrapped around his waist. "I'm guessing you don't own anything in my size." He had used her deodorant and smelled like hot male mixed with baby powder. He reached for the black robe he had hung on the hook on the back of the door.

"I can at least clean it for you." She held the robe and sent a Cleaning Spell through it that left it soft, clean, and scented like lemons and wind-washed sunlight. He smiled at her and pulled on the robe.

They went out and sat on the bed, facing Tobias.

Tobias set aside the script. "I believe the nature of your trouble has changed?"

"Yes," said Opal.

"When I threw the auguries last night, there was urgency implied, and a suggestion to prevent something from happening. My sense now is that I came too late to stop it."

"What did they say? Was it a dire reading?"

"The reading was muddled and confusing. It wasn't dire

enough to make me hurry. I was worried about you—there was a death threat—but here you are, alive, thank goodness."

"A death threat!" Opal glared at Phrixos, who smiled and shrugged. She made a fist and tapped his bicep with it. "There was a death threat?"

"It depends on your definition of death," he said.

"What does *that* mean?"

"There was a death, I think—"

"Who? What else happened while I was out of it? Someone died?"

"You," he said.

She punched him again. "What? I'm a walking corpse?"

"For a time you were alive with your walls down. A state you thought of as death, and so, for you, a little death."

"Uncle?" she asked, turning to Tobias.

"Niece, you haven't introduced us yet," said Tobias.

"What?" She looked at Phrixos. Tobias had met Corvus on the *Dead Loss* set. But now he was speaking to a deeper reality. "My apologies, Uncle. This is—I am not sure, exactly. Some parts of him seem to be Corvus. A portion is an entity I call Phrixos, an agent for the local power that possessed Corvus. There's another part, I think, that is the actual local power speaking for itself through him. Phrixos is capable of deceit, so I don't know whether to believe him when he pretends to be Corvus. All of you inside the body of my boyfriend, this is my great-uncle Tobias, who has come to help me solve the problem you present."

"To whom am I speaking?" Tobias said. Opal heard the undertone in his voice; he was asking a question with more than words.

Phrixos straightened, his gaze sharper, more alert, and then a level of character faded from his face, leaving him still sitting up, but different. Opal flattened her hand over his on his thigh. He flashed her a brief glance, then turned to Tobias. "Corvus Weather," he said.

"Were you really here when Phrixos sounded like he was you?" Opal asked.

"Some of the time. It got complicated. He decided to bribe me instead of continually putting me to sleep."

"Were you you while we——" She stopped, conscious of Tobias's regard.

"Bribe you with what?" Tobias asked.

"Presence."

"Explain," said Tobias.

"Phrixos tells me I invited him in, but I don't remember that. I was sleeping through my days while he walked around in my body and did my job. I woke up and time had passed. While I was asleep, he hurt my friends and colleagues, and used me to do it. I don't understand much about this, except that most of what I've believed all my life isn't true, and I have even less control over myself than I thought I did. Anyway, this visitor in my head figured out that Opal responds better to me than to him, so he lets me wake up for key parts of the day now. Sometimes he even tells me what he wants to do next, and gives me the chance to ask people for their cooperation, instead of him trying to force his plans on people."

"Do you know what he wants and why?" Tobias asked.

"Sometimes I know a minute before he asks. I don't have the big picture."

Opal squeezed his hand. "Not even a little part of the big picture?"

"Some of the outlines. But he's already told you some of that. They were asleep and they want to be awake, and now they have a bunch of people they can use to help them wake up."

"Who are they?" Tobias asked. "The auguries——"

Corvus shook his head. "I don't know enough. He guards himself from me. Also, he's so different, even when I see some of his thoughts, I don't understand them. They're in a different language, or they happen at a different speed, or there's an extra dimension I don't grasp."

"You get nothing at all?" asked Tobias.

Corvus bent his head. His hand turned upward under Opal's, and his fingers closed over hers. "There's a shine to it. It's too bright for me to look at."

"Is it something that hurts people?" Opal asked.

"I don't know. I don't think so. It's—it might change people, but I'm not sure it's supposed to hurt them. I would hope I could stop them from jerking me around if I thought it was going to hurt people, but since it's unclear to me, I can't—stand against it."

"Some part of you understands it on a deeper level," Opal said.

He shook his head while saying, "Maybe."

"You're not frightened of it."

"I am, a little. But Opal—cliché, I know, but this gives me power beyond my wildest dreams. I had no idea any of this was possible. What you can do, and what they can do. I've been playing monsters for fifteen years, and I never believed in any of them except when I was being them. God."

"What do you want power for?"

He hesitated, staring toward a wall. "I hit my growth spurt when I was around thirteen," he said. "It didn't all happen at once, but it came before any of the other kids my age got that tall. By the time I was sixteen, I was seven two, and no one else was my size. Nothing fit—clothes, furniture, doorways, social situations. People didn't know how to respond to me, and I didn't know how to get my body to work. I tried basketball, because that was the best typecast I could think of, but back then, I had no coordination. I retreated into quiet, studying too much, exercising on the sly at three A.M., when I could count on being alone. Most of the teasing wasn't meant to be mean. The only girls interested in me, though, were looking for a freak, and that wasn't what I wanted to be."

He frowned. "One of my friends from the nature club decided he wanted to be a moviemaker, and he asked me to be the monster. At first I was really mad at him, but then I thought, why not? I loved being a monster, because I could take off the costume and turn back into myself afterward, pretend I was normal. When I made the jump into real movies, things got much better. Everyone involved in this business is weird one way or another, so they can accept me the way I am, pretty much. There's still no way for me to step out into the regular world and not be noticed, and I—I can't help wondering what that would be like. Phrixos says—" His voice trailed off and he stared down at his feet.

"That's the bribe he offered you? He can make you shorter? I can make you look shorter, if that's what you want," Opal said.

"Can you?"

"Illusion is my business," she said. "I can make you look like whatever you want."

"But you never would have told me that."

"True. Probably. I don't know. If we got involved, I might have told you."

"He offered first."

Tobias opened his bag and pulled out a smaller bag, unzipped it to reveal compartments filled with different ingredients. "Maybe the auguries will tell me more, now that I'm in the presence of what's been warping them."

Opal stood. "Can we do that after supper? We haven't eaten in hours."

Tobias frowned. He opened one compartment, pulled out a pinch of yellow fragments, rubbed them between fingers and thumb, and tossed them into the air with a muttered phrase. An image formed and faded. "I guess it can wait," he said.

"If you can make me look like anything," said Corvus, "make me look like a normal guy now. Let me try having a meal as someone besides me or a monster."

Opal closed her eyes, so deeply tired she wasn't sure she could handle anything demanding. She went to her study and checked her power reservoir. It held an assortment of shades of power. She held out a hand toward a streamer of blue that looked friendly and uncomplicated, and it rose from the array, touched her palm, slid into her. The blue power revived her, like three sips of water on a hot day—a temporary but convincing state.

She envisioned a Corvus shorter than the one she knew, shrank his features and his stature until he looked—strangely normal, almost nondescript. She decided to dress him in a brown sports jacket, pale blue shirt, dark slacks, and brown shoes. When she had the vision complete, she flicked it over the tall black-robed man in front of her and opened her eyes.

Corvus reduced: she wouldn't have looked twice, except he smiled, and his eyes lit up, and then he was present in a way she knew and loved, from the inside. "Done?" he asked.

"Done. I haven't changed your size, just how you look. You'll need to be careful moving around; you take up more room than it appears. Or did you want the complete transformation? I'm not sure I have enough energy for that right now."

"You can do that?"

She smiled, shrugged with shoulders and eyebrows.

"Let me see." He rose, stared into the mirror over the dresser. His eyes widened. "Heavens. Do you see what I see?" He turned to Tobias, eyebrows up.

"Opal is very good at what she does. You look like someone I would pass on the street without a second thought."

His eyes danced. "Let's go out. I want to walk this one around. Possibly the most peculiar part I've ever played."

In the elevator down, Opal tried to make sense of her impressions of Corvus. She was aware of the space he took up. He hovered over her, even though she looked at him and saw someone only an inch taller than she was, smiling at her. She refined the illusion to damp the space-taking vibes he was giving off. By the time the door opened on the lobby, she had made the transformed Corvus so convincing she believed his apparent size herself.

Tobias bumped into Corvus's elbow as they got off; he had tried to occupy space Corvus was already using.

"Sorry," they both said simultaneously. Corvus made his first frown in his new face. "I see what you mean," he said to Opal.

"This might not be the best idea I ever had," she said. "I should do the whole thing. I'm too tired, and it might hurt you, though. I was never big on total transformations, so I'm out of practice. My brother could do a better job."

"Your whole family has skills?" Corvus asked as they exited the hotel.

"Opal," said Tobias.

"Sorry, Uncle. Corr, we don't talk about that."

"I met a bunch of siblings," he said thoughtfully as they crossed the parking lot. "I—" His eyes glowed green for a second. She would have missed it, but she was still studying the effect of her magic, still trying to reconcile what she knew and what she saw. "Oh, yes. There were three more of you, and two parents, yes?" he said. Though his voice hadn't changed much, she knew Phrixos was the one asking.

She smiled and didn't answer. She had four siblings; one hadn't made the meeting. No need to correct Phrixos's impressions. The less he knew, the better.

Corvus strode ahead to open the door to the IHOP for them. She brushed his arm without intending to. He shifted so there was no more contact.

It took a while for the waitress to notice them. Corvus smiled the whole time. The waitress was Jenny again, and she looked very frazzled. "You movie people?" she asked.

"Not right now," said Corvus.

"Booth or table?"

"Booth," said Opal. Less chance of someone bumping into the invisible parts of Corvus if he was in a booth.

Jenny waved toward a booth. It was next to the corner booth where Travis and Bethany were sitting, again, their laptops out, scripts scattered around. They both had headphones on and gave off an aura of not knowing the other existed. They frowned ferociously at their screens, unconsciously mimicking each other.

Opal wondered if they had been on location that evening. Maybe her party should sit farther away from people they knew. The waitress hadn't recognized Opal from earlier—what casual acquaintance would notice Opal when Corvus was with her?—but surely Bethany and Travis would know her . . .

Corvus took her arm gently and steered her toward the booth beside Bethany and Travis's. Tobias followed. Corvus moved in first, pushing the table out with what appeared to be air in front of his stomach. Tobias and Opal slid in on either side of him.

Bethany took off her headphones and tapped Opal's shoulder. Opal turned to look at her over the back of the booth. "Hey, hon," said Bethany, "whatcha doing here?"

"Need food," said Opal.

"Were you on location tonight?"

Opal relaxed. "Yeah. You miss the whole thing?"

"Yep. We were right here, reworking some of the kid scenes. What the hell happened? No one answers their phones! But Neil came along and dropped a bunch of changes on us. He wouldn't say anything, either, except the whole script is scrapped, practically!"

"Let me eat, and then I'll try to explain it," Opal said.

"Okay," Bethany said, but she looked frustrated, and so did Travis, who hadn't taken off his headphones, but was listening to their conversation. Bethany looked past Opal. "Oh. You've got company. I'm sorry. I'm being rude. But it's like—he's throwing out everything we did! He wants the movie to be romantic! Maybe with a brand-new female lead, but can he give us any background on the new lead? No! I can't believe he's throwing out everything we've done. What about all those days of filming? He didn't seem to care whether he can use any of the stuff he already shot. He can't have talked to the producers. When do they *ever* scrap everything? God, Opal, the whole thing's going to hell!"

Jenny returned. "Have you decided?" she asked, poof-topped pen poised over her order pad.

Corvus ordered a club sandwich. Opal hadn't thought to disguise his voice; the rich words came from his mouth, making the sandwich sound like luxury.

"Hey!" said Bethany.

He glanced over at her and smiled.

"No way!" Bethany said. "Corvus? How can that be you? What the hell?"

17

Travis tore his headphones off and stared.

"I'm not Corvus," said Corvus. "I'm his shorter brother."

"You sound just like him. It's eerie!" Travis said.

"No, seriously," said Beth, "how the hell are you doing that?"

Corvus drank coffee and smiled.

"This is my uncle, Tobias." Opal pointed to Uncle Tobias. "Uncle Tobias, this is Bethany and Travis. They wrote the script for the movie. Dreams came into Beth's head while she was visiting here, and she wrote from them. She grew up here."

"Ah," said Tobias.

Opal turned to Jenny, who was still waiting for their order, though her gaze had settled on Corvus. "Can I get one of those sandwiches, too? Tobias?"

"Just coffee," he said. "I ate on the way."

Jenny smiled, nodded, and headed for the kitchen.

"Stop jerking us around," Travis said, "and tell us what you did to Corr."

"I didn't do anything to him," Opal said. She had only altered the air around him; he remained internally intact.

"Corvus, how is that—what happened?" Bethany asked.

"Nonmovie magic," Corvus said.

"What?" Bethany asked, her voice almost a whisper.

"It's just an illusion, Beth. I wanted to see what it was like to look normal for once. So far, it's very interesting. I'm not used to being ignored. I rather like it. In the short term, anyway."

"How could you possibly get that to work?" Bethany asked.

"Opal managed it. You do miss out on a lot, not being on the set," Corvus said.

Jenny put a coffeepot and plates full of sandwiches on the table, and Corvus said to Bethany and Travis, "Excuse us, please. It's been too long since we ate, and we really used up a lot of energy today—"

Opal socked the air near where his arm appeared to be, and hit an elbow. He flinched and smiled, so strange with his smaller face, nearer to hers. It made her wonder how the illusion worked; he could still use his face as an actor did, even though it was far from the face he actually lived in. She had worked with light to create his false self, but hadn't noticed how intimately entwined this atmosphere she had created was with his actual person. She knew what she had done, and still she found him completely convincing.

Bethany and Travis stared at him. Then Bethany waved a hand, and she and Travis put their headphones back on.

"We can't plan strategy here," Tobias said.

"We'll go back to the room afterward." Opal ate. The first bite was bliss, the second even better. She had eaten half the sandwich before she knew it, and Corvus scarfed his even faster. She watched him eat. It really looked like the sandwich went into his illusion self's mouth. How on earth was that working? She was a better craftswoman than she knew.

"Why are you staring?" asked Corvus.

"What does it look like from inside?" she asked.

"You're staring at my chest," he murmured. "Maybe this is what it's like for well-endowed women. I'm imagining you're looking into my eyes, and responding accordingly. Are we making eye contact?"

"Yes. I can't figure out how the food gets into your mouth."

"How strange," he said, and stared at his empty plate. "I guess I've had enough."

"You haven't," she said. "You've got a lot of self to maintain." She handed him the other half of her sandwich.

"Thanks. I'll eat it in the room." He wrapped it in a napkin and made it disappear somehow. She couldn't remember if his robe had pockets.

She ate her fries. He had already eaten his. "Okay. You finished?" she asked Tobias.

Tobias drank the last of his coffee and didn't pour more. Even the parsley had vanished from Corvus's plate. Opal rose. She grabbed her messenger bag. This time, she would pay; Corvus didn't match his ID.

"Hey," Bethany said. "Not so fast! You promised us an explanation after you ate."

"We're not going to tell you here," said Opal.

Bethany packed her computer, headphones, and script pages and was on her feet before Corvus even finished getting out of the booth. Travis, slower on the uptake, stared after her with confusion on his face. "You pay, hon. I'll be back once I find out what's going on. Opal, you're in a little bitty single room, right? Trav and I have a suite. We needed work room, even though we spend most of our writing time over here. You can meet in our room."

Opal glanced at Tobias, then up where she suspected Corvus's real face was. Both of the men shrugged. "Lead the way," Opal said.

On the elevator, Opal said, "Are you ready to be yourself again?" to Corvus.

He glanced into the mirrored back wall of the elevator, smiled at his smaller self, turned to Opal with a faint smile still in place. "Okay. Which one?"

She poked his chest and let the illusion dissolve, and then, there he was, taking up a fourth of the available space, dressed in the black robe of his monstrous self. Bethany and Tobias gasped and stepped back against the wall.

"How the *hell* did you do that?" Bethany demanded.

"I forgot how large you are," said Tobias.

Corvus beamed. "It was educational, wasn't it?"

"Come on," Bethany said, "that works in movies and on-stage, but—how the hell?"

The doors opened and Opal marched out onto Bethany's floor, ignoring the rumble of Corvus's voice behind her. The other three caught up with her when she paused in the hall. She realized she didn't know Bethany's room number. Bethany gave her three eyebrow waggles and walked past to open double doors into a suite with the legend "Senator" over the doorway.

As soon as Bethany dumped her backpack on the coffee table and they all sat on the two couches in the suite's sterile-looking living room, Bethany said, "All right, tell me what happened on location today."

"What have you heard?" Opal asked.

"Zip! Zero! Zilch! Nada! We're in our usual booth, arguing about how bad to make the kids' trauma, when in walks Neil, his shirt and pants stained in interesting places, his hair sizzling around his head, and his eyes shooting lasers.

Bam! He hits the table so hard the coffeepot wobbles. 'This changes everything,' he says. Travis and I go, 'What? What?' like dummies, and he says, 'The film's going in a different direction. We'll know more after we look at the dailies. You people are going to have to be ready for a lot of rewriting. Just so you know.' Like that's any help at all!"

Bethany went to the sideboard and grabbed a bottle of whiskey, whipped off the cap and drank. "This job is already so stressy," she muttered. "Do something you think works, you're proud of it, it's great, he says it's great, then an hour later somebody else complains about something and then he hates what you've done, and you have to do it all over again, and there's no guarantee any of it's going to work, and it's not because of anything you can control. I mean, I've worked like this before, don't get me wrong, but Neil is the worst slave driver I've ever worked with. All directors piss on your work to prove it's theirs, but he's just a big gushing fountain of urine." She recapped the bottle and set it on a tray again. "Yesterday, though, it felt like everything was going to work out all right. We were sliding right along toward getting out of here. What the hell happened today?"

"The whole cast and crew were possessed," Opal said.

Bethany strolled over and dropped onto the couch beside Tobias. "Possessed? That makes no sense. You know that, right? Possessed. Huh. By what?"

"The spirit of the place. Same thing that stole women in the fifties, and made your childhood scary, and crawled into your dreams at the B&B while you were writing the script."

"But that's—but you—but that's crazy."

"Get over it. There's something underground here that's been sleeping a long time, and it's awake now. It's been messing with the production all along, one way or another, and today it went crazy and we all had a great big lovefest out there in the woods, with the cameras rolling. So maybe this turns out to be porn."

"Porn? Porn? Goddamn it. Not again."

"I was kind of out of it while it was happening, so I don't know if anybody got decent tape. But—" Opal felt her cheeks heat. Maybe she should just say it now. Tobias, watching alertly, needed to know this, too, no matter how embarrassing it was. "Corr and I were the stars out there on the altar. Not that we were the only ones. Just—we were the ones with the good lighting and camera angles. But pretty much everybody went nuts simultaneously."

"Whoa," said Bethany.

"So that's what happened." Opal slumped back on the couch. Corvus eased an arm around her shoulders. She wasn't sure that was what she wanted, given how little she knew about who he actually was, but it felt good. She relaxed into the embrace and closed her eyes.

Other Opal was waiting for her on the inside of her eyelids. "Do you remember what happened this afternoon yet?"

"Go away."

"Come on, this is part of our journey now. You stop running away from who you are and what you've done. Remember what you know about this guy's body, and what else we touched while we were with him. Decide from an informed place whether you want his arm around you right now."

"Is there a reason why I might not want that?"

"I'm not going to tell you. You need to decide for yourself."

Opal let her memory open on the afternoon. She had been in two or three places at once: on the altar; on a version of the altar in a dream; inside her own mind, flying around and looking at her fortifications, which guarded against some things and not others. An edge of the memory flapped at her like a flag in wind. What was that? She leaned over and gripped the loose corner, lifted it, opened a door into a fourth reality.

Lying under a bumpy transparent surface like a frozen sea

lay a rivery network of lights and darks, a lacework in three dimensions through which green and blue colors pulsed and flowed, although they were running slowly, and many parts of the network were dim. There was such depth to the vision she could not see the bottom, only that the roots of the rivers twisted down into darkness and faded from view. From the surface of the sea rose many tall columnar shapes with nets of faint light threading through them, but they were hard to see in this dark expanse.

In one place the lines of light converged, braided amongst themselves and rose upward into one of the surface bumps, upwelling, reaching tendrils up toward—

Two forms in the rough shape of humans lay on top of one of the shorter bumps; it was squat, like a table. The larger one, whose body was interwoven with the same sorts of light rivers as the ground, and another, smaller, beneath the first, who was laced through with interlocking snowflakes of red and orange fire.

Opal focused and found herself drawing closer to the two. She stared at the transparent hands of the lower figure, which were bright with internal mehndi lacework, the fingertips alight with whorls and flowers of pulsing red light. The hands, the arms, reached up from the lower figure to embrace the other on top of her, and where their bodies intersected, his cooler colors of light exploded into her, and her own fires dived under his transparent skin to mix with his, to feed his, until the dimmer lines of light inside him grew brighter, their colors shifted toward the red end of the spectrum. This was where she had surrendered, let her shield drop, and she and whatever it was that laced all through the ground under Lapis, whatever it was that had invaded Corvus, had connected. The ground brightened and stirred with the influx of light. Though she fed her energy into the other's net, she did not become depleted. The rivers of green energy had flowed into her as she had flowed into them.

So he, the presence under the ground, Phrixos, whoever it was, had drawn from her even as he put himself into her— and where was Corvus in this equation? She hadn't had a moment alone with him to find out how much of Corvus was left.

A rosy flush ran all through the networks, then faded, leaving the whole of the webwork brighter than it had been before. All around the two figures were other faint networks she had ignored while she had watched herself. Where these networks touched the surface, water from the underground rivers flowed up into them. The whole of the film crew and cast, doing whatever they had done while she and Corvus's body had been engaged with each other. Lines of green force ran through everything, faintly, then faded again, leaving the people more transparent, still alive in faint lingers of light, but not as influenced from the underground as before.

This was when they woke.

Opal opened her eyes. Tobias and Bethany were staring at her. "What?" she said.

"Waiting for an answer," said Tobias.

"Was there a question?" She glanced toward Corvus.

"Where were you?" he asked.

"I was thinking back to what happened in the clearing." She watched as his face rippled in search of an expression. Two or three people inside him seemed to be trying to decide who would control the surface. She felt a brief prickle of grief at the thought that she was losing Corvus before they'd had time to explore each other.

He settled for looking worried.

"So was there a question? I'm sorry I missed it. Could you fill me in now?"

"Your uncle wants to know what you want him to do," said Bethany.

"Yes," said Opal. "That's a good question. Corr, you stay here, all right?" He shifted his arm, tightened it around her.

She straightened, and he relaxed his grip so she could rise. "Tobias, will you come with me?"

"Assuredly," he said. He followed her out of Bethany's room and down two floors to Opal's.

They sat facing each other across the table. She stretched out her hands, and he laid his own on them, staring into her eyes. "What on earth has been happening?" Tobias asked.

"Oh, Uncle," she said, and lifted her hands to press them to her eyes.

He was beside her then, his hand on her arm, the weight of a fallen leaf, a chance gift. She lowered her hands and took one of his, careful not to squeeze. When she was younger, she had thought Uncle Tobias would go on forever, like the tides and the moon, but ever since Christmas Eve, when her sister's spell had given her a glimpse of the hidden ways of things, she had known her uncle was ancient and more fragile than he appeared. His skills and wisdom still burned with clear flames, some of them clearer and stronger as his physical powers faded. He had lost his role as the all-powerful elder, though, whether he recognized it or not. His hand was warm, but felt breakable.

He sat silent while she explained the changes Corvus had undergone since they started filming, the surges of power she had felt underground, her own confusion and participation, culminating in the orgy that afternoon. "Nobody's blamed me for that, as far as I know," she muttered, "but I'm no longer hidden in my talents. Four or five people know I'm not just another normal human being."

"Given the circumstances—forces acting on them, and the peculiar atmosphere that gives people permission to believe the unlikely," Tobias said, "this is not terribly surprising."

"I think it's the first time since high school that I might need to clean up after I've made a mess, though."

"Or maybe not," he said.

"Not? After yesterday?"

"Let's wait and see how all this plays out. It sounds like it's already self-correcting. One of my questions now is, are you in personal danger? Should we work some wards for you?"

"Flint sent me some nonstandard energy that works as a shield."

"What? Explain that."

She told him about Flint's attack over the phone, and he said, "I keep forgetting to watch that boy! This is fascinating! Can you manifest some of this power for me?"

She closed her eyes and went into her mental study. The fire was faint in the fireplace. She stooped before it and held out her hand. "What's the matter?" she asked.

"You don't need us anymore," it said, flames reaching out to brush her skin with heat.

"I do, though. Don't go away. You're some of the best stuff I've got."

"Are you sure?" The flames grew.

"I'm sure. Thanks. Please stay lively." She fed the fire sticks of dried, seasoned wood. She didn't remember putting wood into this room, but it was handy that there was some close at hand. Then she wondered if someone had meddled with the wood, but by that time the fire had eaten three big sticks and burped.

Opal sat on the floor and laid her hand over the remaining wood, sought through it for an explanation.

"I put it there," Other Opal said from behind her.

"Did Phrixos mess with it?"

"No. It came from our own forest. Flame, eat more. We need you. I didn't mean to dismiss you altogether; I just needed you to lie low for a while." Other Opal fed the fire with Opal, and the flames reached up to lap at her hands as she added wood.

"We have a forest?"

"There are a lot of rooms here you haven't seen. We have all kinds of things." Other Opal held a hand near the fire, and a flame jumped to hover above her palm. She turned and held it out to Opal, who accepted it. It melted down over her hand like hot butter, a golden haze of light. "Open your eyes," Other Opal whispered, and Opal opened her eyes to stare into Tobias's face as he leaned over her.

She lifted her hand, and it wore the flame like a translucent glove, a beautiful color of yellow orange like sunset light. Tobias sucked in breath, untucked something from a pocket and held it out to the flame. The flame wicked toward it, a twist of pale string, made the jump, sizzled at the end of the twine for a moment, then faded. The string turned ocher. Tobias held it close to his face and sniffed it.

Opal rubbed her hands across each other. The flame seeped under her skin, a transient warmth, a continuing comforting presence.

"Strange and elegant," said Tobias. "And, of course, unprecedented. Is it entirely Flint's?"

"I had to transmute it so I could use it, but I think it's the Flint part that makes it work."

"His gift may lie in mixing his magic with others'," Tobias muttered. "But that's something to explore another time. This worked as a shield?"

Opal spoke to the Flintfire, asked it to shield her the way it had before, and it rose up and enveloped her, not visibly, but in an embrace she could feel. She held out her hands palms facing her uncle, and he closed his eyes and sent questing fingers of power toward her. They stubbed against her shield. He opened his eyes. Their normal pale blue flared brighter, and he sent a spear of power at her that made her gasp. If she had seen it coming toward her in a regular argument with someone in her family, she would think she had really hurt someone's feelings and they wanted to kill her.

It splashed against her shield and parted, went around her and sizzled against the chair she was sitting in. "Uncle!" she cried, leaping up. Parts of the chair were history; some of them were still smoking.

"As I thought. An amazingly effective tool."

"You could have killed me!"

"True," he said, "but I didn't think you would let me, and I was right. I'm glad you've got this kind of armor, Opal. The situation calls for it."

"What do you see as the situation?"

"You already know it. An uppity dormant god power has grasped opportunity and seeks to rise again. It's a smart one, and it sees you as its chief vehicle. This is a role you've been preparing for much of your life. You know, when I was teaching you as a teenager, you took some of the lessons wrong. I never meant for you to suppress your powers; I just wanted you to learn to use them responsibly. Don't let this thing take you over and use you, Opal. Make your choices. Lay it to rest. If it gets out, who knows what it will do?"

Opal felt strange, listening to Tobias. He said aloud things she had been worrying about, and suddenly she felt contrary and didn't want to believe them. Or she wanted to reframe them.

"The question is: Do you need my help?" he said. "You have your armor, and you have your powers; there's some shifting going on inside you that I'd like to explore; it feels weighty. I think you have the power to stop this yourself, but I'll help if you want me to."

"Would you turn around and go home now if I asked you to?"

"Yes," he said.

"Even though you never leave home, and now you have? Seems like a long time since you went out in the world. I appreciate your coming. Would you be mad at me because you made this trip for nothing?"

"It was not for nothing. You're right, it's been a long time since I was out in the world, and I know now I should do it more often. Santa Tekla is not the world. I feel invigorated, in fact, by having brushed up against so many different kinds of powers and people and communities on my journey. Will you dismiss me, Opal?"

"What would be wrong with your staying, at least overnight?"

"Is that what you want?" He was staring at her as though her answer was important.

She sat back and closed her eyes, and inside, she found herself in a forest, facing her other self. "What is he up to?" she asked Other Opal. Had she seen this forest before? While they were making love to Corvus, these were the trees that surrounded them. And yes, some were dead and could serve as firewood. Twilight made the trees into silhouettes. Other Opal glowed with a pale radiance of her own. One of her hands was still gloved in the warm orange of Flint's fire.

"You can ask him," Other Opal said, "but I don't think he'll answer."

"What's important about this choice?"

Other Opal looked off toward the trees. An owl flapped out of the forest, crossed the clearing where they stood, and was gone. "We left home, and none of the rest of them has," she said slowly.

"Yes," said Opal.

"Since we left, have we ever asked for help before?"

"No. Well, just with Flint."

"If we accept his help now," said Other Opal, "we're binding ourselves back to the family."

"I never left all the way," Opal said.

"From their perspective, it looks as though you've left."

"I come back every year."

"You're the only one Mama doesn't have bound to her with all those strings she laid on the other kids. We really got away from her."

"Do you remember if Tobias was bound up in that web?"

Other Opal looked at her and they both thought. No, Tobias had not been tied to Mama with the network of threads she'd laced into the siblings.

"There are other ways of being bound," said Other Opal. "That vision only showed one surface. Gyp was checking for what she needed to know. She wasn't looking at the whole constellation. She most needed to know how Mama was controlling them all. Look now."

Opal opened her eyes and studied Tobias, but he just looked like himself, waiting, maybe a bit exasperated, or maybe that was just his normal expression. His white hair still bushed up in an untidy bunch, and his face, though weary, was almost more familiar to her than her own, after all the hours of lessons and training he had put her and the other kids through. She had relied on him in many ways to be her compass while she navigated the world of her powers. She had used her skills and strength to care for her siblings when their mother hadn't had the attention to pay them, and Tobias had been one of the powers who supported her in that. A surge of love and gratitude warmed her as she studied her great-uncle. She smiled, and he smiled back.

"Look again," whispered Other Opal inside her. "Widen your eyes. Here. I'll help you."

Other Opal settled into Opal like a dream self coming home, blinked her eyes, and then Opal saw the world draped in webs and colors. Tobias was wrapped in ragged threads of silver and gold, the way he had looked under Gyp's reveal spell, but beneath that lay a soft cashmere-looking layer of blue green, with strings that led away, including one that led from Tobias's chest to Opal's.

"Family ties," Other Opal murmured, using Opal's voice. Tobias, dimly seen through his wrappings, frowned and leaned toward her.

Other Opal pulled back from Opal's edges and retreated to the forest, where they could talk without being overheard.

"So the question is, do you want to lean on your family now, or stand on your own feet? You've been standing on your own feet for years. Do you want to slide back?"

"It's not a final decision, is it? If I ask for help once, I don't become dependent again. Or do I?" Opal had structured her life so she didn't have to depend on anyone. She didn't remember when that had become her goal. But even before she had seen an enmeshed vision of her family, she had felt that their mother was strangling them. She had burned herself out making sure that her younger brothers and sisters were okay, and then they had grown into their powers and gotten snotty. They didn't want or need her help.

So fine, she had left and found other communities where she was necessary and appreciated. They were temporary communities, lasting the length of a shoot, but once one was gone, she could always find another. She had more job offers than she could accept.

Other Opal answered her: "I don't know if it's a final decision, but Tobias is making it seem extra important. You could tell him to go fuck himself."

"Great way to ask for help," said Opal.

"Look at the question he really asked. Do you need help, Opal?"

Opal thought about everything that had happened. The gradual shift toward what Phrixos and the thing under the ground wanted, and then the not-so-gradual shift. Everyone blinking and waking up after the orgy—a change that they had yet to process. Could she grasp the various forces at play and turn them back? Could she send the underground thing, the no-longer-dormant god power, to sleep, and make the world safe for moviekind?

She hadn't bested Phrixos in most of their encounters. Had she truly tried? Did she have the power to control him, make him let go of the other people he'd laid claim to, Lauren, the girls, Erika, Magenta, others she might not know about?

"Do you like it when Tobias says you've spent your life preparing to be a handmaiden?"

"Not a lot," said Opal.

"Who do you really want to be?"

All her life, she had built skills that made her a consummate helper, except those times in her teen years when she experimented with being a user, like many people in her extended family. Helper had felt better, and the fallout was pleasure rather than regrets and pain. She took care of people. She stepped in when a job needed doing and did it. She made people look better, or worse, or whatever way they wanted to look, and in Hollywood, that was a significant power.

"Who else *could* I be?" she asked.

"Mother. Builder. Witch. Fortune-teller. Wife. Sanitation worker. Wizard, baker, actress, seamstress, director, writer, musician, retail worker, teacher, nurse, president, cook, accountant, whore. Soldier. Folklore collector. What do you want? You could spend the rest of your life being lazy, or you could be a drudge, or you could turn into an animal and ditch all human responsibilities."

"Huh."

"It's taking you a long time to make a simple choice," said Tobias in her ear.

"There's nothing simple about this choice, is there?"

"Do you want my help?" he asked. "Yes or no?"

"I don't know if I can handle this on my own," she said slowly. "What if I need your help, whether I want it or not? Is there something wrong with wanting to be safe and sure?"

"Set those questions aside and answer: do you *want* my help?"

"No," she said.

He smiled. He leaned forward and kissed her forehead. "All right," he said. "Now that I'm away from home, I think I'll do some exploring. I've taken a room in a hotel in Salem. Give me a piece of paper and I'll write down the phone number. I won't be in the room during the day, but I will check for messages. I may not be able to respond right away, but I'll try to come if you need me."

She dug a scrap of paper out of her messenger bag. Tobias wrote the name and number of a chain hotel on it. "Good luck," he said, picked up his duffel, and left.

18

She sat alone in her hotel room for the first time in a long time. "What am I going to do?" she asked.

She went into the bathroom. The damp towels from her and Corvus's impromptu shower were still neatly folded and stacked on the floor under the sink, and she didn't have any fresh ones left for the next morning, but the steam had cleared off the mirror. She looked at herself, really looked at herself: violet eyes just like her mother's, the gleam of gold in the soft brown of her hair, her clear features: her birth self, not altered in any of the ways she could have altered herself.

Her reflection doubled. Other Opal stood shoulder to shoulder with her, the nose, cheekbones, mouth the same, hair black with a white streak above her left temple, her eyes golden and softly glowing, lit from within.

"What's our next move?" Opal asked her second self.

"What do you really want?" Other Opal said.

"I don't know! I don't know! You must know if I don't, right? You're all the me I don't let out."

"Not all of you. There are more of us; we have different jobs. Baby you is one, and—"

"Do I need to know this now?" Opal asked.

"Maybe not." Other Opal smiled, a little sadly. "I asked you what we really want, and that's a complicated question, because we want a bunch of different things. You're the one who lives out there in the visible world, though, the one who has the riskiest job. What *you* really want is to go to sleep."

"That's what I want?" Suddenly Opal sagged, feeling the exhaustion of the day catch up to her. The shadows under her eyes darkened.

"Yes, but we can't do that, can we? There are too many things left hanging. So I'll help you." Other Opal laid hands on Opal's shoulders. Opal felt fire shift through her, burn away fatigue, energize her.

She hunched her shoulders, stared at herself, paused long enough to get a glass of water from the tap and drink it, then straightened again. "All right. Ready for our next move."

"Do we want to do the job Tobias outlined? Put the god-let back to sleep?"

Get the movie back on track, make everything go back to normal? Wash out whatever memories people had of strange events? Turn back into Opal, shadow-person, attached at the hip to Corvus, with no current role outside of making him look like a forest god?

Sink into that comfort, that invisible existence. That would be okay.

Lose the friendships she had started with Magenta and Lauren.

Force Corvus back into his unmonsterlike self.

Warp a lot of images taken earlier in the day, make the orgy unhappen, quiet the exciting energy under the ground, relieve Bethany's mind of all the dreams her home place had laid on her to make her write the script. Take the magic out of the movie.

If it had magic. She hadn't seen any dailies. She wasn't sure what the end product was going to be. She usually didn't concern herself much with what the movie looked like when it was finished. She just made sure her work was done well.

This project would have been different if everything had gone according to plan. Corvus was her focus, and he had so much to do in this one. She wanted to see him on the screen in a role that would take him to a level where his talents wouldn't be wasted anymore.

There was little chance in a movie like this there'd be any award-level recognition—most horror movies never got noticed by the Academy—but producers would see her work and think of her when they needed excellent makeup in films. They would see Corvus act.

Now, who knew.

Other Opal shook her shoulder. "Quit thinking about long-term career goals and get back to the present," she said.

Someone pounded on her hotel door. Opal sighed and snapped back together, with Other Opal inside again.

She went to the door, wondering if it was Bethany or Corvus knocking. She opened it to find Neil.

"You're the goddamned special effects makeup artist," he yelled.

"That would be me, yes."

"You're not the producer or the D.P. or the A.D. You're not anybody important. How come you're now central to this godforsaken movie we're stitching together?"

Opal crossed her arms over her chest. The fingers of her left hand tapped her right upper arm. "What do you want?"

He pushed past her into the room, slamming the door behind him. "Violating every order I gave when we started on this shit-spewing project, one of our cameramen took a digital movie of events this afternoon, and he gave it up when I threatened to fire him if he didn't. Of course there hasn't been time to process what was in the real cameras, but we took a look at his movie. George and Basil and I have been reviewing every shit-spattered thing that happened today," he said, still at pretty high volume. Opal glanced at her watch. After three A.M. She wondered if anybody in a neighboring room was going to call the front desk to complain about noise, but then she realized most of her neighbors were probably crew, and would either recognize Neil's voice or be out cold with exhaustion after the day they'd all had. "And even though we can't quite figure out how, you have somehow become central to this bleeding project. My first impulse was to kick you off the film, because I don't like having people around who can screw up my work. I've thought twice, because what started out as a nice little money-maker has the potential to turn into something wilder, something that could take off if we figure out how to frame it. So we've decided the thing to do is pick your brain."

Opal sighed and sat on the bed. Neil dropped into a chair facing her and leaned forward, his hands gripping his thighs, his face thrust toward hers as though he were about to bite off her nose. "What the hell have you done to my film?" he yelled.

Opal took a breath and felt her Flintfire spark up. Suddenly her shield was back, a second and invisible skin. She laughed, because she hadn't thought of the fire in terms of shielding her from a normal human assault, but she still felt better than she had without it.

"What are you laughing at?" Neil yelled, even louder.

"What the hell *could* I do to your film?" she asked.

"Rumor has it you're some kind of witch," said Neil, in a more conversational tone of voice. "After what I saw in that flaming handheld playback and what I know about where I've spent our special effects budget, I believe it. Of course, I absolutely do not believe in anything supernatural. I know how people get effects. I can debunk anything—one of the reasons I relish making monster films. Gives me a chance to see what fools these mortals really can be. But this afternoon, you—and he—and good Lord, the rest of us—Fran can say anything she likes about spiked water or hallucinogenic mold spores or some kind of hypnotism, but that doesn't explain what I saw on the handheld."

"I like the mold spores theory," Opal said.

"I don't give a damn what you like. Tell me what happened today, and whether you can make it happen again."

Tobias had talked about the atmosphere of people believing what they usually wouldn't. Atmosphere. Hmm. "I'm not making strange things happen. There's a local power that's doing it," she said.

"What does that mean, *a local power?*" Neil jumped to his feet and paced the narrow aisle between the end of the bed and the dresser. "Politics? I've met the mayor in Lapis. Fran told me I had to make nice. Guy couldn't sell shelter in a blizzard."

"Do you have a religion?" Opal asked.

"Religion is for idiots. Will you quit stalling and get to the point?"

"All right. A local god wants to use your movie to get famous."

"What?"

"He gave the writers the idea for the script. He influenced the choice of locations. That altar stone and all that, what did you think when you saw it? Those were naturally occurring rocks?"

"I thought the locals were very odd. I assumed some local lunatic built it for some weird thing they do at a harvest festival or something. Then again, the rocks are very solid, and—right, it was there already, wasn't it? Even getting permissions from the owner of the site—Fran said it was dead easy."

"There's a god in the ground there, and people used to

worship him, and he wants them to start up again. If the movie gets distribution, and people see it and feel even the slightest hint of belief, maybe he gets——"

"He *wants* the movie to succeed. He's not trying to sabotage it," Neil said. "Well, what the bloody hell was this afternoon about, then? That footage isn't going to edit well with everything else we've done. What was the point? Was he trying to communicate with us? Are we reduced to hand signals and semaphores? Can't we just ask him what he wants, and give it to him?"

"Well, we kind of can," she said, "because he's been possessing Corvus."

"The god wants to fuck you! What's it like being fucked by a god?"

"Do you want to try it?"

"Hell, yes, or the possession—no, cancel that, I don't know what it means. It could be like a really bad drug and leave me a wreck. I don't take chances like that anymore. But if he could possess Blaise——"

"Don't even think it," Opal said, her voice freezing.

"Why not?"

"Possession is a serious business for everybody concerned."

"If it makes your boyfriend more convincing in the part, then it's a good thing . . . Hmm. The script is about an evil god who makes his followers suffer." He dropped into the chair again and peered at her. "Are you suffering?"

"I think Bethany came up with the suffering part," Opal said. "I don't know for sure what this god wants his followers to do. The jury's still out on whether he's evil, though I've seen him do some things I thought were questionable."

"If the god didn't hurt people, would you support him? I'm pretty sure we can't use most of what we shot this afternoon without going to a completely other market, but maybe there's some other way we can salvage this. I mean, even though I resent him like hell, I have to confess Weather is a genius in the part. He could *make* this film, if we can finish it. I need a success. My last film tanked."

"I don't know what the god wants," Opal said, "or if I'll ever get Corvus back. Did you see what he did to Erika?"

"Erika? Who's that? Oh, that p.r bitch? What happened to her?"

"He laid her on the altar and drank her blood. Hell, you were there. You almost interrupted. But then Phrixos—" Phrixos had pressed Neil's forehead. Neil had changed from a yelling tyrant to someone calm.

"Phrixos?"

"That's what I call the entity possessing Corvus."

"Phrixos. All right. What did Phrixos do? I don't remember anything about this."

"I guess he messed with your memory," said Opal.

Neil looked thoughtful. "That doesn't sound good. How was the woman afterward?"

"I don't know. Right afterward, she was mad about it, but then we went back to work. I had other things on my mind, and I haven't seen her since. When's the last time you saw her?"

"Can't remember. Didn't care enough to pay attention." Neil shifted in the chair, frowned mightily. "That's neither here nor there. What I want to know is whether we can get back to work tomorrow." He heaved himself to his feet, gripped handfuls of hair. "Gawd," he said. "I can't believe I'm discussing this with the makeup girl!"

Opal dug through her messenger bag, sorting through various pieces of multicolored script pages, looking for the call sheet for the next day. All she dug up was a couple of crumpled call sheets from earlier in the shoot. "What are we shooting tomorrow?"

Neil went to the door, stooped, lifted an envelope lying on the floor. "George didn't get them made up until after we finished our meeting. He was supposed to wake everybody up when he passed them out, make sure everyone knows what the plan is for tomorrow. Guess he figured I'd clue you in." Neil slipped a finger under the envelope's flap and pulled out a call sheet. "First we'll shoot the girls on the soundstage, and then the seduction scene between the devil and Serena on location. What I really need to know is whether *I'm* going to be the director, or if everything will go to hell again."

"I don't know," Opal said.

He glared at her with intense dislike. His eyes narrowed, and he said. "Very well, then. One more day like today, though, and——" He snarled and paced away from her, then glanced down at the sheet of paper in his hand, which he had crumpled in his fist. He straightened it, then handed Opal the sheet. "You're supposed to prep Weather at ten A.M. We shoot at noon. George said you budget four hours for prep time, but it doesn't take that long, does it?"

Opal stared down at the call sheet.

"Rod said you whiz through it," said Neil.

"It's true," she said in a low voice. "It's been going much faster than I expected. The possession helps speed it up." Rod was ratting on her now? She'd have to find out what that was about.

"I don't care how you do it. I don't want you padding my budget and charging for extra hours you don't need, understand?"

"Yes," she said.

"Get some sleep and be ready for anything, all right? Did you put my star to bed yet?"

"No."

"Is he here? I could take him back to the B&B." Neil shuddered, then firmed his chin. "If you come with us."

"I think we'll stay here tonight," she said.

"Where is he?"

"In Bethany's room."

Neil glanced toward the ceiling, shook himself, and headed for the door. "Get him to the location on time and in costume," he said over his shoulder.

19

When she went upstairs, Opal found that Travis had come back from the restaurant, and he and Bethany were knee-deep in arguments, which continued even as Travis answered the door and let her in. Corvus sat on the couch, arms along the couch's back, eyes closed, head back, apparently asleep. *Death takes a holiday,* she thought, appreciating the contrast between his large, black-robed presence and the standard beige furniture and vanilla floral prints and landscapes on the walls.

There was an energy in his presence that hinted he was awake on several levels.

Opal sat down beside him, touched his hand. His arm slid around her shoulders, though he didn't open his eyes. "Who's awake in there?" she whispered to him.

He opened his eyes and smiled at her. The green glow showed in a subdued rim around his irises, so she guessed he was both Corvus and Phrixos. Maybe that was who he would be from now on. "Where's your uncle?" he asked.

Travis and Bethany paused to look toward her, interested in her answer.

"Gone," said Opal.

Corvus leaned closer, studying her face, his own concerned. "Why?"

"I wasn't sure what to do with him," she said.

His fingers tightened on her shoulder, then relaxed.

"Let's go to bed," said Opal. "We've got a ten o'clock call tomorrow."

"Shooting what?" asked Bethany.

"Did you get a call sheet?" Opal said. She looked at the floor by the door and saw another envelope, production stationery. "I guess George dropped it off. But he didn't knock and give it to you. Do you guys ever get called?" She tried to remember. During the shoot Opal had never seen the writers on the set except on their own time, and then, if Neil noticed them, he chased them off.

"Just on the phone," said Travis, "or when he comes in here to scream at us. That's one of the reasons we write in the restaurant. Even Neil doesn't want to make a scene there. Fran really gets on his case when he alienates locals, especially in places where cast and crew need service. When Neil needs something, though, we better be ready to write it, print it, leap in the car, and drive it to wherever the hell he is, and he needs it yesterday." He went over, picked up the envelope, opened it, and shook out the call sheet.

To save him time, Opal said, "We're shooting the seduction of Serena tomorrow."

"Which draft are we on with that?" Travis asked Bethany.

"I think it's the marigold pages," Bethany said, searching down through her stack of many-colored papers, some sheafs of them fastened together with brass brads.

Opal had left her messenger bag in her room. She couldn't remember if she had any marigold pages. "Do you have an extra copy? I didn't get the call sheet until about ten minutes ago because everything was so chaotic on the set today. Neil just stopped by my room—"

"Why?" said Bethany, her expression a mixture of fascination and distaste.

"To pick my brain, ask me if I could make whatever happened today not happen again."

"He thinks you're the agent of strange?" asked Bethany.

Opal smiled. "He did. I told him it was really the local god. He doesn't believe in any of this, but he kind of believes in that."

"Oh?" said Corvus.

She looked at him directly. "As long as you support the film instead of trying to sabotage it, he's happy. When we go back to the forest location, are we all going crazy again?"

He smiled. "Wait and see."

She held a fist up to his chin, tapped it. "Don't tease me. I've had a long, weird day."

"The answer is, I don't know."

Bethany pulled some pages out of her stack, leafed through them, brought them to Corvus and Opal. "This hasn't changed a whole lot. This *is* the most recent version we've written, though with Neil, who knows, maybe he wants the pink pages or something. It's my only copy, though, so don't you dare lose it. I want it back when you're done."

Corvus took the pages and read through them. "Pretty close to what I've already memorized," he said. "Let me just make sure." He went back through the pages and reread them.

"Travis, we're going on location tomorrow," Bethany said.

"But the retool on the big finale?"

"I don't think we should do any more work until Neil gets his head out of his ass and figures out where the film is going. Which probably depends on what happens on location tomorrow. Can we ride with you, Opal? Maybe he won't notice us if we come in one of those black cars instead of that powder blue Nissan we got."

"Corvus?" Opal said.

"Fine with me."

"Okay." Opal slipped from the claim of Corvus's arm and rose. "Breakfast at 8:30, and we're out of here by 9:30." She took his hand and tugged him toward his feet. It helped when he got the message and cooperated with her. "See you tomorrow."

"Night," said Travis.

Downstairs, Corvus sat on the bed and Opal on a chair and she ran his lines with him. The energy she had given herself from her internal stash was wearing thin; she read the lines without paying attention. Corvus tried several different readings on some of his lines, but he noticed her sagging at last, took the pages out of her hands, lifted her onto the bed, and pulled off her shoes. She was asleep before he stripped and crawled in beside her.

The next morning, Opal didn't recognize the waitress at the IHOP, a teenager with pink hair, black lipstick, and an eyebrow piercing, but the girl seemed to know them. She nodded to Bethany and Travis and put them all in the big corner booth. "Will you have enough room?" she asked.

"We're actually eating today and then leaving," Bethany said with a smile. "We don't need to spread out."

"Oh, so you're down to two pots of coffee instead of six?"

"Probably," said Travis. "Thanks, Tera."

"You guys have the menu memorized already, right? What would you like this lovely morning?"

They ordered, ate, paid, and left. Opal called Hitch at about 9:15. He had the car waiting out front by the time they got to the parking lot.

On the drive to the location, Opal glanced at Corvus. He looked back at her, his gaze quiet. *Where do we go from here?* she wondered.

The closer they got to the location, the stronger and wilder grew the buzzing under Opal's skin. The ground was wide awake today. She put up her shield as Hitch drove, thickened it as more and more energy radiated against it. She wasn't ready to collapse into Other Opal this time.

By the time they parked, Corvus's face had already changed partway. Leaf outlines lay just under his skin.

"How'd you do that?" asked Bethany as they climbed out of the car.

He gazed at her. She swallowed, backed up, and grabbed Travis's arm. Corvus raised the hood of his robe to cover his head.

"Do you sense anything different about this place?" Opal asked Bethany. On this project, Bethany had been the first one influenced by the god under the ground. Was she still being affected by it? To Opal, the trees shimmered with energy, and there was a glow surrounding the altar stone she wasn't seeing with her eyes.

"I'm totally spooked by Corvus," Bethany said, "so yeah, I'm feeling kind of fucked up."

"Anything else?"

"I've got this crawly feeling under my skin," said Travis. "More static than anything else. I feel jumpy."

"Want to leave?"

"No way," said Bethany, as Travis said, "Are you kidding? We've got to see what happens next." He grabbed Bethany's hand and pulled her toward the altar.

Opal shrugged and headed to the Makeup trailer, trailing Corvus.

Kelsi intercepted them, gripped a fingerful of Corvus's robe. "So that's where that got to," she said. She frowned. "Did you clean it?"

"I did," said Opal.

Kelsi narrowed her eyes, leaned closer, peered at the material, sniffed it. "Looks like you didn't destroy it, so okay. Next time, ask before you take something off the set."

"We didn't have anything to change into yesterday."

"Sure," said Kelsi, "that's what everybody says. And yeah, I was there, so I guess I know it's true, though I'm kind of fuzzy on what happened. You should see what the kids did with their clothes, damn it. Yesterday was a nightmare with those kids' clothes! First the blood, and then the dirt! There wasn't one intact dress for either of them, so Betty and I were up all night making new ones . . . Glad you took good care of this robe. The other two we have are still spattered with that damn peppermint blood. It's supposed to be washable, but I soaked them all night, and they're still not right." She released Corvus's robe and headed for the Wardrobe trailer.

Inside the Makeup trailer, Lauren was sitting in one of the normal-sized chairs, with Magenta working on her. Rod lounged in another chair, flipping through a magazine. Blaise sat cross-legged in the chair next to Rod's. She wore a gauzy purple and gold Indian-print hippie dress her character wouldn't have worn, and she gripped her bare feet with her hands. She gazed at Opal and Corvus as they passed the other chairs to get to Corvus's custom chair.

"Blaise?" Opal paused next to the actress. "You're not on the call sheet."

"Right, I'm not working today, but I decided to come watch. Neil was interesting and mysterious and way too secretive when he got back last night."

"We heard we missed the party of the year yesterday," Lauren said.

"Don't talk." Magenta was outlining Lauren's lips.

"Sorry," Lauren said, without meaning it. "Would someone please fill us in? Blaise said Neil wouldn't tell her much. Everybody in town seems to know something except us; my hostess at the B&B was all, 'You wouldn't believe what happened at the altar yesterday,' and then she wouldn't give me any details."

"The townies know?" Rod said. "Oh, God. Can the media be far behind?"

"Neil was trying to keep it under wraps," said Magenta. "I wonder how they found out."

Rod said, "Everybody and his sister was out here working yesterday. It's hard to keep every mouth shut. I didn't think the crew knew the townsfolk, though, since we're all staying by the highway."

"Some of the hotel staff live in Lapis," said Blaise. "One of the grips is sleeping with the desk clerk, and the desk clerk's parents are second-generation Lapislanders. That could be one avenue of information."

"How do you *know* these things?" Lauren asked.

"Please," said Magenta. "Keep still."

"It pays to be informed," Blaise said. "Stop being evasive and tell us what happened. Opal?"

"Drugs in the water, or mysterious spores, that's what I've heard," said Opal.

Blaise glared at her. "Right, those are the fake stories Neil's telling. Cough up a few actual details, witch."

Opal grinned. "Calling me names, great way to get me to talk to you. I've got something else on my mind." She turned to Rod and lost any impulse to smile. "Why'd you tell Neil it doesn't take me long to put Corvus in his makeup?" Corvus moved past her and settled into his chair, his head still hidden in his hood.

Rod glanced at her, then back down at his magazine. Without looking at her, he said, "All these years, Opal, working side by side, I thought we were friends."

"I did, too."

"But I don't even know you," he said to his magazine. "Blaise is right, you're a witch. You never told me."

"I never tell anybody. That's your excuse to snark about me behind my back?" She leaned forward, tilted Rod's chin up so he was looking at her.

"A small, petty revenge, but mine own," he said.

"You were friends with the person I used to be," she said. "Due to circumstances beyond my control, I don't think I'm that person anymore. You might think about whether you want to be friends with who I am now. I imagine I'm a better friend than an enemy."

"Do you really care about your hours, Opal?" asked Rod, staring unflinchingly into her eyes. "Does any of that matter to you, given what you can do? The minute I said that to Neil, I regretted it, but I couldn't take it back. Now that you're acting like Threaten-Me Barbie, I'm not sure what I want. Would you quit being such a badass?"

"Um," she said. She released his chin and straightened, felt the starch drain from her shoulders. "Okay. Sorry about that. I'm pretty confused."

"And scary," muttered Magenta.

Opal glanced at Magenta before she headed for Corvus and her tools. Magenta was focused on her work and didn't meet Opal's gaze. Another thing to worry about?

Not right now.

Opal opened her locked cupboard and pulled out Corvus's head mold, with its mask of leaves. It looked alive, the blank eyes forbidding. She knelt and searched the cupboard for the leaf skin she had taken off him yesterday, but there was no sign of it. Well, that was going to be trouble—today's scene had chest nudity in it, and the leaf skin had made that simple. She might need more time after all.

"You guys, sorry to interrupt a personality conflict, but nobody's answering my questions. We're not the public," Lauren said. "And we're not just asking for fun. We *need* to know what happened yesterday, and if we're expecting more of the same today. I didn't volunteer for total insanity."

"Stop talking!" Magenta said. "You made me smear!"

"Opal, please. Please tell me *some*thing," Lauren said, even though Magenta looked mad enough to spit fire.

"Yesterday we were all possessed by a spirit of sex, and some of it got on tape," Opal said. "We fucked like rabbits. No one was in their right mind except Magenta, who was protected. Something's going to happen today, but I'm not sure it'll be the same. That's what I know. Okay?"

"Um," said Lauren. "No."

"If you would let me do my job," Magenta said, "maybe we could film everything and get out of here before another sexquake happens. Will you *please* shut up now?"

Lauren subsided.

"Why were you protected?" Blaise asked Magenta.

"Opal fixed me up way before it happened."

"Like with a charm or something?"

"I don't know. Don't say it," she said to Lauren. She finished filling in the lip color, having repaired earlier mishaps, and Lauren sat still for it.

"Opal," said Blaise.

"Give me a break. I have work to do." She tapped the mask, whispered, "Shed, skin." It split neatly down the center of the face. It was warm in her hands as she fitted it over Corvus's head. It molded to his skin immediately, and a gilded flush ran over it. Buried leaves rose from the skin of his neck, raced down under his robe. She undid the brooch at the throat and bared his chest, which was now as leafy as his head. "Good," she said, and got out yesterday's Polaroids for comparison. He looked exactly the same, down to the green glow in his eyes.

She put the Polaroids in a drawer and came back to take more pictures and another look at him, just to make sure everything worked together.

He pulled her into his lap and kissed her.

At first she resisted. This was where she worked, not where she kissed. She was working with materials she didn't understand and wasn't sure she could fix if they got messed up.

But her work was done, by someone other than herself, and

even though she didn't like or trust Phrixos, his kiss felt wonderful, promising that she could relax into the self who didn't have to be in charge. He tasted of forest and sleep and comfort. Her Flintfire kept her from sinking into him completely, but she let herself respond to the promises as though she believed them.

Someone tapped her shoulder. She opened her eyes, broke contact with Phrixos's mouth, and looked up. Magenta stood above her, frowning.

Opal pushed away from Phrixos. He let her go, his fingers lingering and sliding along her hips as she pulled away.

"It pisses me off to no end that he doesn't smear," Magenta said. "Anyway, it's time to get to the set."

"But I thought—" How long had the kiss lasted? Lauren and Blaise were no longer in the trailer. Opal checked her watch. All the time budgeted for applying makeup had melted away. Weird that a kiss could relax her instead of exciting her, and weird that whatever it was had happened in spite of her shield. Things had changed while she'd been lost; a kind of nervous energy flooded her now, something ambient that almost sounded like a song. "Come on, big guy." She tugged Phrixos to his feet.

Everything felt electrified. Phrixos's hand in hers was hot and buzzing, as though she touched bees. "What is it?" Opal asked. The mirrors on the trailer walls reflected back scenes brighter than the one they were standing in.

Magenta looked around, too. Rod glanced up from his magazine. "Here we go again," he said. "I think I'll lock myself in the restroom this time. I didn't like who I ended up with last time."

"Is that what's happening?" Magenta asked.

"Don't you feel it?" asked Rod. "That urge to merge—but maybe different from yesterday. I don't—I'm not sure what I want, but—"

Magenta cocked her head. "There's some kind of weird

sound, like one of the generators is running too fast or something, but I don't feel anything."

"You are shielded," Phrixos said. "Do you want to open to this?"

"Nope, no thanks," said Magenta. "Rather sit it out, like I did yesterday."

"As you like." Phrixos tugged Opal with him toward the door to the trailer. She grabbed her messenger bag on the way. Rod headed toward one of the trailer's restrooms. Magenta took her duffel and followed Opal and Phrixos out, locked the door as she left the trailer.

Everyone they passed on their way to the altar looked alert and itchy, most glancing this way and that in search of something nobody seemed to find. Suspicious glances followed Phrixos.

"This is where I get off," Opal said as they came abreast of the cast corral. Phrixos's grip on her hand tightened, then released.

"Don't go anywhere," he said. "I need you."

"Sure," she said, uncomfortable. Did he really need her, or did he just want to own and control her? "Something's going to happen today."

"If everything works out," he said.

"It's not going to be the same as yesterday, is it?" she asked.

"No," he whispered, and walked on, toward where Lauren, in her character's dumpy-phase clothes, stood. Lauren looked lost and sad. Corvus's stand-in, Fred, walked into the circle of light and stood facing her. They murmured to each other. Everyone glanced around uneasily.

Blaise stood in the trees, out of sight of where the cameras aimed at the moment, a pale forest dryad spying on invaders.

Magenta set her duffel on the ground and sat in Lauren's chair, her hands gripping each other in her lap.

Opal settled in Corvus's chair and closed her eyes. "What's going on?" she asked Other Opal.

Other Opal took shape in the air beside her, glanced around. "Interesting," she said. "Gearing up."

"For what?"

"Can't tell, but it feels like everything around us is awake." Other Opal looked toward the ground. "We're standing on another kind of person. He lies there and smiles at us. He's glad we're here. He wants us."

Opal stroked her shield. Part of it had opened for Phrixos's kiss, but now it gloved her. She could resist what was about to happen. As long as that door Phrixos had made in the shield stayed shut. *Damn.*

"You gonna keep that shield up the rest of your life?" asked Other Opal.

"Maybe," said Opal. She had lowered it during the kiss, though, and whatever Phrixos had done to her still resonated inside. She sighed and opened her eyes to the outside world.

Neil yelled by the altar. "Am I surrounded by dolts and donkeys? Would you all stop shaking the equipment? News flash: we're not sitting on a volcano!"

Opal went to the Props department to get a camera-eye view.

"Blocking rehearsal's over," Joe said. "Looked good. Neil's like a cat on a hot griddle today."

"Who isn't?" asked Opal.

"Good point." They watched Lauren and Phrixos. The scene took place after Caitlyn had practically kidnapped Serena and forced her back to the forest, where Serena had sworn she would never go again. Caitlyn told Serena she had to help Caitlyn figure out how their mother had died. At this point, the flashback of the mother's death would show, as Serena regained her lost memory. And then the Dark God would talk her into accepting his proposal. There was a lot of verbal persuasion involved; it was one of Corvus's best scenes in the movie, all talking instead of anything that smacked of scare tactics. Opal had drowsed through the scene the night before, even as she mouthed Serena's lines, but this time she leaned in close as Phrixos and Lauren spoke the lines. Joe's TV didn't pick up sound, but as Opal watched the actors' lips, she remembered.

> DARK GOD
>
> All your life you have denied your power and hidden from yourself. It is time for you to become who you really are.

> SERENA
>
> Wouldn't my sister be better? She's already given heart and soul to you.

> DARK GOD
>
> *You* are the one with the gifts I want. Accept your destiny. How long will you hide in the shadows? Show the world your true self. Open to your power.

"Last looks," the A.D. called.

Opal and Magenta went to check their respective charges. Phrixos's leaves had darkened, turned more realistic. Opal wasn't sure how to reverse that. "Can you step it down a notch? This is bad for continuity," she said to him.

"I can't," he said. "It's not in my control. It never really has been." The green in his eyes was only half-lit, and he spoke to her in Corvus's voice. She stepped back and stared up at him. The nervous energy in the air vibrated against her shield.

"I can't wait until you get all trampy and rampagy," Magenta was saying to Lauren. "That's going to be the fun makeup."

"Looking forward to it." Lauren's voice sounded tight.

From just behind Opal's shoulder, Neil said, "What's the

problem here?" He touched a leaf on Corvus's cheek and grunted. "The color palette changed, eh? Why's that?"

"Um," said Opal, "it wanted to, I guess. I don't know how to change it back, unless I cover it with something lighter, which would take a while."

"Oh fuck oh dear." He stepped back. "Well, maybe we can fix it in post. Prognostications for today?"

Opal shook her head.

"Damn and thunderation. All this itchy energy, too. Please. Just let us shoot the scene as written at least once, all right?"

Opal wasn't sure who he was talking to. She knew she couldn't say yes to that; like Corvus's makeup, the whole situation was beyond her control.

"Maybe if we do it quickly," Corvus said.

"I despise *quickly*," said Neil, "no matter how many people tell me it's important. Today, though—let's do this thing right now."

"Clear the set," George yelled.

Opal and Magenta hid behind the backdrop. Someone yelled for quiet on the set. The bell rang, sound rolled, the camera assistant called scene and take number, the slate was bumped, Neil yelled, "Action," and the lines ran.

How long will you hide in the shadows?

20

Corvus spoke with a clarity that brought the lines to her even this far from the set. Was she hiding in the shadows still? No, people were looking at her in the light, more than she was comfortable with. She wanted to fade into the background again.

Which was hard when everyone was aware of her now. She glanced at Magenta, Blaise, random other not-working-at-the-moment crew. Everyone was silent while the scene played out, but none of them were reading, puzzle solving, distracting themselves today. They all stood listening, and many of their gazes rested on her.

Were they remembering her as half of the center of yesterday's tossed human salad? Or was everyone remembering she was a witch equivalent?

Oh, come on, thought Dark Opal, *it's not always about you.*

It's almost never about me, thought Opal. *That's the way I like it.*

Keep telling yourself that. I'll hang on to the other thoughts for us.

Are you saying I want to be the center of attention?

Every little once in a while, thought Dark Opal.

Opal straightened, pushed her shoulders back, and took a deep breath. *Okay. Yesterday was enough of that for now. Agreed?*

Dark Opal laughed. *You got it, sister.*

Maybe everyone was tense because of the ubiquitous hair-raising, nerve-tingling energy, its pitch rising, that tightened the air until it was hard to breathe.

Barefoot, an almost unrecognizable Erika came to stand beside Opal. This Erika's hair was loose around her shoulders, and she wore not a single camera around her neck. She had on some kind of springy, flower-laden dress and wore an unfamiliar nongloating smile.

Brainwashed, Opal decided. "You okay?" she whispered.

"I'm so happy," Erika murmured. "I've found my true happiness."

"Cut. Print," called Neil and two bells rang.

"Weren't you happy before?" Opal asked Erika. "Taking pictures and torturing people?"

A shadow of Erika's triumph smile flashed across her face. "Yes," she said. Then she looked confused. "This is different."

Handmaiden, thought Dark Opal. *She's a total handmaiden. Don't go there. I'm sick of being a handmaiden.*

I'm with you there.

The cast and the director came off the set. Phrixos took his own chair. Lauren retreated to the cast trailer.

Neil grabbed a cold frappuccino from the Craft Services cooler and came over to Opal. He said, his gaze directed between Opal and Phrixos, "The master shot is in the can. Three takes, at least one of which is good enough, if we revert and follow the original script, and ignore everything that happened yesterday, which, at this point, I'm inclining toward."

She wasn't sure why he was telling her this, or how to respond. She tried a smile.

He scowled and strolled off to where Blaise was lurking, then wandered back to watch people position equipment. Lauren returned from the trailer and sat in her chair.

The undertone of frenzy intensified.

"What is it?" Opal asked Phrixos. "What's going to happen?"

"It takes the right trigger," Phrixos said.

"And then what?"

"I'll ask you a question. I'll ask everyone a question."

"What's the question?" Magenta said from beside Lauren's chair. Lauren looked anxious and sweaty. She was drinking orange juice.

"You have to wait for it."

"Waiting is driving us all crazy," said Lauren.

"Only a little longer, and all the steps will be complete," said Phrixos. He closed his eyes and leaned back, cutting off the conversation.

The next shot was of the Dark God, speaking seductively to Serena, or, more realistically, directly into the camera. Lauren wasn't in the shot, but she stood nearby to speak her lines off camera. Opal hovered behind one of the cameras filming the shot.

The energy erupted while the Dark God spoke.

DARK GOD

Will you spend the rest of your life hiding from your true nature? Now is the time to surrender all the things that keep you locked up inside yourself. Come to me. Worship me. Give me strength, and I will set loose the power you already have.

His voice, Corvus's best voice, reasonable, enticing, seductive, was everywhere. Opal heard it in her ear, felt it sliding through the clearing and even into the trees. Her heart raced. Heat flooded her face. She yearned toward him, almost stepped past the camera, then recalled herself, glanced at the cameraman and the focus puller, and saw that they were leaning forward, too.

> DARK GOD
> All you have to do is say yes. Will you say yes to me?

He held out his hands, palms up. His voice was irresistible. The green rose from the ground, coruscating around his hands and face. He smiled, turned to look straight at Opal, then swept the crew with his gaze.

"Yes," said Lauren, her line, but "yes," cried everyone else, everyone, boom mike operator, electricians, grips, director, cameramen, set dressers, wardrobe, props, supervisors, writers, everyone.

Opal opened her mouth, a "yes" shaping her lips. Dark Opal invaded her muscles and changed her response to "No!" spoken in a whisper. *No! You don't need him to make you whole. You have me! You have all of us. Frozen baby, marble child, your internal forest, all those rooms you haven't looked in, all the yous you've locked up, and even Flintfire that's you and not you. I can help you out of the shadows.*

Can you help me let go of everything holding me back and locking me up?

Oh, yes, thought Dark Opal. *You know I can.*

After the chorus of "Yes!" swept the clearing, the Dark God laughed and held out his hands. Green rushed from him, enveloped each one of them and sank under their skin. It tried to enter Opal. She could feel its promises and whispers: warmth, love, safety, the death of worry, the comfort of being cared for. She held out a hand, but it shone faintly orange—shielded—against the invading green.

"You are mine now," said Phrixos. He turned and stared at each of them in turn. *Not in the script.* "I thank you and welcome you. We will do great things together."

He smiled, a benediction. Even shielded, Opal felt its glow.

"Is that it?" said Magenta, and everyone turned on her.

"Cut," cried Neil. "Damn you! How dare you interrupt my take?"

Everyone did their jobs; stopped taping, finished the shot. Second bell rang shrilly through the clearing.

Everyone again turned on Magenta.

"What? It's a special effect? Everybody gets a green dot? What?" she asked.

"A green dot?" Neil said. People glanced at each other and saw that she was right, everyone else had a small, glowing green dot just above their noses.

Nice redirect, thought Dark Opal.

Opal touched her forehead, glanced at Magenta, caught her attention, and lowered her finger. Magenta's eyes widened.

Corvus stepped out from under the lights, touched his own forehead, and frowned. Opal walked to him, stared up into his leafy face. There was green among the leaves; she couldn't tell whether he had a dot. His eyes were his own color, no trace of Phrixos in them. "What just happened?" she asked.

"I don't know."

"Um," said Magenta. She pointed past them, and they turned.

A giant green figure faded into view on the altar, spinning out of air, sunlight, and diffused klieg lights. People gasped.

"Cameras," Neil yelled, and dazed camera people started film rolling.

The green mist took vaguely humaniform shape as a seated person. It pushed stumpy arms toward the sky, opened a hole the shape of an orange slice in the lump that was its head, and sighed with pleasure. "So long," it said, its voice warm and musical, "since I've had the strength to manifest. Thank you, my new children."

"What are you talking about?" Magenta asked, striding toward it.

"My poor orphan," said the creature. Something Opal could barely see was rising from all the people in the clearing, including those who had come from behind the backdrop and out of the trailers while Phrixos was talking. A faint mist lifted from each of them and flowed toward the green thing. The form got solider and better defined. It looked cheerful, benevolent, and enormous; it stopped being lumpy and turned nearer to human, as muscular, sculpted, and sexless as an Oscar. It smiled at all of them and rose to its full height, perhaps nine feet tall.

"Do you want to join the rest of your people, or are you determined to be alone?" It leaned toward Magenta, its face blank but somehow attentive.

"Join my people in what?" She thrust her jaw out. "Did you turn them all into your handmaidens? What kind of verbal contract did they just agree to, huh?"

"Nothing that will kill them," it said gently.

"That covers a lot of ground, some of it pretty bumpy. I say no thanks."

The god brushed Magenta's cheek with a fingertip—she flinched from his touch, and he smiled gently—and walked past her to Opal. He towered above her. He bent, his face kind, his eyes irisless almonds.

"You," he said. "My most ardent supporter."

"Me," Opal said.

"We have made homes in each other. Why do you cast me out now?"

A whir of replies whizzed through her head—I don't like your use of force/I'm not sure who you are or what you want/I don't trust you, and for good reason/You hurt me, and you hurt my friends. Ultimately, she said, "I got a better offer."

He looked sad. "I want you back."

She studied everyone else. They stood quiet, almost like the trance state they had been in yesterday, waiting. Opal shook her head. "No."

He gazed at her, his attention concentrated, a force that almost made her take a step back. Then he rose. "I will never stop wanting you. For now, I don't need you. I'll ask you again later." He straightened to his full height. "Now," he said to all of them, "where shall we start?"

Everyone woke. "We start with making this a damn good film," roared Neil, "and that's going to take the lot of you working like demons, hear me?"

"We hear you," said someone, and the rest of them laughed.

"So what else is new?" muttered Magenta. She grabbed Opal's hand and stomped back to the Makeup trailer while the crew, supervised by the tall green man, set up for the next shot, which would be Lauren saying her lines on camera, with Corvus interpolating his lines out of sight. The god helped the electricians and grips move equipment. No one said anything about him being nonunion.

Corvus and Lauren followed Opal and Magenta.

"What just happened out there?" Magenta asked after she had slammed and locked the door with the four of them inside. "Did you become happy little cult members? Who *is* that guy, anyway?" She stomped up to Corvus and stared up into his eyes.

"Isbrytaren, I guess. Who knows who that is."

"I Googled it," Magenta said. "It's not a god's name. It means *icebreaker* in Swedish."

"*Icebreaker?*" Corvus repeated. He started laughing, and fell into his chair clutching his stomach.

"Yeah, it's these ships that go out and break ice to let shipping operate in the winter in the northern ports—what's so funny about that?"

He leaned his leafy head over the back of the chair, trying to catch his breath, his belly rippling the black robe as he laughed. Opal and Lauren exchanged a glance. For Opal, it was almost a reflex; she had become used to exchanging glances with her friend. Who had Lauren become since she had said yes to the god?

Lauren shrugged. She smiled the same smile she had used before her conversion. So maybe you didn't have to go all the way into goofiness, the way Erika seemed to have, under the influence of the god.

When Corvus conquered his laughter, he said, "*Icebreaker*. I was thinking more in terms of conversation starters at parties. Weird function for a god."

"Does this mean he's some kind of Norse god? How'd he get here?" Magenta asked.

"I don't know," said Corvus. "Why don't you ask him?"

"Maybe I will. But you never did answer my other question. What are you now that you said 'yes' to him? Slaves? Clones? Handmaidens? Religion pushers?"

"Lauren?" Opal asked.

"I don't know. I don't think the terms were outlined anywhere. I feel really weird, like I just agreed to be the evil girl in the movie, and now I'm going to have to curse all my friends, sacrifice small animals, and run around in slut makeup. But when he asked me, it wasn't like that, it was sort of like he was saying, 'I'll love you the way no one else ever has, accept you as you are, help you do what you most want, no matter what it is.'"

"Corr? You were saying all the lines. You didn't say yes. Are you included in this agreement?" Magenta asked.

Corvus straightened, stroked a forehead leaf. "Uh—

another good question. I'm not sure. I've already been invaded and possessed. I don't really understand whether the person who's been walking around in my skin, the one Opal calls Phrixos, is the same as the green thing we saw outside. But I didn't answer Phrixos's question with a yes, and I didn't feel quite what Lauren felt. I just felt like I loved everybody. A lot."

"If that thing walks in here right now and orders you to lick its feet, what do you think will happen?" Magenta asked.

Lauren made a face. Then she made a different face. The first conveyed disgust, and the second dismay. "Shit."

Someone tapped at the door. Magenta huffed a sigh and went to peek out.

George stood there. "We need Lauren and Corvus on the set."

They all went back outside.

The god walked behind Neil as the director strode around the set, peering through the camera, speaking with the crew at a much lower volume than he usually employed. Neil stopped to consult with the script supervisor and the director of photography, and finally got mad. "Would you cease *looming*? Why must you be so green?" he yelled up at the god.

"Oh, God," muttered Lauren. She lifted her skirt and hurried past her lighting stand-in to take her mark.

"Am I bothering you?" the god asked, his tone jolly.

"The green. The glowing. It's fucking with my light balance."

"I don't want to interfere with your work. I'll go out of sight," said the god, but instead of backing off, he leaned closer, lowering his face to Neil's as though seeking a kiss from a reluctant partner.

"You great gob, that's worse—" Neil cried, and the god turned to mist and flooded into his mouth. Neil shrieked. His belly pushed out against his clothes like the surface of boiling water, bumps rising and collapsing. He stopped screaming and pressed both hands against his stomach, which continued to bubble under its taut layer of shirt, skin, muscle, and fat. Finally he let out a belch and wiped his forehead. "That's better," he said.

"Is it?" Magenta muttered.

Neil turned toward Opal and Magenta, his eyes alight with green glow, and said, "Yes. It is. Now let's get this done. Serena?"

Lauren, standing on her mark beside the altar, had her hand over her mouth. Her eyes were wide.

"Don't worry, love. We'll smooth it out. Ready? Last looks."

Magenta edged past him and checked Lauren's makeup, then ducked away. She gripped Opal's arm and pulled her toward the backdrop.

"Dark God. You set?"

"I am," said Corvus.

"Right, then. Sound the bell."

The bell rang.

"Quiet on the set," George yelled.

Behind the backdrop, Opal and Magenta collapsed into the actors' chairs, muffling the crack of canvas an instant too late. They both froze, waiting for a scream from the set, but the only sound was Lauren and Corvus, continuing their lines, with the same energy and passion they'd used all day, barring Corvus's brief foray into ad-libbing with the whole crew.

Magenta tugged her duffel out from under Lauren's chair, pulled out a pad and a pen. *Do you think he'll keep being creepy?* she wrote.

Opal took pad and pen and wrote, *I'm not an expert.*

You slept with him.

Still doesn't make me an expert. I'm not even sure it's the same guy.

Great.

They both sighed and sat back. The Props table and Joe's monitor were near. He stared at the screen, transfixed. Finally Opal rose and went to look. It was only Lauren, or Serena, really, looking alternately horrified, fascinated, and excited. Her face was so expressive. Her hesitation, her final surrender, the naked ecstasy of the moment—

Lauren opened her eyes and stared as though she were looking at Christmas morning.

"Cut. Print. Next setup," Neil's voice called.

"He swallowed a god and he's just going to go on directing?" Magenta muttered.

"Looks like it," said Opal.

By suppertime they had finished all the filming for the day and shut down the set.

This time, Opal had to use solvents to remove Corvus's makeup, and he scratched frantically at his chest. "I forgot how irritating this can be," he said as she collected scraps and damp cotton balls into a trash sack.

"Me, too."

"Could you cheat?"

She cleaned leaves off his face and moisturized his skin. "Maybe. It might invite Phrixos back, though. Is that what you want?"

He sighed. She finished wiping leaves off his neck and gently detached the points elongating his ears.

One of the A.D.s came by with a call sheet for the next day, and Opal paused to study it. Dark God invaded the bed-and-breakfast where Serena was staying—dream or haunting? After lunch, a scene with Caitlyn, her betrayal, eclipsed in all ways by her renegade sister. Lauren would finally get to be evil.

Magenta set her call sheet on the counter. "That's it?" she asked. "We just keep going?"

Opal, too, felt the sense of waiting for something to fall, a boulder, an avalanche, an earthquake, tornado, or tsunami. She glanced toward the door, saw that Neil, eyes still glowing, stood there.

"Is that it?" she asked.

He smiled and nodded. "We'll finish the project. I'll follow it south into postproduction, and give it all the extra help I can, weaving the right kinds of influences into it, and then—"

"Then what?" Magenta asked.

He smiled wide, like someone with a bellyful of good food, and said, "Distribution! People see it. They meet me." He nodded a head toward Corvus. "Or one part of me. They think about me, and send me energy, and I stay awake."

"Unless it totally tanks," said Magenta.

"In which case—in any case—we move on, and make another one. I know I have the support of the crew."

"What about everybody who wasn't here today?" Magenta asked.

"There's time. We're all working on the same project already. I'll speak to them."

"In your own special way," Magenta said, with a sneer in her voice.

"Yes. Will you join us?"

"Not yet," said Magenta.

"Your choice," said whoever was inside of Neil. He looked kind.

Opal thought of Other Opal, dressed in knee-high black boots and tight black clothes, like a thief who might need to slip through slender openings. Her black hair was tied back, the white streak swooping along the side of her head and diving into the clubbed ponytail at her nape. She stood, arms crossed, ass toward the fire as she leaned against the mantel. Her amber eyes glowed golden.

No way we're going to join him, not if I have my way, said Other Opal. *Gonna miss the wild sex, though.*

Corvus rose, took her hand. "Let's go home," he said.

Or maybe not, one of them thought. Perhaps both of them.

Over the past twenty-some years, **Nina Kiriki Hoffman** has sold adult and YA novels, juvenile and media tie-in books, short story collections, and more than 250 short stories. Her works have been finalists for the Nebula, World Fantasy, Mythopoeic, Sturgeon, Philip K. Dick, and Endeavour awards. Her first novel, *The Thread That Binds the Bones*, won a Bram Stoker Award. Her short story "Trophy Wives" won a Nebula Award.

Nina does production work for *Fantasy & Science Fiction* magazine and teaches short story writing through her local community college. She also works with teen writers. She lives in Eugene, Oregon, with several cats, a mannequin, and many strange toys.

Explore the outer reaches of imagination—don't miss these authors of dark fantasy and urban noir that take you to the edge and beyond.

Patricia Briggs	Karen Chance	Anne Bishop
Simon R. Green	Caitlin R. Kiernan	Janine Cross
Jim Butcher	Rachel Caine	Sarah Monette
Kat Richardson	Glen Cook	Douglas Clegg

THE ULTIMATE IN FANTASY!

From magical tales of distant worlds to stories of those with abilities beyond the ordinary, Ace and Roc have everything you need to stretch your imagination to its limits.

Marion Zimmer Bradley/Diana L. Paxson

Guy Gavriel Kay

Dennis L. McKiernan

Patricia A. McKillip

Robin McKinley

Sharon Shinn

Katherine Kurtz

Barb and J. C. Hendee

Elizabeth Bear

T. A. Barron

Brian Jacques

Robert Asprin

penguin.com

M12G1107